PRAISE FOR
THE WORLD OF THE NARROWS SERIES

"A daring, swashbuckling adventure, complete with—no matter how hard they try to resist—a heaping helping of romance."
—*Booklist*

"Rich, poetic prose that beautifully underscores the two main characters' strengths, weaknesses, and beliefs . . . Returning and new readers alike will find much to love in this absorbing tale."
—*Kirkus Reviews*

"As an author, Young's strength is in her ability to craft both strong female protagonists and worlds that are filled with realistic details."
—*Culturess*

PRAISE FOR
SKY IN THE DEEP

"This is a gripping story, richly told."
—Renée Ahdieh, *New York Times* bestselling author of *Flame in the Mist*

"Fierce, vivid, and violently beautiful."
—Stephanie Garber, *New York Times* bestselling author of *Caraval*

"A stunning debut."
—Roshani Chokshi, *New York Times* bestselling author of *The Star-Touched Queen*

"Bleak, beautiful, and deadly."
—Traci Chee, *New York Times* bestselling author of *The Reader*

"Wholly unique and instantly addictive."
—Kerri Maniscalco, *New York Times* bestselling author of *Hunting Prince Dracula*

"Heartrending, heart-mending."
—Kayla Olson, bestselling author of *The Sandcastle Empire*

PRAISE FOR
THE GIRL THE SEA GAVE BACK

"Lyrical prose . . . and an evocative atmosphere elevate Young's tale of war, identity, and fate."

—*Publishers Weekly*

"Young's lyrical writing and lush descriptions make this world of fjords and forest come alive."

—*Culturess*

"A fast-paced and fierce atmospheric story with a heavy dose of fate and a light touch of romance."

—*YA Books Central*

"Gripping and exquisitely written. *The Girl the Sea Gave Back* tore at my heartstrings until I was completely unraveled. Readers will fall in love with this story, whether they are fans of *Sky in the Deep* or new to Adrienne Young's breathtaking world."

—Stephanie Garber, *New York Times* bestselling author of *Caraval*

"Eerie and beautiful, *The Girl the Sea Gave Back* is set in a world so vivid, you can almost touch it. I devoured this story of a lonely, powerful young woman with the ability to change the fate of her world and the brave young chieftain who must stop her at all costs."

—Kristen Ciccarelli, bestselling author of *The Last Namsara*

"Ignore this omen at your own peril—you will love this book! Perfect for fans of *The Last Kingdom,* it really immersed me in the Viking world that felt so mystical, complex, and fully formed. From the moment we first meet them, Tova and Halvard unravel the complicated threads of family, fate, and destiny."

—A. C. Gaughen, author of *Reign the Earth*

ADULT BOOKS BY
ADRIENNE YOUNG

Spells for Forgetting
The Unmaking of June Farrow
A Sea of Unspoken Things

YOUNG ADULT BOOKS BY
ADRIENNE YOUNG

Sky in the Deep
The Girl the Sea Gave Back
Fable
Namesake
The Last Legacy
Saint

FALLEN CITY

ADRIENNE YOUNG

SATURDAY
BOOKS
NEW YORK

This is a work of fiction. All of the characters, organizations, and events portrayed in this novel are either products of the author's imagination or are used fictitiously.

First published in the United States by Saturday Books, an imprint of St. Martin's Publishing Group

EU Representative: Macmillan Publishers Ireland Ltd, 1st Floor, The Liffey Trust Centre, 117–126 Sheriff Street Upper, Dublin 1, DO1 YC43

FALLEN CITY. Copyright © 2025 by Adrienne Young. All rights reserved. Printed in China. For information, address St. Martin's Publishing Group, 120 Broadway, New York, NY 10271.

www.saturdaybooks.com

Designed by Devan Norman
Sunburst art © Net Vector/Shutterstock
Case stamp and endpaper illustrations by Eleonor Piteira
Designed edges © Olga 27/Shutterstock

The Library of Congress has cataloged the hardcover edition as follows:

Names: Young, Adrienne, 1985– author.
Title: Fallen city / Adrienne Young.
Description: First edition. | New York, N.Y. : Saturday Books, 2025.
Identifiers: LCCN 2025009250 | ISBN 9781250794192 (hardcover) | ISBN 9781250794208 (ebook)
Subjects: LCGFT: Fantasy fiction. | Novels.
Classification: LCC PS3625.O932 F35 2025 | DDC 813/.6—dc23/eng/20250317
LC record available at https://lccn.loc.gov/2025009250

The publisher of this book does not authorize the use or reproduction of any part of this book in any manner for the purpose of training artificial intelligence technologies or systems. The publisher of this book expressly reserves this book from the Text and Data Mining exception in accordance with Article 4(3) of the European Union Digital Single Market Directive 2019/790.

Our books may be purchased in bulk for specialty retail/wholesale, literacy, corporate/premium, educational, and subscription box use. Please contact MacmillanSpecialMarkets@macmillan.com.

First Edition: 2025

10 9 8 7 6 5 4 3 2 1

FOR ETHAN,
MY GREATEST TEACHER

FALLEN CITY

GODS AND FEASTS

THE FIRST FEAST
Eris, goddess of life

THE SECOND FEAST
Phaedo, god of peace

THE THIRD FEAST
Thekla, goddess of craft

FOURTH FEAST
Calisto, goddess of fertility

THE FIFTH FEAST
Remillion, god of wealth and abundance

THE SIXTH FEAST
Hermaus, god of health

THE SEVENTH FEAST
Musaeus, god of hearth and home

THE EIGHTH FEAST
Kali, goddess of death

THE NINTH FEAST
Alkmini, goddess of wisdom and enlightenment

THE TENTH FEAST
Eleni, goddess of love

THE ELEVENTH FEAST
Toranus, god of bloodlines

THE TWELFTH FEAST
Aster, goddess of war

PROLOGUE

Some stories begin at the end. This one does—of that, I'm sure.

The difficult part is figuring out exactly when that beginning was. Some would say it began with the Philosopher. Others would say it was the first season of withering crops. It could even be said that it began with the first sword drawn in the Old War.

If I am to be the one to tell you this story, I can begin only where my own ending started—with the shadow of wings on the stone floor of the temple. With the smell of ink and parchment, and the first seeds of a secret.

My name is Casperia. Maris Casperia.

Perhaps we should begin there.

CHAPTER 1

NOW: LUCA

There were no gods left to pray to.

The short sword glimmered as I tilted its edge against the sharpening stone, the metal warm against my calloused fingers. A line of recruits watched in a kind of daze, their focus trained on my grip as the high-pitched vibration drowned out the sounds of early morning in the camp.

Sharpening your blade correctly is a means of survival, I'd told them. As necessary as cleaning your armor or fastening your boots before battle. What I didn't tell them was that there are times when none of those things matter. That no amount of preparation could prevent the kind of death many of them would meet.

The motion of the wheel sank deep into my hands as I leaned my weight into the sword, turning it again at just the right angle until it held steady against the stone with almost no sound at all.

"Give it a try." I handed the sword to the man beside me.

The unsteady look in his eye did little to reassure me. If I had to guess, I would say he had once been a mason or one of the laborers who maintained the city walls. He didn't look as if he'd ever swung a sword in his life.

He was at least ten years my senior, but he gave me an obedient nod and took the sword, eyeing the blade. It was a humble weapon, the iron a flat gray and missing the faint shimmer of the swords that had been forged and strengthened with godsblood. With the right blow, the metal would fail him.

He got to work, stepping into my place so he could position its edge against the wheel as it cranked back to life. The sound of metal on stone filled the tent, and I watched his eyes focus, his strong hands turning the sword a bit clumsily until it slipped, sending an eruption of sparks into the air. He caught it by the handle before it fell to the cobblestones underfoot, eyes wide as he looked up at me.

I motioned for him to try again, and when he set the blade to the wheel this time, it took only seconds before he had the feel of it. The medallion that hung around his neck signified him as a citizen of Isara, but I paid no mind to the family name engraved on it. These recruits weren't the apathetic privilege-born legionnaires I'd sparred with in the training ring. The ones who grew up in the Citadel District, enlisting for their parents' political gain. They weren't the zealous, hot-blooded youths I'd fought beside when the first breath of rebellion flooded the streets, either. These were dwindling remnants of the Lower City. Broken pieces of lost family lines who'd joined up for the rations and the protection of the New Legion. I'd stopped looking at their faces months ago, eager to keep myself from recognizing them when we pulled the arrow-pierced bodies from the streets. But the questions still hung in my mind as I drew the smell of the hot metal into my lungs. How many children did this man have? How many would miss him once he was gone?

He lifted the blade from the wheel, and when I gave him a nod of approval, he stepped back in line.

"Next."

I gestured to the man behind him, an old Isarian with a white beard and sun-worn skin that sagged. As soon as he drew his sword, I exhaled a little. He had strong hands and arms. That, at least, was something. But that meager sense of hope withered when I saw the talisman that hung alongside his medallion. The braided cord lay beneath the opening of his tunic, a sign that this was a man who believed the gods would protect him.

He tried to be discreet when he glanced up over my head, but then forced his eyes down with a look of shame. He wasn't the only one in the group I'd caught staring at the mark. That was something I hadn't gotten used to. I didn't think I ever would.

It had been almost six months since the gods had marked me, placing a faint circlet of light over my head. It wasn't as visible in the glare of the sun, but in dim, shadowed light like this, it glimmered just enough to catch the eye.

The scrape of the wheel sounded in fits and starts as the man got started, and I tilted my hand in the air silently, showing him the correct angle. He made the adjustment, giving me a grateful nod, but my attention was slowly drawn to the opening of the tent, where I could hear the low hum of voices. Dust had been stirred into the air.

My brow creased, my arms falling from where they were crossed over my chest, and I watched the light outside change just a little. Far beyond the walls of the city, the sun was just rising over the horizon, but the stillness of the camp had shifted somehow. I could feel it.

One by one, the recruits were sensing it, too. They looked up, faces turning toward the sunlight, and the man lifted the sword from the wheel, waiting.

"Every blade," I ordered, leaving them.

I pushed outside, expecting to find my tribune waiting, but he was gone. The moment the Centurion's medals had been placed on my chest, I'd been assigned a handpicked legionnaire honored for his talents in battle. A tribune's only job was to protect the highest-ranking soldiers, and in the last three months alone, I'd watched two of them die. This one would be the third.

I looked up and down the street, trying to spot him. I hadn't been able to shake him from my shadow for more than an hour at a time. So, where was he?

The Loyal Legion's barricades were erected along the riverfront, where the soldiers who'd been our brothers-in-arms less than a year ago were hunkered down and waiting for the end we all knew was coming. They'd chosen their side, just like we had. And most of the time, I could hardly blame them for it. The only question was how much blood would be spilled before it was finally over.

Our sprawling camp marked the hard-won front line, flanking the opposite edge of the river that cut the walled city of Isara in two unequal parts. The first was the Citadel District, where the Citadel sat on a hill, encircled by the villas of the Consul, Magistrates, and other highborn families. It was still dark, save for the lights of the Forum's great dome, the streets empty. The commotion wasn't coming from there.

Behind me was the Lower City, ten times the size of the district and filled with everyone else. It had taken months to fight our way through the compact maze of streets and buildings all the way to the edge of the Sophanes River, and for twelve nights, we'd held what was left of the Consul's Loyal Legion on the other side. It, too, was quiet. Just beginning to stir as the temperature warmed.

It took a few seconds for me to realize what was off. It was the camp itself. By this time each morning, there were already legionnaires going about their daily tasks, and in preparation for what lay ahead, there was more than enough work to be done. We outnumbered what was left of the Loyal Legion, but the last stand in the district would be a bloody one. In a matter of days, we'd be crossing the river.

I took a step forward, where the tents opened up enough to see past the camp. It was all but empty now, a stream of red tunics spilling down the bank of the river. Except for one. My tribune appeared, pushing through the legionnaires in the opposite direction. As soon as he saw me, his pace quickened. He had one hand clenched to the hilt of his sword.

"What the hell is going on?" I snapped, eyes scanning the growing crowd in the distance.

"It's the south bridge, Centurion."

As soon as the words left his mouth, my gut twisted.

For the first time, I looked the tribune in the eye. His dark irises were sharply focused on me, the set of his jaw firm. There wasn't so much as a ripple of unsteadiness there, but I could sense the faint shadow of something else.

My feet were moving before he could fall into step beside me.

"Three bodies this time—Magistrates." He kept his voice low, confirming what I already knew.

It wasn't the first time dawn had broken over the hanging corpses of Magistrates and their families on the south bridge. They were the reason this war had started, the wielders of the judgment stones that controlled the fate of the city. But now they were being hunted one by one, emboldening the soldiers of the New Legion with the promise of an empty Forum once we crossed the river.

"Are there any women?" I rasped, throat tight.

"Sir?"

"*Women.*" I could barely get the word out. "Are any of them women?"

"Yes. Two women and one man."

My pulse was racing so fast now that it felt like my heart would stop altogether. More legionnaires ran past us, everyone headed to the bridge, and I pushed into the crowd as panic flooded my veins. I could see the pillars of the stone archway ahead, but there were too many people. I couldn't get a view of the water.

The tribune stayed close to my side, one arm shoving into the bodies before us to create a path. But it took only a moment for the legionnaires to recognize me, a collective hush falling over them. They parted until the street was open before me, and their gazes drifted above my head to the mark, a look of reverence falling over their faces.

I ignored them, taking advantage of the opportunity to get to the railing at the river's edge. Once I could see the bank, I struggled to keep my steps steady until I reached it.

Not her. Please, gods, don't let it be her.

"Centurion."

My tribune's voice faded away behind me, my heart turning into a knot wedged between my collarbones. I couldn't breathe for the several seconds it took for my eyes to find them. Three bodies were hung from the bottom of the bridge, their forms limp and heavy. The river ran below their feet, the water whitecapped and quick as it traveled from one side of the city to the other.

The dead man's face was turned up to the sky, his neck gruesomely broken, and his bulging red eyes open and empty. He had a crescent ring of hair that crested his balding head and a bloom of dark blood stained the front of his fine white tunic. It looked as if he'd soiled himself, too.

I nearly lost my balance, catching the railing as my vision focused on the pale blond braids of the woman who hung beside him. She was missing a sandal, her bare foot blue and misshapen, as if it had been crushed.

Not her.

But the third body was turning slowly in the air, the face hidden by a curtain of dark hair. My hand tightened on the railing, slick with sweat. My chest felt like it was caving in, my whole body bracing for what I was about to see. The green silk chiton fluttered in the breeze, gently caressing the pale hands that hung limp in the air, her skin almost completely drained of its color. The tassels of the belt at her waist were caked in mud, the ties unraveling, as if she'd been dragged through the streets. A shaking breath escaped my lips as the glint of a gold ring caught the light.

I swallowed down the urge to retch, as slowly, the body continued to turn on the rope. The wind picked up, blowing the length of hair across her face, and by the time I could see it, black was pushing in along the edges of my vision.

It wasn't her.

The image of the woman suspended from the bridge was instantly replaced by my memory of another, which was cast across my dreams each night. Salt water dripping from her hair, the sound of her laugh. The shape of her body beneath the wet silk as she waded out into the sea. The memory flashed in my mind, flickering in and out until the blue-tinged face of the dead woman finally came back into focus.

Not her. Not her.

A sharp, tingling feeling spiraled from the center of my belly as I finally inhaled, and then I was pushing back into the gathered legionnaires, away from the river.

"Centurion?"

The tribune followed at my back, but I kept my eyes on the cobblestones until I reached the edge of the crowd, certain that I was going to pass out. I barely made it to the corner of the building across the street, my legs threatening to give out beneath me with every step. I caught my balance on the stone just as I vomited, and I was only half aware of the tribune taking position behind me to hide me from view.

I retched until my stomach was empty, the rush of blood in my head making me dizzy. By the time I was steady on my feet again, my tribune was waiting, discreetly holding a cloth between us. I took it, trying to catch my breath.

"Are you alright, sir?" he said, eyes still fixed to the street. He'd been like a splinter beneath my skin for weeks, but he at least did me the courtesy of not watching as I wiped the vomit from my mouth.

The crowd at the bridge had multiplied now, and the sound of cheering had begun to fill the air. The collective chant took shape slowly, growing louder as more voices joined in.

"Thirty-three! Thirty-three! Thirty-three!"

The number changed every time a Magistrate's body was hung from the bridge—it was the number of them left in the Citadel.

"Centurion Roskia," my tribune murmured.

I wiped the sweat from my brow, trying to breathe through the sick feeling still gripping my gut. I knew he was right. The Centurion Roskia and his cohort of forty-eight legionnaires were some of the best soldiers we had, and there was no doubt that they were one of the reasons we'd managed to push the front all the way to the Sophanes River. But he was also the most brutal and barbaric Isarian in our ranks, and he'd made a name for himself by hunting down and killing every Magistrate who attempted to flee the city. After more than two dozen unsanctioned skirmishes and executions, he'd been relegated to the gates in an effort to contain him until we crossed the bridge. But that hadn't kept him and his legionnaires at bay.

"Thirty-three! Thirty-three!" The sound of the words warped in my mind.

The seats in the Forum were now half empty. And it was only a matter of time until I saw Maris Casperia hanging from one of those ropes. And when that happened, it wouldn't just be the end of me. It would be the end of everything.

I pushed off the wall, stalking back toward the camp, where the smoke from the temple fire was still rising from the Illyrium. I glanced back one more time at the crowd, at the fists lifting into the air, the sound of a bright, fragile hope in their voices.

Traitors, they'd called us, when we first revolted. Defectors and rebels. When the first arrows flew over the Forum. When the first barricades went up. But it wasn't until I saw the bodies in the streets that I realized what we'd done. And for that, I didn't know if there was a name.

CHAPTER 2

NOW: MARIS

If I could cut the name from me, I would.

The paintbrush moved over the canvas in an arc, bristles twisting as the portraitist rolled it between his fingertips. The pale yellow pigment was a shock against the background he'd chosen to depict, a dense forest of trees you wouldn't find anywhere within the walls of Isara.

He waved the brush in my direction and I lifted my chin a little higher.

"This is a waste of time." My hands clenched beneath the fabric of my robes, back aching as I sat erect on the stool.

"Almost finished now," he murmured.

My own face stared back at me from the enormous portrait, the details of my eyes, mouth, and hair so perfect that it almost made me sick to look at it. The pure white Magistrate's robes draped around my figure, coming to a neat point where my medallion sat just below the center of my throat. The round, flat pendant forged in the temple wasn't just my identification. It was the token of my citizenship. The engraved name of Casperia was legible, even from where I sat, but the portrait was like everything else in this city—a lie.

The portraitist dipped his brush into the smear of green on his palette, and my eyes fixed on the glimmer of the pigment. The paint was mixed with godsblood, giving the canvas an eerily lifelike effect when the light hit it.

"We're going to be late," I said through gritted teeth, trying to hold my face still.

"We won't be late." Nej's crackling voice echoed in the chamber before he appeared in the doorway.

His robes were only half tied, the folds of the fabric loose. My uncle had never been distinguished in appearance, but somehow he always managed to clean himself up enough to look the part of a scribe. He smoothed down the side of his hair that almost never lay flat, stopping beside the portrait to study it with a serious expression.

He winced. "She needs to look older."

"I've painted her as she is," the portraitist snapped, retaining a sense of defensive pride for his work even now, as the city was days from falling.

"That's the problem," Nej pressed. "They're already suspicious of her. The least you could do is make her look dignified."

That made me drop my pose. I turned my head to fix him with an icy stare.

He shot me a dismissive look. "You know how this works. The only reason you have that seat is because your mother chose a cup of poisoned wine over her duty to the Citadel. The first question people will ask about you is if you're a coward, like she was."

My throat constricted at the harsh, unbridled words. Not because I had any semblance of feeling for my mother. That was a title she gained merely by birthing me. What made me stiffen was the reminder that what she'd done was a shadow over my place in the Forum. I'd always known I'd take the seat of a Magistrate, but not like this. Not in the middle of a war that had destroyed the city.

For my whole life, I'd dreamed of wearing the robes so that I could do the exact opposite of my mother and the Magistrates who'd driven our city to rebellion. I'd had a plan. A carefully wrought one that had cost me everything. But the day my mother cast her vote to execute the Philosopher Vitrasian was the day that plan fell apart.

Nej *tsk*ed, impatiently crossing his long, lanky arms. He glanced from me to the portrait and back again. "I suppose there's nothing we can do about the fact that you look like a child."

"I'm not a child. I'm twenty-four years old," I corrected him.

He ignored me. "It doesn't matter. The only thing they'll be thinking about when you take your seat in the tribunal today is Ophelius."

That, he was right about.

I'd taken a place as a novice to the Priestess Ophelius almost four years ago to avoid the attention and scrutiny of the Citadel. While other sons and daughters of the Magistrates took noviceships in the legion or as a scribe, I had bided my time quietly in a prestigious but low-profile position so that once I took my robes, I would have as few enemies as possible. My uncle thought that devoting myself to the myths and customs of the gods was beneath our family name, as did my mother. But no one could have predicted that the Priestess would wind up being the tip of the first spear thrown in the rebellion. In that, my noviceship had been almost ill-fated.

"It certainly doesn't help that you spent so much time in that blasted temple that no one knows a thing about you," he continued. "Now you don't have a single ally in the Forum."

"I have you, don't I?" I said, letting my eyes meet his. It was an actual question. I was almost sure that my uncle cared for me, which was more than I could ever have said about my mother, but he was as mercurial as the rest of them.

The hint of a smile softened the pinched look on his face. "I'm not a Magistrate. I'm a scribe."

"The Consul's scribe," I corrected him. Some would argue it was a place more prominent than any other in the Forum. He had the ear of the most powerful man in Isara. That wasn't nothing.

"You'll always have an ally in me, Maris."

Hearing him use my given name made me want to believe him. A name was a thing of intimacy and closeness when spoken, and the permission to use it was a rare gift. It was customarily reserved for those with whom you shared blood or soul, and Nej was family.

That was why, six days ago, when I'd found my mother's lifeless body on the floor of her study, the first thing I'd done was walk the dark, empty streets of the district to my uncle's villa. He hadn't shed a single tear for his sister, nor had he shown even a shred of surprise at the news she'd poisoned herself. Instead, he'd sent a message to the Citadel and a strict protocol as old as the city was enacted. With the death of my mother, a seat in the Forum was open, and as the only child of Magistrate Casperia, I would be the one to fill it.

Two days later, my robes arrived and the portraitist was commissioned to paint my official portrait. It would be hung in the Tribunal Hall, replacing my mother's. Just in time for the Citadel to burn.

I let my gaze trail to the window, where I could see more of the city than I wanted to. The streets and alleys that snaked between the rooftops of the Lower City were a tangled maze where the flash of sunlight on swords and scale armor flickered in the shadows. In every direction, the encampment of the New Legion was spreading. They were everywhere, growing by the day as more lowborn Isarians continued to join their ranks.

After months of battle, the New Legion had made it to the banks of the Sophanes River. Now, they were waiting to cross it—a reality that, only months ago, the Magistrates had sworn was impossible. No one had actually said it yet, but we were trapped. The Citadel District had slowly become a prison guarded by a dwindling band of soldiers who were losing resolve by the day. The only reason the New Legion hadn't stormed our streets and cut our throats was the grain. What remained of Isara's food stores was sitting beneath the Citadel, and taking the last of the city meant nothing if everyone was doomed to starve to death. And that wasn't the only priceless thing down in the catacombs.

There were still some left in the district who believed the Consul would win the war. That once the legionnaires crossed the Sophanes, the gods would intervene and they would meet their end. But I'd seen the number of their fires growing each night from the roof of our villa. I'd seen the Magistrates' bodies strung up along the bridge.

After a moment's hesitation, I finally let my eyes wander to the white walls of the Illyrium in the distance, where the insignia of the New Legion had been rendered only days before. It was clearly visible from the windows of the Citadel, which, I assumed, was the intent.

The insignia was the sharp silhouette of a kneeling legionnaire, face gazing up toward the heavens, as if waiting for a blessing from the gods. The gold ringlet that encircled the figure's head only confirmed that he'd received it.

Luca.

The moment his name wormed through my mind, heat flooded my chest, making it difficult for my lungs to draw a breath. I found the soft skin at the crook of my arm beneath the sleeves of my robes and pinched, trying to ward away the lump that came up into my throat. It was the same feeling I had every time I cast my eyes across the river. Like the hot oil from a lamp spilling from my heart into the rest of my body. That insignia was the closest I'd come to seeing Luca since all this began.

Nej gave me an almost sympathetic look, following my gaze to the window. "I know this isn't how you imagined taking your robes."

That was true in a way he could never know, but I said nothing, letting him believe that my grief for Isara and its people was the source of that excruciating burn behind my ribs. But it wasn't. Every time I looked across the Sophanes and saw the torchlight of the New Legion, I wasn't thinking about the Citadel or the Consul or even the district that was my home. I was thinking about the last time I'd seen the face I was supposed to grow old with. I was remembering the gleam of lamplight in eyes the color of the sea and the sound of my given name spoken by a voice that was only a ghost in my mind now.

"As for the tribunal," Nej continued, clasping his hands behind his back, "do you remember what we talked about?"

I let out an irritated breath. "I am not to speak unless addressed by the Consul."

"And what else?"

"I am not to look at anyone as if I want them to be hurled from the windows of the Forum."

Nej gave me a firm nod. "Exactly. Now, the Consul will call the tribunal to order and then—"

"Nej, it's not my first tribunal. It's not even my fiftieth."

I'd grown up attending them with my mother, a practice that most children of Magistrates were expected to partake in. If we were to inherit their seats one day, we had to be instructed from a young age. And it wasn't just procedures and formalities we were learning. We were meant to be ingrained with the politics that no one gave speeches on or plastered onto the sides of buildings. There was a bigger game afoot—one that influenced the turning of the judgment stones in every single tribunal. The highborn families and the ever-shifting balance of power between them was the tide that controlled the tides of our city.

"It's your first one as a Magistrate." His voice deepened just a little, and I could tell that he was worried. I could see it in the way his mouth twitched. "There's also the dinner with the Consul."

I let my eyes trail to him, managing to hold my pose still for the portraitist.

"I hope I don't have to tell you how important it is that you make a good impression."

"I know."

"If there's anyone who can win you the favor of the Magistrates, it's him. There isn't a single one among them who isn't trying to ensure their place after this war."

My fingers tangled tightly in my lap. Every time Nej mentioned *after,* it made my heartbeat slow just a little. There would be no after if the Consul didn't try to negotiate the peaceful transfer of power when the New Legion took the Citadel. That was exactly what I intended to use the opportunity of the dinner for—a plan Nej would never approve of.

"Can I ask you something?" I said.

Nej turned to face me. "Of course."

"You really believe it? That all of this is going to end with the Forum intact?"

His eyes cut to the portraitist, whose paintbrush slowed on the canvas.

"I know as well as you do that there is only one way for this to end," he said, voice tight. "With this rebellion crushed and the Citadel reinstated with its power over all of Isara." The words were a warning that such conversations were not meant for the ears of those we did not trust. "The more you show that faith in the Forum, the more leverage you will have with your judgment stone. Don't forget that."

I didn't answer, but I held his gaze long enough for him to be satisfied that I wouldn't argue. I knew he was right. We were far past the point of entertaining those thoughts. More than half the Loyal Legion was gone and the Citadel District was trapped between the river and the walls. They'd once existed only to protect us—the gates far across the city so that we'd be shielded from any breach. Now they had become a cage we were trapped in.

He walked to the south window, his eyes cast out over the city. But then his sauntering steps faltered, the expression on his face falling.

"What is it?" I asked, studying him.

Nej didn't answer.

I got to my feet in the next breath, crossing the room as the portraitist groaned behind me and his brush hit the palette with a clatter. Nej leaned into the window ledge with both hands and I followed his gaze to the river, where a swarm of red tunics was gathered at the south bridge. From this distance, I could just barely make out the three bodies suspended over the water. I didn't need to see their faces to know they were Magistrates.

Nej was silent, the vein at his throat pulsing.

I dropped my eyes, trying to quell the sick feeling blooming inside me. "How many?" I whispered. "How many are left?"

"If all three are Magistrates?" Nej exhaled. "Thirty-three. The gods do not reward cowardice."

The wretched souls hanging from the bridge weren't the first to try to escape through the Lower City. They wouldn't be the last, either.

The low-pitched peals of the bell tower rang out, calling the Magistrates to the Forum.

"Come," he said, squeezing my wrist. "We don't want to be late."

When I turned back to the study, the portraitist already had his paint box closed up.

"I'll be back in the morning." He rose slowly from his chair to stretch his legs, shooting a glance at the south window before he left.

Nej tied the strands of his robe clumsily as he looked me over. He straightened the medallion around my neck, brushing off my shoulders before he gave me an approving nod. Instead of turning for the door, he went to the desk, gathering up an armful of scrolls.

"What are you doing?"

He set a few of them into my hands. I inspected them, turning the parchments to try to read what was inside. "What are these?"

"Just something to make you look like you know what you're doing."

I expected him to laugh, but he didn't, making me think that there was more riding on this than I probably knew. When I tried to imagine myself in the grandeur of the Forum, sitting in my mother's seat, the truth settled in the pit of my stomach. I had *no* idea what I was doing. And now, more than ever, I wondered if I'd made the right decision that night. For so long, I'd been telling myself I'd had no choice. I didn't know anymore if that was true.

"Ready?" Nej asked, setting his gaze on mine.

I drew from the confidence in his eyes, that steeled look of surety he'd always had, and I pushed the memory away. "Ready."

CHAPTER 3

BEFORE: MARIS

The air was full of rose and spice.

I wove through the market with quick steps, sending a glance to the sundial's shadow cast on the outer wall of the Illyrium. The morning's tribunal had gone long, and while Priestess Ophelius didn't like it when I was late, she also wouldn't let me through the doors of the temple on a feast day without an offering.

Carts filled with silk, bread, and herbs littered the walkway where the citizens of the Citadel District were haggling over wares in their own preparations for the festivities. There would be parties, rituals, and ceremonial gatherings for the next three days to observe the First Feast, honoring the goddess Eris, keeper of life itself. Once the sun set, a new year would begin.

When I spotted the cart I was looking for, I tugged the length of my chiton higher, turning to the side to wedge myself through the crowd. A hunchbacked woman was perched on a stool over a collection of jars that glowed like liquid gold in the sunlight.

Large slices of honeycomb were suspended inside, the bright amber color signifying them as a delicacy from the most remote coastland meadows. The honey was tinged with the scent of orange blossoms, the very fruit that the goddess Eris used to divine the future.

I already had my drachmas in hand, studying the jars carefully before I chose one. Eris would receive countless offerings in the next few days, and if I wanted to garner her favor for the year ahead, I needed a gift that would stand out among the others.

As soon as I plucked one from the cart, the coins were clattering on the table and I pushed back toward the bridge with the honey clutched to my chest. The market edged along the outer wall of the baths, and from the look of it, they were full. The steam lifted into the air behind the carved stone walls, where the Citadel District's residents were preparing for the events that would go well into the night. My mother would spend her afternoon in our family's private chamber there, being bathed by our servant Iola before her skin was scrubbed with herb-scented salts. By sundown she'd be covered in the glow of rare oils, her hair intricately braided and dotted with jewels. Our family had been given the honor of hosting this year's First Feast for the Magistrates, and my mother had had Iola polish her obsidian mirror weeks ago. There was no room for anything but perfection tonight. Not when the whole of the Forum would be in attendance.

Scores of people were streaming in from the Lower City, on their way to work in the villas and shop fronts of the Citadel District. By nightfall, every window would be illuminated with firelight, the celebrations drowned in wine. The Lower City would have to wait until the residents of the Citadel District were sleeping off their drunken stupor to hold their own parties.

Two men with large wooden dowels propped on their shoulders barreled up the bridge, nearly knocking me into the street lantern as they passed. A gutted pig carcass was strung up between them, its hooves bound, ready for roasting. The smell of the raw flesh made my stomach turn.

When I finally made it across the river, I walked faster, sweat beading between my shoulder blades. The courtyard of the Illyrium was bursting with people who'd come to collect the blessed water in the fountain. It was the only temple in the city dedicated to all twelve gods, and on feast days, people lined up for half a mile along the river, ceramic vessels cradled in their arms or dangling from ropes. Tonight, they would be placed at the doorways of every home so that guests could cleanse themselves before paying homage to Eris.

I took the stairs up to the Illyrium's entrance, where a marble carving of the three faces of the god Phaedo painted a shadow on the steps. The huge marble walls of the temple blocked out the noise of the city, and the thick smell of incense curled softly in the air. The great hall was lined with enormous statues of the gods that watched with empty eyes as I crossed the polished floor with quiet steps. In the three years I'd been a novice to Ophelius, the Illyrium had become a second home. A place where I found myself moving by memory.

I passed the chamber that housed the temple smith, where he worked over the smoldering forge. The sound of water on hot gold hissed as he cooled a newly made medallion, sending a metallic scent into the hall. I slipped off my sandals and went to the nearest stone washing bowl, where cold, perfumed water from the fountain outside was replaced every hour. The customs of entering the temple had been ingrained in me since I could walk, even if my mother had never had much reverence for the gods. I scrubbed my hands and arms methodically before I washed my face. My feet were next, dipped into the hammered bronze troughs along the wall, and then I pulled back my hair from my face, tying it at the nape of my neck. The perfume of quince and rosemary replaced the dusty smell of the city that clung to my skin, washing away the last bit of the outside world before I entered the inner chamber of the temple.

I held the jar of honey in both hands as I stepped inside, where Ophelius was already standing at the altar. Her long silver hair trailed down the center of her back, her shoulders square beneath a robe embroidered with a shimmering gold thread that had been spun with godsblood. It was the one she wore only on feast days.

She didn't turn to greet me when she heard me coming, but she didn't turn to greet me. She never did. I came up the aisle with steps slow enough to be considered respectful and dropped to the ground to press my forehead to the stone. But when I rose and saw what Ophelius was doing, I all but ran to the altar.

She had the ceremonial knife clutched in one hand, suspended in the air as she watched her wrist drain into the porcelain bowl before her.

"You started without me," I rasped, setting the jar of honey down haphazardly and pulling up the sleeves of my robe.

"You are late," she said, letting me take the knife. It was carved from the bone of a whale with a design of gentle waves that commemorated the sea. The shining blade was smeared with godsblood.

I took over the ritual with quick hands, setting down the knife and taking Ophelius' arm to balance it over the bowl. The blood that dripped from her wrist was laced with the metallic sheen that signified the magic of the gods. The deep crimson glimmered as the light touched it, as if gold dust had been stirred into it.

The altar was stacked high with bundles of basil, baskets

of pomegranates, and strings of garlic. A sea of gold and silver drachmas had also been littered throughout in an offering to Eris.

Ophelius' eyes lifted to the tapestry strung up above the altar as her wrist dripped. A flock of doves was depicted in the scene there, little golden halos stitched in godsblood thread set atop each of their heads. The symbol identified them as those who were *gifted* by the gods, a distinction that could come in the form of a mark like this one or even an object that had been given to a mortal. Whatever the gifts, their meaning was the same. They were bestowed only upon those who'd been chosen to enact the will of the gods. But the days of the gifts had long been over.

"Recite the story," Ophelius said, waiting.

I exhaled, wondering if the test was meant to punish me for being late. The Twelve Feasts took place on the first day of each month, with a different god or goddess honored as the seasons passed. It was a time for telling stories and recounting the history of Isara, and by now I knew most of them by heart.

I studied the tapestry, eyeing the details of the background. The only words were written in the first language, which Ophelius had refused to teach me. She insisted that there was no good that could come of speaking to the gods in their own tongue. But I could tell the scene was a banquet. A long table was set with a feast, and the doves hovered over the heads of the gods who were seated there. I recognized the imagery but couldn't quite place them in a sequence of events.

"I do not know it, Priestess," I said.

I didn't have to see her face to know she was disappointed in me. In three years, the woman had never criticized or praised me. That wasn't her job. It didn't matter that I was the daughter of one of the most powerful women in the city. As a novice in this temple, my only function was to learn.

Ophelius' eyes moved from one dove to another. "The goddess Aster was at war with a greater god, Remillion. But she lacked the strength to conquer him."

Aster. The goddess of war, the very one to whom the city of Isara was consecrated. It wasn't the typical kind of story that was revisited on the First Feast, especially since the feast was dedicated to Eris. Not Aster. She wasn't honored until the Twelfth Feast.

"She'd been parted from her sister, Eris, throughout the fight. But when she heard that Eris was to marry the god Toranus, Aster took seven perfect white doves from the sky and sent them to Eris as a wedding gift."

My gaze trailed over the golden halos that crested the delicate brows of the birds.

"Eris accepted the generous gift," Ophelius continued, "instructing her servants to bake the doves into pies for the wedding feast. But upon taking the first bite, Eris fell dead, as did her entire wedding party."

My head turned, and I looked at Ophelius. Her expressionless face was still cast upward, toward the tapestry.

"Why?" I asked.

"To incite the wrath of Eris' new husband, Toranus." Finally, her eyes drifted to mine and they caught the light with a silver glow. Her narrow face was lined in soft wrinkles, her irises the color of moonbeams. "Aster could not beat her enemy, so she found someone who could. She told her new brother that the doves had been cursed by Remillion, and Toranus sent his armies to join Aster's. The battle was swift, and after only two days and nights of fighting, Remillion was vanquished."

I wanted to ask the meaning of the story, but I'd learned a long time ago that I had to be sparing with my curiosity. There were only so many questions Ophelius would tolerate from me. So, I waited for her to impart some lesson that I was meant to take with me to the Forum in my days as a Magistrate. Or some deeper wisdom I could use as a novice. But Ophelius just looked at me, eyes moving over my face as if she were looking for something.

The Priestess was like water, filling space and receding in a flow that made her seem as if she weren't as material as the rest of us. And she wasn't. She was the third-generation daughter of Priestess Ursu, who'd stood at the side of the legion on the front lines of the Old War.

I could see the fierceness of her ancestor in her eyes. The one who had performed the blood rites to secure the greatest bounty Isara had ever won. When the legion conquered the great city of Valshad, it wasn't gold and silver they were after. The legion laid waste to the city in search of only one thing—the gifted magic that had made Valshad prosper. Godsblood.

There were five Valshadi Priestesses in the temple when they stormed the gates, all souls within whom that magic dwelled. Two successfully took their own lives rather than give the godsblood to Isara, but the three who failed were subjected to the blood rites when they refused to gift their magic to three Isarians. Leah, Cadie, and Ursu—Ophelius' great-grandmother.

The act of the blood rites was a shameful desecration. One that hadn't been performed since and that Ophelius never spoke of. There were only two ways for the magic to pass from one mortal to another. It had to be given or it had to be taken. And the only way to take the godsblood was to drink it. Every single drop.

Over the last hundred years, the stolen magic of Valshad had bolstered the city of Isara with the favor of the gods, sparing us famine, disease, and even war. It was bound to the bodies of the three Priestesses who dwelled in the Illyrium until the day they chose to gift it to someone else. But Ophelius had no child, and it was no secret that the Magistrates were growing concerned over the fact that she hadn't yet passed on her magic. She was a stubborn woman who wasn't easily controlled, and the Citadel was eager for a young Priestess who could be tended. Coaxed to grow in one direction like a loyal grapevine.

The gold-tinged blood dripped into the bowl, and once it was filled, I tilted her arm carefully. The wound slowly healed, knitting itself back together. I reached for the thin, flat mother-of-pearl stone set on the cloth before me and placed it against her forearm. Gently, I scraped it against the skin until the last of the godsblood was gathered onto the stone, and I set it into the grooves of the bowl so that it could drip.

From there, the precious liquid would be siphoned into vials and delivered to the Citadel. A single drop of godsblood lent the strength of the gods to mortals. The entire city had been built with its magic. It was sown into the fields, baked into the clay bricks of the Citadel, infused into medicines, and even forged into the weapons of the legion. But over the course of one hundred years, its use had been all but defiled. Now the godsblood was cast into jewels, spun into thread, painted onto trinkets—anything the highborn of Isara desired. There were even vials sold to the highest bidder, an idea that made my stomach turn.

Ophelius' eyes fell to the jar of honey on the altar stone. "Very good, Casperia. But be careful. You don't want to become a favorite of the gods."

"I thought it's an honor to chosen by the gods," I said.

She glanced back up at the tapestry, to the halo-crowned doves that arced across the scene. "I'm not sure the doves would agree."

I didn't notice until then that she was a shade paler than usual, a darkness hovering beneath her eyes. Down the hall, the hiss of the temple smith working sounded again.

"You don't look well, Priestess." I touched her elbow gently, but she pulled away from me, taking a stick of incense from the silver bowl at her side.

"Are you ready for tonight?" She ignored my concern, changing the subject.

"I am."

"I hear Matius will finally be introducing his heir to the Magistrates."

I'd heard the same, but her mention of it surprised me. Ophelius didn't usually take any interest in the frivolous, vain world of the Magistrates. In fact, there was nothing she despised more.

My mother had talked of almost nothing else since the rumors of Magistrate Matius' illness started circulating. He was her rival in every sense of the word, the leader of the opposing political faction in the Forum. My mother had spent her entire time in the Citadel slowly chipping away at his majority hold, and she was close to balancing the scales of power. But now, he was dying.

It had been years since Matius had adopted his nephew in order to secure the inheritance of his seat in the Forum, but for the most part he'd kept his heir out of sight. Everyone in the Citadel District was talking about the succession of the seat that would open upon Magistrate Matius' death. He had managed to ensure it would stay with his family name, but no one knew anything about the nephew who would wield the judgment stone.

He didn't bring him to gatherings in the Citadel District or parade him on the balcony of the tribunals the way other Magistrates did with their children. He'd waited. For what, I didn't know, but it was no coincidence that the night he chose to finally bring his new son into the light was the same night my mother was hosting the First Feast. It was a slight. A declaration of war, even.

Matius' faction was determined to keep its majority in the Forum after his death, and the most reliable way to do that was to find a reputable Magistrate family to marry his nephew into. There were those among my mother's faction who could be swayed by the prospect of joining with a family name as prestigious as Matius. The party tonight would be a perfect opportunity to make that kind of alliance.

"I want you to get a sense of him," Ophelius said.

My eyes narrowed on her. "Matius' heir?"

She nodded.

"I'm not sure my mother would—"

"If the favor of the gods is truly what you seek, it will take more than a clever gift to gain it, Casperia," Ophelius said, cutting me off. "You can't lead a city with a jar of honey."

I swallowed, instinctively glancing again to the gift I'd left on the altar.

"You will hold your mother's seat sooner than you think." Her voice lowered, the words making me shiver.

Her pale silver eyes shone just a little brighter as she said it, her tone ringing with prophecy. It was one of the gifts the magic afforded her, but it was incredibly rare for Ophelius to share her insight into the future with me.

"You will meet Matius' heir. You will learn what you can of him," she said again.

She waited for me to answer with a nod before she reached into the sleeve of her robe and produced a small scroll that matched the many she'd had me pen for her in the past. She held it in both hands, fingers careful, as if considering its weight.

"A message?" I reached for it, but she moved it from my reach.

Her eyes were searching mine again with that same penetrating look.

After a long moment, she finally let me take the scroll, but her eyes followed it as I tucked it into my chiton.

"Where would you like me to take it?" I asked.

"The Philosopher Vitrasian." Ophelius turned back to the altar, dipping a stick of incense into the fire. Once it was lit, she waved it through the air, letting the smoke drift over her. "Now go. I must pray."

The smoke began to billow, the sound of her voice already taking on the monotone timbre of chanting. I picked up the bowl before me, the godsblood gleaming in the light, and cradled it in my steady hands as I made my way down the aisle. When I reached the doors, I glanced back, tracing the hazy image of the Priestess enveloped by the smoke.

She always spoke in riddles and stories, forcing me to unearth the meaning of things. But her request had been simple and direct, and that could mean only one thing. Ophelius had taken an interest in Matius' son.

CHAPTER 4

NOW: LUCA

I stalked back through the camp, headed to the Illyrium with the sound of the crowd at my back. The rows of tents grew wider as I neared the towering colonnade that had once served as the entrance to the Lower City. Beyond its archway, the Illyrium was still whole.

I glanced up as I entered the courtyard, a familiar discomfort bleeding into me. The temple's entrance bore the likeness of the god of peace, which was an irony that I took no pleasure in. It was one of the oldest buildings in Isara, constructed long before the Citadel that sat across the river, but now it belonged to the New Legion.

Great white pillars carved in deep, uniform ridges stood shoulder to shoulder atop the temple's steps, where six legionnaires were posted with swords in hand. Along its roof, archers were at the ready above the three carved stone faces of Phaedo looking out over the square. In its center sat a large round fountain where Isarians used to come collect the water blessed by the

Priestesses. Now, for the first time in nearly three hundred years, it was dry. But it was the smooth white stone wall that faced the river that drew my eyes now.

The insignia of the New Legion had been painted in red, black, and gold across the pale stone. The symbol stretched at least thirty feet high, like a flag that couldn't fall. Couldn't burn. Couldn't be shot down. The depiction was of a soldier on his knees, bloodied short sword hanging from his hand as he looked up toward the sky. A gilded halo encircled his head, and every time I looked at it, I couldn't help cringing.

It wasn't just any legionnaire. It was me.

No one knew who first drew the symbol, but in the days after the Philosopher died, as I sat in the catacombs awaiting my own death it began to appear all over the Lower City. This image, this record of what had happened, was the match that lit the fire of rebellion. Now it was a battle cry.

The Commander's tribune, Asinia, stood at the top of the steps, his javelin clutched in one hand as I passed beneath the ornate entry. His was one face I did look at because I'd known it before all this began. But it was different now. The scar that marked the curve of his jaw disappeared into his tunic. The result of a javelin's hook thrown in the second battle at the gates. He was one of the few who knew the version of me from before the fighting began. By the time it ended, maybe there would be none.

"Has he been told?" I asked.

Asinia fell into step beside me. "He has. The medallions arrived before dawn."

The thick smell of incense swelled around us as we entered the chamber. The windows encircling the great domed roof filled the Illyrium with bright, scattered light, and a number of soldiers already had their hands busy with the day's work. I followed the corridor that led to the gallery on the north side of the building. Inside, more tapestries were hung against the expansive walls, their bright colors dulled with a layer of dust.

Before the rebellion, the Illyrium had been one of the city's jewels, filled with ornate marble statues and colorful frescoes. Now some of the tapestries were torn from their rods, the beautiful golden tassels piled on the ground. The enormous granite slab that had once held offerings to the gods was now stacked with the leather strips used to make armor and finely sanded wooden rods waiting to be crafted into arrows.

My eyes landed for just a moment on the altar, where the mother who'd borne me had spent her days and nights begging for favor from a god who didn't know her name. She'd wasted away on that floor until my noble uncle took me in, determined to make me his heir. I had no way of knowing then that it would all lead to this. Now.

When we reached the gallery, I stopped, turning to face Asinia.

"How is he?" I kept my voice low, trying not to draw the attention of the guards posted on either side of the doors.

Asinia waited longer to respond than I liked. As tribune, it was his job to protect the Commander with his life. Not just in body, but in reputation. I could see him weighing his answer before he finally spoke.

"His color is better today." He gave me a knowing look.

I pushed through the doors, the length of my cloak rippling out behind me. The Commander stood over the table at the far end of the gallery, his attention on the unrolled maps before him. I was glad to see that Asinia was right. The pallor of his face had warmed since the night before, even if just a little. His black hair was longer than I'd ever seen it, making him look much older than his twenty-seven years. The scruff along his jaw was thickening, too. I caught myself wondering when exactly it had happened—the two of us becoming men.

"This has to stop." My voice echoed in the room, drawing the Commander's eyes up from the table.

He let the edge of the map curl up beneath his palm, exhaling. "Luca."

My given name was almost unrecognizable to me now. The Commander was a friend who'd been made my brother by war, and one of two people who could call me Luca without me drawing my sword. To the legionnaires and everyone else in this city, I was called by the name engraved on the medallion that hung around my neck. Matius, son of the family Matius. In the same way, the Commander was Saturian, son of the family Saturian. I, however, knew the Commander by his given name—Vale.

I stopped in front of the table, gaze dropping to the stack of three medallions that held down one corner of the maps. The gold discs still hung on their chains, bearing the family names of the bodies on the bridge. Each time Roskia and his men executed someone attempting to flee the district, the medallions were delivered to Vale. A kind of trophy that allowed him to maintain the claim that it was the work of the Commander, not a rogue Centurion.

"We're losing control of him," I said through gritted teeth.

"We've *lost* control, Luca. Surely you can see that." His stare fell to my hands, which were still trembling just slightly. I balled them into fists.

"She's not a fool. She won't try to flee the Citadel District. She wouldn't dare set foot in the Lower City," he said, addressing the true source of my panic.

I wanted to believe that. Maris had missed her chance to leave

Isara, and the New Legion's thirst for Magistrate blood was growing by the day. This was the wire I'd been walking for months now—balancing my commitment to the cause with the fact that there was still someone across that river I was protecting.

He waited for me to respond, but I didn't.

"I want you to go see him—Roskia," he said.

I straightened. "When?"

"Tomorrow."

"I'm not leaving you at the front. Not when you're like this." I grimaced, gesturing to the wound concealed beneath his armor.

A swift anger lit in Vale's eyes, where dark circles made the cut of his cheeks deep and shadowed. In an instant, the old Vale, the one I'd spent my first years in the legion with, flashed in my mind. Bright-eyed, with words always on the edge of sharp humor. The man who stood before me was a different creature. One of my own making.

"I'm not *asking* you," he snapped, snatching up one of the medallions and holding it between us. "If we're going to make a deal with the Consul for surrender, we need Roskia to support it."

"He won't. You know that," I argued.

"We can't afford to have him oppose us. There are too many in the New Legion who would be happy to slaughter every single soul left in the Citadel District when we take it."

He met my eyes again, this time with a look I couldn't quite read. He was nervous, and I could guess it was because there was more than one kind of battle waiting for us across the river.

"Are you sure you can do it? See the Consul?" I asked.

Vale swallowed. "My father is a difficult man, but I understand him. I can get him to negotiate."

"And if you can't?"

When Vale crossed the bridge with me and the rebellion began, he'd chosen to stand on the other side of the line from his own father. It was a betrayal that had garnered him the respect of the New Legion, but the rift between the Consul and his son had started long before that.

"When we take the district," he continued, "the legionnaires will look to *Roskia* for permission to take out their vengeance. Not me."

I stared at the medallions on the table, the gold shimmering with godsblood. Like every Isarian, I grew up with the tales of the Old War, when our legion took the city of Valshad and planted its stolen magic and seeds of wealth in our own soil. But the blood of that fight had never painted the streets of our city. It wasn't an outside enemy who'd turned its gleaming spires to crumbling dust. Now Isara was a husk, a crumbling sandcastle compared to what it had been just a year ago. The weight of that lay on one person, and one person alone.

"Summon Roskia and we'll talk," Vale pressed.

"I—"

"You're going to the gates." His voice invoked his rank, reminding me of my place.

I gritted my teeth, swallowing down a curse.

"If we're going to push into the Citadel District, it will take all of us. And I can't afford to have a Centurion who is waging his own separate war," Vale reminded me. "And you're not going alone."

I stared at him.

"Asinia says you have yet to accept your new tribune."

I clenched my jaw, shooting a look over my shoulder to where Asinia was posted at the door. The argument was one we'd had more than once now, and it was the last thing I wanted to discuss.

"I told you I don't need a tribune," I said.

Vale's expression went flat. "You're a Centurion. Every Centurion has a tribune. That's how we keep you from dying."

"I've kept him busy enough," I said.

"He's not your errand boy," Vale snapped, irritated now. "He goes where you go. He fights where you fight. If I have to assign you three tribunes so they're more likely to keep track of you, I will."

I glared at him.

"I mean it," Vale said. "The last thing I need is to find out that an archer on the other side of the river took you down while you were taking a piss because you were too proud to let a tribune cover your flank."

"It's not pride," I said, defensive.

"Isn't it?" He shifted on his feet, wincing as he pressed a hand to his ribs. His face blanched a shade whiter.

He waited to see if I'd continue arguing, but he wasn't the one I was angry with. Asinia reporting my actions to Vale wasn't surprising, but he should have known better than to bother the Commander with it at a time like this. We had bigger things to worry about.

"How is your wound?" I changed the subject, glancing at the right side of Vale's breastplate, where the bandage wrapped around his ribs was concealed.

He gave a frustrated sigh, as if he resented being reminded of it. "Better."

"And you're letting the physician treat you?"

"Luca," he said, clipped. "*Stop.*"

I relented, recognizing that look in his eye. Almost two weeks ago, as we took the Illyrium, I'd watched from only yards away as a legionnaire from the Loyal Legion drove his short sword into the seam of Vale's armor. The man was dead before Vale even hit the ground, Asinia's blade catching his throat. There had been several hours while the physicians worked over the hole in Vale's chest when I thought he was going to die. Since then, I'd done a poor job of hiding how much it had terrified me.

"Now, if you're finished." Vale paused. "There's something I need to show you."

He didn't bother with the cloak he usually wore at his back, leaving it behind as he came around the table and headed for one of the arched doors along the wall. I glanced at Asinia before I followed Vale up a tight staircase that curled like a seashell as it rose. Tiny slits in the stone walls let in the sea air, but it was still dark and dank with the smell of sour mud. He stopped when he reached a small platform, moving aside in the tight space to make room for me.

A young boy dressed in stripped-down armor stood at one of the rectangular openings, his bow in one hand, a fresh arrow in the other. He looked up at us, a nervous fidget finding his stance. But his eyes widened when they landed on the arc of gold that hovered in the air over my head.

"Show him," Vale said, crossing his arms as he leaned against the wall.

The boy blinked, shaking himself from the trance. He instantly obeyed, sheathing the arrow and setting the bow down before taking up a small woolen sack at his feet. He handed it to me and I peered inside, my jaw instantly tensing. The soft silver shine of feathers gleamed in the dim light, and I stepped closer to the opening, lifting the sack higher. They were falcons.

Across the river, the tower of the Citadel that housed its scribes was painted red by the setting sun. The day we took the Illyrium, the Citadel's aviary released a single bird. The next day, another. The day after that, three.

"How many now?" I asked, reaching inside and picking up one of the stiff, cold carcasses.

"Eight since yesterday morning," the boy answered.

One of the bird's black feet was encircled by a bronze ringlet that held a small wooden tube. I opened it, sliding the rolled message from inside. But like always, it was blank. The parchment gleamed with a warm iridescence, the evidence of godsblood. Whatever it said, we couldn't see it.

"There are more each day," Vale said.

I dropped the bird back into the sack before my eyes moved over the blank scroll again, willing something to appear. Behind the gilded doors of the Citadel, the Consul was sending messages hidden in the magic of godsblood. But to whom?

Isara didn't have allies, one of many mistakes the Magistrates had made in their policies in the hundred years since the Old War. There were only a few places that messages from the Citadel went. To the farms that fed the city or to the ports that brought in trade, which had all but stopped. The only other thing I could think of were the remnants of the Loyal Legion who'd been posted at the borders, but every soldier had been called in when the fighting began. There was no one else out there to talk to.

"You said you understand the Consul. What do you think this is?" I asked.

He shook his head just slightly.

"I don't know how much it matters now, anyway." I tried to believe my own words. "We'll be standing on the Citadel steps in a week's time."

Vale didn't look convinced. I could see his mind was working at something he wasn't saying aloud. He turned out of the chamber, and I handed the sack back to the young soldier, tucking the small piece of parchment into my tunic's pocket beneath my armor. The boy was standing at the ready with bow in hand again before we were even out of sight.

I followed Vale back down the spiraling stairs. "What is it?"

"It's not just the district I'm worried about. It's the Lower City, too. How much longer do you think they'll believe in this cause? How much do they have to lose before they turn on us, like we turned on the Citadel?"

"That's not going to happen," I said, though I'd thought the same thing. Many times.

Vale walked me to the opening of the gallery and stopped, holding out a hand for me. I took his arm, gripping it below the elbow, and he did the same to mine.

"I'll see you when you get back," he said.

My hold tightened on him. "And if they cross the river before I do?"

"They won't."

I bit the inside of my bottom lip to keep myself from challenging him again. I didn't like the idea of being deep in the Lower City if the Loyal Legion took a chance to attack.

Vale let me go and turned on his heel, steps heavy as he crossed the gallery. His voice echoed out behind him. "And take that damn tribune with you."

I watched him round the table and open the maps again before I started for the gallery's entrance, where Asinia was still waiting. When I reached him, I muttered a curse.

"Could have warned me."

The look Asinia gave me said that he couldn't. More important, he *wouldn't*. That alone was the reason he was the only person I trusted to keep Vale alive and the only one worthy to serve as his tribune.

"He relies on you," Asinia said.

I knew that. More than Asinia could possibly know. And I relied on Vale, too. I let my gaze drift back to the gallery, where Vale's shadow was cast on the marble floor. Only days ago, I'd stood over his barely breathing body, calling out to every god I could think of to save his life. And not only because I loved him. Vale had taken the role of Commander in part so that I didn't have to. If something happened to him, it would fall to me. There was no one who dreaded that fate more than I did.

"He doesn't leave your sight until I get back," I said. "Understand?"

Asinia gave a sharp nod in answer, hands clenched tight around his javelin.

The sound of my boots bounced through the marble hallways until I was coming back down the steps of the Illyrium. When I was a boy, if I'd been able to peer into the future like the Philosopher and see us, three scraggly boys leading the charge of a rebellion that was bleeding Isara dry, would I have believed it? I didn't think so.

CHAPTER 5

BEFORE: LUCA

"Again, Matius."

The Philosopher Vitrasian stood at the top of the steps that led down into her study, watching me scrawl the last of the sequence on the smooth surface of the parchment. The pain in my wrist had crept up to my elbow in the hours since I'd first started.

I dropped the stylus to stretch the cramp in my palm. "I've completed it sixteen times. I know the axiom."

"Again," she repeated.

I looked up, ready to argue, but Vitrasian's attention had already left me. Her eyes were cast up to the bronze-and-silver orbs suspended in the air overhead as they slowly rotated in the breeze coming through the windows. The shining metal spheres were erected in an apparatus that replicated the orbits of the six planets. I watched as she reached up, touching one and gently nudging it through the air to make the entire solar system spin.

She'd had me working the sequence to triangulate the orbits' arcs for the last month. The equation was one she'd solved years ago, but each day that I came to the theater, she had me work it again from scratch.

"I think my time would be better spent on the archives. Or the trials you're running on the new infusion from the Citadel's physicians."

She turned the small scroll she was holding over in her hands, rolling it between her palms. "I thought you were here to learn, Matius. In fact, from what I remember, you *begged* for this noviceship."

"I did, but—"

"So, that is what you will do. You will learn."

Her gaze held a finality that I knew not to challenge. Angering Rhea Vitrasian would only end with me cataloging the hundreds of scrolls in her study or cleaning the equipment for her experiments in the catacombs for the next month. This noviceship was a place I wanted to be.

It had taken almost an entire year to convince Vitrasian to agree to the noviceship, which was triple the time it took to persuade my uncle. I'd had to show up at the theater before dawn for an entire month before the Philosopher would even begin to discuss it, and there were times when I regretted my persistence. Vitrasian was unrelenting in her instruction, with standards that felt impossible to reach. On top of requiring me to master and memorize countless mathematical equations and scientific theories, she had also begun to teach me the first language—the language of the gods. Only those who held the highest seats in the temples could read it, and that alone had me up late studying every night.

The first time I saw Rhea Vitrasian, she'd been giving a talk to a group of Magistrates at the Sophanes River on hydro propulsion and water purification. I was a child, no more than six or seven years old, but I'd marveled at her use of technical terms and concepts that felt more like magic to me than they did ideas.

The next time I saw her was after my uncle took me in. After years of trying to produce a child with multiple women who went on to carry children for other men, he'd been forced to face the fact that he wasn't capable of fathering an heir. As fate would have it, he had a nearly orphaned nephew who carried his blood living right across the river. My uncle was a Magistrate, and his sole purpose in taking me in and giving me a life outside the Lower City was that I would fulfill the duties of an heir—to carry on the family name, maintain its honor, and build upon its power. For most noble boys in the Citadel District, that meant a career that began as a legionnaire.

I was attending my first-ever tribunal as a spectator when Vitrasian was called to give an account of Isara's inefficient trade routes that had stifled the Citadel's profits. I watched in awe as she countered the arguments of the Magistrates and defied their resistance to her recommendations. The Philosopher didn't mince words, and I had never seen anyone speak to the Magistrates that way.

The next day, I asked my uncle if my place as a novice could be with the Philosopher. He'd laughed, and then he'd refused, enlisting me in the legion like the other Magistrates' sons. Kastor's plan for me was a military career that would bring me glory and fame. It was months before I could convince him that serving as both a novice to Vitrasian and a legionnaire would strengthen my place in the Forum when I took his seat. The only reason he'd finally agreed was to ensure that even if I failed to make a name for myself as a soldier, I'd have connections elsewhere. Now I was tenuously juggling the hours of my day between the two, all while trying to learn the rules and constructs of the Forum.

Vitrasian came down the steps of the theater, hands clasped at her back. The violet stola draped over her white chiton trailed down the stone behind her bare feet, the gold brooches at her shoulders bearing the mark of the Citadel. Beyond that, she bore little resemblance to the other women of the district. Her hair wasn't adorned with jewels, and she didn't have a single possession that was made with godsblood, nor did she use it in any of her studies. She didn't even wear a talisman to signify which god or goddess she worshipped. And I wasn't the only one who'd noticed.

She was the city's most accomplished Philosopher in the last six generations, with discoveries and breakthroughs that spanned biology, the cosmos, mathematics, and medicine. She was even gifted in the arts, having written multiple plays and literary works that were celebrated as cultural pillars. But the way she stood on the edge of society was a point of contention among Magistrates, and the longer I served as her novice, the more I realized that she was anything but favored. The Citadel considered her a necessary evil, merely tolerating her in exchange for the advancements she made for the city. She wasn't nearly as afraid of them as she should be, and that concerned me.

I slid the parchment to the side and took a new one from the stack, starting the sequence again.

"You know, I can tell when you're worrying about something, Luca." She grinned, using my given name in an attempt to force me to relax. She thought I was too rigid. Too serious. She pressed the tip of her finger to the place between her eyebrows. "You get a crease just here."

"You don't worry enough," I murmured.

I didn't call her by her given name out of respect, though she allowed me to use it. The lines of our relationship had blurred over the years that I'd served as her novice, and there were times when she felt much more like a mother to me than a mentor. It was a feeling I tried to keep in check when we were working.

"Are you nervous?" One of her eyebrows lifted.

"About what?"

Now she was smiling. "Your public introduction at the feast tonight."

I didn't give her the satisfaction of an answer, my attention focused on retracing the numbers on the parchment. They'd nearly lost their meaning to me now, becoming just a blur of ink.

"Your uncle will want to make a show of you. I hope you're ready."

"Not much to show, I'm afraid."

Vitrasian clicked her tongue disapprovingly. "You're too modest, Luca."

I gave her a knowing look. From what I'd heard, the Magistrates tended to use the feasts as an opportunity to display their sons and daughters like goods in the market. Marriages were arranged adhering to schemes that had been in play as far back as the Old War, sometimes even planned from birth. The other heirs had spent their entire lives grooming themselves for the Forum, but my mother had been disowned after taking vows with a lowborn trader who ruined her, so I hadn't been reared like the children of the Citadel District. While they spent their young years being taught the ethics of government and economics by tutors and advisors, I was laying bricks with calloused hands in the Lower City. I was just a sick woman's son who'd been adopted by a desperate, dying man.

You didn't have to see the blood on my uncle's handkerchief to know that his days were numbered. The death growing in Kastor's eyes was looming. The physicians predicted he had mere months to live, and as a faction leader who'd slowly been losing his majority to Casperia in the Forum, he'd finally been forced to unveil me at tonight's feast.

"It's important you make a good impression," she said. "And whatever you do, don't disrespect the gods in front of them. That's the quickest way to make enemies in the Forum."

I stifled a laugh.

"It's not a joke," she said, words sharp.

I glanced at the room around us. Her theater was one of the only places that was wiped clean of any evidence of the gods. "It is. You don't revere the gods any more than I do."

"You don't have to worship them to understand that they are an important part of playing this game."

My jaw clenched. I didn't like it when she referred to the happenings of the Citadel as a game. I heard enough of that from Kastor.

"That's what it is." She countered my unspoken rebuke.

"When you talk like that, you sound like one of *them*." As soon as I said it, I could feel my body tense. I was edging the line of insulting her—something I never did.

"You were dedicated at the temple, weren't you?"

My eyes flicked up, my fingers tightening on the stylus. "I didn't tell you about my mother so that you could use her in a debate against me."

Rhea watched me for a long moment, and I could almost feel the change in the atmosphere of the theater. Her mind was like that solar system drifting through the air—always spinning. It was the reason she was brilliant, but it also meant she could always see more than I wanted her to.

"There is only one insect that can invade the great fortress of a beehive. Do you know what it is?" she asked.

I set down the stylus, attempting not to appear irritated. "No."

"It's a beetle. A parasitic beetle."

She walked to the shelf behind her desk, surveying the jars there until she found what she was looking for. When she had it in hand, she walked back in my direction and set it on the parchment before me.

I picked it up, studying the creature inside. "How?"

"They mimic the scent of the female bees, which attracts the males. When the males come to gather pollen off the vegetation, the young beetles attach themselves to those males, who unwittingly fly back to the hive with them in tow. There, the beetles gorge themselves on pollen and nectar and eggs. They grow and get stronger, surviving off the spoils of the bees' opulent kingdom. And once winter has passed, the adult beetle emerges as both a child of that place *and* an enemy."

The illustration made me uncomfortable. I wasn't sure I wanted to understand it.

"I don't worship the gods the way others do, because I know well enough not to trust them. Magic, favor, miracles—they are like sand that slips through the fingers. But science—" Her chin lifted. "It does not change. It does not shift with the wind. Science is truth."

She had a heavy look about her now, her face just a bit paler than it was a moment before.

"Tonight, you will write the first line of *your* story in the Citadel. You may not have grown up with the advantages of the other Magistrates, but a clean slate—a lack of history—is more valuable than all of that. Don't discount their hunger for new blood." She walked back to her desk, where she'd been sketching the geometry of a collection of seashells. "They can't resist it. You may be of Matius' lineage, but you represent something the Magistrates rarely see—possibility. It's been generations since a seat in the Forum turned over to someone who isn't *one of them*."

I looked up, not able to hide my own pride at her words. I didn't *want* to be one of them, and Vitrasian seemed to be the only person who understood that.

"And it's not just any seat, Luca. Your uncle is a faction leader. With that place comes power, and there isn't a soul in the Forum who isn't wondering what you'll make of it."

Vitrasian held the small scroll out before her, an empty expression cast over her face. I watched as she tipped it toward the candle. It took me a moment to realize what she was doing. The flame caught the parchment slowly, growing as it consumed the end of the scroll. She stared at it, unblinking, before she dropped it into the bronze bowl on her desk. Smoke trailed up into the air as it burned in a tangle of fire that died down a few seconds later. I hadn't paid much attention to it before, but it looked like a message.

Her eyes flicked up but I dropped my gaze before she could catch me watching. And I wasn't even sure why. There was something strange about the way she'd almost nervously fidgeted with the scroll, and I'd never seen her burn one. But Vitrasian was full of secrets. I'd learned that much by now.

From the corner of my eye, I could see her return to her sketches, and I focused on the sequence, working the sums methodically until it was finished. But before I'd even lifted the tip of the stylus from the parchment, the Philosopher was already speaking.

"Again, Matius."

CHAPTER 6

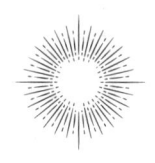

NOW: MARIS

The thick wooden doors of my mother's chambers—now *my* chambers—swung open, and we spilled into a sea of white as the Magistrates streamed down the Tribunal Hall toward the Forum. The sound of sandals sliding over marble and the rustle of scrolls floated up into the tall ceilings, where the limestone was cast in a warm glow. That dim light reminded me of my days in the temple.

Nej had never approved of my noviceship with the Priestess Ophelius, even before she was considered a traitor to Isara. But my experience as a novice was the only reason I was even somewhat qualified to wear the Magistrate's robes. The Priestess had never been kind, but she'd taught me more about politics and people than my mother ever did. You couldn't understand the city or its problems without understanding the Old War. And you couldn't understand the Old War unless you understood the magic we stole from Valshad. The very godsblood that ran through the Priestess's veins.

FALLEN CITY

The Magistrates' portraits looked down on us as we walked, lining both sides of the hall with one stoic face after another. My steps slowed when I saw two men balancing on a ladder ahead, carefully lowering one of the enormous paintings with a pulley. It was of Magistrate Heraldes, an old member of my mother's faction, which meant his was one of the bodies on the bridge. The rest of the Magistrates who filled the hall were making an effort not to look.

For my entire life, there had been sixty-five portraits to represent the sixty-five Magistrate seats of the tribunal. Now, every few paces, there was a missing one. Some of the Magistrates' families had left the city when the first battle against the New Legion was lost. They'd streamed to their summer villas to wait for what Consul Saturian said would be a swift victory over the revolt. Once we lost the city gates, our only way in and out of Isara, there were those who tried their hands at escape or being smuggled out. Every one of them had ended up strung from the bridge—a warning of what would happen to anyone else who attempted to flee. But still, nearly every week, there was someone willing to try.

When we passed beneath the place my mother's portrait had once hung, I kept my eyes on the white robes in front of me. Like Magistrate Heraldes', it had been taken down only hours after she died, and soon my own portrait would replace it.

The moving crowd began to slow and the bellowing sound of the Magistrates' names echoed out ahead.

"Osturan! Philosta! Trestis!"

The names of prominent, powerful political families rang out in the Forum as the Magistrates entered. They were names I knew, some of them belonging to my mother's rivals or even those who had sons she had thought of marrying me to. She'd had no idea, even at the end, that I'd taken control of my own fate in more ways than one.

I took a step forward as the line formed, clasping my hand around the medallion resting against my chest. I tilted it in the light so that the gold flashed along the rim, the weight of it heavy. The godsblood forged into the metal gave it a luminescence, and the branch of a cypress tree and the feather of a dove encircled my family name.

Casperia.

The medallion had been cast in the temple three days after I was born. The name it bore signified wealth and reputation. It had endowed my mother with a seat in the Forum and our family a villa in the Citadel District. But now it was no more than a myth, like the ever-changing will of the gods. Now it was just a noose around my neck.

Nej pressed his elbow into mine and I blinked, realizing the scribe seated at the entrance of the Forum was waiting for me. I dropped the medallion and took up the length of my robes so I could climb the rest of the steps.

The man was seated beside a small table with an unrolled scroll nearly falling over its edge. He dipped the tip of his quill into the pot of ink, eyes finding my medallion before they snapped up to my face. There was a long pause before his quill touched down, dragging the letters across the parchment in the glistening ink.

"Casperia!"

His voice filled the chamber before me, and every set of eyes within it turned in my direction. The Forum was carved from pure white stone with twelve rows of tiered levels encircling the floor below. It was here that Isara had been born, consecrated to the goddess Aster. Beneath this golden dome, wars had been declared, laws written, and lives taken by the voices that still echoed here. I could almost hear those voices now, my mother's among them.

I was nudged by the Magistrate behind me before I took an awkward step into the Forum. Every man and woman in the room was watching me, gazes dragging from my head to my feet. I had the sudden feeling that I was naked, parading before them without even a stitch of silk to hide me.

I walked toward my seat, not slowing when a man called Lechronis blocked my path. The length of his robes brushed the ground when he was forced to shuffle aside and a few other Magistrates coiled around him as he clutched his scrolls to his chest.

No one wanted to catch the ill favor of the gods, and as Ophelius' novice, I was drenched in it. Ophelius and the two other Priestesses took the fate of Isara into their own hands and did the unthinkable. The unforgivable. Now Ophelius was the last living keeper of Valshad's magic and imprisoned beneath our very feet, in the catacombs of the Citadel.

I didn't breathe until I made it to my seat, a high-backed chair upholstered in a rich floral tapestry. It was secured to the floor and enclosed on all four sides by stained wooden walls that reached as high as my waist. Within it, a small folding surface served as a desk, and a golden plaque that bore my family name was secured to the outside. At the corner of the desk stood my family's judgment stone. The smooth, perfectly round face was polished and gleaming. On one side, the marble was a bright, spotless white and on the other it was an onyx as black as ink.

I pushed through the little door of the enclosure with my hip and sat, busying my hands with the scrolls Nej had given me. The Magistrates were divided into two factions: those who clamored for the fickle favor of Consul Saturian and those who sought to replace him once they had enough votes. My mother had led the latter faction, determined to take the place of Consul herself.

News of her suicide had flooded the district as soon as it was reported, and it had caused a shift in the precarious balance of the Forum. With nearly half the Magistrates gone, the factions barely existed, but that didn't mean that the remaining Magistrates weren't wondering which side I would fall on.

I forced my gaze ahead, ignoring the penetrating eyes of the room. The interior of the Citadel was the only thing in Isara that had remained untouched by war. There were plenty of buildings in the district that had been hit by catapults or damaged by firebombs cast across the river, but the white marble floors of the Forum were polished and shining. They reflected the domed ceiling overhead, where colorful paintings of the gods looked down on us and the light from the flaming oil lamps made the scenes look like they were moving. There were even a few of the gifted—Isarians who had been chosen to help deliver the will of the gods.

Below, the circular stone at the foot of the Magistrates' seats was marked with an enormous twelve-pointed star, and every time I looked at it, I was there again—that single horrifying moment that had changed everything. The Philosopher Vitrasian had stood at the center of the Forum, the fine silk of her chiton fluttering along her shoulders only seconds before she was executed. I could still see the pool of dark blood that had smeared across the spokes of the star. I could see the heavy drop of Vitrasian's body, her head hitting the stone.

And I could hear *him*. Luca's ghost of a voice. I could still hear him screaming.

My fingers curled around the fabric of my robes so tightly that they creased the silk, and I forced myself to unclench my hand, stretching it out before me. My own mother had sat in this very chair that day and cast her judgment stone against Vitrasian. Her hands had been painted with the blood that started the rebellion, but now the seat was mine.

Slowly, my eyes trailed to the empty seat of Magistrate Matius, where Luca should be sitting now. If he'd taken his uncle's place, like we'd planned, the balance of the Forum would have already been tipped. But everything changed the day Vitrasian died.

The doors that opened across the Forum swung so quietly that I hadn't noticed Consul Saturian entering until I saw the brilliant blue of his robes flash like liquid sapphire in the corner of my vision. He took purposeful but patient steps in the direction of his seat, which rose higher than the rest in the room. White hair crowned a young-looking face, with skin that hadn't yet given way to wrinkles. He looked almost as if he existed between two times.

My uncle followed on his heels, a stack of scrolls clutched in his arms. He didn't look at me, but I could tell he was making a great effort not to. That was more than I could say for the other Magistrates, who were still glancing in my direction between whispers.

The last of the Magistrates took their seats as the Consul stopped at the podium, waiting for silence. The low hum of the fires burning in the bronze bowls overhead resonated in the room before he began.

"On this thirteenth day in the month of Aster, I call this tribunal to order." The monotone syllables of the words bled into the ambient noise of the room as he executed the formal duties of opening and recording the events of the tribunal.

Seated beside him, Nej was already scribbling.

Legionnaires and rebels aside, the Consul was the man whose

unyielding resolve had been the downfall of our city. His was the fist that held tightly to the Old War and the stolen magic that had once filled our dwindling storehouses with grain. Now there was almost nothing left to hold on to.

I'd seen the Consul many times at tribunals, but I hadn't met him until the first Magistrate dinner my mother took me to when I was old enough to be put up for the silent auction of marriage. It was expected, encouraged even, to be sure all forms of your wealth were visible to the tribunal. As a Magistrate, having a child was like having treasure to trade. Marriages between highborn families were alliances that couldn't be dissolved. They had the power to change the entire course of the future. In fact, they had many times.

My mother presented me to the Consul, and I remembered how he'd seemed to almost look *through* me. Like his silver eyes didn't actually possess the ability to see. Even now, as I watched him look out over the Forum, they had an emptiness to them that was unsettling.

"Before we begin." Consul Saturian paused. "It is my unfortunate duty as Consul to report to you the deaths of two Magistrates who served this body."

There was no sudden stillness in the room. No intake of breath. The whole of the district had seen the bodies that morning.

"Magistrates Furia and Heraldes. As well as the daughter of Heraldes. May the gods keep their souls."

The chill of the silence seeped into my bones, that stillness finally falling. There wasn't a single Magistrate in the room who wasn't thinking what I was—that each of us would find ourselves hanging from those ropes eventually. The only one who seemed not to know it was the Consul.

"Rest assured the gods will have their retribution. The fate of the warlord who calls himself Commander of the New Legion has been written. Just as ours has."

The Consul didn't even flinch as he spoke of his son. I hadn't heard him refer to Vale using their family name even once since the fighting began.

His hands clenched on the edge of the podium, the tenor of his voice changing. "The subject of this tribunal is to witness the oath of Magistrate Casperia," he continued.

Below, Nej shifted in his seat and my pulse quickened. There was a long pause, giving way to the murmurs of the Magistrates, and again, their eyes found me.

I instinctively stood, trying my best to keep my stoic expression in place. The silk of my robes fell past my hands and I clenched my fingers into tight fists to keep them from shaking. This wasn't how it was supposed to happen. That was all I could think. This wasn't how it was supposed to go.

The Consul's gaze met mine. "Do you, Casperia, pledge your body and soul to the sons and daughters of this city?"

"I do." My voice just barely shook.

"Do you swear by your family name to lay your hands only to that which honors Isara and her future?"

"I do," I answered, louder this time.

"And do you pledge your life in service to this Forum?"

I swallowed, a pain igniting in my throat. "I do."

"I hereby grant the Magistrate seat to you, Casperia, daughter of Casperia. May the gods bless you, protect you, and guide your hand on the judgment stone."

A chorus of voices lifted, filling the Forum in a string of rites administered to cement my place among the Magistrates. But the sound was warped, twisting in my mind, because one voice was missing among them.

My eyes landed on the twelve-pointed star at the center of the Forum, the gathering storm of thoughts in my head circling only one thing—Luca Matius. The feel of him slipping through my fingers before he ran down those steps. The sight of him taking Vitrasian's limp body into his arms. The shine of crimson covering his hands as he pulled the sword from the legionnaire's belt.

That blade severed more than his own life, his own future. The blood on that sword cut him from me. Cut me from my vows. And when he crossed that river, he hadn't just left the Citadel. Luca had left *me*.

CHAPTER 7

NOW: LUCA

The goddess of death did her work in threes. That was all I could think about as I stood at the opening of my tent, watching the tribune work my armor.

He was hunched over the bench with a cloth in one hand and a tin of oil in the other, and he didn't look up when I stopped at the entrance. His attention was narrowed and focused, as if the only things that existed were the tools set at his side and the task before him. My armor was separated into pieces so that he could clean it, painstakingly oiling the leather until the grit from the last battle was gone. Even the worn straps of the belt's baltea had been replaced with new material and the brass studs polished.

Iola stood behind him, setting down a bowl of fresh water before she smoothed the blanket neatly over the cot. Without the fine silks she wore as a servant in the Citadel District, she looked like any number of the women I'd grown up with in the Lower City. She glanced from me to the tribune, judgment in her eyes. When she showed up in the New Legion's camp looking for work, I'd made sure she secured a place where I could keep an eye on her, because that was what Maris would have wanted. But she never passed up an opportunity to cast her disapproval on me.

She caught my eyes for another moment before she slipped back outside, leaving us. Even I couldn't deny that the sight was a humiliating one. To see a legionnaire of his caliber occupied with such a menial chore almost made me cringe, but the thought was immediately replaced by another—no one died cleaning armor.

Kali, the goddess of death, was equally attentive in her work, and along with ushering souls from this world to the next, she was tasked with deciding the precise moment a life would end. But every life was a tether entwined, and when death touched you, it came three times. After watching two of my tribunes die, I was keenly aware of the fact that I was due the third.

The first tribune who had been assigned to me was forty-six years old. Deriti was his family name—one I'd recognized because it wasn't an uncommon one in the Lower City. He'd enlisted in the New Legion only days after the rebellion began, emboldened by the death of the Philosopher. He'd quickly gained notice at the front line of nearly every battle we fought in those first weeks.

I'd avoided having to take on the place of Commander, but I was made a Centurion almost as soon as we took the gates, and soon after Deriti was posted as my tribune. Only six weeks after that, he took a javelin to the gut that was meant for me. I could still feel the way his hot blood had bubbled beneath my hands as I pressed my palms to his wound. I could still see that empty look in his eyes as he stared at the clouds overhead.

The second tribune was named Proctes, a nineteen-year-old legionnaire who wasn't a stranger to me. I recognized him from the training grounds, because he'd risen in the ranks below me before the Philosopher was killed. Then he joined up with the New Legion. He'd been a strong-willed, passionate nephew of a Magistrate who'd turned his back on his family in the Citadel District. Just like me and Vale. I'd thought more than once that he and I were the same—angry and vengeful. Self-righteous and stubborn. But he'd been with me for only three weeks when he was killed at the battle for the Illyrium, crushed beneath the crumbling wall of a building hit by a ballista. It took three and a half days to recover his body and it was already rotting when I burned it. That was a memory that still followed me, too—the smell of decaying flesh in the air. The way it had clung to my clothes.

Watching my new tribune now, that sick feeling was turning in my gut again. I couldn't see a young, zealous believer in the rebellion or a lowborn son of some Magistrate's servant. The only thing I could see was a boy just barely turned man who was days or weeks away from becoming the third strand in the tapestry of death that Kali was weaving.

The tribune picked up one of the brooches that I wore at my shoulders, tilting it toward the light and checking the metal for imperfections. I hadn't asked him for his name or paid much attention to him since he was posted with me, convinced that the moment I did, his fate would be sealed. But I let myself really look at him now, realizing that he was at least a few years younger than me. That made him twenty-three, maybe twenty-four years old, a fact that unsettled me even more. His light brown hair was cut short on the sides and back, but the length on the top was knotted in a style that reminded me of the boys I'd grown up running through the streets of the Lower City with. A pointed nose and chin made his brown eyes appear sharper, and the set of his mouth was tense with concentration.

"I didn't ask you to do that," I said, breaking the silence.

The tribune's hands fumbled with the brooch, nearly dropping it before he rose from the bench, straightening to attention in front of me.

"I'm sorry, Centurion, I was . . ." He swallowed. "I was just . . ."

"You don't touch someone's armor without permission," I reminded him.

There were legionnaires who would draw their own blood before they let someone else handle their armor. The armor and weapons were the same ones we'd worn as new recruits in the Isarian legion, freshly plucked from the noble families of the Citadel District to try our hands at glory in the hopes that we'd buy ourselves favor and win our own seats in the Forum. Only a lazy Centurion would trust the job to someone else rather than do it himself. I'd known Centurions like that, but they were all dead now.

"I noticed it needed repair and thought I could make myself useful."

I clenched my teeth, stepping inside. It was a polite way of saying that he had nothing else to do. That I'd *given* him nothing else to do. He wasn't wrong.

"It needs to be done before we cross the Sophanes," he added.

We. As in, he and I. Together. I didn't like the sound of that.

"I can manage it myself."

The tribune set the brooch down on the table, dropping his eyes to the ground by my feet. To his credit, I hadn't caught him glancing up at the mark of the gods that hung over my head even once since he'd been assigned to me.

I could see the argument trapped in his mouth, the way it

made the muscle in his jaw twitch. He had enough self-control to keep it unsaid. "Yes, sir."

I took a step toward the table, eyeing the armor he'd already finished with. It was good work. Skilled work, even. But the moment I wanted to ask what his trade had been in the Lower City, I swallowed the question down. The less I knew about him, the better. It might even spare me the weight of guilt that would follow the moment I had to find the dry wood it would take to burn his body.

"Are you feeling better, sir?" he asked.

It took me a moment to realize what he was referring to. Only hours ago, he'd stood watch on the street as I vomited my guts onto the cobblestones.

I let the silence stretch out between us, waiting for him to look at me. When he did, his eyes met mine without blinking. There was something unnervingly certain in them. He was too steady for a legionnaire of his age and experience, too calm, and I wondered not for the first time how exactly he'd managed to get appointed to me.

"Why did you take this post?" I asked.

The tribune didn't react, but he shifted on his feet just slightly. That was as close to seeing him falter as I was going to get.

"Every Centurion has a tribune."

"That's not an answer."

He lifted his chin. "It's an honor to serve as your—"

"If this is about that insignia out there"—I lifted a hand toward the opening of the tent—"or some childish idea of winning the favor of the gods, you'll be sorely disappointed."

"I don't care about favor." His reply came more quickly this time, taking on the slightest edge. "Not from the gods. Not from you."

My hand dropped to my side. He wasn't afraid to disrespect

me, and I liked that. But it made me even more curious how he'd ended up here in the first place.

"Then what are you doing here?" I asked.

"The same thing you are," he answered, gaze still not wavering from mine.

The words felt like a trick. Like a thread asking to be pulled. The look of him changed as he spoke, sharpening enough for me to see the fierce warrior that lay beneath his armor. It wasn't zeal or fervor I heard in his voice. It was something more deeply anchored than that.

He was already taking up the scale armor as I stepped past him to the small desk erected beside the cot. The pages I'd been writing were carefully stacked, the stylus cleaned of ink. I didn't like the idea of him seeing my work. My pathetic attempt at salvaging some of what Rhea Vitrasian had taught me had become a fixation I didn't want anyone knowing about. I reached into my tunic for the message I'd taken from the Citadel's falcon. Again, I let my eyes scan the blank parchment before I opened the small wooden box on the table and stowed it inside.

When I turned back to the tribune, he was waiting with my scale armor lifted in his hands. I raised my arms out to the sides, and he moved quickly, dropping it over my head and positioning it over my chest before securing the straps over my shoulders and across my back.

I studied him as he worked, but he was unreadable, unflinching in his expression. My gaze dropped to his throat, where only the chain of his medallion was visible.

"You don't wear a talisman," I said, meaning it as a question.

"I don't worship the gods."

That caught me by surprise. Maybe the tribune wasn't mad after all.

"Good," I said. "Because they can't protect you. Not from what's coming."

The tribune's hands slowed, his chin lifting just a little. As if he were daring that fate to come. I wondered if he had any idea that it really would. He returned his focus to the armor and worked methodically, tightening the straps and cinching the ties until everything was in its place.

The sequence was too familiar now—my gaze fixed on the opening of the tent with a tribune's hands tugging at the seams of my armor and checking for the imperfections that might get me killed. I let myself look at his face for a fraction of a second, thinking that this tribune was definitely Kali's third.

"Come with me."

I stalked out of the tent and the tribune followed, fixing his sword to his belt as he tried to catch up. The sun was setting behind the mountains in the distance, but the view was obstructed by the western wall. I turned when I reached the end of the row of tents, headed for the riverbank. The crowd that had been gathered at the bridge that morning was gone, the bodies still hanging, but that wasn't where we were headed.

I followed the path I took every night, ignoring the way the legionnaires stared as we passed. Every few steps, I could see the glow of the gods' mark just barely visible in the air around me, and they could see it, too.

Slowly, the lights of the camp faded behind us and the air grew quiet. In this corner of the Lower City, so many buildings had been damaged that they were almost all uninhabited. I stopped when I reached the statue of Alkmini, goddess of wisdom and enlightenment. The stone that shaped her right shoulder was busted, half her face missing from the hit of a scorpio's ammunition. She looked out at the Citadel District with one eye.

The tribune came to a halt beside me, following my gaze across the water. But I didn't move. I didn't speak. My eyes were fixed on the villa in the distance, on a shadowed terrace covered in sprawling vines. It was here I sat every night as the sun went down, waiting for Maris to finally get up and light the oil lamps. Any moment now. But this was also always the time each day I held my breath. Terrified the lamps *wouldn't* light. Because one day, they wouldn't.

The water lapped below as we watched, the draining sunlight cooling the breeze. And the moment the amber glow ignited in the window, every muscle coiled tight around my bones instantly relaxed, the breath unevenly leaving my lungs. She was there. Behind that window, beneath the roof of Villa Casperia, in a city that was dying, Maris was there.

I turned to the tribune. "You want to be useful? Consider this your most important task." I lifted a hand, pointing to the small square of orange light. "Each night at sundown, I want you to come here. And if that light does not appear, if that window ever stays dark, you tell me. Wherever I am, whatever I'm doing, you come tell me."

The tribune's brow wrinkled, his eyes studying me. "Yes, sir."

"Now get some sleep. In the morning we're going to the gates."

"The gates? But we cross the Sophanes any day," he said.

"The Commander has asked me to deliver a message to Centurion Roskia. We'll leave after dawn."

Still, the tribune stared at me. "And you'd like me to come." He couldn't quite manage to hide his confusion. After weeks of me bogging him down with pointless errands and chores fit for a servant, he didn't know what to make of this.

"I would," I answered.

For maybe the first time, the tribune visibly reacted. He stood a little taller, shoulders drawing back before he gave me a single nod.

I moved past him, headed back the way we came, but I glanced once more to the window across the river. I could feel it all bearing down on me, the scales tipping farther and farther, ready to come crashing down. We were days away from winning the war I had started. With the tip of a single blade, I'd bled all of Isara dry. But the closer we came to crossing that river, the less sure I was of what it had all been for.

CHAPTER 8

BEFORE: LUCA

My existence had never mattered to Kastor Matius until he could bear no child of his own.

My uncle brushed off the shoulders of my tunic as we waited in front of the closed door of Villa Casperia. He looked more like a corpse with each passing day, his face pale and gaunt, his eyes losing their light. When he'd succumbed to a coughing fit that morning, I'd been sure he wouldn't be able to attend the party and that I'd be spared the ridiculous charade. But somehow, he'd managed it.

I stared at him as he intently straightened the elaborate toga that draped over my tunic. He'd spent days having me try different ones before he made a choice, and now he looked as if he were doubting his decision. I waited for some instinctual feeling of compassion or pity to surface inside me as I surveyed his withering face, but it didn't come. It seemed there was no bottom to the well of hatred I had for the man, and I could guess that he would say the same for me. Our fates had been irrevocably bound, whether we liked it or not.

I was sixteen years old the first time that I met Kastor. It was only months before my mother died, and he'd shown up to make her an offer. In addition to the purse of drachmas she could use to die comfortably in the bowels of the Lower City, he promised education, wealth, and a future in the Forum for her son. He hadn't even finished speaking before my mother agreed, and that night, she laid the drachmas on the altar of the temple, choosing to give the fortune over to the gods and die in some filthy gutter instead.

The custom of adoption wasn't an uncommon one. Magistrate families had been taking on the sons and daughters of relatives in order to secure heirs for their Forum seats for generations. Knowing what I did now, it was even possible that my mother had been the one to first suggest it. But when the deal was struck, neither of them knew that Kastor would meet an early death, succumbing to a sickness slowly consuming his lungs. In the last few years, he hadn't been able to hide the stain of blood at the corners of his mouth, and now the entire Forum was waiting for him to die. When he did, his seat would immediately be passed down to me.

"It's very important that you make a good impression." Kastor's scrutinizing gaze ran over me again as he unknowingly repeated Vitrasian's words.

I looked up at the home of my uncle's enemy, which towered behind him. The sound of music and the scent of roasted boar drifted down from the open windows of the villa. The terrace overhead was bursting with vines that snaked down the walls with bright red blooms, and the shadows of the people inside rippled over the buildings around us. This was where I would make my debut.

Hosting the First Feast was a great honor bestowed by the Consul, and my uncle had put his own name forth for consideration. But Saturian was desperate to garner favor with Casperia, and when the announcement was made, Kastor had thrown his wineglass against the stone wall of his chambers. Nothing made him angrier than losing to Casperia, who'd managed to beat him at almost every turn of his political career. It was especially cruel that she'd taken his chance to host the First Feast when it would be his last.

"The Magistrates are looking for good stock, and despite what you lack in sight and conviction, that's exactly what you are. A cock that can put a child in a womb." He slapped me on the back painfully. "In the end, that will have to be enough."

I gritted my teeth at the implication that I was nothing more than cattle, but I was used to the callous speech. Kastor had kept me mostly out of sight when it came to the social customs of the Magistrates so that when he finally did bring me into the fold, I'd have something of a military record and other accolades to tout. It would do him no good for people to remember that I wasn't actually his son. We shared blood, but I'd been raised in the Lower City long enough for it to show if anyone was looking closely enough. Still, I was expected to marry someone who would strengthen his position and bridge us with another powerful family.

"There are a few in particular who would do well for us." He was still talking, despite my obvious disinterest. "Magistrates Umbria and Osturan both have daughters who will not inherit seats in the Forum. They'd make strong alliances, and Magistrate Trestis has a very handsome son. His family owns more than ten miles of the southern coastline, and I'm told there is talk of a new port."

The hinges of the heavy door creaked as it finally opened, and a servant in a red tunic edged in a gold pattern appeared. It was the same design that had decorated the invitation to the feast.

"Welcome to Villa Casperia." The man had been cleaned, trimmed, and dressed for the sake of appearances, but beneath the adornments, I could see the reflection of the Lower City in his eyes.

He stepped aside, letting us pass, and my gaze hungrily roamed the interior of the villa. I couldn't help but be curious. Everything I'd heard about the family Casperia was from Kastor, who painted them more as bloodthirsty dragons than political opponents. The matriarch's brother was Consul Saturian's scribe, which her critics believed was the reason she'd been able to scrape together such an advantage in the Forum. Whatever the reason for her success, she had Kastor walking a thin line of panic.

What was evident from the moment we crossed the threshold was that Casperia had spared no expense for the party. The celebration was themed after the colors and symbols of the goddess Eris, and it served as a rare chance for Magistrate Casperia to flaunt her riches before the whole of the Citadel District. No one in attendance would question the wealth of the family, and that held a different kind of power from the judgment stone.

Garlands of fragrant red blooms were draped from the ceiling, and the faint glow of godsblood made everything look like a dream. It was everywhere—visible in the jewels that adorned the women's necks, the trim of their gowns, and the golden chalices perched in their delicate fingers. It glinted in the low lantern light, filling the room with an ethereal aura that was almost disorienting. The sight of it made me sick.

Kastor made his best attempt at composure as his eyes scanned the splendor, but I could see that he was already seething. Before us, the entry hall opened up to an enormous atrium, where trees planted in glazed pots were arranged in varying sizes and species. Gilded cages filled with birds were strung from the branches, and the shadows of fluttering wings were cast on the walls and ceilings. Three tiled steps took us down to the floor of the atrium, making the entire spectacle feel like an enchanted forest from one of the great myths.

I searched the faces around me for Vale's. The sons of Magistrates were trained as future Centurions, while the young legionnaires from the Lower City were engineered for frontline battle. It had taken years for the recruits to stop considering me one of the lowborns, and that had been mostly because of my friendship with the Consul's son.

My uncle's demeanor transformed into his well-rehearsed performance as soon as we crossed to the center of the atrium. He shook the hands of the guests as if he himself were the host, his charm making him look a little less like he was dying. He was known for that skill as well as his inspiring oration, and that was what would be expected of me, too. His elbow tapped mine with the reminder.

I turned to stand at his side, where he was already introducing me.

"My son, Matius." He set a hand on my shoulder in what would appear as an affectionate gesture.

That word—*son*—still made me stiffen, and not because it felt like a betrayal to my mother. I didn't like that it made people expect me to be like Kastor. To follow in his footsteps.

I gave a wooden smile to the Magistrate he was speaking to, an elderly woman who was just bones beneath her luxurious chiton.

"I know I speak for many when I say we've been looking forward to meeting you," she said, teeth flashing.

Kastor was already listing my virtues, sparing me the responsibility of a reply. This was the part of the performance I hated most. Casperia had built her advantage in the Forum on the pretense that she was a defender of the Lower City. A voice for the people who didn't have one. What better way for Kastor to undermine her than by showing off his own lowborn son?

But as his voice drawled on, my attention drifted, following a stroke of bright emerald green flitting in and out of view between the plants in the atrium. The sound of my uncle's voice faded as a young woman appeared and then vanished, hidden by the wide, flat leaves of the potted trees. Glittering gold earrings peeked out from beneath dark brown hair that fell over her bare shoulders, and my head turned almost involuntarily, following her. When she finally reached the atrium, the light caught her face.

Her dark, focused eyes took in the party, moving over the figures that filled the villa with an expression I couldn't quite read.

"*Not* that one."

My uncle whispered lowly near my ear, playing off the exchange before anyone noticed. But I could hear a hint of what sounded like trepidation in his voice. That was new. I'd never known Kastor to be afraid of anyone.

I watched the woman from the corner of my eye, tracking her through the crowd until she stopped beside someone I did recognize. Magistrate Casperia, the host of the feast, was making her rounds with the guests. The woman stayed close to the Magistrate's side as we continued the greetings, and I only half listened as Kastor introduced me to another string of faces. He listed my sellable qualities in the same order every time, a rehearsed speech he'd been practicing for weeks. But as we moved through the villa, my gaze was pulled again and again to that emerald-green stola and its gold adornments.

My jaw ached from smiling by the time I finally spotted Vale.

He and the Consul were enveloped by a throng of admirers at the top of the gallery steps. When Vale caught my eyes, he politely excused himself from his father's side to weave through the crowd on the staircase.

I exhaled, feeling my shoulders draw down my back when he reached me. His dark red toga was the color of garnet, the brooches at his shoulder studded with blue gemstones. I eyed the ornate bracelets around his wrists, smirking.

"You look just as ridiculous as I do," he muttered, clasping his hands behind his back and turning to face the room. He gestured to my uncle, who hadn't noticed I was no longer standing behind him. "Wasn't sure you'd make it."

"Neither was I. It seems not even death is stronger than his fear of losing the Forum's respect. He thinks I'm doomed to embarrass myself."

Vale kept a close watch on his father from where we stood, ready to be summoned at any moment. "He's not the only one."

"What?"

He discreetly turned toward me, gaze roaming the atrium around us. "The closer your uncle comes to the end, the more concerned my father is about you. He's asked me to be sure that you're worthy of the seat."

My jaw clenched, an embarrassed flush warming my face. It wasn't like Vale to talk about his father, especially anything that might have been said in confidence. He'd despised the man as long as I'd known him, because the Consul had cast Vale's mother from the city, forcing her to give up her citizenship when he was just a boy. But Vale also had the sense to fear Saturian. For the most part, we steered clear of the political web we both lived in. But if Vale was mentioning it now, it was because he was worried.

"Well, you can tell him that the dust of the Lower City isn't contagious, if that's what's bothering him," I muttered.

"It's more than that. You know it's more than that."

He met my eyes knowingly, making me swallow hard. Kastor's seat wasn't just *any* seat. It was the seat that ruled the Forum majority. The fabric of Isara's leadership was precariously constructed, and the faction leaders were an important part of that. If I lost the majority, it would go to Casperia, and although the Consul was supposed to be impartial, he wasn't. It was in his best interest that our faction control the votes.

The door to the street opened again, making the garlands sway as the air turned, and again my eyes found the young woman with Magistrate Casperia. As if she were a flickering light I couldn't help staring at. My gaze followed the valley that ran from the nape of her neck down to the divot of her lower back, exposed by the draped opening of her stola. A single gold godsblood chain was suspended there, a delicate rope of links that glimmered in the low light. It was the same glow that emanated from the rings on her fingers, the earrings that dangled over her shoulders. Everything from the pin in her hair to the straps of her sandals was an overt display of extravagance. It was as nauseating as she was beautiful.

I leaned in closer to Vale. "Who is that?"

He followed my gaze. "Magistrate Casperia's daughter."

That explained my uncle's warning. Casperia was his rival on the floor of the Forum and leader of the opposing faction, so there was nothing to be gained by an arrangement between our families. If anything, it would be dangerous.

Vale stiffened when his father gestured to him, and he gave me another look before he left me, making his way up the stairs.

When I turned back to Kastor, he was still deep in conversation with a Magistrate, but his posture was rigid, his attention half pulled to the other side of the atrium. Kastor pretended not to be aware of Magistrate Casperia and her daughter as they slowly made their way toward us, but there wasn't a single set of eyes that wasn't on them.

And I understood why. They were both the kind of beautiful that was hard to look away from, but that wasn't what made my stomach drop when I saw Casperia's daughter. It was that look in her eyes—something almost violent. She was missing the feigned gentleness that the other Magistrates' daughters had. Like at any moment, she might actually open her mouth and scream.

"Isn't that right, Matius?" My uncle's voice pulled my attention back to him.

I'd missed what he'd said, but I nodded anyway. "Of course."

Kastor went more rigid when Magistrate Casperia finally stepped into the circle around us, a thin smile on her lips as she cast her eyes on my uncle. There seemed to be a hush in the room as he extended his hand.

"Casperia," Kastor said, dipping his head respectfully.

"Welcome, Matius."

The woman's smooth, raspy voice was familiar from the times I'd seen her speak in the Forum. Her blue stola was held up over her sheer white chiton by a brooch at one shoulder, her long dark hair twisted back into an intricate knot of braids. The Magistrate was known for her lewd relationships in the Citadel District, and there were a number of men who wanted into her bed. The rumors had run through the recruits of the legionnaires for years. Casperia's daughter, on the other hand, had stayed out of the public eye. I knew absolutely nothing about her.

She stood only feet away now, the hem of her chiton swaying around her feet as the breeze coming from the terrace picked up. My eyes followed the fabric up the form of her, tracing the shape of her hips and waist to her breasts and shoulders. Her skin had a warmth to it that made her look painted into the room, and the more I looked at her, the more I could feel a heavy, hungry pit forming in the center of my chest. There was a prickle of heat dancing beneath the collar of my tunic as I studied the line of her throat, and when my eyes found hers, she was watching me.

My skin flashed hotter and I swallowed, feeling it redden my face again. If she was offended by my close examination, she didn't show it. Her chin tipped to the side just a little, her eyes narrowing like she was almost amused by it.

"You haven't yet met my son, Matius." The formality in Kastor's voice made the words sound like a song.

The introduction snapped me out of the locked hold my gaze had on Casperia's daughter, and I cleared my throat, returning my attention to her mother. She was looking at me closely, eyes slowly falling from the top of my head to my feet, like she was sizing me up.

"I've seen you observing in the Forum," she said, taking my hand.

She squeezed it, fingernails dragging against my palm before she let it go. The sensation made me clench my hand into a fist.

"He's quite eager to take the seat when the time comes. I have no doubt he'll make a formidable opponent in the Forum." Kastor's chest was puffed out, but I could see the curl of his lip.

"I hear you're a novice under the Philosopher Vitrasian?" Casperia met my eyes directly as she licked her lips, the tip of her tongue poised at the edge of her teeth.

I nodded. "That's right."

"A strange placement for someone of your family rank."

"He's a legionnaire, first and foremost," Kastor cut in again.

"Well, that must be a relief to you." She smiled at my uncle. "An association with Vitrasian won't do him good for much longer."

I swallowed back a sharp reply. Rhea Vitrasian was becoming less popular with the Magistrates by the day. Her outspoken nature and controversial views were beginning to cost her the credibility her accomplishments had afforded her.

"I wouldn't be surprised if you're forced to denounce her before long."

Casperia's words made Kastor almost visibly cringe. This woman knew exactly where the opening in his armor was and she'd wasted no time putting her blade there. The only thing my uncle cared about was his legacy. The idea of his heir bringing him shame by his association with a pariah would be unbearable to him.

"Her fall has been painful to watch." Casperia snorted. "Pathetic, really."

My mouth was moving before I'd even realized I was going to speak. "I'd open my own veins before I ever denounced Philosopher Vitrasian."

The words were so sharp, so precise, that they surprised even me. My blood was boiling hot now, a defensive rise of anger rushing through me, and all three faces before me looked unabashedly shocked.

"The Magistrates are quick to forget the work she's done, and I can't help wondering if it's because they're so good at taking the *credit*," I said.

Kastor was breathing heavily beside me now, but Magistrate Casperia looked almost entertained, a wicked grin transforming her subdued expression into a sinister mask. It made her even more beautiful. Her daughter, on the other hand, had a look I couldn't even begin to interpret. Her gaze dropped from my eyes to my mouth, down the center of my chest, as if she were searching for something.

"If you'll excuse us, Casperia." Kastor's smile was still polite, but his tone was taut now. I knew what that meant.

He discreetly took me by the arm, leading me toward the open doors of the terrace, and I could feel Casperia's daughter still watching me, her eyes leaving a feeling of fire at my back. We made our way down the winding paths that snaked through the gardens, Kastor silent and fuming beside me. The terrace was enormous, with views that looked out over the city in all but one direction. Oranges hung heavy on bowed branches and climbing roses clung to the stone. Even the gravel beneath our feet was pristine and white—made of crushed seashells from the beaches at the coast.

It wasn't until we were out of sight that my uncle rounded on me and his hand flew through the air, striking me hard across the face. Sharp pain shot through my jaw, whipping my head to the side, and I let out a breath before I lifted my chin again. Kastor was looking at me with a disgust that was almost palpable in the air.

"What the hell do you think you're doing?" he spat.

I didn't answer because he didn't expect or want me to. This was the underbelly of my charming, magnetic uncle—the part of him that resented me because I wasn't like him. It was moments like this that he had to face the fact he was being forced to leave his seat in the Forum to a creature who wasn't of his own making. There was a steady stream of panic in that knowledge. It was always there.

"We can't afford for Casperia to start talking about your undying allegiance to the Philosopher. You'll be sitting at the lowest rung of the Magistrates by the time you inherit my seat."

Again, I only stared at him, letting my silence reply for me. The thing that twisted his gut the most was that I didn't care. About any of it.

"You will *not* embarrass me," he seethed.

I took a step toward him, letting the fact that I was now a larger man than he was sink in. I was a legionnaire. If I wanted to, I could wrap my hands around his throat and watch him die in a matter of seconds. And sometimes, I wanted to. But there was a more painful blow I could deal than that.

"When you're rotting in the grave, Uncle, I will take the seat in the Forum. But I will cast the judgment stone according to my own mind. There's no threat you can wield over me, no marriage you can push me into, that will change that. Your power, your influence, will die with you." I spoke calmly, letting each word land. "And the next time you hit me, I *will* hit you back."

Kastor swallowed, his face on fire. He stared at me for a long moment before he shoved past me, disappearing up the path. As soon as he was gone, I crossed the garden to the edge of the terrace, where a silver tray with an open bottle of wine had been left. I set my hands on the stone railing, looking out over the city as the pain in my face swelled. It wasn't the first time my uncle had hit me. It wasn't even the hundredth time. But I could guess it would be the last.

"You'll never make it as a Magistrate." A voice wove through the warm wind, making me still.

I looked back over my shoulder to see Casperia's daughter standing in the path, framed by garlands of red geraniums. Instantly the shame of her having witnessed my uncle striking me twisted in my stomach. The guarded, stoic look I'd seen on her face in the atrium was gone now. It was softer. There was a glint to her eyes as she surveyed me.

"They'll do a lot worse to you in the Forum. There, they cut you where no one can see," she said.

I leaned against the railing as she took a step toward me, and when I saw the braided cord around her neck, I stiffened. She was wearing a talisman, the sign of a devout Isarian who followed the gods, and the sight of it only made me judge her more harshly. It was easy to have faith when you wanted for nothing.

Her hand lifted between us when she was close enough for me to catch the scent of her in the air. Gently, her thumb brushed over my lower lip and the breath held in my chest suddenly felt like a painful gust of wind. When she took her hand away, there was a streak of dark red blood on her finger.

She let the scarf draped across her arms fall into her hands, offering it to me. I stared at it, the dark green that matched her stola nearly black in the waning light. Her eyes dropped to my lip, where I could still feel blood dripping down my chin, and I pressed the silk there, wiping it away.

She took the bottle of wine from the silver platter and handed it to me, stepping up onto the stone.

I stared at her. "What are you doing?"

She tucked the length of her stola and the chiton beneath it into her belt so that the fabric swept up and across her thighs, revealing her bare legs. I swallowed hard.

She swung one foot over the railing, pausing when I didn't follow. "Are you coming?"

I looked back over my shoulder to the glowing windows of the villa. "We can't just . . ."

"What?" She raised an eyebrow. "Don't tell me you're afraid of them. Not after that little speech you gave in the atrium."

My eyes fell down to the perfect skin of her thigh. "Maybe I just can't bear the thought of you ruining that silk."

Her mouth flattened.

"Looks like it could feed a dozen families in the Lower City for a year." I couldn't help myself.

Slowly, her eyes darkened, and to my surprise, it seemed as if the insult meant something to her. "If you think I had any more choice about what I'm wearing tonight than you did, then you're wrong," she said.

My jaw clenched, but before I could speak, she was climbing down the vines. I hesitated, checking the shadowed paths of the gardens one more time before I followed. She reached up to take the wine as I lowered myself down, and when my feet hit the ground beside her, I saw the smallest hint of a smile at the corner of her mouth. She sat on the marble ledge, folding her legs beneath her, and I watched as she raised the bottle to her lips and drank. It was so dark that I couldn't see the details of her face, but the godsblood in her jewelry glinted like tiny sparks.

The view of the Lower City from here was like a sea of stars, nearly every window lit with the celebrations of the First Feast. Most households were likely missing at least one member who served in the Citadel District, but I remembered the way the parties spilled out onto the streets and bled into one another. The offerings piled at doorsteps and on household altars. The Lower City didn't have the same borders and boundaries that existed on this side of the river.

She passed me the bottle and I leaned on the ledge beside her. "Your mother won't mind you leaving the party?"

"Oh, there will be a price," she said.

"One that's worth it?"

"I guess we'll see." She gave me that sharp look again, her eyes meeting mine so directly that I almost looked away.

I took a long drink.

"You lived down there?" she asked quietly.

I watched her, curious. "I did."

"And do you miss it?"

I looked out over the blinking lights. "Some things I do. Some things I don't." But the answer wasn't as simple as that.

"What's something you miss?"

"Swimming in the sea."

Her eyes widened in a childlike awe, catching me off guard. "Really?"

I grinned. "I used to leave through the gates in the evenings and go down to the beach. I would swim until it was dark and sleep on the sand, then wait for the gates to open at dawn."

I could see her imagining it, the scene playing out behind her eyes.

"You've never done it," I guessed.

Her face turned back to the view of the city, where the salt-tinged air rolled over the rooftops. "I don't know how to swim," she said softly, clearly embarrassed by the admission.

It didn't surprise me. The residents of the Citadel District left the city only to go to their grand countryside villas. What *did* surprise me was that glimmer of wonder that had lit in her eyes, like the strike of flint in the dark.

Casperia fell quiet, letting the silence draw out between us. I wasn't sure what was happening here, and that made me uneasy. Not even an hour ago, I'd been watching Casperia's daughter in a kind of trance in the atrium, and now she was sitting inches away, looking at me like she was waiting for something.

Vale's words about his father came back to me. How he'd been told to watch me. To manage me. That was how things worked in the Citadel District, and when I thought about it like that, all this made sense. Magistrate Casperia had a reputation for getting what she wanted. And she knew how to use her own beauty and charm to get it. Maybe her daughter had the same gift.

"What is this?" I set the bottle between us. "Did she ask you to come out here to find out what you can about Matius' unworthy heir?"

Casperia flinched. "Are you asking what I think you're asking?"

I stared at her.

A bitter smile curved on her lips. "You don't know me, Matius."

"No. I don't." I didn't look away from her, wanting her to catch my meaning. I wasn't a fool, and I couldn't be played with.

"Well, allow me to tell you everything you need to know." She slid off the ledge, peering up into my face. "I'm no different than the birds in those cages." Her eyes flicked to the villa windows above us. "And neither are you." She took the wine bottle from my hands, turning toward the narrow path that led down to the river. "But there might be hope for you yet, Matius. Because you're no good at this."

"What?" I called after her.

She disappeared, swallowed by the night, her voice softly drifting behind her. "Pretending."

CHAPTER 9

NOW: MARIS

The north wing of the Citadel held the warmth of the afternoon sun, but as I made my way deeper into the heart of the winding corridors, the air turned cold.

If I'd been told a year ago that I'd be descending into the dark catacombs to perform my duties as a novice, I never would have believed it. The open-air temple of the Illyrium was only a memory now, as was the woman I'd served.

I'd had the sense to shed my tribunal robes and pull the jewels from my wrists and ears before I made an appearance before the Priestess. In her eyes, I would never be Magistrate Casperia. To Ophelius, I wasn't a woman at all. I was still just the child who'd been her novice in the temple.

As the halls narrowed, the ornate adornments that covered the walls and ceilings bled away and the black iron doors came into view. The legionnaires posted at either side were expecting me, already reaching for the bolt before I'd even made it down the corridor. There was a time when I performed the rites only once a month—on the eve of each feast. Now I was bleeding the Priestess every week.

A deep, vibrating groan rang out as the heavy doors were opened, and the cool, damp smell of the catacombs filled my lungs. The first time I'd taken the steps down into the belly of the Citadel, my chiton had been soaked in blood. I could still feel how my heart had raced, fingers dragging over the stone wall as my feet flew down the stairs on Vale Saturian's heels. The start of the rebellion would be marked two days later, but that was when it had really begun—with Luca Matius dragged into the catacombs while Vitrasian lay dead in the Forum. The first breath of this war was the flash of his blade as it arced through the air. It began with the sound of him screaming.

I started down the staircase and the walls grew tighter around me as I descended, the echo of my steps coming from every direction. The torches that lined the narrow passage flickered with amber flames, and the last of the sunlight from above snuffed out as the doors closed above me.

When I reached the main artery of the catacombs, the stone walls finally opened up again. There were a dozen legionnaires posted along the chamber, standing at the ready with javelins in hand. When the Priestess was brought here, I was told that the guards were here to protect her, and at first I'd believed it. The Lower City was falling, the Loyal Legion losing ground, and Ophelius had been shut away from danger, guarded day and night. But as weeks turned to months, I'd come to see what Ophelius had long before—that she wasn't being protected from what lay outside the Citadel. She was being held prisoner inside. And I still couldn't help feeling that, in part, it was her own doing.

The stone walls glistened with the trail of moisture dripping from above, reflecting the glowing square of lantern light at the end of the corridor. There, a small window was cut into a closed door.

I walked straight toward it as the legionnaire closest to the chamber pulled the ring of keys from his belt, and again, the memory flashed through my mind. Luca's face lit by amber torchlight, his hands finding me through the iron bars. The feel of him shaking in my arms as he wept.

I stopped beside the door, slipping my feet from my sandals before I dipped my fingers into the crude wooden basin on the floor. I washed my face, followed by my hands and feet, and then I pulled my hair back, tying it into place.

The second guard was already waiting with the carved alabaster box that held my tools, and he didn't meet my eyes as he handed it to me. They never did.

I drew in a breath, bracing myself before the door opened. The Consul had allowed me to continue as Ophelius' novice, but the woman who'd taught me the tales of the gods wasn't here anymore. She was something else now.

The legionnaire stepped forward to unlock the bolt and the door screeched, swinging out into the corridor. Light flooded the darkness, making me squint, but as soon as my eyes adjusted, I could see her—a lump huddled in the shadows.

The room was small, with solid stone walls that still bore the crude marks of chisels, and it was sectioned into two parts divided by a wall of iron bars. Ophelius sat on one side and the bronze bowl filled with the fire that kept her warm was on the other. It also served as a makeshift altar, lined with a few offerings and bronze bowls to burn the incense.

Ophelius had all but lost the face I remembered. The woman who'd painstakingly instructed me in the ways of the gods was encased inside a withering body, a tangle of bones beneath a chiton she'd been dressed in that morning. Now she was just a creature determined to die.

"You're late," she said, out of habit more than anything. Down here, she had no sense of time.

"I'm sorry, Priestess."

I opened the alabaster box on the altar as the legionnaire unlocked her cell and helped her to her feet. I tried not to stare. Her stringy, thin hair had been braided, her skin washed clean. But when she looked up at me, it was like being stared at by a half-living corpse.

I gathered up the length of my chiton and lowered myself to the ground, sinking onto my knees. My palms pressed to the cold floor before I let my forehead touch the stone in the same way I'd done in the temple.

"Have you brought an offering?" Her voice scratched as the legionnaire closed the door.

I reached into my belt, producing a small clay vessel fixed with a glass stopper. For a moment, Ophelius' eyes flashed, a question lighting them.

"It's only olive oil," I said lowly, watching her expression fall.

Ophelius had been branded a traitor before Vitrasian's body had even gone cold. At the very moment the Magistrates had been casting their judgment stones in the Forum that day, the three Priestesses in the Illyrium had been bringing their own judgment down on Isara. They were found in a pool of godsblood that dripped over the altar in the Illyrium, their veins opened by their own hands.

The plan had been in motion for months, and in the days that followed, I would stand before the Forum and be questioned as to what I'd known. The truth was, I hadn't suspected even for a moment what the Priestess was planning. I never saw what was coming. She'd made sure of that.

No one knew exactly what transpired that day, only that the Priestesses were guilty of the worst kind of treason. Vitrasian had committed the first true act of rebellion, and the Priestesses committed the second. If Isara was to turn its back on the will of the gods, then they would take the only thing that gave the city its power—the magic. But Ophelius didn't succeed as the other Priestesses had. By some cruel twist of fate, her heart had failed to stop. And when her eyes first opened after the physicians saved her life, she'd used what little strength she had to curse them.

The magic could only be given from one to another, and it was the single reason Isara's legion marched from the sea and spilled the blood of Valshad in the Old War. Isara wanted the favor of the gods that had allowed Valshad to flourish for generations, and they'd gotten it.

Now the last little flame of its power was dwindling in the eyes of Ophelius, only days away from snuffing out. She'd been dying long before the rebellion. The greedier the Citadel became, the more blood I drew. The more blood I drew, the less life it left her. But Ophelius seemed to welcome the ritual now, and each time I came to see her, she was closer to death, determined to let her body die. More than once, she'd made it clear that as her novice, it was my duty to make sure she had that choice. But conspiring with Ophelius in her own death was a crime that would end with my execution. I loved her in my own way, but the only person I'd give my life for was across the river.

"Not so different from your mother after all." Ophelius came to stand beside me, her thin fingers brushing the stone.

I bristled, giving her a questioning look.

"I don't need to see the robes to know you've taken your oath. I could smell the stench of the Forum on you before the door even opened."

I turned away from her, taking a stick of incense from the urn on the altar. "Not as if I had much choice."

"That's the question, isn't it?" A sound that resembled a laugh bubbled deep in her chest. "How much choice belongs to us, and how much belongs to the gods?"

I ignored her, not in the mood for one of her cryptic lessons. I lowered the incense into the fire, blowing on the small ember until the smoke bled into the air. I was almost halfway through the names of the gods before her hand landed gently on my wrist.

"Let me look at you, Maris," she said softly.

Using my given name was something Ophelius almost never did. Not even in the last few months, when I was the only soul permitted to enter this room. I turned my back to the incense and faced her, steeling myself before I let my eyes land on hers. It was difficult to look at her like this when I remembered the brazen, bold face she once wore.

Her pale gray eyes ran over me, the color shifting as they focused. A deep exhale escaped her lips. "Just as I suspected. Your fate has changed. Again."

I felt my heart sink at the deep disappointment in her voice. Ophelius had never hidden her opinion of the Magistrates from me. She saw them for who they were—a body of highborn strategists who played their roles in exchange for the power their seats afforded them. She'd taught me as much in the temple, her treasonous teachings like a knife hanging over us both. I hadn't fully known then what she'd risked with those words, but she had. And now that judgment in her eyes was set on me.

I drew in a deep breath, letting it out before I picked up the names of the gods where I'd left off, hoping she would let it go.

"Does *he* know you've taken the oath?" she asked.

My eyes shot to the door, where I could see the legionnaire's shadow on the wall. Talking about Luca within the confines of the Citadel was a risk that I didn't think even Ophelius would take. But I'd been wrong about her before.

"You fool yourself into believing that you aren't like the rest of us. That you've chosen the bloodless way to peace. But you're no different, Casperia. And it's only a matter of time before you realize that."

The words slowly diffused into the air, sounding vaguely like a threat. Ophelius was the only person in the Citadel District who knew what I'd done. Again, I looked to the door. My pulse was climbing now.

"It's time to go see him."

"You know I can't do that," I whispered. "There were three more bodies hanging from the bridge just this morning."

Ophelius blinked, falling quiet as she reached for the incense smoke and wafted it toward her. I could see her thinking. Considering.

I finished the prayer, reaching into the box and taking the marble bowl from inside. I set it between us as Ophelius pulled up the sleeve of her robe, already offering me her wrist. She didn't even blink as I pressed the whalebone knife to her skin. Her face was blank as the first drops of godsblood drained into the bowl.

"The gods are at work, child. It will do you no good to refuse them."

"You think all of this is the work of the gods?" I spoke through gritted teeth. "You really believe all of this is fated?"

She let her silence answer for her. Ophelius had been speaking prophecies in riddles for years, and I wasn't sure even she knew what they meant anymore. Her mind seemed as lost as her body was.

"It's time," she said again, the words sticky in her mouth. "Something has changed. He will need you for what comes next."

The blood began to slow to a drip, but Ophelius' eyes didn't leave my face. I avoided her gaze, binding the wound as the skin knit back together, but her wounds were much slower to heal now. Sometimes, they took days.

From the corner of my vision, I saw her hand inch toward the knife, her fingers twitching as she looked at me. There was a question in her eyes. An intent that chilled me, no matter how many times I saw it. This was a woman who wanted to finish what she started and we both knew I was the only one who could help her do that. And I could. I could conveniently forget to place that knife back into my box. Let the door shut behind me as Ophelius tucked it into her pocket. By morning, she would be dead. But the death of the last Priestess, the end of the magic, assured destruction for Isara. Without it, what was all this for? What would come after?

Carefully, I set my hand on hers, sliding it back to the edge of the altar before I took up the knife. I wiped it on the satin before I closed it in the box and she swallowed, the wrinkles that framed her face deepening.

"Keep your offerings." She picked up the small vessel of oil I'd laid on the altar and pressed it into my hand, her fingers enclosing mine. "This is no temple."

My eyes rose to meet hers, disquiet filling me. The touch was a tender gesture I'd never seen from her before. It scared me.

"You told me the gods dwell everywhere." The bitterness that had lived inside me for these last months hardened the words.

A weak smile pulled at one side of her mouth. "Because I used to believe it. But the wrath of the gods is coming, Maris. Which side of the river will you be on when that fire begins to burn?"

She knew exactly what I was thinking. She could see the thoughts unfolding as if she'd put them there herself. I had every reason to believe she was mad, that every word to come from her mouth was poison. But I couldn't shake the faith knit into the fabric of who I was. The faith that she herself had planted in me. I had seen too much to still give my allegiance to the gods. I had no reason to hold fast to all I'd learned in those years at the temple. But impossibly, despite everything, I somehow still believed.

CHAPTER 10

NOW: LUCA

The only cleared path from the Illyrium all the way to the city gates was a winding one, littered with the debris and broken cornerstones of collapsed buildings. Most of the Lower City had fallen victim to the Loyal Legion's catapults, leaving homes and humble shop fronts crushed beneath. That was how everything was now—broken into pieces. The streets that I'd once memorized as a child had been erased, forming a new map that changed by the day.

My tribune stuck to my flank as we walked, unbothered by the fact that I all but ignored his presence. He had the sense to make the journey a quiet one, and I imagined it was because he didn't want to risk fracturing the only bit of trust I'd given him.

Glass and shards of clay crunched beneath our boots as we navigated the wayward route, following the path marked by the New Legion's insignia. It was painted on crumbling walls and facades, the red stain dried in drips along the stone. The gold that encircled the figure's head shimmered in the setting sun as I passed—a sight that always made me swallow hard.

I'd never imagined, that day in the Forum as I stood there with Vitrasian's blood on my hands, that the moment would be immortalized. Early on, I'd insisted that Vale reject the symbol and order that it stop being used. I'd argued that the actions of one man shouldn't be a battle cry—that what we were doing was bigger than that. But the fervor the image stoked in the citizens of Isara couldn't be discounted, and now it was everywhere, a constant reminder of what I'd done. I couldn't help thinking it wasn't so different from the statues of the Consul that littered the city. The praise of one man was a treacherous path for a people.

A group of men carrying baskets of cloth remnants stopped when they spotted the Centurion brooches that fastened my cloak, and it took only seconds for them to recognize me. The tribune picked up his pace, putting himself between us, and I watched as their gazes shifted from me to the insignia on the building. I could see them measuring me against the figure, but the man painted there was like a character in the stories of the gods. He wasn't real. He never had been. The old Luca Matius was buried beneath that rubble with the rest of the city.

Two of them lifted a respectful hand in the air, and I gave them a nod despite the burn beneath my skin. I didn't want to see them glance up at the godsmark or mutter prayers beneath their breath as they touched the talismans at their throats. I didn't want to watch that change of light in their eyes, either. The one that revealed just how close they all were to not believing in what we'd started.

A few whispers passed between the men, but as soon as they saw the tribune's hand fall to the hilt of his sword in an unspoken warning, they continued walking.

"The last thing we need is for them to fear us, tribune," I breathed, voice tired. "Our enemy is across the river. Not here."

"Nothing tests loyalty like desperation."

I stopped walking. "What does that mean?"

The tribune bit back his words, clearly second-guessing his choice to argue.

I waited.

"You may be chosen, Centurion, but that insignia has more than one meaning," he said. "I would be willing to bet those men have lost sons, nephews, even grandchildren since they first laid eyes on it. If they haven't yet, they will."

The tone of his voice was so even, so steady, that I found myself clenching my jaw as his meaning took root. Most of the Lower City had welcomed the war, eager to force change in the Citadel and ward off famine, but their lives had only gotten worse since the day all this started. They'd gone from poor to destitute, from hungry to starving. And while most considered it a necessary sacrifice, the tribune made a valid point. One I'd considered more than once. There was no way to know how long their steadfastness would last.

Two of the men threw glances over their shoulders before they turned the corner up the street, but the tribune didn't move from his place beside me or drop his hand from his sword until they were out of sight.

We didn't speak again until the gates came into view. The silhouettes of legionnaires posted up on the walls that encircled the city flashed against the harsh midday light. Three rings of barricades had been erected before the gates, and I stopped before the outermost one made up of a collection of overturned shop carts and stacked broken stones. For once, I let the tribune do what he was trained to do. His dark eyes roamed over the empty windows overhead, marking the number of men above us. He was quiet and solemn, taking his time before he gave me a nod.

I lifted a hand into the air to let the guards ahead see us before one of them had cause to draw an arrow. "Centurion Matius, here to speak with Centurion Roskia!" I let my voice carry out.

There was a beat of silence as more figures gathered up on the wall. Roskia's soldiers could be identified by the blue sash tied at one arm, a visible distinction of brotherhood that unnerved me to my core. For months, I'd felt the nagging sense that it was more than morale. He and his men were becoming more separate in identity by the day.

"Welcome, Centurion!" a voice finally called back.

I lifted myself up over the barricade, feet hitting the ground on the other side. The tribune was right behind me, his sleeve brushing mine as he kept pace close to my side. Roskia's legionnaires stood tall at attention, chins lifted. A number of low acknowledgments were uttered, a reverberating string of the word *Centurion* weaving through the air. That was at least some sign that they still respected the New Legion's leadership, I thought. But it did little to reassure me.

My tribune, too, looked unconvinced. His hand clutched the hilt of his sword again, a gesture I found reckless, given that we were in our own camp among our own soldiers. He looked ready for something, though I didn't know what.

The legionnaires fell in line, ushering us through the crates and sacks of supplies toward the three-spired tent erected beside the barricades. Being sent to guard the gates was an order Vale had tried to spin as a great honor entrusted only to the New Legion's most skilled soldiers, but it was a job Roskia resented. He'd made no secret of the fact that he hungered for a fight on the front lines, and that was exactly why he was here, where he couldn't do more damage than necessary. That was what I'd thought, anyway, before I'd seen the bodies on the bridge that morning.

It only made me more concerned about what the next few days would bring. With so few of the Loyal Legion left, the push across the Sophanes River would be swift and precise. But we'd still need every single one of our legionnaires' swords once we were standing in the Citadel. There were those who would welcome the end of the fighting, but we were a city that drank blood now, and peace would be an uncomfortable transition for some.

I found Roskia bent over a short man with a scroll when we came into the tent, his red tunic clean and his freshly shaven head uncovered. He was clad in only half his uniform, relaxed beneath the weight of the shining scale armor. But it was the sword at his hip that made me pause. The glimmer of godsblood shone in the blade, indicating that it had been made for a high-ranking legionnaire of the Loyal Legion. The weapon had probably cost more drachmas than Roskia's family had seen in a lifetime.

Stacks of ammunition were neatly organized on wooden risers in the makeshift courtyard, guarded by legionnaires at each corner. No one had ever accused Roskia of negligence. He took his posting seriously, even if he could see through the charade that it was.

He picked up the parchment and rolled it tightly, taking up the stick of red wax beside it. I watched as he held it over the flame of the oil lamp and it bubbled, dripping over the parchment's seam. He curled his fingers into a fist so that he could press his signet ring into it.

"Matius." Roskia said my name without the courtesy of my rank, which caught the attention of both the man sitting at the table and my own tribune.

I ignored the insult, returning the favor. "Roskia."

"It's an honor to have you in our humble camp." He smirked.

It had been a long time since a friendly word was exchanged between us. Roskia wasn't a proud man, and he'd never been interested in the decadent lives of the Magistrates. He was a legionnaire with a different kind of power, rising through the ranks of the rebellion and earning the favor of not only his own soldiers but also the entire legion. He'd been a recruit from the Lower City only a year after Vale and I had been enlisted by our families. But Roskia had gotten his footing quickly and made a place for himself among the legionnaires despite his low birth. What he lacked in integrity, he made up for with charisma, and there were few legionnaires who weren't inspired by him.

"I hope this is a friendly visit," he said.

"Why wouldn't it be?" I asked.

His eyes floated past me. "I see you've got a new tribune."

The tribune didn't so much as flinch beneath Roskia's attention, his jaw set and piercing eyes focused. I had to admit it was impressive. Roskia was an intimidating man.

"How many does this one make? Four? Five?" Roskia mused.

From the look on his face, he'd noticed the instinctual clench of my jaw. Again, my mind went to the insignia that painted the Lower City. It was one thing to inspire a rebellion. It was another for it to put a target on your back that got others killed.

When I said nothing, Roskia gestured to the wooden bench on the other side of the table. "Would you like to sit?"

"No, thank you."

"I imagine you're here to thank me for the gift." His smile flashed.

The memory of the limp, colorless bodies dangling from the bridge recast itself across my mind, making my stomach turn again.

"I'm sure the Commander will want to speak to you about that himself," I said.

Roskia glanced to his tribune with a smug smirk. Demás stood stoically at the back of the tent. I'd heard only a handful of words spoken by him since I'd first met him, but he always seemed to be listening. I'd gotten the sense that he'd become something of a trusted advisor to Roskia, extending his role of tribune beyond protection.

Roskia's eyes returned to me. "If he's worried about his father, the Consul, tell him that I'd at least give him the courtesy of letting him cut the man's throat himself."

"I'm here to summon you at the request of Commander Saturian," I said, getting to the point.

"Summon me? For what?"

"You'll have to ask him."

The grin crept back onto Roskia's lips. "A bit beneath you, isn't?"

I didn't take the bait. "You're expected at the Illyrium in the morning."

We stared at each other, the silence making my tribune visibly nervous. He didn't strike me as timid, but I'd already observed that he had a sense about people. Roskia was the only legionnaire I knew who hadn't been changed by war. He was the same sharp-eyed soldier with measured words he'd been in training.

The only difference was the pattern of scars that now covered his arms, disappearing beneath the sleeves of his tunic.

"Demás." He knocked a fist onto the table and his tribune stepped forward, helmet low over his eyes. "It seems we've been invited to the Illyrium at last. Gather a small contingent. We'll leave command with the morning patrol."

Demás nodded in reply before turning on his heel. Once he was gone, Roskia's hand lifted between us so I could grip his forearm and he, mine. "Tell Saturian that I'm grateful for his invitation and that I'm happy to accept. We'll be there before the sun rises over the gates."

My fingers tightened around Roskia's arm and I held him there just a moment before I let him go. "*Commander,*" I corrected him. "It's Commander Saturian."

It wasn't an innocent slip. It was the palest shade of disrespect, and he'd wanted me to bear witness to it.

"Commander," he repeated, mouth tilting in a wider grin.

I started toward the tent's opening, where my tribune was still waiting, hand gripped even more tightly to the hilt of his sword.

"Matius." Roskia leaned on the table with both hands, eyes still on the maps.

I stopped short, turning back to him. "What is it?"

"Just a reminder that in a few days"—his gaze lifted slowly—"everything changes. We won't be rebels anymore. We'll be rulers."

His eyes flicked to the sky behind me, in the direction of the Citadel. I could see him imagining it—standing in the Forum in the white Magistrate's robes. It was a fate that would have never been possible before all this. That had been our purpose, hadn't it? To open the streets of the Citadel District and take its power from the Forum? To build a city that was for all Isarians, not just the highborn?

I met his gaze, trying to see what lay beneath that look. "And?"

"And then you'll understand." His voice lowered. "You're not the only one the gods are watching."

CHAPTER 11

BEFORE: MARIS

Iola was waiting for me at the top of the villa steps when I returned from the Illyrium, but she should have been across the bridge hours ago.

I'd spent most of the last two days in the temple with Ophelius, performing the rites of the First Feast ahead of the grain's arrival from the coastlands. I could already hear it—the beat of the drums at the gates far in the distance. The procession would make its way through the Lower City before it crossed the Sophanes, and every Isarian would close their shops and leave their homes to watch. Even the servants who worked in the villas of the Magistrates would pause their work, crossing the bridge early.

When she saw me, Iola's face turned grave, and my feet slowed on the steps. She hadn't waited for me like this since I was child, but even then, it hadn't been with that look.

"What are you still doing here?" I stopped a few steps below her.

She hesitated for a moment before she let the hand at her back come forward, and a slow panic began to churn behind my ribs when I saw what she was holding. Clutched in her fingers was a tangle of emerald-green silk.

It took only seconds for me to recognize it. It was the scarf I'd given to Matius' son in the gardens. When my gaze traveled up to meet Iola's again, there was reproach in her stern eyes. She'd been a young woman when I was born, destined to raise me instead of having children of her own. It wasn't like her to be rigid with me. In fact, any semblance of parental tenderness I'd gotten in life had been from her. But there were lines I couldn't cross, even with Iola.

"He came here," she said, keeping her voice low.

The windows of the villa were open overhead, and the curtains that hung in my mother's study were slipping out into the breeze. Iola wouldn't risk my mother overhearing.

"You're lucky she wasn't here," she whispered.

I let myself lean into the cool white stucco wall of the stairway, bracing myself for Iola's ire. She wasn't just angry, she was afraid.

"Are you going to tell me why the nephew of Matius was knocking on this door for you?"

"I met him at the party for the First Feast. I lent him my scarf for the bloodied lip his uncle gave him. That's all."

Iola wasn't convinced. She crossed her arms, tucking the scarf into her elbow. "That isn't the impression I got from him. He wanted to see you, Maris."

I avoided her gaze, trying to move past her. "You should go. Zuri will be waiting for you."

She stopped me, her fingers tight around my wrist. "This is dangerous. Do you have any idea what would happen if your mother knew he was here? If she thought there was something going on between you and a Matius?"

"There's nothing going on," I rasped.

"Then you'd better see to it that he doesn't come here again." She let me go with a sigh. "You're a woman now, Maris. You have to know what your mother is capable of. What lengths she would be willing to go to if . . ."

The implication made me stiffen. No one knew better than I did how ruthless my mother could be. She wanted to be Consul, and the Magistrates had no idea just how heavy-handed she'd been in her pursuit to control the future of the Citadel. She was behind nearly every tumultuous upheaval the Forum had seen in her time as a Magistrate, and she'd chipped away at Matius' majority hold far beyond what anyone had imagined. But when I'd listened to his son insult her in the middle of her own party, I'd been too busy trying to quell the thrumming in my chest to even consider what the consequences might be. It had been like watching an eclipse. It was a rare phenomenon, a disturbance in the balance of things. And I'd been utterly mesmerized by it.

"You need to be very careful," Iola said, reluctantly handing the scarf to me. "I've done my best to raise you. But I won't always be here to protect you. Not from them. Not from yourself."

When I took it, she started down the steps to the street, leaving me alone in the shaded corridor. I balled up the silk and tucked it into the belt of my stola, opening the door and going inside.

The atrium was cooler than the sun-warmed steps, and the caged birds flitted on their perches, wings fluttering as I entered.

"Maris?" My mother's voice echoed.

The door to her study was cracked open and the shadow of that curtain danced on the stone. I walked toward it like a moth to flame.

She was standing over her desk, a vial of godsblood open in her hand as she dripped the liquid onto a blank, shimmering parchment. A sense of gravity pulled at the center of my gut as I realized there was a chance she'd been listening. But with the sound of the wind coming up from the south, I could barely hear the street below.

She pressed her thumb to her tongue, sucking the godsblood from her skin, and then she methodically opened up a scroll, letting it unroll across the desk. My eyes narrowed on the vial in her hand. Whatever she was working on, she didn't want me to see it. Over the years, she'd begun to trust me with more and more, letting me peer into the background of the Forum's inner workings, but there was still plenty she was hiding from me.

I gazed out over the Lower City, where the gates had been opened wide. The procession of the grain had already begun, and though it was impossible to see from this distance, the caravan of carts could be discerned by the rising dust and commotion in the streets. Once it crossed the bridge, the year's harvest would be stored in the Citadel's granary.

My mother had dressed for the display out on the street in a pale yellow stola the color of morning sunlight and a rich blue chiton. Her skin looked two shades darker beneath them, and the jewels around her neck were an opaque lapis lazuli cut in perfect circles. The Magistrate families had a place at the riverfront to watch the grain cross the bridge, and the other side served as a kind of observation point for the spectators in the Lower City as well. They stood on one side of the river, and we stood on the other, gems sparkling and silks shining.

"Cutting it quite close," my mother murmured.

"We have time."

"This business at the temple is getting ridiculous, Maris. You all but sleep there these days."

"I'm a novice," I reminded her.

She finally turned toward me, one eyebrow arched. "And there isn't a day that goes by that I don't regret letting you take that on. It pains me to say it, but I should have listened to my brother."

My uncle's place as a senior scribe had afforded him more power than anyone in the Citadel knew. The role was considered a humble one but was held only by highborn Isarians. He'd wanted me to serve as a novice in the Hall of Scribes, arguing that it was the perfect place to go unnoticed until you took your seat as Magistrate. But I'd hungered for a noviceship that would be out of my mother's sight. Serving her brother wouldn't afford me that.

The rattle of the door to the villa echoed through the atrium and my mother sighed. "You'd better be here to tell me that Magistrate Matius has died!" she called out just before my uncle pushed into the study.

"He hasn't, I'm afraid." Nej smirked, giving me a wink.

"What will it take for that man to finally choke on his own blood? Honestly. I have half a mind to take care of it myself."

A shiver raced up my spine as she said it, but Nej didn't even blink. He was dressed in one of his nicest togas, a pair of amulets strung across his chest.

"You don't have to. He'll be dead long before the Twelfth Feast." He pulled a scroll from his belt, handing it to her. "The one you requested."

Having a brother in the Hall of Scribes meant unfettered access to the Citadel's library. It was the reason my mother's own collection of scrolls was so robust. But there were texts even she didn't have access to, and Nej was a solution to that problem.

"Then I'd better get to work on that son of his." She unlocked the cupboard on the shelf, stowing the scroll inside before she reached for the iridescent bottle she kept there. "That's one legionnaire I wouldn't mind in my bed."

I cast my eyes back to the window, teeth clenched. My mother wasn't just known for her political maneuvers in the Forum. The means by which she achieved them were the talk of the Citadel District. There wasn't a week that went by that she wasn't inviting someone into her chambers or taking illicit meetings at the baths.

She placed the vial of godsblood back inside its cupboard, locking it, and the memory of the legionnaire's words came back to me. That the stola I'd worn at the party could have fed a dozen families in the Lower City for a year. That single bottle of godsblood tincture could feed infinitely more than that.

My mother had successfully portrayed herself as a voice for the Lower City, and that had worked in her favor in the Forum. But she had no love for the citizens on the other side of the river. She was just smart enough to know that there would come a time when she would need them.

"Don't tell me you didn't notice that he's beautiful," she said.

I wished I *hadn't* noticed. Matius' son was strikingly handsome, his form cast like one of the statues in the temple. He had the look of a god, and I wasn't the only one who'd thought so. The other Magistrates, along with their sons and daughters, had been whispering about him throughout the night. But now the memory was spoiled with the knowledge that he'd likely end up in my mother's chambers. They all did, one way or another.

"I thought he offended you," I said.

My mother squared her shoulders in a way that felt almost like a challenge. "The days of the gifts are over, Maris. The gods don't just hand out power like they used to. You will have to learn to use everything at your disposal to move the pieces on the board. And one of the most effective tools you have, whether you like it or not, is between your legs."

She gave me a snide look before leaving the room, her voice carrying out in the atrium. "We're going to be late."

Nej caught my eyes. "She's right, you know."

Nej's affairs were almost as notorious as my mother's, and I'd heard rumors more than once that he was often summoned to the bed of the Consul himself.

"We'll see," I said.

Nej's expression turned pitying. "You think the favor of the gods is enough."

"I do," I admitted.

He and my mother thought my piety was foolish, but I'd resolved a long time ago to wield the judgment stone with more conviction than my mother once I had it in hand.

"I wish this were a world where you could go on with childish notions like that one, Maris. But soon enough, life will show you how brutal it can be. And even the gods can't save you from that."

He came lower to kiss me on the cheek, giving my arm a gentle squeeze before he went out into the atrium. I waited for his footsteps to grow faint before I pulled the scarf from my belt, letting the fabric unfurl in my hands. I almost couldn't see it against the dark green silk, but it was there—the stain of Matius' blood.

CHAPTER 12

NOW: MARIS

I twisted the bracelet around my wrist, staring at the carving of the goddess Aster in the chamber door. Her braided hair was cast out around her, floating in the wind, and the end of each strand was tied in a noose that tethered the skeletons of her enemies to her—an eternal reminder of victories won.

An inscription written in the first language was carved across her chest, its meaning lost to me.

I let go of the bracelet, pulling my shoulders back and lifting my chin before I pushed the door open. The vestibule that served as the entrance to the Consul's chambers was quiet, the guards posted on either side of the next set of doors, which were propped open, framing the view of a polished wooden table adorned with garlands of olive leaves. The fresh green fragrance filled the rooms, made heavier by the scent of the burning oil in the lamps.

The customary invitation had come with the Magistrate's robes that were delivered to the villa less than two days after my mother died. I'd recognized my uncle's penmanship immediately, and I imagined him writing it at his desk in the Consul's study, recording the dictation. A private dinner with the Consul was the last of the ceremonial traditions that marked the induction of a new Magistrate. It was considered as much an honor as an opportunity. When I left these chambers, I would be either a friend or an enemy of the Consul. There was no place in between.

I studied the table as I entered, eyes trailing from one lavish platter to the next. The head of a pig was the presentation's centerpiece, the tip of its tongue just barely visible between its lips. To either side, mounds of figs and apricots dotted the spread of roasted meats and flame-charred artichokes. Fragrant cut wedges of lemon were arranged among them like little stars.

It had been months since I'd seen food like this. The market had been emptied only weeks after the fighting began and the dole to the Citadel District was a mere portion of grain and salted fish. Almost as soon as the legionnaires began to tear the Citadel's insignia from their chests, Iola had gotten to work. She didn't say she was leaving, but I could feel it. For three days she'd harvested what fruit and herbs could be found in our gardens. She preserved and dried what she could, lining the shelves of the kitchen with jars and wax-sealed crocks. When the last loaf of bread came out of the oven, she kissed me on the cheek and pressed her forehead to mine. And then she was gone. Just like Luca.

There had been a table much like this one at our villa the night I first met him. I'd watched through the tangle of climbing roses as Magistrate Matius hit him in the face. I'd been so shaken by the sudden violent act that when Luca's eyes lifted to his uncle's again, steady and still full of light, I'd been trapped in a kind of awestruck daze. I hadn't been able to walk away. Not ever. But Luca had found a way to walk away from me.

The chamber doors opened and the Consul appeared, the backlight from the sun hiding his face and that of the figure who entered on his heels. The boots of the guards knocked together at attention, and I lifted a hand to stave off the glare. The man with him was my uncle.

I dropped my hand, mind turning at the sight of him. It wasn't usual for the Consul's scribe to attend a dinner like this one, and Nej hadn't mentioned that morning that he would be joining us.

My gaze returned to the table, where a third place was set. I hadn't noticed it before.

"Magistrate Casperia." The Consul looked me up and down, his attention lingering a beat too long on my breasts.

Beside him, Nej's eyes were conveniently pinned to the floor. I knew this game well enough to know where it led. There was an expectation here. An unspoken request. If I wanted to garner the goodwill of the Consul, one way to do it was to end the night in his bed.

"Consul, it's an honor to be your guest." I dipped my head respectfully.

He gestured to my seat before he took his at the end of the table and Nej followed, sitting across from me. He didn't look me directly in the eye, his entire countenance different from what I was used to. There was a stiffness to him that I didn't recognize.

A servant entered the room with a jug of wine tilted in her hands and she filled the glasses, beginning with the Consul's. He was still watching me, a look of curiosity in his eyes.

"It grieves me greatly that your mother chose a coward's ending after so many faithful years as a Magistrate," he said, picking up his glass. He stared into it, as if imagining my mother taking that poisoned sip. "Some just cannot stand beneath the weight of true leadership, and in the end, weakness outweighed her sense of duty." He looked at me for a long, silent moment before he took a drink.

This, I could guess, was some kind of test. A way to put me through a sieve and see what came out the other side.

"The Citadel was my mother's first and greatest love, Consul Saturian," I said.

"I'm not sure I would agree with that. The writers of Isara's most enduring tragedies would have us believe that there is no greater honor than to die for love."

"Maybe, in her own way, she did," I said.

My instinct to defend my mother wasn't something she'd earned, but to hear her loyalty to the Citadel questioned was something even I had difficulty swallowing. Her preoccupation with the Forum and everyone in it had always come first. Even before her own daughter.

"I'm relieved to see that you still bear pride for your family name, Casperia." He gestured to the medallion around my neck. "The legacy of your line is honorable, and the failure of one link in that chain can be mended with the right heir."

The Consul took up the knife at his side, skewering a slice of pork and setting it on his plate. I understood his meaning. He was saying aloud the thing we both were thinking—that the seat I was inheriting had been disgraced. And the name Casperia didn't hold the unblemished record it once had.

Across the table, Nej unstopped a bottle of olive oil. I spooned the apricots onto my own plate, stilling when the utensil gleamed just a little too brightly. Slowly, I turned it in the lamplight, watching the liquid gold shimmer. The Consul even ate his food off silver cast with godsblood. The thought made my stomach turn.

"My scribe has told me a lot about you. He would have me

believe that you are the future of this city." The Consul took another drink. "I must admit, I hope he's right."

"I'm ready to play my part, Consul."

He stabbed his fork into the bleeding meat, sawing at it slowly. "And what part would that be, exactly?"

Reflexively, I glanced at Nej again, but the reassurance I was looking for wasn't there. He hadn't so much as acknowledged my presence from the moment he walked in.

"To fulfill my vow to the Citadel," I answered.

"That's the problem with the vows, Casperia. They're so . . . nonspecific." His knife waved in the air. "Yours is an interesting background for a Magistrate. I understand your noviceship took place in the Illyrium," the Consul said.

"It did." I tried to rein in the irritation sharpening my tone, but Nej seemed to catch it. He sat up a little straighter, shifting in his seat.

"And was Ophelius a gifted teacher?"

I watched the Consul's face for any hint of where this was going. But it was blank, his attention still directed at his overflowing plate.

"She was."

"Did you find your instruction thorough?"

I studied him.

"What does a novice in the temple learn exactly?" he added.

"Ophelius instructed me in the history of the city, the myths, the ways of the gods."

"Rites? Rituals?" he asked.

"What exactly are you asking, Consul?"

Finally, Nej looked up, meeting my eyes. There was a silent warning in them that filled the air between us.

"The new dawn of Isara is mere days away. The warlord who

calls himself Commander of the New Legion will find his rebellion over, and the first thing we will do is fill the empty seats of the Forum so that we can rebuild all he has destroyed."

His voice didn't so much as tremble as he spoke of his son, Vale. There was a coldness in his eyes that made them a lighter shade of blue.

"The gods are at work, Casperia. The days of the factions were over even before Magistrate Matius died and his son committed treason. What we must decide now is how we will unify the Forum."

"I don't understand."

"It's time for Isara to remember we are but servants of the gods. There will be decisions to be made. And when the judgment stones turn, it's important that they turn in our favor. That's one thing your mother understood very well. It's the reason I recognize her loss as a great one."

"You can count on her, Consul." Nej's voice was deep and certain. It swelled with pride.

But I was still trying to sift through the cryptic words the Consul had spoken. He seemed too calm. Too sure that we were days away from peace. More disturbing was the implication that my mother's work in the Forum had somehow been in league with the Consul. From everything she had said, she'd hated the man.

"Can I?" The Consul turned to me, waiting.

There was a tension in the room that made me uneasy, the weight of his words sinking deeper each time my heart beat. Something was happening, something that made the Consul certain that he'd won. He was already stacking the seats of the Forum, eager for my allegiance. He was plotting. Strategizing. This wasn't the game of a madman.

"Casperia? Are you with us?"

I met the Consul's gaze straight on. "I am."

"Then it is time for me to ask what it is I can do for you."

Nej's gaze moved to me again, and I was suddenly grateful for his presence. This was the part of the pomp and circumstance when there was an exchange to be made. My loyalty pledged as payment for something I wanted.

"I plan to initiate a vote at the next tribunal."

Nej stopped chewing.

"Oh?" The Consul set his elbows on the table. "Calling a vote at only your second tribunal? That is quite ambitious." His eyes slid to my uncle. "A family trait, I think. And what is the motion?"

"A meeting. A formal negotiation with the Commander of the New Legion for a peaceful resolution to this war."

Nej's knife hit his plate, the sound ricocheting in the room.

The Consul stared at me, waiting. He looked genuinely confused. Typically, these requests came in the form of a countryside villa or a more advantageous family seat in the Citadel's theater. But I wasn't interested in any of that, and it seemed to catch the Consul by surprise.

"I'd like to propose a—"

"I heard you," the Consul interrupted. "But agreeing to negotiate with those who have committed treason is a validation of their cause. And I'm sure that is not what you are suggesting."

"It's not." I was struggling to keep my voice even now.

"Then the only thing I can conclude is that you wish to spare the rebels the vengeance of the gods. Because it *is* coming for them, Casperia."

"With respect, sir, that's what we said before they took hold of the gates, before they took the upper hand in the Lower City. Before they took the Illyrium."

Nej wiped his mouth, struggling to swallow down his food. But the Consul didn't appear to be angry. He gave me a look I couldn't read. Curiosity, or intrigue, maybe.

Nej finally found his voice. "I'd like to apologize, Consul, I—"

"Don't apologize." The Consul's hand lifted, silencing him. "There is untempered arrogance and then there is brazen foolishness. Our new Magistrate has not yet proven which of these ailments she suffers from." His face was unreadable, but he didn't break his gaze from mine.

Across the table, Nej let out a strange sound, muffled at the back of his throat. He set down his wine, plastering a smile on his face. This was exactly what he'd warned me not to do, but I wasn't going to waste the chance to influence the outcome of this war or miss the only opportunity I had to save Luca's life. But it was clear to me now that Nej had been wrong. There was no power to be gained here. You couldn't wager against odds like these.

I glanced down at the spoon, turning it in the dim light just enough to see the shimmer of godsblood. Ophelius' words came back to me. *It's time to go see him. Something has changed.*

I was beginning to think she was right. And if the Consul wouldn't negotiate with the New Legion, I would have to do it myself.

"I can assure you my niece is ready for what lies ahead," Nej said, conviction deepening his voice.

The Consul took another bite, speaking around a full mouth as he chewed. "I supposed we'll see, won't we?"

CHAPTER 13

NOW: MARIS

The Citadel's bell tower rang out each night when the sun dipped below the horizon, just as the evening painted the intricate maze of white stone a delicate pink. That was the only thing that had remained from *before*—the way the daylight skewed the colors as the hours ticked by, like an ever-changing prism. No matter how broken Isara became, that light still cast the city in the hues of seashells and pearls.

But the once busy shop fronts that lined the market below now mostly stood abandoned behind merchant carts that had been toppled over. Even the colorful awnings that stretched over windows were shredded or missing altogether, and the tall marble statues that flanked the plaza were no more than a pile of rubble. The river, too, was different. Before the fields began to fail, it was filled with boats loaded with dried meats from the pasturelands, fruit from the south, or decorative glass bottles of wine.

The atrium of Villa Casperia was an impossible contrast to what lay outside. Lush green plants spilled from terra-cotta urns, vines climbing in their search for the light pooling at the center of the room. There, mosaic floors depicted the gods on a hunt. Musaeus himself was crouched low in the brush, spear in hand as he stalked a deer.

Even the birds seemed to be unaware of the blood that painted the streets of the city. Their gilded spindle-tipped cages in varying shapes and sizes were strung from the beams overhead—an obsession of my mother's. The birds hopped and fluttered at my back as I unclasped the medallion from my neck, their songs like the tinkling of bells that stopped only with the periodic boom of an explosion somewhere in the city. That was a sound that had once made my blood run cold, but now it was the silence that terrified me.

I closed a small sack of grain into my satchel and slung the strap over my head so it lay across my chest. The smell of paper and ink was in the air, and I looked up to see the door of my mother's study cracked open. I walked toward it, hand lifting before me. It hovered there for a few moments before I pushed the door open. Carved wooden shelves that reached almost to the ceiling covered the entire back wall of the small room, stacked carefully with my mother's scrolls. I didn't let my gaze linger too long on the things she'd left behind. Trinkets, spyglasses, and little pottery vessels filled with birdseed dotted every surface, bringing to life the sounds that had once filled this house. The slide of the scrolls as she unrolled them across her desk. The absent-minded tap of her stylus against the inkpot. The soles of her sandals brushing over the floor.

I blinked the thoughts away, firmly replacing them with the last memory I had of my mother. Not of her lovely narrow face or her delphinium-blue chiton or her almost-whisper voice. The memory was of her hand. Her slender ringed fingers smeared in the blood that covered the floor.

I pulled a small bronze box from one of the shelves, setting it on the desk before I opened it. The brooch was cast in silver and set with an ornate bouquet of gem-studded blooms. Its weight in metal alone would fetch a very good price, and I hoped it would be enough for what I needed.

The bells finally chimed, and I tucked it inside my chiton, making my way back out into the gallery. The finches chirped, hopping on their little perches as I dropped the cloak over my shoulders. I'd unearthed an old chiton left in a forgotten trunk by one of the servants and a pair of sandals that were a bit too small. But if I was going to do this, I needed to look the part.

The bells rang out again as I closed the thick mahogany door of the villa behind me. The winding stairs were covered in dust and crumbling stone with no servants left to sweep them. In fact, the villas that lined the entire street were nearly empty now, the dark windows like gaping holes.

In the old days, the district would have been filled with the sounds of the market, with men and women calling out the prices of their pottery and their silks ready to be cut into elegant stolae and distinguished togas. Now it was littered with broken marble from the toppled arches hit by the ballistae.

Ophelius' warning that something had changed was like a splinter under my skin, driving deeper the more I turned the Consul's words over in my mind. We were only days from the Citadel District being taken, a fate that anyone who looked across the river could see coming. So, why didn't the Consul?

My deep blue chiton was nearly invisible in the waning light, but there was no one to see me, because there was no one who dared to go out after dark. Terrified of being accused of trying to flee the city, the remaining occupants had their villas shut up tight before the bells rang. The Citadel District was silent, no drifting notes of a song coming from someone's window or a conversation of a couple on an evening stroll.

The fires of the New Legion stretched along the other side of the river, their glow wavering on the surface of the black water. I watched from the shadow of the scaffolding, waiting to be sure that the street was empty before I started toward the eastern bridge.

I could see Zuri tucked into the darkness. Iola's younger brother was almost two heads taller than her now, close to becoming a man. He leaned against the pillar of the stone wall, arms crossed over his chest in an almost bored manner. But I could tell, even from a distance, that he was nervous.

I stuck close to the embankment until I could cross the street unseen. The legionnaires patrolled both sides of the river, the rebels on one side, the loyals on the other. When I reached him, I concealed myself in the shadows at his side.

"Wasn't sure you'd come." He watched the street behind me, wary. "After those bodies on the bridge this morning."

I pulled the satchel over my head, handing it to him as he took the empty one from his own shoulder and offered it to me. Iola wouldn't approve of our weekly meetings, but even she couldn't deny the value of grain at a time like this. Despite the rebellion's best intentions, most people in the Lower City were starving.

"I need a favor," I said, reaching into my chiton for the brooch. "And before you say no, it's one I can pay for."

Zuri hesitated before he took it, eyes widening as his vision focused on the glint of the gemstones. It wasn't the purse of drachmas I usually pressed into his palm. "What kind of favor are we talking about?" His gaze turned wary.

"I need you to take me across," I whispered.

"You can't be serious," he scoffed.

"I need to see Iola."

"I'm not taking you over there. You won't last an hour before someone catches you."

"I'm not asking."

He stiffened, the line of his mouth flattening. "We're not servants anymore, Casperia."

"That's not what I meant." I sighed.

"You get yourself killed over there and it won't just be the New Legion trying to cut my throat. My sister will—"

"*Please,*" I pressed.

He studied me, mouth twisting to one side as he thought. "You're not trying to get out of the city, are you? Because that cohort at the gates has caught every poor bastard with the same idea."

"I don't have a death wish."

"That's debatable." He exhaled, holding the brooch to the light and testing its weight in the center of his palm. After a moment, his hand dropped to his side and he shoved it into his pocket. "You sure you know what you're doing?"

I nodded.

He looked out over the moonlit water. It was several seconds before he glanced back at me, gesturing for me to follow. He turned into the darkness and stepped onto the ledge. The narrow stone shelf below the bridge followed its length to the other side, hidden from the glow of the oil lamps that lit the path above. I'd seen Zuri walk it countless times, but the emptiness of the air below us made my stomach drop.

When I didn't immediately follow, Zuri waved me forward.

I kept my eyes on the flickering flame of the streetlamp on the other side, willing myself not to look down as the ground dropped out from beneath us. The warm wind swept around me, pulling at the length of my chiton as I moved onto the ridge of stone.

I fit my hands into the grooves of the bridge's base and inched myself along the narrow ledge. It was just wide enough for my small feet, and I kept my body close to the wall as sweat trailed down the center of my back. We inched along in a silence that woke gooseflesh on my skin.

When voices on the other side of the bridge rang out, I stopped, pressing myself to the stone wall and trying to slow my breaths. It was the sound of drunken laughter from a pair of legionnaires crouched around a fire for the night's watch. Their shadows played on the walls ahead, the unmistakable shape of their armor giving them away. They were throwing dice.

"Quickly," Zuri called back in a hoarse whisper.

My sandals silently found their way along the ledge behind him. His feet stepped from stone to stone, and when he reached the end, he sank low, holding one hand in the air. The only way to the street from here was crossing the mouth of the bridge or scaling the wall that was lit with firelight. If we were caught doing either, we'd have an arrow in our backs before we could slip into the darkness on the other side.

I studied the distance between the legionnaires and the archway, counting the number of steps that would take us around the wall. Thirty, I guessed. Maybe a few more or less.

Two high-pitched *ping*s rang out, followed by a brief silence, and the two legionnaires erupted into cheers, sending their shadows dancing ahead. One of the men grabbed the other by the shoulders, shoving him aside as he crouched down to scoop up the dice. The other one stood, murmuring something I couldn't hear before his silhouette moved into the street.

Zuri shifted, getting ready to stand, and I took hold of the stones overhead, following his lead. A few seconds later, I could hear the legionnaires relieving themselves in the distance. Zuri moved aside, making room for me to pass, hands at my back as I climbed.

The darkness beyond the archway swallowed me up and I tucked myself behind the wall, waiting for Zuri. He appeared a second later, pulling me along the alley and away from the river. He didn't stop until we'd made it to the next street.

His eyes scanned the empty windows overhead before his voice broke the eerie silence. "Iola's going to kill me for this."

The path through the congested streets was etched in my mind like the faint trace of a dream. Iola's lavender palla fluttering in the breeze as I followed her through the Lower City was an image that was still vibrant and alive inside me.

We kept to the wall, staying close enough that I could drag my fingertips along in the dark. The streets grew narrower as we made our way deeper into the labyrinth of buildings, every corner empty, every passageway silent. The emptiness of it all made a shiver jolt up my spine.

We had to go only a few blocks before I saw it. The white domus that sat at the corner of the cross streets was aglow in the moonlight, the smooth white walls like snow. Unlike the villas I'd grown up in, the domus had flats on every level, reaching four to six stories high. Iola's was on the second, with trailing vines of wisteria draped across the windows.

Zuri watched the street, listening for the sound of boots before he crossed into the dim torchlight of the lamps. The soft sound of someone scrubbing floated down in the silence, punctuated by a faint voice somewhere in the distance.

He waved me forward once it was clear and I took the narrow steps. The stucco cracked in a maze of veins that reached up to the sliver of night sky between the rooftops.

Zuri stopped before the door and I stared at the talisman that hung from the handle. A blessing of cornstalks bound together, folded in the shape of the god Toranus to protect the home from evil spirits. Zuri hesitated for a moment before he knocked and I swallowed hard when the sound of the wash bin instantly ceased.

The quiet was replaced by timid steps over tile floor until the light beneath the door flickered.

"Who's there?" a voice called on the other side. It was Iola.

"It's me," Zuri said lowly.

When the door swung open, I exhaled, my throat tightening. Iola's face was aglow in the little flame dancing on the wick of the oil lamp in her hand. Her eyes widened as they fell on me. "Maris? What are you doing here?"

"Iola," I breathed. "I need your help."

CHAPTER 14

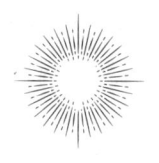

BEFORE: LUCA

"Don't tell me you're going to refuse her." Vale's voice was at my back as I led us down the corridor that connected the Citadel to Vitrasian's theater. We followed the vines that snaked between the pillars lining the walkway, where the early mist was still dripping down the stone. Every few steps the sound of our boots sent birds fluttering from their nests tucked up in the eaves.

"Really, Luca. Don't be an idiot," Vale muttered.

I ignored him, exhaling when we turned the corner and I saw that the gallery was empty. Any moment, the doors to the theater would open and the Philosopher would expect me to be standing there. I couldn't afford for her to find out that I was late again, this time because our drills in the sparring ring had gone long. I'd had to visit the physician for stitches after I caught Vale's blunted sword with my forearm, but it wouldn't matter to Vitrasian that I was juggling my noviceship with my training as a legionnaire. If anything, she'd use it as proof that I was overcommitted. And I was.

"Luca." Vale gave an exasperated sigh, snatching the folded message from my hand.

I finally stopped, turning to him. He was still wearing his dust-smeared armor, his hair damp with sweat. It fell across his forehead as he opened the parchment, reading it.

"I'd be an idiot to accept the offer." I adjusted the belt around my tunic, checking that it was straight. The last thing I needed was for Vitrasian to accuse me of being unpresentable.

Vale's eyebrows lifted as he finished reading the message. Once it was refolded, he pressed it to his nose so that he could inhale the scent. The parchment was perfumed with coriander and jasmine.

It was the third one I'd received from Magistrate Casperia, inviting me in no uncertain terms to sleep with her. The first had arrived three days after I'd met her at the First Feast. The message had been delivered to the training grounds by a servant waiting for me outside the baths, and my stomach had dropped when I saw the seal of Casperia on the scroll. But the message wasn't from the girl who'd given me her scarf. That tipped-over feeling in my gut soured when I read what was written inside.

If you're going to insult me, at least have the decency to do it in my bed.

The second message had been the same. So had the third, and I suspected it wouldn't be the last one.

"You can't deny that she's beautiful." Vale waved it between us. "And if she smells half as good as this parchment . . ."

I gave him a flat look.

"You wouldn't be the first legionnaire to accept an invitation from her. Most people would consider it a compliment."

"It's a political play. That's all."

"One that could benefit you both."

"She holds the leader's seat of the opposing faction, Vale. She thinks that I'm young and impressionable. That she can bend me to her will."

"Who's to say she doesn't just want you to bend *her*?" He held in a laugh and I snatched the message from his fingers, shoving it into the pocket of my tunic.

"There's one side of this I don't think you've considered," he said. "If there's anything that would finally finish off your uncle, it's you sleeping with his enemy. Might save you some time."

"Maybe that's what the Magistrate is counting on," I muttered.

Vale's mouth quirked to one side just as the doors at the end of the corridor opened, sending a screech echoing between the stone pillars. A horde of Centurions spilled from the theater, dressed in their armor with their polished gold brooches gleaming.

Vale shoved me toward them, folding himself into the current of the crowd and almost immediately falling into conversation with one of the high-ranking soldiers. He was a pet of the legion, talented and admired. Most of the Centurions had known him since before he was weaned from his mother's breast, and when the Consul cast her out of Isara, it had only garnered Vale more loyalty from those who opposed the decision. He had the favor of the whole city, a fact that made his friendship with me even more unlikely. In fact, most considered him to be the natural heir to the Consul's seat. But few in the district really knew just how different he was from his father.

I turned on my heel, weaving through the bodies until I reached the threshold of the theater. The high walls opened up to the sky, where a sea of stars served as the ceiling on nights that a play was performed. Every member of a Magistrate family had a regular seat, and tickets sold for more than what some people in the Lower City earned in a year.

Down on the stage, Vitrasian was gathering up a stack of loose parchments on the podium. I came down the steps quickly, raking my hair back from my face before she finally noticed me. But it wasn't with the sharp attention her eyes usually held. The wrinkle in her brow made her look distracted, as if she'd forgotten I was coming.

"Luca." She spoke my given name in a weary tone.

"How did it go?" I asked, watching the last of the Centurions slip out the door.

"It went well." She managed a smile. "Thanks to you."

I nodded, a bit of pride swelling in my chest because she didn't give praise often. She'd been preparing to deliver a half-day lecture to the legion's Centurions on the mechanics of siege warfare for weeks and she'd tasked me with working on the historical figures for her. It was one of the only times my experience as a legionnaire had aided me in my noviceship.

"The Consul should be pleased. The Centurions are now equipped to lay siege to any city he may choose. To starve, isolate, and trap. To target resources, poison water supplies, and even perpetuate widespread sickness." She tapped the edge of the parchments, gaze flicking up to me. There was a bitterness in her voice that dimmed the light in her eyes.

This was a look I'd seen on Vitrasian more and more lately, and I wasn't sure what to make of it. She'd always been critical of the Consul, the legion, and the Forum, but there was something wounded about her in the last year.

She walked across the stage with the parchments tucked beneath her arm, and I followed her through the door that led to her study. She usually kept it propped open so that she could go stand in the empty theater and try out lines from whatever play she was writing or practice her teachings.

Her desk was covered in an array of plans for medicinal experiments, a half-assembled skeleton of a bat, and the little metal cogs she was using to test a new, more blade-resistant form of scale armor.

"This is where it begins, I suppose," she murmured, still lost in thought.

"What does?"

"War." She set her fingertips on the surface of her desk, face lifting to look at me. "It always comes back to the Philosopher."

"I thought the work of the Philosopher is quite opposite to the work of the legion."

"How so?" she asked, perking up a little. The weight that had seemed to settle on her shoulders looked lighter now. She was always ready for a debate.

"Philosophers build, create, discover. The legion attacks, destroys, conquers," I offered.

She considered the argument, her eyes going to the doorway behind me for just a moment. "Do you know what made Isara successful in the Old War? Do you know how we were able to take Valshad, one of the greatest cities to ever exist?"

"The legion," I answered.

Her mouth twitched in a way that told me I was wrong. "We had a legion and many lost battles against Valshad before the Old War."

That was true. My military history was sound and there had been a number of failed attempts. At least a few generations' worth.

"So, how did we do it?" she continued. "What did we have in the Old War that we did not have before?"

It took a few seconds for the answer to come to me. "Ballistae."

She nodded. "That's right."

I watched as she went to the corner of the study, where she took a large hunk of something gray from the shelf. "And how did we make the ballista?"

"It was . . ." I hesitated, thinking. "Made by the legion."

"Using?"

"Iron," I said.

She walked toward me, placing the gray lump in my hand. It was ore. "Where do you think iron was first smelted? Where do you think lead and copper were first forged and formed?"

"Here," I said, realizing what she was getting at.

She nodded. "Yes. Here. In this very study. By a Philosopher." She looked around us. "There is no one with more blood on their hands, Luca. Because everything we make, everything we study, will be used in the quest for power. You wanted this noviceship because you didn't want to be a soldier. But we are *all* soldiers in Isara. We are all cogs in a machine meant for a single purpose and you will not be useful to me until you understand that."

I bristled at the sharp words. She didn't sound like herself. She didn't look like herself, either. Again, she glanced at the entrance, as if she was waiting for someone to appear.

"If I were you, I'd be asking myself why the legion is preparing to lay siege."

My eyes narrowed on her. "The legion educates every soldier on warfare tactics. One lecture doesn't mean we're going to war."

Her gaze flicked up to me before it darted away again. There was something in that look that I couldn't quite sift from the tense conversation. Something was bothering Vitrasian. I'd been the Philosopher's novice long enough to know when she was stuck on something. When she was working a problem that had a difficult answer, she would all but disappear. As if her mind had been swept up to the heavens with the gods.

"Is it something I can help with?" I finally asked, acknowledging the taut silence in the room.

She shook her head, distracted by the thread of thought she was still holding on to. A few seconds later, she was pacing the length of the room. I'd lost her now. She was folded deep into the shadows of her own genius, and when that happened, it took a long time for her to surface.

I'd noticed a shift in her over the last few months, but Rhea Vitrasian was a secretive woman. She'd been anxious, her mind divided, and she'd been giving fewer lectures. I hadn't seen a single invitation arrive for her in weeks.

I crossed the study, putting the ore back where she'd gotten it. The parchments strewn across her desk weren't neatly stacked like they usually were. Now that I thought about it, they hadn't been in quite some time. Her work was consumed by recording and testing her scientific findings or writing reports on her experiments, but the records on her desk were missing the usual formulas and sums.

"What is this?" I asked.

She didn't stop pacing, hands clasped behind her back and gaze fixed on the floor. "A new play. For the Fifth Feast."

I studied the parchment. The messy ink looked like the words had been written quickly. Almost compulsively. Vitrasian's handwriting slipped from its usually uniform script to a slanted stack of lines that nearly ran off the page.

"It's a tragedy, of course," she said, her voice sounding far away again. "Always a tragedy."

I opened my mouth to speak, but footsteps echoing in the theater's gallery stopped me. They stopped Vitrasian, too. Her pacing ceased, and she looked up at the doorway with an almost fearful expression.

I set down the page and went out into the theater, taking the steps up to the entrance. But when I saw who was coming down the corridor, my feet slowed. Casperia's daughter flitted in and out of the sunlight cast through the columns that lined the walkway, her lavender palla like the delicate petals of a lotus flower.

When she spotted me, the look on her face shifted, like she was as surprised to see me as I was her.

I picked up my pace through the gallery to meet her halfway down the corridor. My heart was already in my throat, the same way it had been when I stood only feet from her on the terrace that night.

She stopped, letting me make up the distance between us, and by the time I reached her, the look of surprise on her face had been replaced by a cool, even expression. I couldn't resist the urge to really study her, letting my gaze fall down her face to the hollow of her throat, where the braided cord of her talisman hung. The sight of it immediately made my jaw clench.

She was quiet for a long moment before she spoke. "You shouldn't have come to the villa," she said.

After the servant's reaction when I asked to see Casperia's daughter, I hadn't been sure that she would even tell her that I'd come. She'd made it clear by the way she looked at me that she didn't approve of the gesture.

"Seemed rude not to return what belonged to you," I said.

Her eyes narrowed. "Is that really why you came?"

I swallowed. I wasn't used to people speaking so bluntly, and she seemed to be taking pleasure in my discomfort. There was nothing hiding beneath the tone of her voice or that glint in her eye. Casperia's daughter was a different creature from the class of Magistrates I'd been surrounded by since my uncle brought me to the Citadel District. It made me more than a little uneasy.

"You clearly don't know enough about my mother to be afraid of her," she said, this time with a little wariness in her tone.

I was suddenly aware of the message folded in my pocket. The one that bore the seal of her own house. It burned against my hip like a flame.

If she knew about her mother's invitations, she wasn't showing it. And it was possible she was even involved with the plan. She and I would eventually hold the two faction leader seats, which meant that the daughter of Casperia had just as much reason to oppose me as her mother did.

"You should take more care," she said. "This game we play is a very long one."

I studied her. Those words didn't feel like the warning of an enemy. And I didn't know why, but I was almost sure that there was part of her that *liked* that I had come to see her.

"I came to the villa because I wanted to see you." I gave her an answer as blunt as the question she'd asked.

"Me? Or my mother?"

My jaw clenched. So, she did know, or at least suspect, that her mother had set her sights on me.

"I'm much more curious about Magistrate Casperia's daughter," I said.

There was a flash of something in her eyes again. A quicksilver glimmer that came and went in an instant. She took a step backward, and the pull of her in the air was like the water moving in the river below. It was a current that tried to take me with it.

She reached between the folds of her stola and chiton, producing a small scroll. "I'm here to deliver a message from Priestess Ophelius for the Philosopher."

I took it, eyes snagging on the carved red wooden dowels that secured the parchment. They were the same as those on the message I'd seen Vitrasian burn the day of the First Feast.

"What's a Magistrate's daughter doing delivering a message for Ophelius?" I asked.

"I'm her novice." When I said nothing, she smirked. "You find it strange that someone in my position would serve as a novice in the Illyrium?" she guessed.

"It's . . ." I searched for a word that wouldn't offend her. "Unexpected."

"So are you." She said it so quickly that I wasn't sure I'd heard her correctly. And in some way I didn't fully understand, the words felt like a knife. "You're an heir to a seat in the Forum. A legionnaire, even. What are you doing serving as a novice to the Philosopher?"

She took a step toward me until she was close enough that I could feel her warmth filling the space of the cold stone corridor. She was alive and full of heat, like the life inside her was bleeding out into the air around us. I had the sudden urge to draw it deep into my lungs, and when I did, the scent of rose and cinnamon made me drift even closer to her.

A voice echoed out of the shadows as three men appeared in the next corridor, making me instinctively take a step back to hide myself behind the column. When I looked up, Casperia's daughter had done the same. She was tucked behind the next pillar, a square of sunlight between us.

We stared at each other, an unspoken understanding taking hold. If we were seen together, there would be no end to the rumors. And we both knew what speculation like that could do in the Forum.

Her cheeks flushed just a little, her chest rising and falling in a steady rhythm. Her reaction had caught her by surprise, revealing a softer, more vulnerable version of her face than I'd seen before. As if she could hear me thinking it, her breaths slowed, her chin lifting to an arrogant angle. In a matter of seconds, the woman in front of me changed color, like the fish that swam through beams of sunlight on the reefs.

Casperia's eyes went to the open door of the theater behind me. "What is she to you—the Philosopher?"

There was a blatant suspicion in the words. I could see her trying to riddle it out—something that would explain the strangeness of me. It seemed to truly bother her. But I didn't know how to answer that question. Rhea Vitrasian was a kind of hero to me. A leader and a friend. Aside from Vale, she was the only soul in the Citadel District I trusted.

"A teacher." I gave her the simplest answer I could think of.

Casperia's eyes met mine, the sunlight turning her brown irises to a glowing amber that almost seemed to swirl. She was studying me now.

She blinked suddenly, as if snapping out of a trance, and she immediately took a step backward. "Don't come to the villa again," she said, her voice a breath.

"Then where should I go if I want to see you?"

That faint flush colored her cheeks and the sight of it made my stomach clench.

She fixed her gaze to the center of my chest. "Matius, son of Matius, of everything you could want in this city, I am the very worst thing."

She turned and my hand instinctively lifted to reach for her. But my fingers only encircled air, narrowly missing the edge of her palla. And I was instantly relieved that they did. Because if I had been able to touch her, I wasn't sure what it would have done to me.

CHAPTER 15

NOW: MARIS

There were three whole seconds when time wound back, like light spinning backward over a sundial. Iola stood half veiled in shadow, the glow of firelight soft and warm behind her. It was terrifying how quickly I forgot the last six months, memory wiped clean of it all. My mother's blood on the floor, the bodies hanging from the bridge, Luca's voice whispering my name in the dark. For those few seconds, the sight of Iola drove it all away.

She leaned out of the doorway, checking the stairs behind me before she took hold of my chiton and pulled me inside.

"What are you doing here?" she rasped.

Zuri slipped in behind me before the door shut and the bolt dropped into place. Iola's eyes ran over me, wide and bright as if she couldn't believe I was standing there. I wasn't sure I could, either. I'd been sure I'd never see her again, and I found myself studying the lines of her face, the curl of her hair, to convince myself she was real.

"Maris," Iola whispered again, impatient, "you shouldn't be here. It's not safe. For any of us."

She led me deeper into the flat, where the glow of the oil lamps swelled in the back room. The window was open to a western view of the city, but the Citadel District was completely dark, its boundary visible only by the moonlight that sparkled on the surface of the river. There was a time when the district shone brighter than anything in the city. Now it was just a place that had lost all its light.

"By the gods, I thought you'd be on the other side of the walls by now." She pulled the curtains closed.

My eyes drifted past her to the kitchens, where a small round of dough was rising. There was a steaming pot of water that smelled of herbs and jars of what looked like prunes cooling. It was a sight too familiar, the woman who'd raised me fluttering in the kitchen with the scent of food in the air. When the fighting first began, I'd been kept awake by nightmares of her and Zuri starving or sick, the domus flattened. But it appeared they were making do better than most.

When she finally stopped to look at me, a long breath escaped her. She softened, hand finding my face. "Do you know what they're doing to members of Magistrate families if they find them on this side of the river? You need to get out of this city. Now."

"I can't." My voice was a small thing.

"Families from the Citadel District have paid to be smuggled out. Gods know your mother can afford it."

"She's dead," I said flatly, and it was maybe the first time that it felt true.

The lack of emotion in my words mirrored the look on Iola's face. For years, she'd cared for me as if I were her own, but she'd never had a drop of love for my mother. When Iola came to our household, she'd barely been fifteen, tasked with raising me like so many other young women from the Lower City. She'd done it for a meager wage that barely helped to keep her and Zuri fed. Now I was a woman, a far cry from the girl she'd put to sleep each night.

I swallowed against the thick feeling in my throat. "I need your help," I said again.

"I can't get you out," Iola whispered, paling just a little.

"That's not why I'm here."

"Then what is it? What do you need?" she said, breathless. As if whatever it was, she was ready to give it.

"I need you to get me into the Loyal Legion's camp."

Iola's hands fell heavily to her sides, her owlish eyes widening. "Are you *mad*?"

Behind her, Zuri watched us nervously.

"I know you work in the camp." I moved toward her, but she stepped out of reach. "I know you serve Centurion Matius."

The cold, sterile mention of his rank and family name was all I could muster. Even thinking about letting his given name pass through my lips made my heart feel like it was in my stomach.

Iola gave Zuri a quick, furious glance. She didn't need to voice the reproach for it to be felt in every corner of the room. "If I'd known you were spying for a Magistrate—"

"I'm no spy," he snapped.

"What are you thinking, putting him in that kind of danger?" Iola turned her attention back to me. "Nearly every moment of my day is spent keeping him from joining up with the New Legion and getting himself blown to pieces."

She stared at me, the tightness of her mouth relaxing just a little. It took me a moment to realize she wasn't waiting for an explanation. She was already putting it together herself.

"The grain," she said. "It's from you."

Zuri cleared his throat awkwardly. I didn't know what explanation he'd given for the grain he'd been bringing home, but it was clear Iola didn't know about him crossing the Sophanes. The dole was the city's allotment of grain to its citizens. A sacrifice the people of the lower city had made when they chose a side.

"I need to get into the camp. I need to see him." Again, I couldn't bring myself to speak his name aloud.

"They will kill you, Maris. Especially now." Her voice rose in pitch. "And you're not the only one. They'll turn on Matius if they think he's got any allegiance to you. You're putting *him* at risk."

"It's time now, Iola." I reached up, finding the talisman at my throat and squeezing it in my palm. She was a devout woman who'd taught me to fear the gods. I didn't know how or why, but they were the reason I was here.

A sound lifted in the kitchen and I fell quiet, listening. The sound was a broken, fragile thing. A soft, whimpering cry.

I took a step toward the doorway, hands slipping from the talisman when I saw the linen blanket in the basket moving. It was the sound of a baby.

Iola pushed past me, scooping the tiny thing up and tucking it against her breast. The swatch of pale cream linen unraveled until I saw a tiny face. Full, round cheeks were warmed with a flush, lips pursed and parted as Iola opened her chiton. The child stretched in her arms, arching its back and rooting to nurse.

I stared at Iola, trying to understand what I was seeing. It had been only six months since the rebellion began and I had last seen her.

"You have a child," I murmured.

Iola gave me a look I couldn't read. It wasn't guilt or shame. It almost seemed as if she pitied me. And for a moment, I pitied myself.

"You're a mother," I said, feeling the sting of tears in my eyes.

"I am."

Iola's place as a servant had made the choice of motherhood for her—she wouldn't bear a child she couldn't care for. She was young enough to be my sister, but I'd become her daughter. Looking at her now, with her own flesh and blood cradled in her arms, I could see for the first time how foolish it all was. I'd come to Iola because I trusted her. Because I had no one else. She was the closest thing to a mother I had, but now this woman had a real child.

"When? How?" I stumbled over the half-formed questions, trying to think back to those days before she left.

"Does that matter now?"

My gaze trailed over the flat again, looking for any sign of a man, but there wasn't one. Whoever fathered the child didn't live here.

The weeks before the Philosopher died were a hazy blur in my mind, like paint smeared over a canvas. The baby still had a frailty to its cry that sounded new. If I had to guess, I would say the child was less than two months old. That meant Iola had been pregnant before I last saw her. How had I missed that? Why hadn't she told me?

"You were already leaving," I said, putting it together. That was what she'd been trying to tell me that day when Luca came to the villa.

I won't always be here to protect you. Not from them. Not from yourself.

She'd been leaving long before the Philosopher was killed. And why wouldn't she? I was a grown woman now. No longer the child that skipped along on her heels in the market, one hand clutched to the length of her chiton.

Iola stepped back into the light, gaze moving over my face. "They're saying the New Legion will take the Citadel District any day." Her mouth twisted in a way that was so familiar that it hurt to look at. "You should leave, Maris."

I could feel it suddenly—the teetering weight of the city around us. She was right. It was all about to come crashing down, and when it did, the child she held to her breast would inherit what was left.

"I shouldn't have come here," I said, voice lost to the heavy silence in the room. "I'm sorry. I shouldn't have—"

The baby's wide brown eyes were open and looking up at me now. The child didn't make a sound, both arms now freed from the wrap, feet kicking.

I pulled a bracelet from my pocket, setting it on the table. The lamplight gleamed on the polished gold like a writhing flame. It was a pathetic gesture, but the only one I could make. When all this was over, Iola and this child would have a life to build.

Iola's voice dropped low. "You're going to need that, Maris." Her eyes were on the bracelet. "On the other side of the walls."

I felt a sad smile tug at the corners of my mouth. "I'm not leaving."

The meaning of the words fell heavy around us. If I didn't leave, like Iola said, I was damning myself to an inevitable fate we could both see coming. But I'd sworn by the names of the gods that I wouldn't walk through those gates unless Luca was with me. And he'd made the choice for both of us.

Iola pressed the bracelet back into my hand anyway. I looked down at the baby, who was still watching me with calm, wide eyes. "What did the gods name your child?"

Iola stroked the little face in a gesture that was so maternal and foreign to me. "Muriel," she said. "Muriel Rullias."

Iola's family name had been meant to die with her and Zuri, the last children of their lineage. Now it would live on. When all this was finished, her family would lay the bricks to rebuild this city. Without me.

I started for the door and Iola reached for me, pulling me into her, the baby silent and warm between us. Her arm wrapped around me and I instantly stilled, the tenderness of her touch allowing a single tear to fall down my cheek.

I let my hand brush across Muriel's brow, seeing the faint echo of Iola in those eyes. She smelled of the blooms that crested the villa's terrace in spring. She was new. Innocent. Clean of the blood and ash that covered the rest of us.

"Goodbye, Iola." My voice was a breath.

This really was the last time I'd see her. If there was still a city to return to when all this was over, there would be no more Magistrates. The New Legion would purge Isara of highborn blood. And they were mere breaths from doing it.

I let her go and lifted the bolt, opening the door. The clean night air rushed into the flat and Muriel started to cry. I let myself look back one more time to see Iola cradling the back of her head gently as she pressed the baby to her shoulder. She didn't say goodbye.

When I reached the bottom of the steps that led to the street, I stopped mid-stride. The insignia of the New Legion looked down on me from where it was painted on the white plaster wall of the next building.

The tears I'd managed to swallow only moments ago were a tightening vine around my throat. This time, I couldn't breathe through them. I pulled up the silk of my chiton, pressing it to my mouth to muffle the sound of the cry before it could escape. I knew this pain—the fractured remnants of the broken thing buried like a knife in my chest. There were times when I couldn't keep that wave from running ashore. Not when I could still feel Luca's hands on my face. When I could still taste his tears as I'd kissed him for the last time.

That pain was the reason for everything.

I drew in a long, steadying inhale and pushed that feeling back down to the place it lived, the damp chiton slipping from my fingertips. I let myself look at the insignia for the length of another breath before I forced myself to turn and walk away.

"Maris." A whisper broke the silence. "Wait."

Iola stood at the top of the steps, Muriel propped gently against her chest.

"I'll get you into the camp. But he won't like it."

My chest deflated, my lungs emptying in a relieved exhale.

"Wait there."

She disappeared through the open door to the flat, and I leaned against the wall, wiping a stray tear with the back of my hand.

But I went still when the shadows along the wall of the building beside me suddenly shifted, and I jolted when I caught sight of a red cloak in the darkness. Across the next street, a legionnaire was unfolding himself from the embrace of a woman, her soft laughter echoing over the cobblestones.

Up the stairs, Iola reappeared with her palla draped over her shoulders, pulling the fabric up over her hair, but when she saw me, she froze. Silently, I shook my head, and her gaze trailed the street until she saw what I did. I could see her debating what to do. Weighing the cost of the risk. So, before she could make up her mind, I slipped into the darkness, disappearing.

As soon as my feet started moving, the woman's laughter

lifted again and then it abruptly cut out. I kept walking, trying to keep to the shadows, but when I glanced back, the man was already scanning the street around him. It took only seconds for him to spot me, and my pulse skipped into a run.

"You!" His voice sounded at my back.

The legionnaire was pulling himself from the woman's arms. Now her eyes were on me, too.

I kept walking, the trembling in my hands now finding my arms. My legs.

"You there!" The word rang out in the silence. "Stop!"

I did, halting so fast that my chiton swirled around me. I stared into the cobblestones, mind racing before I slowly turned to face him. He was stepping into the street, hand lifting to the hilt of his sword. His eyes squinted as they tried to focus on me.

"Medallion," he ordered.

I looked one more time at the door of Iola's flat. It was shut now, the flames of the oil lamps blown out. I had two choices, neither of which ended with me breathing. Anyone without a medallion would be considered suspicious, and it wouldn't take long for the legionnaire to decide I was lying about who I was. I knew what lay at the end of that path—I'd seen it that morning, hanging from the south bridge. But if I ran . . .

I didn't give myself time to think it over, turning on my heel and taking off in the opposite direction. My sandals slapped on the cobblestones as I reached the corner of the next street, and I caught the wall with my hand, scrambling into the alley. The legionnaire's footsteps pounded behind me, but I didn't look back. Shouting erupted, cracking open the stillness of the Lower City, and I threw one foot in front of the other with my chiton clutched in my fists. I turned again, and then again, sliding to a stop when something flew past, slamming into the closed window shutters before me. I stared at it with wide eyes, heaving. An arrow.

"Stop!"

The voice called out and I turned in a circle, searching the alley. A pair of eyes watched from one of the high windows, but the silence grew more still. More sinister. There was nowhere to go. Nowhere to hide.

I sank down, hands coming over my head as more than one set of footsteps stormed toward me. I screamed as fingers took a fistful of my hair and wrenched my head back. When I opened my eyes, I was looking up at a soot-streaked face. The legionnaire's flat mouth was the only thing visible in the darkness. His other hand searched at my throat for the chain of my medallion and when he didn't find one, he let me go.

"Name," he spat.

I stared at the ground, palms pressed to the stones.

"Name!" he said again, louder.

A light in the window overhead went out, shutters closing. I tried to think. If I gave them the name Casperia, I'd be dragged into some dark corner of the Lower City and gods knew what they would do to me. If I was caught lying, I'd find the same end.

"Get her up." The man sheathed his sword and two others appeared. They took hold of my arms, dragging me forward.

My sandals slid beneath me as I tried to find my footing, and another cry escaped my lips as we turned the corner back onto the street. Panic snatched the breath from my lungs as they shoved me forward and I looked around me, searching for an escape. If I took my chances and ran for the river, I could jump. If I was lucky, it would be too dark to see me in the water and their arrows might miss. But that wouldn't keep me from drowning. It wasn't hard to decide which fate was worse.

I wrenched forward, freeing one arm, and threw myself toward the ledge. But before I'd made it more than two steps, the men had hold of me again, yanking me back. A sharp sting lit across my cheek and I looked up to see one of the legionnaires standing over me, his face like ice.

"Try that again and you'll be hanging from that ledge by a rope."

He jerked his chin toward the opposite direction and the other man dragged me forward, scraping my knees along the stones. More voices lifted outside, followed by footsteps, and nausea rolled in my stomach when I saw what lay ahead. Rows of tents. The glow of fires. The three carved stone faces of Phaedo, peering out in the darkness.

They were taking me to the Illyrium. They were taking me to *Luca*.

CHAPTER 16

NOW: LUCA

It was still dark when the tribune woke me. The sound of my name dragged me from shallow sleep and I opened my eyes to see him standing at the opening of my tent. It took a few seconds to register that there was something wrong about this. From the look of the light, morning was still more than an hour away. As soon as that detail clicked in my mind I sat straight up, my consciousness coming so fast that I was dizzy.

"What is it? What's wrong?"

My first thought was Vale and that hole in his ribs. But the tribune's hands instantly lifted before him in an attempt to calm me. "Nothing. Nothing's wrong."

I exhaled, rubbing my face with both hands. "Then what the hell are you waking me for?"

The tribune hesitated. "Roskia is coming this morning. I imagine he'll arrive soon after dawn."

"And?"

"And . . ." The tribune hesitated again. "You may not have time to . . ."

"To what?" I grunted, impatient.

"Pray." His voice softened on the word.

I stilled, eyes lifting to meet his. This tribune had been paying closer attention than I'd realized. Every morning at dawn, I went into whatever temple was nearest to our camp and I prayed. But I hadn't realized the tribune had ever noticed. I was sure no one else had.

When I said nothing, he took a small lit torch from the fire outside and ducked back in, lowering it to the lamp. When the flames caught, the corners of the tent illuminated around me. A smooth, unwrinkled tunic hung over the end of my cot and my bronze scale armor was already laid out, cleaned and shined. On the table, my morning rations were set on a plate—half a small loaf of bread, salted fish, and a thick slice of hard cheese. How long had he been up preparing for the morning? He couldn't have gotten more than two hours' sleep.

"That's all," I murmured, dismissing him.

Without a word, the tribune disappeared, taking his post outside to wait. I stood and picked up the armor, slipping it over my tunic before setting the breastplate into place. The worn bindings slid together as I buckled the brooches, and I hooked the thick cloak at my left shoulder so that it fell down my back. It, too, had been cleaned of the dust that had covered it only the day before.

I fastened the belt around my waist, leaving the sword but taking the knife, and tore a piece of the bread from the loaf. I didn't wait for the tribune to follow, pushing out of the tent and starting in the direction of the Illyrium. The open doors were lit with orange light that spilled down the white stone steps into the square. The tribune followed on my heels, a feeling I liked even less now that I knew how closely he'd been watching me.

The guards at the doors stepped aside as I entered, following the hallway to the chamber that held the altar. It didn't matter which god or which temple, I'd take whoever was listening.

The tribune's footsteps stopped at the door, giving me the privacy of the room. The enormous marble slab was mostly whole, covered by figures of galloping horses in the waves of the sea. Within their mouths, fires were lit, and the stone was carved so expertly that it felt as if those eyes were following me as I made my way up the aisle.

I knelt on the floor, taking a stick of incense from the agate cup to dip the coated timber into the golden flames. I turned it slowly as I mouthed a string of words I'd had memorized for most of my life. Here, kneeling in the Illyrium, the sound of my voice echoed in the way it never did at our family altar. The sound reminded me of all those nights watching my mother waste away here.

I reached into my tunic, taking my talisman from where I kept it tucked beneath my armor. The strand of dark braided hair was tied at both ends, fixed in a circle. I pressed it into the palm of my hand, reciting the prayer again. I believed in the gods. You'd have to be a fool not to. What I didn't believe was that they could hear us. I doubted there was a wind strong enough to carry Isarian prayers to them now, but I lit the incense anyway. I spoke the prayer again as the smoke encircled me like a shroud, the sweet smell of spice clinging to my tunic and my hair. It curled into ghostly ribbons as the rolled stalk of frankincense caught fire, and its pungent scent poured deep into my lungs.

I didn't pray for the city or the soul of my uncle or even for the war. There was only one thing I asked for. The only thing I cared about protecting. And I could only hope that her faith in the gods was enough for both of us.

Shadows flickered on the mosaic floor as legionnaires passed on the other side of the open doors. When one of the shadows appeared and stopped, I turned. A young man was standing at the opening, leaning close to my tribune. I could hear the low resonance of his voice.

The tribune nodded and turned to me, waiting for my acknowledgment before he came into the chamber.

"What is it?" I asked, voice still dragging with sleep.

"Neatus is asking to see you. Something about a thief caught in the Lower City last night."

"And?"

"And they have them here in the Illyrium."

I stared at him, waiting for an explanation.

"They say they think they're from the Citadel District. I thought you'd like to deal with it yourself before someone hands them over to Roskia."

I sighed as I got back to my feet, leaving the incense to burn. I'd had to play a light hand when the legionnaires caught a fleeing rat from the Citadel District. Every week, there were more of them, but the tribune was right. We couldn't afford any more trophies hanging from the bridge.

We followed the legionnaire back through the Illyrium to a circular chamber lined with several doors. We'd been using it as a temporary confinement for prisoners, but only one of the makeshift cells had a cluster of legionnaires gathered around it. Neatus was already waiting.

He straightened when he saw me, glancing at the door behind him. "Sir."

"Thief?" I asked.

"That's what I thought at first. She was out alone with no medallion. Didn't think much of it until she ran. But then I saw her."

"And?"

"Well, she just . . . she doesn't look like she's from the Lower City. There's something off about it."

"Did she give you a family name?" I asked.

"No, sir. She hasn't said a word."

I sighed. "Alright." I gestured for him to move and he obeyed, stepping aside.

The door opened and the two guards waiting inside turned toward me. The air was filled with a veil of smoke trailing up from the hanging lanterns. It took a moment for my eyes to focus on the figure in the corner. And in an instant, every muscle in my body tightened into a rope that wrapped around my bones.

I didn't need to see her face, because I had every part of her memorized. There wasn't an inch of her skin I hadn't touched. There wasn't a single curve on her body that I hadn't pressed my mouth to.

Maris.

Her blue chiton was mussed, the hem smeared in mud where her half-untied sandals peeked out from beneath the silk. Dark hair fell over her shoulder on one side, the ends of it touching the ground in an inky black pool.

Several seconds passed as I stood there in silence, mind racing.

"Sir?" Neatus leaned forward to catch sight of my face.

I had to clench my fists to keep my hands from shaking, making me remember the talisman. It was still wound tight across my knuckles.

"Name." I forced the word out.

There was a moment when I still hoped that when she looked

up, I'd see a different face from the one I expected. But the way she stiffened when she heard my voice told me I was right.

Slowly, her head lifted from her arms and her chest rose and fell as her gaze trailed across the floor to my boots. I could feel it as soon as it touched me, like the burn of the sun as it rises over the horizon. It crept up the length of me until, finally, her eyes landed on mine. As soon as they did, pain exploded in my chest.

Maris Casperia was only feet away. Alive. Breathing the same air I was.

I swallowed hard when I saw the blood dried at her lip. There was a bruise on her chin that was darkening, and once her arms unfolded from her legs, I could see the stain of more blood on her chiton. Spattered on her ankle.

"Why is she injured?" I managed to keep my voice even despite the strangling ache in my throat.

"She tried to escape. Ran for the river," Neatus answered.

There were several seconds when I wasn't sure if I was going turn around and put my hands around his throat. The look in Maris' eyes said that she was wondering the same thing.

She'd made an effort to look the part of a lowborn, but she hadn't done a good enough job. It was the small things that people from the Lower City noticed—her clean fingernails and smooth, unscarred skin. Even her attempt at simple clothes had missed the mark. There wasn't a single loose thread in the stitching.

Neatus stepped forward, waiting. "What do we do with her?"

"I'll deal with it. Get your breakfast before the rest of the night patrol leaves you with nothing."

Neatus didn't look sure, but he wasn't going to argue with me. There weren't many legionnaires who would. He motioned toward the door and the two guards followed him out. I stood silent, listening to the sound of their boots grow faint. When they did, Maris let out a shaking breath, catching a tear at the corner of her eye with a knuckle. She'd put on that cold, angry face she knew how to wear so well, but beneath it, she'd been terrified.

We stared at each other and I waited, trying to guess which of us would have the guts to speak first. But just when I thought she might, another voice was at my back.

"Centurion." This time, it was the tribune.

I turned to him, and his expression was watchful. His eyes ran over me, as if trying to find the source of the tension in the room. It looked as if he could see that I was about to come out of my own skin.

His gaze went to Maris before it moved back to me. "It's Roskia. He's arrived."

I looked at the floor between us, still trying to think. Maris had been lucky the legionnaires hadn't recognized her. Recruits from the Lower City who hadn't spent any time in the Citadel District most likely wouldn't. But the minute anyone born across the river saw her, there was a good chance they would know exactly who she was.

The tribune waited, and I changed my mind more than once before I spoke. I still wasn't convinced I could trust him, but I didn't have much choice now.

"Take her to my tent."

His brow pinched. "What?"

"Clean her up. Get her something to eat." I took a step toward him. "No one gets near her, understand? No one sees her. No one talks to her."

Again, he looked at Maris, but after another unspoken question turned in the air between us, he answered with a nod. I shouldered past him, and it wasn't until I was out of the Illyrium that I was able to draw a full breath. The sunrise had broken over the city, and I could feel her, that warmth drawing farther away with each step I took. But it was never really gone. It never had been.

CHAPTER 17

BEFORE: MARIS

I lit a row of incense with a steady hand, letting the smoke gather in the eaves of the vestibule. Compared to a feast day, the altar was bare, but the gifts and offerings from the most devout Isarians still cluttered its vast surface. In the early hours of the morning alone, small treasures had been left—glass vials of oil, painted pottery, and spools of dyed wool. A basket of lemons and a bundle of dried lavender.

Ophelius would bless the offerings after the sun went down and then the items would be collected and burned in the altar fire. As a novice, gathering the ashes to be cast into the wind from the top of the temple's spires fell to me.

The dark dust still marked my hands as I waved the incense smoke into the air. Once the glow of the embers was visible, I hauled the vessel of ash up onto my hip. The sound of my bare feet on the stone was a soft echo as I made my way back to the corridor, but I slowed my pace when I saw the shadow of a figure painted on the floor ahead.

I came around the corner to see the brilliant red of a legionnaire's cloak and immediately stopped short. The man leaned one shoulder against the stone wall, his hand resting on the hilt of the sword at his belt. He was half hidden in the darkness, but I recognized the sharp cut of his face.

Magistrate Matius' son.

He straightened when he saw me, hand slipping from his belt.

"What are you doing here?" I whispered, arms tightening around the vessel of ash as I tucked myself around the corner, out of sight.

I hadn't seen Matius since the day I delivered a message to the Philosopher for Ophelius. The celebrations of the Second Feast weren't as grand as the first. The factions mostly kept to themselves until the Fourth Feast, when the whole of the Forum would gather again.

"You don't come to observe the tribunals," Matius said. "I've attended every one in the last month and I haven't seen you there once."

Three young women with colorful pallae pulled up over their heads appeared in the entrance to the Illyrium's library, and Matius fell quiet. Their kohl-rimmed eyes settled on his face before dragging down the length of him. But when I looked back to Matius, his gaze was still set on me.

I was all too aware that this wasn't just a low-ranking legionnaire. Matius' name had been everywhere since the First Feast. He was the heir to a faction leader's seat in the Forum and had a face that made a traitorous flush burn in my cheeks. But he seemed wholly uninterested in the attentions of the district. For the last few weeks, he'd been trying to see me. Not only that, but he was also admitting it.

"If I can't go to your villa and you won't come to the Forum, then I have no choice but to come find you here."

I glanced over my shoulder, watching the women turn the corner of the corridor. "We really shouldn't be seen together . . ."

"What happened to that girl at the party who climbed down the garden wall?" He grinned. "The Casperia I met at the First Feast didn't seem to care much what other people thought."

"Don't pretend you don't know what I'm talking about." My gaze fell to the short sword still fastened at his hip. It was sign of blatant disrespect. "And you can't have that in here."

He eyed the vessel of ashes disapprovingly.

"You don't fear the gods," I guessed.

"I don't." His attention was on the talisman around my neck now, making it burn like a coal pulled from the fire. "My mother died before the altar in this very temple. I think she said enough prayers for the both of us."

"If you're here to insult the gods . . ." I said, tone taking on an edge.

"I told you. I'm here to see *you*."

He took the vessel from my hands, setting it on the ledge, and then he opened his hand in the air between us. I stared at it for a long moment before I looked up to meet his eyes.

"What are you doing?"

"There's somewhere I want to take you," he said.

Again, my gaze fell to his extended hand. I bit down on my bottom lip, trying to quell the upside-down feeling in my stomach. I knew I shouldn't be glad he'd come. I knew the fire stoking to life inside me could very well swallow us whole. I could feel in my bones that there was a chain reaction of fate beginning to take shape. But it wasn't enough to keep me from folding my fingers into his or following him out of the cool shade of the temple into the sunlight.

No one looked twice at the legionnaire walking through the

city gates or the Magistrate's daughter trailing a few steps behind him. No one so much as blinked when we disappeared into the crowd of people on the road. The farther we got from the city walls, the more alone we were, and it wasn't until the water came into view that I understood what we were doing.

Matius started down the slope of pale, hot sand, not bothering to see if I would follow. The cove was empty, with only two boats visible far out on the horizon and cliffs that jutted up so far that the beach was hidden from the road. I stood on the crest of the dune, watching him get smaller below, and my feet suddenly felt like they'd grown roots down into the ground. It was rare that I was ever outside the city walls, and when I was, it was never without eyes watching me or whispers tangling in the wind.

Matius finally turned back when he reached the bottom, a wry grin on his face that made him impossibly more handsome. There was a dimple at one corner of his mouth that I hadn't noticed before. Maybe because I hadn't really seen him smile. But it was just as likely that I hadn't *let* myself look at him. Not too closely.

He waited, patiently meeting my eyes with what felt like a dare. The moment I moved, he looked like he knew he'd won. I started down the slope and his smile widened. He pulled at the fastenings of his legionnaire's uniform, dropping his cloak on the sand.

I glared at him. "I told you, I can't swim."

His belt was next, and then he was pulling his tunic over his head. "That's why we're here."

The skin that stretched over his shoulders and down his back was pulled tight over the line and groove of muscle that made up the shape of him. The width of his shoulders narrowed down to his waist, where the sunlight cast shadows beneath every edge of muscle.

"Are you serious?" I said, chest growing a little tighter as I imagined myself beneath the surface of the water.

He slid his trousers over his hips, leaving only a pair of low, short breeches. "Very serious." The wind caught his hair, pulling it across his forehead. That dare was in his eyes again.

I looked up at the cliffs, afraid that someone would be up there watching us.

"It's just me and you, Casperia," he said.

"And the gods," I replied.

The thought made me suddenly nervous. There was no one listening. No one watching. I wasn't used to that feeling.

He walked into the water as a wave climbed up the sand, and he followed it out, the surf churning around his legs. I hesitated before I reached for the cords of my palla, unknotting them with trembling hands. Matius turned around as I unwound the belt, and he didn't look back as I let the stolla and chiton fall down my shoulders. The fabric landed in a heap at my feet.

The wind bit at my bare skin, protected by only the thin linen sheath I wore beneath the chiton. When I stepped into the water, it was even colder. Matius waded farther from shore, where he could still stand, his sun-darkened skin sparkling with seawater. When he turned back around, he stared at me unapologetically, eyes slowly tracing my hair, my throat, my hips.

He waited patiently as I made my way toward him with careful steps, feet sinking into the fine sand below. When I nearly lost my footing against a wave, he caught hold of my hand and pulled me through the water.

He held on to me for several seconds to be sure my feet could reach the bottom, and when he let me go, I could feel his warmth racing away from me. His hand lifted out of the water to rake back his hair.

I was suddenly too aware of the fact that there were only inches between us. The sense of not being watched felt like a dangerous thing now. I could do anything, say anything, and the only one who would know about it was a man I had no reason to trust.

I turned in a circle, watching the glitter of light sparkle on the pale turquoise water. The crash of water on the rocks was the only sound, the smell of salt and fresh seaweed thick in the air.

"Is this the place you used to come?" I asked.

"It is."

"With your mother?"

He didn't answer at first. He didn't look at me, either. "No, not with my mother."

The medallion around his neck gleamed, flashing sunlight across his family name.

Magistrate Matius' sister was a mysterious figure, and I'd never heard the full story of how she was cut from her family line. I wasn't sure anyone really knew what happened, other than the fact that she'd had a bastard child with a lowborn man. I wondered now if she was who I saw when I looked in her son's eyes. I certainly couldn't see any trace of his uncle.

"What is it?" he asked, brows coming together.

"If you could change one thing in Isara when you're a Magistrate, what would it be?"

He regarded me with a wary expression, as if I'd spoken a riddle.

"Don't tell me you haven't thought about it."

"I have," he admitted.

"And?" I sank lower, letting the water come up to my chin.

"I'd make it so the seats in the Forum can't be inherited." His voice was full of steady conviction. Like he'd known the answer to that question for a very long time. In the next five years alone, there were maybe a dozen seats in the Forum that would turn over to heirs. It was a system that ensured nothing ever changed, but if seats weren't inherited, the very fabric of the Citadel would be torn in two.

Part of me had hoped that he would say something foolish. That he would provide me with some evidence that he was just like every other man in the district who had power placed in his hands. But I'd also somehow known he wouldn't.

"What about you?" he asked.

I didn't have to think about it, but the words didn't readily come to my lips, because I wasn't sure I could trust him with them. I didn't know exactly what we were doing here. It felt too much like irrevocable lines were being crossed.

"I would dissolve the factions," I said, throat tight.

I expected him to make a joke or point out my hypocrisy, but he didn't. He just looked at me like he was slowly reading the thoughts skipping through my mind. The very idea made me shiver.

The muscle in his jaw clenched, the tendons that wrapped around his throat tensing. The same feeling that was twisting deep in my chest was visible in his eyes. He looked out at the horizon, where one of the boats had raised its sail. It was moving along the surface of the water, a tail of foaming white in its wake.

"The message you delivered to Vitrasian," he finally said. "Did you write it for the Priestess?"

"What?"

"Did you draft the message for her?"

I hesitated. "No. Why?"

I could see him filtering the conversation in his mind, carefully picking and choosing what to say. "Does Ophelius usually have her novice deliver her messages?"

I gaped at him, a deep disappointment settling inside me. "I see." Matius looked confused.

"If you want information about the Priestess or her dealings, you won't get it from me." I started back toward the beach, but his hand found me beneath the water, pulling me back.

"What are you talking about?"

"I misjudged you, Matius. I take back what I said."

"What you said?"

"That you're not any good at pretending. I didn't take you for a liar, but that's what this is, isn't it? What exactly did your uncle ask you to do? Get some piece of leverage he needs to wield in the Forum? Slip into Villa Casperia so that you can sleep your way into some position of power?"

"I could have done that weeks ago if it was what I wanted."

I yanked free of his grip. "If you're suggesting that I'm—"

"I'm not talking about you." He cut me off, meeting my eyes so directly that the words instantly faded from my lips.

My face flushed hot, remembering what my mother had said about Magistrate Matius' son.

"It's not like a legionnaire to refuse one of my mother's invitations," I said, voice tight.

"It's not like a Magistrate's daughter to spend her days hiding in a temple."

"I'm not hiding," I snapped. "And I'm not a fool. I know when someone is using me."

"I don't care about the Priestess."

"Then why are you asking me about her messages?"

"Because I'm worried about her." The words tumbled out of his mouth in a rush, like he hadn't meant to say them. The muscles in his arms moved under the skin, straining. "Vitrasian. I'm worried about her," he said, more softly. "I am not my uncle. I don't care about the Forum or the factions. I care about Vitrasian. I care about the people in the Lower City who carry Isara on their backs so that you can wear your silk and jewels and play your political games."

"*I* am not my mother," I shouted, squaring my shoulders to his. I was suddenly overwhelmed with the urge to hit him.

He looked down at me, the ghost of a smile just barely discernable on his lips. Like I'd surprised him. We stared at each other for a long moment.

"I think I know that," he said.

I held my breath as he reached for me, stroking a thumb along my cheekbone and down my jaw. The feeling of it made me go rigid, the burn traveling across my cheek. I wanted to move backward, to put space between us, but the way he was looking at me, I couldn't. I didn't want to be the first one to give.

"What are we doing?" I said, my voice weak.

He looked serious now, his eyes moving over my face. "Tell me your given name," he said.

I didn't think it was possible for the knot in my stomach to twist any tighter, but it did. It was a question I would have never dared ask someone I'd only just met.

"Why would I do that?"

"Because I think I should know it before I kiss you."

I swallowed, the taste of salt sharp on my tongue. My pulse was racing now.

"Maris." My name was a whisper.

Before I could speak again, before a single thought could stop me, I was lifting up onto my toes, hands sliding across his skin. And I kissed him. My mouth pressed to his and my blood was suddenly running so hot that my heart felt like it was drowning in it. Like it was being held underwater.

He was still for several seconds before his fingers slid around my waist, down my hips, until he had a fistful of the linen sheath. I leaned into him like I'd kissed him a thousand times over a thousand lives. I almost believed I had.

I wonder now if there were any gods watching that day. If they knew what that kiss would mean. I can only hope they were the same ones I prayed to.

CHAPTER 18

NOW: MARIS

"Up." The tribune's voice broke the spell in the room as I stared into the empty hallway where Luca had just disappeared. I'd spent several seconds thinking that maybe I'd imagined it. That my mind had conjured him in the dim, smoky light or that the gods were playing a cruel trick on me. If they had, I would have deserved it.

But it *had* been him. The way my blood was still rushing in my veins was evidence of that.

"*Up*," the tribune said again.

This time, I obeyed, giving another fearful glance to the empty corridor. This wasn't how I'd planned it. I was supposed to slip into the camp unseen with Iola and be back at the villa by sunup. But now several legionnaires had seen my face, and the moment I was recognized, any chance I had of getting out of here would be gone. The same thought had been all over Luca's face as his eyes jumped over the room, trying to find a way out of this for us both.

I stood, letting the chiton drop over my legs.

"Your palla. We need to hurry." The tribune waited.

I lifted the fabric to drape over the crown of my head and he led us out of the room, turning right out of the chamber instead of left, like Luca had. The tribune's thick wool cloak rippled behind him as he walked, his heavy steps and rigid shoulders the only evidence that anything was wrong. If Luca hadn't had a tribune who was sworn to him when he found me in that room, I wasn't sure what he would have done. But the Centurion brooches fixed to Luca's shoulders had made my stomach drop. They were like targets, drawing every arrow that flew across the river.

And of course he'd risen through the ranks. Luca wasn't just a soldier. What he did that day in the Forum as Vitrasian lay dying was the first whispered word of revolt. No one could believe that a young man who'd been plucked from the Lower City had turned on his own and taken almost half the legion with him. In those first weeks, there had been one question asked again and again in the Citadel. How had the quiet, solemn son of Magistrate Matius inspired a rebellion that had torn the great city of Isara in two?

The tribune led us to one of the doors at the back of the Illyrium just as the first beams of golden sun were reaching over the dome of the Citadel. Even after this part of the city was taken, I'd never seen the temple's fires go out. The smoke from the forge could be seen from anywhere in Isara, and it had become something like a pulse as I looked out my window each morning. A sign that not all was lost.

The camp looked almost empty now, with a few legionnaires making their way toward some kind of commotion in the distance. The largest of the tents was erected away from the river, where the flag of Isara flew over its pitch on a bronze staff. It was the same symbol that was emblazoned on the doors of the Citadel and stamped into the floor of the Forum. Now it was the battle cry of the ones who'd destroyed it all.

"Here." The tribune stopped in front of one of the last tents in the row.

Whatever was going on at the other end of the camp, it had drawn the attention of nearly every soldier. Everyone except the tribune. He held back the opening of the tent and gestured for me to enter. I took a tentative step inside, looking around the bare quarters. *Luca's* quarters.

Only one lamp was lit in the corner over a small table, and the cot was dressed with a single blanket. A simple wooden desk held several stacks of parchment and an array of small items I couldn't make out in the dim light. But I could feel him, like a scent clinging to me. This had been his home in the months since I'd last seen him. This was where he fell asleep each night and woke each morning. It had seemed so much farther away than it was. As if he'd existed in another world. It felt impossible that all this time, we'd been in the same city.

"Are you hungry?" The tribune's voice broke the silence.

He met my gaze straight on with a sharpness in his eyes that told me he didn't trust me. And why should he? He didn't have to know who I was to know I wasn't on his side.

"No," I lied.

I could hardly claim to be hungry when I'd spent the last few months in the Citadel District, where the city's grain was kept. Withholding the dole had been one of the Consul's strategies to turn the tide of loyalty against the New Legion, forcing the Lower City to manage with meager rations. It hadn't worked.

The tribune offered the food on the table anyway, sliding the small plate toward me before he fetched the porcelain bowl in the corner. "Eat."

I waited for him to step outside before I reached for it, taking the wedge of cheese and breaking it into two pieces. I could hear him filling the bowl at the fire outside as I chewed, jaw aching.

The sounds of the camp stirring made me feel uneasy. Across the river, the district was doing the same. I didn't know how long it would take for someone to notice my absence, but if the Consul called for a tribunal, my seat would be empty. With my allegiances already questioned, I would have a hard time explaining that.

The tribune came back inside, placing the porcelain bowl on the table. The water steamed, light rippling on its surface. Draped over one arm, he had a new chiton and palla.

He let them hang over the chair in the corner, eyes avoiding mine now. "Clean yourself up. If you need stitching, I can do it."

"That won't be necessary." The words came out hoarser than I expected.

He gave me a single nod before posting himself just outside the opening of the tent. I took up the cloth at the edge of the bowl and washed, gently wiping the dried blood from my jaw and scrubbing the dirt from my legs. The water darkened by the second and it dripped to the ground beneath me, rust-red trails snaking over my skin.

It hurt—all of it. The tight, broken skin at my elbows and knees. The scrapes on my palm and the cut that scored my lip. The ache in my heart—that hurt more than anything.

I peeled off the chiton and put on the new one, tying the belt around my waist before the glint of gold at the corner of the desk caught my attention. The nib of a stylus reflected the lamplight, a utensil too refined for the humble quarters.

I took a step toward the desk, studying its contents. Luca's handwriting covered the parchment, a slanted but uniform script that marched over the pages even when the ink was fading. He wasn't patient enough to pick up the stylus and dip it in the pot. It wasn't until the writing was illegible that the ink pooled again, sloppy and imprecise.

They were equations, a string of numbers and symbols written in a language I didn't understand. I sifted through the pages, where fragments of mathematical theory, methods of triangulation, and prime numbers were sketched out. They were interspersed with notes on astronomy, biology, and even drawings of the bones in a human hand.

More fresh sheets of parchment were stacked beneath a heavy bronze weight and a small ivory box was at the corner of the desk. I sat down on the chair and lifted the lid, sighing when I saw what lay inside.

It was the ring Luca used to wear—a jade signet his mother had given him. I'd never seen him without it.

I glanced back at the opening of the tent before I picked it up, turning it in the light. The stone was etched with a cypress branch, the gold band scuffed and dented. When had he taken it off? Was it the day Vitrasian died? The day he crossed the Sophanes River? When was the exact moment he decided to tear himself from who he was? From me?

I set the ring back down, reaching for a small curling paper set along the edge of the desk. It was flattened as if it had been unrolled. I slid it toward me with one finger so I could read it. But it was blank, only the sheen of godsblood pressed into the parchment visible. The faint prickle of familiarity stirred in the back of my mind. I'd seen one like it before.

The light shifted as the tribune pushed back inside, and I lifted my hand from the desk. When I turned around, he was already standing at attention in the corner of the tent. His gaze was fixed straight ahead, his posture stiff, like he was ready to draw his sword on me if he had to.

His eyes were the color of amber glass when they caught the light, but his was a face I didn't know from the Citadel District. He was probably a young man from the Lower City who'd been promised grain if he enlisted with the New Legion—the same fate Iola had been trying to avoid for Zuri. Or maybe he was someone hoping for a place of power and influence in the new Isara. The city was filled with both kinds of soldiers.

He didn't say a word as I sat on the edge of the cot and let myself lay back. My hand brushed over the blanket, and, without my permission, my fingers curled in the fabric. I pulled it toward me, pressing it softly to my face before I inhaled, breathing Luca in. All at once, every moment came flooding back. Every moonlit whisper, every laugh, every kiss. Flashes of *before* skipped through my mind like flickers of light. The dimple at the corner at his mouth and the shape of his hands. The way his face looked when he was thinking. But that Luca was gone now. He vanished the day Vitrasian died.

The tribune's eyes landed on me for just a moment.

"You're his tribune?" I asked.

"Yes."

"That means you're sworn to protect him with your life?"

He nodded.

"Then tell me your name."

His expression shifted so slightly that I almost didn't catch it. "Why?"

I reached up, finding the talisman around my neck. "So that I can pray for you."

It was a long moment before he answered. "Théo," he said. "My name is Théo."

CHAPTER 19

NOW: LUCA

The roar of fires and voices filled the street as I walked through the crowd gathering in front of the Commander's tent. Asinia was posted outside the opening, his eyes drifting back and forth from the Illyrium to the river. When he spotted me, he gave a curt nod and the legionnaires stepped aside, making way for me.

Roskia's face was aglow beside the largest of the fires. I watched as he clapped soldiers on the back in a series of greetings. It had been weeks since Vale had extended him an invitation to the front, and he was making the most of it. His wide smile made him look like the politician he was—an opportunist dressed in the worn armor of a seasoned legionnaire. And from what I'd seen, the soldiers who filled our ranks liked it.

Asinia seemed to be thinking the same, his narrow eyes watching the Centurion and his tribune, Demás, closely. Asinia had never liked Roskia, even when we were just barely men learning to swing a sword correctly. Roskia had never made a secret of his dislike for Asinia, either.

Long before he was Vale's tribune, Asinia had been a man of few words, and that was one of the reasons I trusted him. He didn't play games, weave rhetoric, or subtly defy orders. And he'd been with Vale and me since the beginning—the day we'd crossed the Sophanes River. In a few days, we'd be side by side again when we stepped back into the Citadel for the first time.

Vale was standing over an unrolled map when I came into the tent, his focus unbroken by the commotion outside. Carved wooden pieces were set throughout the whole of the Lower City, identifying the territory occupied by the rebellion. It was still strange to see them outnumber the smooth white stones that marked the areas still held by the last of the Loyal Legion. The Citadel District was the only thing left to take.

Immediately, I assessed Vale, unsure whether he seemed better or worse than the day before. He looked as if he hadn't eaten or slept in some time, and my eyes trailed around the tent until I spotted a bowl of untouched stew.

The Commander's brow furrowed, hand tracing the soft hide as he followed a path through the tangle of streets depicted on the rendering. I waited as he set down one of the white stone markers on the map and then moved it twice. We knew those streets. They'd been home for years. And now here we were, plotting how to tear them from the Loyal Legion's hands.

I knew Vale well enough not to interfere when he was concentrating. He was a brilliant soldier, but one who thought only in straight lines. I'd never aspired to wear medals on my chest, but Vale had been a natural leader, even among the young men of our cohort when I was first thrust into the training ring. That would have been true whether his father was the Consul or not. He was a good Commander. A far better one than I could be.

When he finally looked up, his face relaxed a little.

"He's here," I said.

"Alright." He sighed. "Then let's do this."

Vale abandoned the maps, his shoulders straightening as I found a place to stand shoulder to shoulder beside him.

"Where's your tribune?" he asked, eyeing the opening of the tent.

"Obeying orders," I answered.

Vale glared at me. "He's to stay with you. I was clear about that."

"My bow needed stringing," I lied.

Vale dropped it. It would do us no good to appear divided in front of the legionnaires, no matter how small the argument. Not when Roskia was biding his time, waiting for any sign of weakness in the rope that tethered us.

"He's not going to like this," I murmured.

Vale's jaw clenched. "No, he won't."

"We get across the river, then we deal with Roskia," I reminded him.

We needed the Centurion and the loyalty of his legionnaires if we were going to take the district. We weren't fool enough to think we could keep our hold on the city without them. But Roskia was a drought-ridden field waiting to catch flame. And when it did, we'd have to be ready to put it out.

Roskia appeared at the opening of the tent, unfastening the brooch at his shoulder. The cloak fell from his back in one fluid movement before he'd even made it inside. He draped it over his arm in an elegant manner before he handed it to Demás, who immediately ducked out to stand guard with Asinia.

"Commander Saturian." Roskia gave a respectful bow of his head, speaking Vale's family name with a familiar warmth he never pretended at with me.

Vale took Roskia's arm, gripping his elbow in a more casual greeting. He knew how to play on Roskia's ambitions, making him feel like he was part of the fold, and Roskia couldn't help reveling in it. I was tired of watching them play this game.

"Thank you for coming." Vale gestured for Roskia to sit, and he took the stool beside the table, immediately pouring himself a glass of wine from the silver pitcher. In addition to cheese, Vale had also gone to the trouble of having fruit—something I hadn't seen in months. I wondered now how he'd managed it.

"When my Commander calls, I come," Roskia said. "What can I do for you?"

"We're finalizing our plan to take the Citadel District," Vale answered, leaning against the edge of the table beside him. "And I'd like your input."

Roskia shot me a suspicious side glance. "Of course. I'm happy to help in any way I can." He lifted the silver cup to his lips.

"Good." Vale nodded. "I'd like to cross the Sophanes in three days' time."

"Days?" Roskia bristled. "Why wait? There's nothing stopping us from doing it tonight. Now, even."

"It's not just the district we need, Roskia. We have nothing if we don't have the grain," Vale replied patiently.

Roskia set down his cup and folded his hands in his lap. "Don't tell me you want to make a deal with them."

Vale let his silence answer the question.

Roskia looked as if he was trying not to laugh. "You can't be serious." But the smile fell from his lips when Vale made no effort to appease him.

"I am," Vale said.

"They aren't going to accept that." Roskia pointed behind him, where the sound of voices was still loud around the fires. "There have been too many of our men lost, Commander. Someone has to pay for it."

"I plan to meet with the Consul tomorrow. I will propose an arrangement that allows anyone in the Citadel District to leave the city through the gates before we cross the river."

"Sir." The fury could barely be heard in Roskia's voice as he spoke, but it was there.

Vale continued, "Those who choose to leave will forfeit their medallions and, effectively, their citizenship to Isara. Those with seats in the Forum will relinquish them, their villas, their wealth."

Roskia stared at the table, visibly seething. "I think it would be a great mistake to allow those murderers to walk out of Isara with no recompense for what they've done. We're not just talking about the loss of our soldiers. We're talking about the mothers and fathers who have lived beneath their boots. Our ancestors in the Lower City who have survived in squalor while they dine on their rooftops and get drunk on their wine."

"I know," Vale said heavily.

Roskia scoffed. "Do you? *I* was born in these streets, like most of the men in this legion."

And there it was. That was the weapon Roskia always kept concealed in his pocket, ready to fling out at a moment's notice. Vale was their leader, but Roskia was waiting for his chance to remind the legionnaires that the Commander wasn't *really* one of them.

"If you leave the Magistrates and their families alive, they will keep their claim to their seats in the Forum," Roskia pressed. "Even if they're on the other side of the wall, they will want it back. With enough time, they'll try to come get it."

That was something Vale and I had discussed at length. According to Isarian law, the only way to open a Magistrate's seat was for the Magistrate to die with no heir. There were those who wouldn't be upended so easily.

"There have been enough bodies in the streets, Roskia. Enough blood in the river," Vale said.

Now we had ventured into another unspoken argument—the Magistrates hanging from the bridge. Roskia had been toeing the line of defiance for almost two months, bolstering the Commander with the credit for the murdered Magistrates and priming the legion for a bloodbath in the district.

Roskia's hands lifted into the air. "Look, you said you wanted my input, so let's talk about a compromise. One that will work for everyone."

"What kind of compromise?" I asked, already not liking where this was headed.

"Open up the gates and let everyone in the Citadel District who wants to leave. Everyone except the Consul and the Magistrate families. Anyone with claim to a seat in the Forum."

Vale's gaze shot to me and I clenched my jaw, trying to hold my tongue. This was exactly what I'd been trying to avoid. License to exact revenge on Magistrate families was license to take the life of the only person in the district I was trying to keep alive. It had been a delicate and, at times, perilous balance.

"Require the forfeit of their medallions, as you've said. But anyone with the family name of a Magistrate cannot be allowed to leave. The legionnaires will lose faith, Commander. I promise you that." Roskia's face was still turned toward Vale, but his gaze was aimed at me now, and the mask he wore slipped just enough for me to see the familiar look in his eye. "They'll wonder what exactly you're trying to protect over there."

There was a knowing in his voice as he said it, making a chill run up my spine. No one except Vale knew what happened the night before Vitrasian was executed, but it was a secret that had grown into a blade hanging over my head. The legionnaires believed in Vale in part because they believed in me—Matius, son of Matius. Not the man in the Magistrate's robes. I was a son of the Lower City who'd crossed the Sophanes and brought the Citadel District to its knees. And if the legionnaires lost that, I didn't know how far their loyalty to Vale would go.

No one could know, I tried to reassure myself. So, why did I feel like Roskia did?

Vale stood, breaking the tension before it could snap between us. "The Consul will never agree to that."

"I know, which will only work in our favor." Roskia continued, "The Consul can't lose his Magistrates because without them, he has no power. And when he chooses them over everyone else in the district, they'll probably do our job for us. No matter which side of the river you live on, it isn't the Isarian way to separate the sins of a father from his bloodline."

Vale went rigid, the implication bleeding into the air like poison. He had disavowed his father, the Consul, but as long as he was alive, there would be whispers about where the Commander's loyalties lay.

I kept my mouth shut, not wanting to give Roskia more reason to accuse Vale and me of being in league together despite what was best for the New Legion.

Vale looked a shade paler now. "Let me think about it."

Roskia rose to his feet, his tone changing. "You have whatever you need from me when we cross the Sophanes. You know that," he said seriously. He was a soldier first, that much had always been true. He knew how to put his feelings aside, and that was maybe what worried me most about him.

"I do," Vale answered.

Roskia knew disobeying orders would cost him, so he'd found ways to step around them. His leadership in the rebellion would give him fame for the rest of his life, but he'd need Vale's favor if he was going to be granted a position of real power in the new Isara.

He gave Vale another small bow before he left, Demás following on his heels.

Across the table, Vale was staring into the flame of the lamp. "That went as expected."

I leaned forward. "His ambition will outweigh his hunger for revenge."

"I hope you're right." He exhaled.

"We can't do what he's suggesting. We can't just slaughter entire families. If we're building a new Isara, we can't start that way."

"He may be right that we won't have to. We can make the deal and let it play out. Chances are that the Consul will do exactly what Roskia said and dig his own grave," he said.

"That doesn't solve the problem. There's still the matter of what to do with who's left."

Vale nodded.

"Where have you gotten with the messages?" I changed the subject.

"Still working on it." He paused, taking a breath before he spoke again. "You know, if Roskia is already wondering if you have interests left in the Citadel District, he's probably not the only one."

"I know," I said hollowly.

He unclasped his scale armor, pulling it over his head carefully and dropping it onto the bench beside him. "Anything else?"

I swallowed, glancing again at the uneaten food on the table. The last thing Vale needed was to be part of covering up the fact that I had a Magistrate's daughter in my tent.

"No," I answered.

He went back to the maps, picking up one of the white stone markers, and I watched as he lost himself to the endless work of war. The guilt of it weighed heavy on me.

The spiraling towers of the Citadel were visible in the distance, where the window to the Hall of Scribes was open to the view of the city. A lot could happen in three days, like Vale had said. But if Roskia was already convinced there was something I was hiding, I had even less time than that.

CHAPTER 20

BEFORE: MARIS

Luca Matius was a fever that wouldn't break.

He pressed me into the cool stone with his weight, hands dragging up my back and finding the hot skin beneath the folds of my chiton. He smelled like sun and sweat, his tunic streaked with the dust from the training grounds, a scent I found myself craving in the middle of the night.

The Third Feast had come and gone. In the weeks since Luca first kissed me at the beach, we'd carved out minutes and hours between his training, tribunals, and our noviceships, chancing a passing glance in the Forum or a brush of fingers on the street. By the time we were alone, I was so hungry for him that I almost felt sick with wanting. Like a forge that burned too hot.

"I'm going to be late." I broke the kiss, breathless, but Luca's mouth just traveled down my throat.

We were tucked behind the colonnade that housed the Citadel's water cisterns, hidden from the view of the street. Voices and the crack of cartwheels over stone drifted over the wall, where we were concealed in shadow.

"Let me come see you tonight." Luca's deep voice woke goose bumps on my skin.

"I can't. We're hosting the faction dinner."

His hand slipped up and under my chiton, calloused fingers finding the curve of my hip bone. "Then come to me."

"*I can't.*" I laughed, placing my hands on his chest and pushing him away.

He relented, leaning into the wall beside me so that my shoulder touched his. My skin was flushed, my breaths coming too fast.

I still didn't know what we were doing, and neither of us had raised the question out loud since that day at the sea. What had started as a treacherous attraction to Magistrate Matius' heir was quickly becoming more than that. Luca wasn't just beautiful, he was a thinker. He liked to talk and debate. To spin ideas into the air as he fell asleep. He *dreamed*—in an unspoiled, hopeful kind of way that could be born only in the Lower City. My body was getting too used to him, it was true. But much more terrifying than that was my growing admiration for his mind.

"Tomorrow," I said, letting my face turn toward him. "Come see me tomorrow."

A smile tilted his mouth before he leaned down and kissed the top of my bare shoulder. Then he slipped behind the colonnade, disappearing in the stream of people headed to the bridge.

I pressed my palms to my face, willing my pulse to slow before I did the same. The plaza was growing more crowded by the minute, a hum rising in the air that was reminiscent of a feast day. Hands floated up above the sea of people, clutching parchments that rippled in the wind. It was a common sight when the Forum

Record was released, a leaflet distributed the day after every tribunal. When someone shoved one into my hands, I tucked it into my belt and pressed through the edge of the crowd.

I took the Citadel steps up from the plaza quickly, eyeing the sundial to check the time. I was late. I gathered up the length of my chiton, leaving the din behind me as I crossed into the cool, shaded portico of the Citadel. The congested arteries of the pillar-lined corridors were ones I'd had memorized for years now. I hadn't been allowed to step foot into the building until I was twelve years old, when the sons and daughters of Magistrates began their education in observing the Forum.

The first time I got lost in the marble passageways was also the last time. My mother spent more hours in her chambers here than she did at home, and as a servant, Iola wasn't permitted to cross the entrance without express permission. It was only my second visit to the Citadel when she held my hand as we climbed the steps. Then she let me slip into the portico alone. It was the first time she'd had to let me go, and in many ways, I'd felt alone ever since.

I followed the corridors of the Tribunal Hall, the painted eyes of the Magistrates peering down at me from their portraits. The gilded door of the Hall of Scribes had an ornate molding that edged the opening where the family names of the first scribes were carved into the stone. Branches of cypress trees and curling waves of the sea framed a series of characters from the oldest stories of the gods.

I'd spent three years as a novice in the Illyrium, and I'd been sent to the Hall of Scribes many times. Any scroll from the Citadel's collection had to be formally requested from its library, and the management of the scrolls was closely stewarded, with a process for everything. Everyone in the Citadel and beyond who requested a scroll from the library was required to show their medallion to be granted permission by the scribes themselves. Even the Consul. And every scroll had to be returned by sundown.

The sound of the growing crowd outside drifted through the windows when I reached the propped-open doors. Beyond the swag of draped curtains was the desk of the signatory on duty—a novice named Drakon.

"Casperia." He shot to his feet, giving me more respect than was necessary out of fear of my uncle.

Nej was known for his rigid instruction of his novices, but to everyone else in the Citadel, he was the picture of charm and wisdom. Drakon had been unfortunate enough to bear the brunt of my uncle's ire regularly since he took the position.

I gave him a nod as I passed, headed for my uncle's chamber. I found him sitting on the corner of his desk, a stylus in his hand. Behind him, a wall of shelves displayed his collection of rare stones, painted pottery, and gifts he'd received in his tenure as a scribe. An ivory tusk and a rectangular box carved of black obsidian were among them.

"Don't tell me," he said, not bothering to look up. "My sister needs a favor."

I dropped my hand and took the small message scroll from my belt, setting it at the center of the parchment he was reading. He blinked slowly before he picked it up.

"I've told you, Maris. It's better that you are not seen so much here."

"Tell that to Magistrate Casperia," I muttered.

It was considered controversial for a scribe in his position to have any direct connection to a faction leader because it reflected poorly on the Consul, who was supposed to be impartial. There were already rumors about Nej's favor for my mother and her many schemes, but it didn't matter how many times I reminded her, she still had me deliver her messages. It was as if she *wanted* people to talk.

With less than delicate hands, Nej opened the small scroll, eyes skipping over the words impatiently. He was about to argue when the hum of the chaos outside grew so distracting that he snapped his mouth shut, shooting an irritated glance at the window.

"What in the names of the gods is going on?" He stood, throwing back the curtain.

The light flooded in, making me flinch. I came to stand beside him as he eyed the river below. The number of people gathered on both sides of the bridge had multiplied now, with an enormous crowd growing in the courtyard of the Illyrium.

I set my hands on the ledge, leaning out. "What's happening?"

Nej's face twisted in confusion, his gaze sweeping from the plaza to the bridge. "I don't know."

Through the opening of the chamber door, I could see Drakon standing at his desk again, a leaflet in his hands. The crease in his brow as he read it over made me take a step toward him. It looked like the same one that was being circulated down in the plaza.

"The Forum Record," I said, realizing what it was.

Nej's head swung in my direction. "What?"

"What was in today's Forum Record?"

"Nothing." He set his hands on his hips. "It hasn't gone out yet."

I reached for the one I'd tucked into my chiton, unrolling the wrinkled pages before me. It was missing the seal of Isara that always marked the distributed leaflets, and the type was crude enough to give away that it wasn't printed in the catacombs of the Citadel. In fact, it wasn't a Forum Record at all.

Nej snatched it from my fingers before I was a few sentences in, his eyes jumping over the words. His expression was growing more panicked by the second.

"What?" I watched the blood slowly drain from his face.

Nej's eyes lifted to meet mine, but the usual humor was gone from them now. He looked almost . . . *afraid*.

"That bastard!" My mother's voice shot through the room, the door slamming behind her.

Her Magistrate's robes were half tied, a copy of the leaflet clutched in her fist. Her blue eyes were crazed as she stalked across the study toward Nej.

"The man is mad, Nej." She lifted the leaflet in the air, shaking it. "Tell me you didn't know about this."

I took the leaflet, frantically reading. It was a report on the harvest that had been brought in after the First Feast, the one that had been paraded through the city. It claimed that the spectacle was a farce. A performance to hide the truth—that there was no harvest.

Nej went to the cupboard in the wall, opening the long door and taking out his robes. "Gather the faction, Seren."

"It's not true," I said, looking between them. "It can't be true, can it?"

The fact that neither of them answered made my blood run cold.

"Drakon!" Nej knotted the ties of his robe before riffling through the parchments on his desk.

The novice appeared a moment later, peeking through the door with wide eyes. "Yes, sir?"

"Send a message to Magistrate Matius. Tell him to gather his faction. There will be a tribunal in an hour."

Drakon ducked out with an obedient nod, but my mother was still gaping at Nej.

"Only the Consul can call for a tribunal," she snapped.

"And that's what he will do." Nej forced a slow exhale.

There was more going on here than I could pick up from their half-spoken argument. My mother's hatred for the Consul wasn't a secret, not even from his scribe. But voicing accusations about Saturian under the roof of the Citadel was a death wish. Even my mother understood that.

"You will call in your faction and do whatever you can to minimize the damage."

"You want me to find a way to help him save face? For this?" my mother scoffed. "This will be the end of him, Nej. He's lost."

"He can't lose." Nej's voice flattened. "Not when we're about to lose control of this city."

CHAPTER 21

NOW: MARIS

I could feel him. Even in sleep, I could feel him.

My mind was pulled from the black by the tether of my knowledge that Luca was there. There were a few slippery seconds when I could believe that we were still in my room at the villa, waking in tangled sheets with the warm sun on our faces. When I could slide my hands across the bed with my eyes closed and find him.

I blinked, the blurred world coming into focus until I could see his face. He sat on the stool only feet away, his elbows propped on his knees as he looked at me. He was still fully dressed in his armor, his weapons strapped to his hip. But when I saw the glimmer of gold that hovered in the air over his head, I swallowed hard.

I'd seen with my own eyes the moment it appeared. In the very second that he avenged Vitrasian, the faint glow of a halo suddenly hung over the crown of his head. Luca, the man who hated the gods, had been *gifted*.

"How hurt are you?" he said, that voice like a barbed thing

cinching around my heart. He was watching me intently with a look I recognized in his eyes—it was fear.

My head was still swimming, and the fact that Luca was only feet away made it all feel less real than it already did. Only yesterday morning, I'd been sitting for my Magistrate portrait. Taking my oath. How could that be? How had any of this—the last six months—been possible?

I sat up slowly, eyeing the length of the space between us. If I reached out right now, I could touch him. That was something I thought would never be true again.

"Maris?" The sound of him saying my given name was a riptide. "How hurt are you?" His eyes were moving from my mouth to the broken skin that covered my hands and wrists.

I shook my head only once, my dry throat like sand as I swallowed. A cut lip and scraped knees were nothing to the wounds inside me.

Luca exhaled with a visible relief that made him look more familiar. I couldn't help studying him, and I realized that he was doing the same to me. There were marks on his skin where there hadn't been before. His face needed shaving, and his hair was longer than I'd ever seen it. He was still so achingly beautiful that I almost wished that he would vanish into thin air and I'd wake again only to realize that *this* was the dream. How many times had I prayed to the gods that I'd wake and find him there? How many times had I stared out across the river, wishing I could go back and change it?

What differences he noticed when he looked at me, I didn't know. On the outside I probably still appeared to be the arrogant, stubborn Magistrate's daughter who'd given him her scarf at the First Feast. But on the inside, I was something else entirely now.

"You shouldn't have done that—lied for me," I said.

Covering for me was a risk with too high a price. If the legionnaires outside knew he was protecting a Magistrate, they'd string him up on the bridge like the others.

He stared at my hands as they curled into the fabric of my chiton. "I was wondering when you'd finally try to get out," he said. "I wish you would have listened to me months ago and left the city when I asked you to."

"I told you I wouldn't," I whispered.

That day in the Forum, I'd watched in horror as Luca tore down the steps to reach Vitrasian. But he was too late. He wept as he pulled the sword from the legionnaire's belt, screamed as he drove it into the man trying to drag her body away. Then they were dragging *him* away, and the next night I'd held him through the bars of the catacomb's cell.

"If you aren't trying to leave, then what are you doing in the Lower City?" he asked.

"I came to see you."

Luca pressed his mouth into a straight line. There was a split second when I thought he was going to reach for me. But his fingers curled into fists, his muscles tensing.

"You wish I hadn't?" I said, voice tight.

Luca's eyes flashed. "You think I don't want to cross that bridge every single day? You think it hasn't killed me to not see you?"

"No one made you leave, Luca."

"We're not having this argument. Not again." He pressed a knuckle to the crease between his eyes. He looked so tired. "We're crossing the Sophanes in a matter of days. Then all of this will be over."

"That's why I'm here," I said.

He waited.

"I want to negotiate a peaceful transition of power. On behalf of the Citadel."

Luca's eyes lit with a question he didn't ask.

"My mother died seven days ago, Luca."

He swallowed hard, stiffening. The news was clearly a shock to him, but he didn't say he was sorry because he wasn't.

"She dropped a vial of poison into her wine and died the same way she lived—buried in her scrolls."

A long, tortured breath escaped him. "So, you . . ."

"Took her seat. Yes."

He closed his eyes, raking his hands over his face before they went into his hair. "You're a Magistrate."

"That *was* the plan, wasn't it? You take your seat, I take mine?"

He shook his head, voice rising. "All this time, I've been trying to keep you alive and then you take a *fucking* Magistrate seat. Why don't you just walk out into the middle of that camp and show them your medallion?"

"What exactly did you expect me to do? You're the one who crossed the river and didn't come back!"

"I couldn't. You know I couldn't."

"You didn't take me with you, either!" I shouted.

The tribune was suddenly in the doorway, eyes fixed on Luca in a warning. A silent exchange passed between them before the tribune stepped back out.

Luca stood, pacing the ground before me. I could see his mind racing. Looking for a way to make this something it wasn't. But we weren't the idealistic people we'd once been. We hadn't just been born on opposites sides of a line. We were stuck there. I could see that now.

"Exile for anyone in the district opposed to the New Legion." I steered the conversation back on subject. "When you cross the Sophanes, you take the district without bloodshed. In return, those in the district will forfeit their citizenship."

"It's too late for that," he said. "We've already agreed on an offer to bring to the Consul. That was before I knew you'd taken the seat."

I stood, taking a step toward him. "What offer? What exactly are you planning to do with us once you get there?"

Luca's tense gaze was answer enough. They would take the district with one last massacre.

"Do you remember what we said?" My voice wavered.

Luca stared at me.

"We said we wouldn't be like *them*. We swore to each other."

A pained look crossed his face, but he didn't respond. Instead, the muscle in his jaw clenched, his eyes cast to the ground. We'd made the plan one night while we lay naked in each other's arms, half covered by the warm weight of his legionnaire's cloak. I remembered that the sky was studded with so many stars that they nearly outshone the moon. We hadn't known then what was to come. We hadn't known that none of our plans mattered.

"That was before they killed Rhea," he said.

Rhea, Vitrasian's given name, was a reminder that she hadn't just been a mentor to Luca. She'd been a mother, like Iola had been to me. A guardian. A teacher. And the only thing my own mother and Luca's uncle had ever agreed upon was that she had to die.

Luca fell quiet, and I knew what he was thinking of. Vitrasian's chambers at the Citadel. The diagonal light that cast from the high windows. The suspended orbs that drifted through the air and the glass cases of seashells that lined her shelves. Before it had all burned to ashes. Maybe that was what he was doing with all the work written out on his desk. He couldn't resurrect Vitrasian, but he could try to resurrect her work.

"There may be a way to get them to make an exception for you," he said.

"What? How?"

He looked down at me. "What do you know about the messages coming from the Citadel?"

"What messages?"

He gave me a skeptical look. "Come on, Maris."

"I don't know what you're talking about."

He walked to the desk in the corner, picking up the small parchment I'd seen earlier. He seemed to hesitate before he handed it to me, and he watched as I unrolled it. Still, the parchment was blank, the shimmer of godsblood like a thin layer of gilded light painted on its surface. Now, I was sure that I'd seen one like it before. More than one. In my mother's study.

"Falcons have been leaving the aviary, almost a dozen a day now. We've been shooting them down, but I know we're missing some in the night."

I took the parchment. "I don't know anything about messages."

"*Think,* Maris. You must have heard something."

The idea that the Consul was sending messages from the Citadel didn't make any sense. There were only a handful of Magistrates outside the walls and Isara didn't have any allies. Nothing had been discussed in the tribunal, and there'd been no vote. I also couldn't remember my mother or my uncle having said a word about anything like that.

A creeping feeling of dread bled through me. Was this why the gods had brought me here? Was this what Ophelius meant when she said that Luca would need my help?

"We need to know who he's talking to," he said.

My eyes widened, understanding slowly sinking in. "Are you asking me to spy for you?"

"I'm asking you to make yourself *valuable* to the New Legion. Before we cross the river."

"You can't be serious."

"I can't stop this, Maris. I can't keep these legionnaires from killing the Magistrates. In a few days, the Citadel District *will* fall and I will lose my ability to protect you. I already have if you've taken an oath in the Forum. If you have something to give—to trade—maybe there's a chance."

"You stopped protecting me when you left the district."

Luca took a step back from me. "When the New Legion crosses the river, you can't be a Casperia anymore. Do you understand?"

His eyes ran over my face slowly, the gleam of tears just barely visible, and I could see the weight of it all pressing down on him. He'd lost control of the monster he created. And he knew it.

He tried to smooth over his expression, but he'd forgotten that I knew him. He was barely holding it together. The glittering ringlet of faded gold shimmered in the air over his head again, a flash in the dim light. I tried not to stare at it.

I couldn't stop myself from reaching for him then. I closed the distance between us and pulled him into my arms, wrapping them around him so tightly that I couldn't feel the places where I ended and he began. I turned my face into his hair, breathing him in, and he melted into me, his palms sliding up my back. The feeling rushed through me, the pain in my chest so great that it felt as if my bones would crack open with it.

My gaze went back to the opening of the tent, where I could see the shadow of his tribune standing guard. I held on to Luca, trying desperately to draw out the moment. I could already feel it slipping away.

"Come with me," I whispered into his hair. "Say you'll come with me and we'll leave right now. Tonight."

A shaking breath passed through his lips before he pulled back to look down into my face. One of those tears now striped the bridge of his nose, the pain in his eyes changing the shape and light of them.

"I can't." He let me go and the warmth of him bled away, the cold air filling the space between us again.

There was more to those two words than he could possibly say. He wore the yoke of this war around his own neck. He was a prisoner of it all, a man half erased by it.

The distant ring of voices lifted at the other end of the camp and Luca went rigid, going to the opening of the tent. Over his shoulder, I could just make out a few legionnaires drifting into the street.

"Go see what's going on," Luca ordered, and the tribune immediately vanished from sight.

Luca watched through the flaps of the tent, the sharpness of his gaze growing more severe with every second that passed. I wrapped my arms around myself, my pulse climbing. Whatever he saw there, it wasn't good.

When the tribune returned, his voice was low, his attention cutting from Luca to me. "Her brother's come to claim her," he said.

Luca and I looked at each other for a silent moment before I stepped around him. I pulled back the canvas just enough to see the young man waiting on the other side of a line of legionnaires outside. It was Zuri. He was wide-eyed and pale-faced, hands clutched together at his back where his fingers were tangled together nervously. The legionnaire Neatus from the night before stood at his side.

"It's Zuri." My hand slipped from the canvas. "Iola's brother."

Luca's eyes moved over my face for another agonizing moment as the footsteps drew closer and I realized that this—these lamplit, dreamlike moments of being here together—was nearly over. I could feel my heart grasping at them, trying to gather them up before they slipped away.

"Luca." I said his name, hand moving in the air toward him, and that was enough to make him turn and push out of the tent. He was gone.

I stood there staring at the empty space he'd left, the burn of tears lighting behind my eyes. The tribune watched me, waiting.

I pulled the palla over my shoulders, draping it over my head so that the fabric covered one side of my face. The wind caught it as I stepped outside, and the tribune fell into step beside me without a word.

I swallowed down the lump in my throat as the early sunlight fell on the street. Were those the last words Luca and I would say to each other? Was this, truly, the last time I'd ever see him? If he was wondering the same thing, I couldn't tell. He wasn't looking at me now.

Luca and Neatus exchanged a few words before the legionnaire turned his hard gaze on me. Across the square of dirt that served as a kind of courtyard between the row of tents, Zuri was waiting.

"Tell him how you know this woman." Neatus gestured to Luca.

"She's my sister," Zuri answered.

Neatus looked me over. "She was caught in the Lower City with no medallion."

Zuri cleared his throat. "She's foolish, but she's loyal. She at least has the sense to not implicate her own family when she's getting into trouble."

"What family?" Neatus asked.

Zuri pulled a medallion from inside his shirt, holding it up so that Neatus could read it. "Rullias."

Neatus took it, turning it in the light to check for the godsblood. It made a medallion impossible to fake.

The legionnaires that were gathered at the large tent in the distance were moving now, headed in our direction. I turned just slightly so that the palla hid my face.

Luca took a step forward, as if thinking the same thing, and his tall frame mostly hid me from view.

Neatus dropped Zuri's medallion after careful inspection and it swung from Zuri's neck. "If we catch her again . . ."

"You won't." Zuri gave me a reproachful look.

"Rullias?" Neatus said, looking at me this time. He was waiting for my confirmation.

The crowd of legionnaires made it to the row, a few of them looking in our direction as they passed. But they were all lost in conversation, distracted. All except one.

A man I recognized was trailing at the back, a tribune at his side. He spotted Luca, and when his eyes moved over the scene playing out around us, his steps slowed just a little. It was Roskia, the young legionnaire from the Lower City who'd made a name for himself as a Magistrate hunter. Now he wore the brooches of a Centurion, like Luca.

If he recognized me, he didn't show it, falling back into step with the others before they disappeared from view. But I felt like I was swaying, a sick feeling climbing up my insides. I could feel the eyes on me now, like flames held to the skin.

"Rullias," Neatus said again.

A few steps away, Zuri was looking at me intently, waiting for me to respond.

I finally answered with a nod.

Neatus motioned to Zuri and he stepped forward, gently taking me by the arm and leading me in the opposite direction of the legionnaires. When I looked back, Luca was still watching me, the stiffness in his body well concealed beneath his armor. Invisible to anyone else but me.

I can't.

The words he'd spoken to me curled around my heart like a serpent as he disappeared from view. I unclenched my fist, glancing down at what still lay crumpled in my palm. The parchment stared back up at me, the godsblood shimmering across the invisible message. If Luca was right and it was from the Consul, there was more to all this than rebels and godsblood. What I held in my hand was a secret. One that even the Magistrates didn't know about.

CHAPTER 22

BEFORE: MARIS

Every altar in the city was piled with offerings, every temple filled with prayer. But it was too late for the gods to save us.

There was only standing room in the spectator's gallery of the Forum, bodies pressed so tightly that the air was stifling hot. It had been two days since the anonymously authored leaflet had circulated through the Citadel District, and now the copies that had survived the retribution of the Consul had made their way through the Lower City. There was no stopping it now. The whole of Isara knew about the grain.

I'd had my ear pressed to the door of my mother's study as she met with the highest-ranking Magistrates of her faction. She'd even allowed me to sit in on her meetings with Nej, and by the time the panic was flooding the city, a tribunal had been called to vote on changes to the dole.

The state of Isara's fields had been kept secret from almost everyone in the Citadel, and both my mother and Magistrate

Matius had been informed only in the early days of the most recent harvest. For three years, the fields had been failing, the procession of grain through the city nothing but a ceremonial performance. But now there would be a reckoning.

There was no question who would be the first to go hungry if the winds of fate didn't change, but what no one outside the Citadel knew was that the time for intervention had passed. More important, it was clear the gods had spoken. Isara was being punished. But for what?

The secret getting out was maybe the most fortuitous thing that could have happened for my mother, which made me wonder if *she'd* been the one to distribute the leaflets. It was a perfect chance to gain the favor of the Lower City, which had been her plan all along in her rivalry against Magistrate Matius.

More spectators pushed into the gallery as I watched the floor of the Forum below where the Magistrates would enter. I pressed my hands to the marble railing before me, trying to keep my balance against the push of people, and when I felt a burning gaze find me, I looked down the gallery front to the face that was turned in my direction.

Luca stood almost a head taller than the men and women around him, his dark blue tunic making his eyes look like crystal. They were focused on me, his expression grave as the muscle in his jaw twitched.

I hadn't seen him since the day news of the grain overtook the district, but the memory of that kiss was still alive in my mind. That same burning sensation crept over my skin now, but it was followed by the acute awareness of the room around us. We weren't alone in the cove anymore. The last thing my mother could tolerate now was a threat to the power balance in the Forum. And that was exactly what Luca and I were.

He moved toward me, wedging himself through the crowd, but the look on his face was guarded. Suspicious, even. He took the place beside me, his arm pressing to mine.

"Did you know?" His words were a breath.

I stared at him, offended by the question. "Did *you*?" I shot back.

The space between us was too small for the number of eyes in the gallery. He looked as if he was deciding whether to believe me. "I didn't know." He waited for my answer.

"Neither did I," I said, turning back to the Forum.

The tension eased just a little, despite the roar of the crowd. I'd never seen so many people gathered for a tribunal. Even the streets across the river were full, and there was a palpable feeling of fear in the air. Like the city was holding its breath.

The door to the Forum opened and the first of the names was called out as the Magistrates streamed in. Their spotless white robes rippled around them, the silence that descended eerily unsettling. I'd attended countless tribunals in my life, and they were usually filled with the pomp and circumstance of highborn family leaders parading in front of one another. But there was a noticeable timidness among them now that I had never seen before.

"Your uncle?" I whispered.

"I delivered his vote to the Consul's scribe, but I don't need to know what it says."

The news that Magistrate Matius' illness had finally bound him to his bed had now traveled through the district. According to my mother, he was only days away from death.

I, too, could guess what his vote was. Matius had never concealed his hatred of the Lower City and its drain on the city's resources, so it wouldn't be difficult for anyone to imagine that he would vote for changes to the dole that would favor the district.

His faction would follow, and it was predicted that even some of my mother's faction could be persuaded, but the decision would require a three-quarters majority. That, the Consul would never get. Not while my mother was a faction leader.

Keeping the state of the grain stores a secret had broken the political agreements between the Magistrates and the people in a way that had no easy remedy. Corruption in the Forum was nothing new, but the implications of what was to come far outweighed the long history of half-truths and preferential treatment of the Citadel District. Now it was only a matter of time before they were held to account.

"And Vitrasian?" I pressed. "What does she say?"

"She says too much," Luca muttered. What he'd said before about his worry for the Philosopher was all over his face now. It carved deep lines between his brows.

Vitrasian was one person in the Citadel who'd known about the harvests, possibly for years. She'd been commissioned by the Consul to assess the fields, and her findings had been rejected. Now they'd been shared with the whole of the Forum in the deliberations leading up to the tribunal.

The last of the Magistrate family names was called out, leaving only one seat below empty—Magistrate Matius'.

Once the doors of the Forum closed, the crowd in the gallery pushed forward, trying to see the floor below. When someone shoved into me, forcing me to brace myself on the railing, Luca's hand came around me, fingers finding my waist. He moved me in front of him, but once I was pinned between him and railing, he didn't let me go. I stared at his hand, splayed across my hip, following the line of his fingers up his arm. But when I found his face again, his eyes were on the Forum. There was an intensity coursing through him, making the touch almost desperate, like he needed to anchor himself to something.

The crack of the gavel pulled my attention back to the floor, where the Consul was beginning to speak. The rigid set of his mouth almost muffled the words.

"I call this tribunal to order." Again, the gavel cracked.

The silence fell quickly, the spectators almost holding their breath. Whatever happened here would bleed through the entire city, and I didn't know what could come next.

The Consul stepped forward, hands clasped before him as he looked out over the Forum. "The purpose of this tribunal is to address the increasing deficiencies of the grain fields and the claims recorded in the unsanctioned release of reports regarding the harvest."

The choice of the Consul's words was concerning, making the stillness in the room expand. Referring to the leaflet's contents as *claims* implied that it might not be true.

"But first, I stand before you today to account for the Citadel's handling of this difficult situation." He let his gaze drift across the gallery, as if speaking directly to the people. "Upon learning of the challenges in our fields, the Magistrates of this Forum made the decision to conceal the information from the people of Isara while we determined the best course of action.

"This decision was not made lightly. Our city faces its greatest threat since before the Old War, and after generations of prosperity and abundance, we find ourselves confronted with the unknown. But it is now clear to us that this lack of transparency has caused great injury to our people."

The quiet room began to rumble with restrained agreement. This had been my mother's fear. That the city would turn on the Citadel before a decision could even be made.

"For this, we owe the citizens of Isara our profound apology, and we trust that your faith in us will be restored." The Consul's voice echoed.

The silence swelled with whispers, though I struggled to sift a collective feeling from crowd that surrounded us. People were afraid. That was the only thing I was sure of.

I looked up, meeting Luca's eyes. As heirs to seats in the Forum, we were both in the unfortunate position to hear everything not being said. The puzzle of language used among the Magistrates was precise and intentional, crafted for a very specific purpose. The Consul hadn't called this tribunal to issue an apology. My mother and Magistrate Matius hadn't been shut away with their respective factions merely to quell the nerves of the city. No, this Forum was laying the groundwork for something bigger.

"We enlisted the wisdom of the Citadel's advisors, among them the Philosopher Vitrasian," the Consul continued.

At the mention of the Philosopher's name, Luca's hand slipped from my waist.

"For the last year, we have been working with those advisors to identify the source of these weak yields and devise a solution. And now it is our duty to inform the citizens of Isara that, with the favor of the gods, we are well on our way to healing our lands."

My eyes narrowed before I searched the Forum floor for my mother. Her face was calm and serene, her rouged cheeks sharp beneath her dark lashes. There wasn't so much as a ripple beneath the surface of that look. But I could feel a change in the room, the sense of gravity shifting.

"This will take time. And until the gods return the fruit of our fields, we will all make sacrifices," the Consul continued. "And by the favor of Aster, the very goddess our city is consecrated to, the strength of our legion will feed our city."

Slowly, his meaning began to take shape. Aster was the goddess of war, and the only way for our legion to feed the city would be to take from someone else. Like we'd done to Valshad. Isara was going to war.

The consul turned to Nej, who rose from his seat, scroll in hand. I knew what would come from his mouth even before he began to speak.

"It is the recommendation of the Consul, along with the advisors to the Citadel, that the dole be amended to withstand the next harvest. This amendment will constitute a decrease of one-quarter to the Citadel District. And one-half to the Lower City."

A collective gasp rang out around me and my slick palms slipped from the railing. Behind me, Luca was made of stone.

Nej let the parchment close in his hands before he took the small sealed scroll from his desk. When he opened it, he began to read.

"In his absence, Magistrate Matius has submitted his response by messenger. He votes in favor of the amendment."

I reached for Luca's hand, encircling his wrist with my fingers. I could feel the race of his pulse beneath his skin as, one by one, Magistrate Matius' faction turned their stones. Their white faces gleamed across the Forum floor.

This was the moment my mother had been waiting for.

"They won't get the majority," I whispered, knowing the damage had already been done.

It did little to dispel the look of disgust in Luca's eyes. But I held on to him, my grip on his wrist tightening as I watched my mother. My heartbeat began to slow as she reached for her stone, her delicate fingers moving over the smooth surface before she took it into her palm. And then she did the thing that no one, not even I, saw coming.

She closed her hands over the stone, turning it slowly. And when she opened them again, the white marble face was shining.

Like a ripple through water, they turned one by one, until every single judgment stone was cast. The Consul didn't need a three-quarters majority. Not when he had the whole.

I shoved away from the railing as the verdict bled through the throng of onlookers, a feeling of suffocation pressing in around me. I was gasping for air, the light from the open doors bending until my head was dizzy with it.

Luca stopped me on the steps, turning me to face him. Outside the Forum, the sound of the shouting was muffled.

"Look what they can do, Luca." I flung a helpless hand toward the Forum, where the gavel was knocking in a frantic rhythm.

Luca stared at me, the same look of defeat in his eyes that I could feel swelling in mine.

"None of this matters. Nothing *we* do matters." My voice broke.

"That's not true."

"It is," I said, believing it for the first time.

"We don't have to be like them. We *won't* be."

"This is pointless. All of it," I whispered, not talking about the Forum anymore. And he knew it.

On some level, he agreed with me, because he didn't argue. We might have been born on opposite sides of the river, but our fates were the same—a lifetime of doing exactly what we'd just seen down on the Forum floor. The Citadel was a labyrinth of schemes. A maze we were foolish to believe we could escape from. Pretending otherwise was just a self-inflicted wound. One day, we'd be down in those seats and we'd be forced to choose. I didn't want to find out how that ended.

"Are you saying we don't have a chance?" He searched my eyes.

"I'm saying we never did," I said sadly.

I turned back down the steps, pain blooming in my throat. Luca called my name, but I could hardly hear it over the sound of the rising voices. Outrage was swiftly turning into panic as the implications of what had just happened began to settle in everyone's mind. I followed the steps down from the gallery as listeners in the portico ran past me, and I wedged myself along the wall as the crowd pressed in tighter.

"Maris." Luca's voice was louder now.

Behind us, the Forum was erupting in chaos. There was a sudden, terrifying sense that the ground was cracking beneath us. Like it was seconds from opening enough to swallow us whole.

Somewhere in the portico, someone screamed just as one of the hanging tapestries snapped from its dowel, rippling to the floor at the bottom of the stairs, and the doors of the Citadel burst open before a tide of people pushed through. The crushing flow of the crowd picked me up, forcing me in the opposite direction. I stumbled, nearly falling to my knees before a pair of hands grabbed hold of me tightly.

It was Luca. He pushed me forward into the wall of people until we were pressed so tightly that I couldn't breathe. I tipped my head back, trying to find air, and Luca wrapped one arm around me, pulling me with him. Dozens of red cloaks appeared as the legionnaires began to fill the Citadel, and the screams multiplied before my foot slipped on something wet. I looked down to see a thick smear of blood across the marble and the battered, swollen face of a man on the ground. Luca lifted me over him and the man vanished from sight.

When we reached the locked iron gates that opened to the gardens, I gasped. As far as I could see, the mob was devouring the Citadel. There was nowhere to go.

Luca planted his feet as the crowd parted around us, searching for a way out. When his eyes locked on something only a few feet away, we were moving again. We reached the gate and Luca pinned me against it, pressing his body tightly to mine before he hooked his arms through the rods.

"Hold on to me," he rasped.

I slid my arms around him, burying my face in his chest, and he curled around me. I pinched my eyes closed as the roar grew louder and the gate shook on its hinges, threatening to break free. The mob turned into a hungry, snarling thing, a monster that ate up the light. Its darkness pooled in the air around us, and I could feel it changing—the city. I could feel *us* changing. And somewhere inside me, I knew. There was no going back.

CHAPTER 23

NOW: MARIS

It had taken Zuri triple the drachmas to convince the legionnaires posted at the south bridge to look the other way for a second day in a row. It was a bribe they wouldn't have taken if they'd known he was crossing the river with a Magistrate. There wasn't anyone on either side of the river who wouldn't string all of us up on the bridge for that.

The sun had set by the time I was walking the streets of the Citadel District again, and I was grateful for the cover of darkness. I kept to the alleys that ran behind the abandoned market until I reached the steps that led to our villa and crept up silently. When I reached the door, I slipped inside.

There was a still silence before I heard the sound of bare feet brushing over the mosaic tile in the atrium and my uncle's voice lifted on the other side.

"Maris?"

I exhaled, pressing the door closed behind me.

Nej appeared in the forest of potted plants, and as soon as he saw me, his hands dropped to his sides, his shoulders sagging in relief. "Thank the gods."

It was maybe the most vulnerable look I'd ever seen on the man, but he almost sounded angry.

"Where the hell have you been?" He ground out the words.

The birds bounced in their cages, wings fluttering in a movement that mirrored my pulse.

"Out," I said, immediately headed for my room. I was already untying the cords of my chiton as I crossed the gallery.

"*Out?*" He followed on my heels. "You've been gone since last night. You missed the portraitist this morning. You're lucky a tribunal wasn't called!"

When we passed the open door of my mother's room, I stopped, eyeing the blankets that were coiled up in a heap on her bed. The lamp was lit.

I turned to my uncle. "Did you sleep here?"

"Of course I did. I was worried. I came to find out what you could have possibly been thinking."

I stared at him, confused.

"With what you pulled with the Consul last night!" He appeared to be genuinely distressed, and I felt somewhat guilty. He wasn't a warm man, but he looked as if he'd stayed up half the night waiting for me to walk through the door.

"I'm sorry," I said, meaning it.

I continued to my room, where moonlight was streaming in through the windows, casting a pattern on the marble. Nej stopped in the doorway, turning his back to give me some privacy before I let the chiton drop to the floor.

"Well?" He waited.

"I asked of the Consul what any Magistrate *should* be asking. I'm the only one who seems to think we've lost this war."

"I don't think you understand what's happening here, Maris. You're a Magistrate now. People are watching you. What you do and say will not go unnoticed. Especially when you disappear into thin air."

I didn't need to see him to know the look on Nej's face was an exasperated one. He had promised to mentor me as a Magistrate and guide me through the politics of the Citadel, but there was more going on here. And I knew that his help also had to do with his own designs. What those designs were, I didn't know, but if I caught the ill favor of the Consul, neither of us would get what we wanted. I could find myself bleeding on the Forum floor just like the Philosopher Vitrasian had. Maybe Nej would, too.

"This is no time for secrets. If something is going on, you need to tell me," he said.

The blank message from the Citadel's aviary burned in my mind, and I weighed the cost of showing it to him. The Consul was talking to someone outside the city walls. It was possible that Nej had even been the one to pen those messages. But asking him about it now felt too precarious, and I didn't want to risk Nej. Not when he was the only person in the Citadel District that I had left.

"I could say the same to you," I said.

"What does that mean?"

I glanced at the doorway, where he still stood with his back to me. "What's between you and the Consul?"

"What exactly are you asking?"

"What is he? Your lover? Are you something more than a scribe to him?"

He hesitated. "I'm an advisor. He trusts me."

There was no waver in his voice. Nej was an expert at tightrope walking, especially when it came to the Forum. Among the players that warred in the Citadel, he was one of only a few who had maintained ambiguous allegiances. In a way, he was everything that was wrong with the Citadel while also avoiding the worst of its acts falling on his shoulders. He had no judgment stone to cast, but there was no doubt that he influenced the outcomes of the votes. That was one of the reasons my mother had retained so much power.

"Are you at least going to tell me what happened to your face?" he asked, more gently.

I examined the cut on my lip in the mirror, gently pressing a fingertip to the bruise on my chin. "Does it really matter?"

He thought about that for a moment. "Everything we do right now matters. Every decision we make."

I went to the washing bowl beside the window. He was right. I knew that. But I'd crossed the Sophanes anyway.

"Everything is about to change, Maris. In just a matter of weeks. You and I need to be sure we're still standing at the end of this. The gods have turned their faces upon us. I can feel it."

"Days," I corrected him.

"What?"

"It won't be weeks. The New Legion is going to cross in three days, Nej."

He fell silent for several seconds. "And how could you possibly know that?"

I dropped the washcloth back into the bowl and went to the chest against the wall, opening it. I chose the first chiton my hands landed on, a copper-hued silk trimmed in gold.

After the last few days, the scene that surrounded me had become even more ridiculous. Fine tapestries hung from the windows over the bed and the dressing table was littered with vials of perfume and strands of pearls. Only hours ago, I'd stood in Luca's humble tent, aching for him to put his arms around me.

I tugged on the chiton, fastening the brooches and letting the gold godsblood chain drape down my back.

"As stubborn as your mother," Nej muttered.

He wasn't wrong, but the words still stung. I'd vowed to take the Magistrate's seat with honor and integrity, but in the day since I'd put on the white robes, I'd already committed treason.

He finally turned around, leaning one shoulder against the doorframe so he could look at me. "Medallion."

I glanced up, finding him in the mirror. "What?"

"Your *medallion*, Maris."

I reached up to my throat as I remembered it was gone. I found it on the window ledge, letting it swing in the air before I clasped it at the nape of my neck. It hung heavily just beneath my collarbone, the metal cold against my skin, and Luca's voice came back to me.

You can't be a Casperia anymore.

When the New Legion took the Citadel, Magistrate blood would spill. There would be no hiding then.

"How can I convince you to trust me?" Nej asked softly.

I turned to face him, guilt curling like a snake in the center of my gut. He was right. I'd seen Nej and my mother playing the games of the Citadel my entire life, and I knew him. He was slippery and changeable, out for his own gain. But Nej wasn't a liar like my mother had been.

"What do you know about the Citadel sending messages from the aviary?" I asked.

"Messages?"

Again, I debated with myself, trying to decide how much I

was willing to tell him. But I wasn't sure I had a choice anymore. If the New Legion was crossing the river in three days, maybe I was already out of time. Nej wasn't without fault, but he was one of the few in the Citadel who wasn't particularly hated for any specific thing. He had connections and relationships that others didn't. That meant he had information.

I sank to the floor, riffling through the chiton I'd taken off until I found the pocket sewn into the skirt. I reached inside, finding the message I'd taken from Luca's tent. I held it out to him.

His brow wrinkled before he took it. "What is this?"

"I was hoping you might know."

Nej's bottom lip jutted out as he thought. "You're sure it came from the Citadel's aviary?"

"I'm sure."

He looked even more confused now.

"They've been leaving the Citadel by the dozens. The New Legion has been shooting them down."

Nej didn't ask how I knew that and I guessed he didn't want to know.

"You really expect me to believe you haven't heard anything about this? Nothing at all?" I searched his face, looking for the lie. "The Consul still believes that we're going to win this war, Nej. Why? How?"

"I have no reason to lie to you. I have no idea who the Consul could be talking to."

"You pen his messages, Nej."

He turned the parchment around, holding it out to me. "There *is* no message, Maris. For all I know he's writing messages to the gods. The man's mad enough for it."

If he was telling the truth, then he wouldn't like the idea of something going on in the Citadel he didn't know about. He had his hands in everything. There wasn't a single Magistrate whose ear he didn't have.

I took the unrolled scroll.

Nej came to stand before me, his voice taking a wary tone. "Maris, the gods are at work here. It would be a grave mistake to interfere." His hands came up on either side of my face, his expression softening. "Let me deal with the Consul."

I stared into his eyes, trying to sift the meaning from the words. Nej wasn't a pious man, but even he could see there was more going on here than we could know.

"In the end, you and I—we need to be on the same side."

I nodded and his hands dropped, a look of relief flooding his face.

"And no more visits to the Lower City. Not until this is over. I have enough to worry about without you committing treason."

My eyes snapped up, face flushing hot. So, he did know where I was.

He met my gaze for a long moment before he finally turned and left. His footsteps trailed through the villa and then he was gone.

But Nej was wrong. Only the day before, as I'd sat across the table from the Consul, the look in his eyes hadn't been crazed or delirious. It had been steady and purposeful. He'd always been that way, and that was why my mother had feared him. If the man was mad, the Magistrates could have risen against him long ago, overturning his seat to someone who could be controlled. It had taken half the city turning on him to disrupt the hold he had on Isara, and even now, with the New Legion on the banks of the Sophanes, he still thought he had it. He wasn't a madman; he was a man who was sure he'd won.

I looked down at the blank parchment in my hands. I'd seen

a message just like it on my mother's desk, not long before the truth about the harvests got out. I was sure of it. And that wasn't the only thing I remembered.

I waited several seconds after the door closed to step back into the hallway, following it to my mother's study. I pushed the doors open and they hit the wall, hinges rattling.

The key to the cupboard was on the windowsill, and when I unlocked it, I stared at what lay inside. The tincture of godsblood was still there. The last one my mother had.

A gust of wind blew in through the window, filling the study as I stepped down. I smoothed out the blank message on the desk before I unstoppered the small glass vessel. My hand shook as I let the shimmering liquid drip onto its surface. The godsblood beaded on the parchment before I smeared it with my thumb. It was only a matter of seconds before I could see the markings coming to life in a faint color as the parchment wrinkled.

The pattern didn't make sense, the letters forming an arrangement of words that I didn't recognize. The Citadel and its scribes loved their puzzles, and some of them were familiar from my time transcribing for my mother or the Priestess. But this one was stranger than the ones I'd seen. Still, there was something familiar about it to me.

I'd seen the symbols before. It was one of the old languages, no—it was the *first* language.

But the way the characters were spaced and stacked, the message appeared to be a cipher. And in order to read it, I'd need a key. There were thousands of official scrolls and papers in the Citadel District that could be used for that purpose. It could be anything. Geographical records, planting plans for the fields, or even sacred texts written by the priests. The randomization and obscurity of the text ensured its secrecy.

I looked up to the shelves that covered the wall behind my mother's desk. I walked toward them, unblinking, and began to pull armfuls of scrolls from their places. I let them unroll over her desk, dragging a finger down the length of each one, eyes scanning the markings. When I reached the bottom, I opened another. And another. I tore through them, scroll after scroll, looking for anything written in the first language.

I was standing in a sea of curling parchment that filled the study's floor when I dropped the last one, and I looked around me, to my mother's trinkets glimmering from their places on the shelves. Treasures she'd hoarded from the markets and gifts from other Magistrates or the Consul himself. If there was anyone who might know what the Consul was up to, it was her. But whatever secrets she'd had, she'd taken them with her.

CHAPTER 24

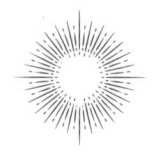

NOW: LUCA

The smell of incense still clung to me as I stood at the mouth of the north bridge, the tribune at my side. Below, the river ran rough, a sign that rain had fallen in the mountains. Now it traveled down to the sea in search of its freedom.

The tribune had taken extra time with my armor, making it shine like it had in the days before the war. It was strange to think of it like that—*before* and *after*. We were mere moments from walking onto that bridge and there, our course would be set.

On the other side, the last of the Loyal Legion was waiting. I knew some of them—older legionnaires who'd trained us as recruits back when no one thought any of this could ever happen. When the fighting began, they'd chosen their side. Some because they hadn't been able to stomach treason, while others just had too much to lose in the district. I didn't envy or judge them, but I wouldn't forgive them, either. None of us would.

"Are you absolutely sure she crossed?" I spoke lowly, so that only the tribune could hear.

He nodded. "I'm sure."

For the second time, he'd proven himself trustworthy, even if I didn't like the fact that now he was in possession of my secrets. What he would do with them, I couldn't guess. I wasn't fool enough to believe there wouldn't be a moment when he would have to choose, too. Only the gods knew what would happen then.

I hadn't been able to focus since I watched Maris walk out of the camp. In the last few months, I'd found a way to live with the gnawing wound, stitched over and concealed, at the center of my bones. It was like poisoned marrow, festering from the inside. I'd managed to keep it from destroying me. But peering down into Maris' face, *seeing* her, had made me wonder if that was true. I didn't like the look in her eyes when they met mine. Like she didn't recognize me anymore.

In a way, I didn't recognize her, either. There was little trace of the fire-blooded girl who used to laugh with her head thrown back, eyes sparkling. That softness I'd found beneath her self-protective exterior was gone. *I'd* done that. I'd been the one to break that part of her.

Not that one.

I could still hear my uncle's words low in my ear the night I first saw Maris Casperia. Looking back, maybe he had been right. Maybe part of me wished I had listened. More than once, I'd wondered if all this would have happened if I had never kissed her. Never touched her. Never held her in my arms. But I was still thankful to the gods that Kastor lived long enough to learn I had.

The memory of holding her was like a vise in my chest. I hadn't known what it would feel like when I left her in the district six months ago. I didn't know that the divide of the Sophanes would feel like a knife twisted between my ribs.

The swing of hammers and chisels behind me silenced, the camp falling quiet, and I turned to see Vale making his way toward the bridge. The legionnaires stopped their work, standing with lifted chins as he passed, every eye watching him. There was a reverence wherever he went, his family name uttered with solemn heaviness. *Saturian.* The nobleborn legionnaire who'd turned his back on his own father and cast his lot with the Lower City. And in part, at least, he'd done it for me.

He stopped behind the granite colonnade that overlooked the river, peering out at the Citadel across the water. Its high dome gleamed in the sunlight, the spire at its top like the tip of a spear piercing the heavens.

Asinia and my tribune placed themselves in front of us, side by side at the entrance to the bridge. A look passed between them with a familiarity that I hadn't caught before.

"Where did you find him?" I asked, leaning closer to Vale and keeping my voice low. "My tribune."

"What do you mean?"

"I mean, where did he come from?"

Vale smirked, a once familiar sight I'd missed.

"What?" I said.

He shook his head. "You don't trust anyone."

"No, I don't."

"He's just a kid from the Lower City. An orphan. I think his father was killed in the first Loyal Legion attack. He volunteered for the position."

"Volunteered?" I studied him.

Tribunes were usually selected by the Commander or the Centurions, which was considered a great honor among legionnaires. It was a quick way to rise in the ranks if you lived through the posting. But it was also the most dangerous position to be in because your life was no longer your own. It was meant only to act as a shield for whomever you served.

"He was quite adamant," Vale added. "I accepted as a favor to Asinia, more than anything."

"Asinia?"

"They belong to each other," he said.

My eyes moved from my tribune to Vale's. The two of them stood side by side, eyes now fixed ahead. I'd known that Asinia had someone, but I hadn't paid enough attention to find out who it was. Vale, on the other hand, never missed anything.

Flags rose on the other side of the bridge, and a contingent spilled from the mouth of the Citadel, where the Consul's brilliant robes were like a drop of blue ink against the white stone.

"Are you ready?" I asked.

"This is what we wanted, right? What we fought for?" he answered.

His tone conveyed his need for reassurance. He wanted me to tell him that it had been worth it. All of it.

I pushed down the image that had plagued me since the first fight broke out in the Lower City. There was no way we could have known how many would die between the Loyal Legion, the rebels, and the citizens of Isara caught in between. The temples had been performing funeral rites almost every day since.

"It is," I answered, nowhere near convinced.

If Vale could hear my lack of conviction, he didn't show it. He seemed to relax a little, resting his hand on his belt as we waited.

"Are you sure you don't want to do this alone?"

He cleared his throat. "I can't."

The Consul had accepted Vale's invitation more quickly than we'd expected, with no qualms about our conditions. He was to meet us at the center of the bridge with only two legionnaires. They wouldn't cross one inch into the Lower City and we wouldn't cross an inch into the Citadel District. But it couldn't have been expected for the Commander to bring a Centurion. Vale had insisted I come, and I wouldn't deny him that. For all his courage and valor, he didn't want to face his father alone.

The Consul crossed the bridge with determined steps that weren't at all hesitant. His eyes didn't even lift to our side of the river, as if he had no concern about what he would see there.

Asinia and my tribune walked in lockstep with their javelins drawn, and the legionnaires on the other side did the same. We followed, the swell of the New Legion at our back like the heat of a roaring fire. They'd all come to the riverfront to watch their Commander meet the Consul on the bridge.

My stomach twisted as the district drew closer. It was the nearest I'd come to it since all this began, and the only thing I could think was that it was too quiet. Like the sound of the forest that edged along the coast. But the smell of the sea was tainted on the smoke-tinged wind. Nearly every window of every villa across the water was completely dark, the streets empty of the sounds that usually drifted through the market and between the buildings.

The tribunes' eyes were on the rooftops and balconies in the distance, trailing along the riverfront and up to the Citadel. The legionnaires were there, but their weapons weren't drawn, and I tried to imagine what they thought when they looked at us. Did they still see the ungrateful, selfish soldiers who'd started a rebellion? Or had they begun to see the Consul and the Magistrates for who they were?

They weren't the only ones who'd come to watch. At our backs, hordes of citizens from the Lower City had begun to gather, ready to see us deliver on our promise. If we didn't, they'd bring their own retribution. On us.

The Consul's legionnaires stopped in the center of the bridge only paces before our tribunes. They stood silent, the rush of the river beneath us, before finally stepping aside. There, the Consul had his hands clasped behind his back as he looked at us. I remembered thinking the first time I saw him that he *looked* highborn. His strong, pointed nose and cleft chin were features you'd see on the statues at the temple. And that blank look on his face made it feel as if he could be thinking anything. As if it would be impossible to predict what he might do. It ignited a prey instinct in people. A lowering and shrinking. And he liked it.

"Saturian, Matius." His tongue rolled around in his mouth as if he didn't like the taste of the words. "Such a shame to speak such honorable names at a time like this."

Vale didn't react. He ignored the insult, getting to the point. "We'd like to discuss the requirements for surrender of the Citadel District."

"There will be no surrender," the Consul said flatly.

Vale stared at him. Even if he refused to look for himself, the Consul had to be aware of the legion at our backs. They were just waiting for the order. Had been for days. And when Vale gave it, the district would fall.

"If you think you can take the Citadel, then by all means try."

There was something else beneath the words, and I searched for their meaning in the faces of the Consul's legionnaires behind him. But their expressions were empty. Hollow. If I had to guess, I'd say they had no idea what he was up to.

"We plan to open the gates in two days' time, at dawn," Vale continued. "Anyone in the Citadel District who wishes to leave will be able to do so, with our word that no harm will come to them. Magistrates, however, will not be permitted to leave. Neither will you."

The Consul's wolflike eyes sharpened.

"Anyone else who chooses to go will be required to surrender their medallion and will be stripped of their citizenship to Isara. Their family names will be wiped from the city's tombs and any other claim they may have within these walls will be forfeit."

"I see," he said. "And what of *your* family name, Saturian?"

Vale and the Consul stared at each other, unblinking. The Consul wasn't the only one who'd posed the question. I'd heard other legionnaires speculating about it over late-night fires. What would Vale do with his family name when his father fell? Would he strike it from the history of the city or remake it in his own image?

"Once the gates close, we will take control of the Citadel," Vale continued.

The Consul smiled. Actually smiled. And when he did, he looked even more like a god. "I understand."

I waited for a threat to follow, but it didn't. There was no mention of grain or the tribunal or bringing the New Legion to justice. There was no resistance to the stipulation about the Magistrates.

A slow, creeping chill slithered up the back of my neck. It was that same feeling I had when I opened the young legionnaire's satchel and saw those falcons. There was something more happening here. Something wrong. And beneath that, there was a panic brewing inside me. I'd counted on Vale and Roskia's prediction that the Consul would refuse our terms and that we'd have to negotiate. But he wasn't even going to argue, and the words had already left Vale's mouth. Maris was a Magistrate in the district. And we'd just made a deal that ensured she wouldn't get out.

"Is that all?" the Consul said, his robes gently rippling in the breeze.

Vale gave a single nod.

"Then I'll see you soon." He turned on his heel, striding back across the bridge, and his legionnaires followed.

Out of reaction more than anything, Vale and I did the same, with the crowd behind us watching.

"What the hell was that?" I murmured.

Vale's voice was clipped. "Good question."

"He didn't even blink about the Magistrates."

"No, he didn't." Vale turned his face toward me. "What are you going to do about your problem in the Citadel District?"

I swallowed hard. He was worried that I was going to be backed into a corner I couldn't get myself out of. There was no question of what would happen if it came down to that.

"I'll take care of it," I answered.

The tribunes flanked us as we stepped back onto the riverbank and Vale took a moment to look out over the citizens and legionnaires who were gathered there. Sunlight glinted on armor as they stood waiting, and when Vale finally began to speak, his voice was the only sound.

"In two days, when the sun falls behind that mountain"—his voice rang out as he lifted a hand, pointing to the towering peak to the west—"we take the Citadel!"

Cheers erupted, filling the camp, and gooseflesh raced over every inch of my skin.

This is what we wanted, right? What we fought for?

Vale's words returned to me.

It was. But now that we were standing here, I was consumed with a fear I'd never known. Not like the one that filled me when I saw Rhea Vitrasian fall to the Forum floor or the first time I saw the bodies of Magistrates hanging from the bridge. This was a different thing. A wild, writhing terror I couldn't contain.

I'd thought I was a man with nothing to lose, but I was wrong.

CHAPTER 25

BEFORE: LUCA

My uncle would die during the month of the Fourth Feast, and there was a kind of poetic justice in that.

The feast day honored the goddess Calisto, keeper of fertility, and it seemed fitting since she was the one who had kept Kastor childless. I'd held the customary vigil for the last three days, watching the sun rise and set through the atrium's window. Each time the stars came out, I hoped it would be the last time they would shine over Kastor Matius.

The Fourth Feast had begun with silence. Isara had been quiet in the aftermath of the tribunal that amended the dole, the Citadel District overturned by what had happened. For the first time in almost one hundred years, there was a unanimous vote in the Forum. Seventeen Isarian citizens died in the hour after the judgment stones were turned, the legion taking up guard along the river. The bridges to the Lower City were closed, and even the Philosopher had been forbidden to send messages from her chambers.

The horror on Maris' face as her mother turned her judgment stone was enough to convince me that she hadn't known what was about to happen. No one had predicted it, not even my uncle. But the victory that had shown in his eyes when he heard the news was enough to make me feel sick.

If Magistrate Casperia had some long-threaded strategy to win over the Forum, no one knew what it was. Not even Kastor. She was a smart, clever woman. One who'd managed to hold tight to the power her seat afforded her. But she'd done something no one had ever achieved—she'd dissolved the line between factions. Either she was brilliant, or she was mad.

The fields hadn't borne enough grain for the city's stores in three years, and while most in Isara were only just beginning to understand exactly what that would mean, my uncle and Magistrate Casperia had been arguing the problem for some time. Now I could feel it bleeding through the city—the foreboding sense that the gods' favor was slipping away.

Now, war was coming. That seemed to be the only thing everyone was sure of. Isara would take what it did not have. Just like it had in the Old War. That was what Rhea had been trying to tell me that day in the theater, after she gave the lecture on siege warfare. She'd seen this coming.

My uncle had not woken in two days, which meant that when his judgment stone was needed again, I would be the one to cast it. The villa had been filled with the members of his faction from dawn to dusk, each intent on determining exactly where my allegiances lay. The seat in the Forum that bore the name Matius would now fall to me. It was the very reason Magistrate Casperia had invited me to her bed. It was also the reason her daughter had stopped answering my messages. It had been seventeen days since

I last saw Maris, and it had taken every ounce of my will to keep myself from going to see her.

I stood in the entrance to the passageway that led to my uncle's chambers, where a large bronze bowl filled with hot coals was smoking. I'd been posted beside it to receive his guests and their offerings. Every single Magistrate and Citadel official would come through to pay their respects and keep the incense burning. Then the smoke would rise until Kastor was dead, taking his spirit to the next life.

It was a soulless custom, like everything else among the Magistrates. A ridiculous dance of appearances. There wasn't a single person who held a seat in the Forum who hadn't wished for this day, and yet here they were, heads bowed in mourning.

I stared into space, only half listening to the voices of the two women who stood before me in their Magistrate's robes. I nodded politely as they offered their condolences and gave vague answers to their half-veiled questions about the Matius legacy. The attention of the Citadel had now turned to me, an adopted son tainted by a birth in the Lower City. And now they were clamoring for my good graces. The whole thing made me violently sick.

A pair of legionnaires was let into the atrium, still clad in their armor from the training grounds, and I sighed when I saw that one of them was Vale. He stood tall over the Magistrates, his hair freshly shorn, and when he spotted me, he cut the pleasantries short and crossed the room.

"Excuse me." I gave a small nod to the Magistrates and went to meet him, guiding us around the pillars until we were mostly hidden from sight.

"So, the bastard is finally dying," Vale murmured.

"Let's hope."

"At least the gods have the decency to let him suffer."

They had. Kastor had been choking on his own blood for days now, his chambers putrid with the smell of iron and rot. There were times I wondered if I hated the man more than I should, but even Vale was filled with disgust when he talked about my uncle. He was everything wrong with Isara and the Forum. He was the incarnation of everything that stood between me and Maris and that day at the beach.

There wasn't a Magistrate, including Vale's own father, who hadn't been betrayed or used by Kastor. He'd seamlessly constructed a web in the Citadel that would depend on him even after death. And now, with Magistrate Casperia's decision to align the vote, he would go into death with more power than he'd ever had. He'd gotten everything he wanted.

Vale turned his back to the atrium. "It's only a matter of time now."

That was what we'd always said. Kastor's days had been numbered for some time, and Vale's father, who held the highest title of Consul, was getting on in years. Vale and I both stood to inherit legacies we were ashamed of, consoling ourselves that we would be different. I'd said the same to Maris. But I didn't believe it anymore.

I'd made a decision only a few moments after the words left my mouth. As I held her, the mob in the Citadel rushing around us like an angry river. Her hands had curled into my tunic and I could feel an ending breaking open between us, even though there was no space for it. There I was, holding her in the middle of the Citadel, and realizing that it was something I'd never do again. Because she was right. In the end, it was all so pointless.

The Forum ran on the structure of the two factions, but that was not how it had been built. The architecture of the body had been permanently altered, like a badly set break, and the only one who stood to benefit was the Consul. There was a time when I thought our greatest act of rebellion could be tearing that structure down once we sat in those seats. But now I could see that none of it mattered. Whether I took Kastor's place as Magistrate or not, this city would devour itself.

"What is it?" Vale studied me.

I'd warred over whether to tell Vale about my plans, and until now I'd decided that it wasn't worth the argument. But with Kastor only hours from death, soon the entire city would know.

The doors to the street opened and closed again, briefly filling the corridor with light. There were more voices in the atrium now.

"Luca?" Vale pressed, gaze tightening on me. He'd picked up on the shift in the air around me, a talent he'd had since the day I'd met him.

"*Casperia.*" A man's voice spoke the name as a flicker of shadow drew my gaze to the pool of light down the corridor. When I saw who stood in its circle, I drew in a breath and held it.

Maris Casperia was framed in the light, her ice-gray stola like melted silver and a stem of braided laurel in her arms. The silk fell over her curves softly, painting her outline against the mosaic wall.

Vale took a step forward, following my gaze to the atrium. When I moved in Maris' direction, he caught hold of my arm.

"Careful, Luca," he whispered.

His expression was as serious as the tone of his voice, which was a contrast to his usual humor. There was a genuine worry in the way he looked at me now.

I pulled free of his grip and crossed the room as Maris placed the laurel on the glowing coals in the basin. Instantly, a fresh stream of fragrant smoke diffused into the air, making the light hazy.

She stepped into it when I reached her, putting her only inches away from me. In an instant, I was back in the cove, kissing her for the first time with that crystal-blue water glittering like diamonds around us. But the memory was quickly replaced by the last time I'd touched her. Holding on so tightly to her in the Citadel that I worried she might break. I didn't know what the name of that feeling was—the magnetic pull that tugged at my hands, compelling me to reach for her. It felt like a curse.

"I'm sorry about your uncle," she said, dark eyes gleaming.

"I'm not."

Her gaze dropped to my mouth, and that impulse to touch her intensified, spreading through me like fire.

"I meant I'm sorry for you." She glanced behind me, to the entrance of the chamber where Kastor lay dying. "This will be your life now. Protecting the seat of the family Matius."

It almost sounded as if she were trying to reassure herself that the break between us was destined somehow. Like there was no possible outcome other than that moment in the Citadel.

"That's what we were born for, isn't it?" I said, giving her the confirmation she needed.

"Isn't it?" she echoed.

She looked at me for a long moment before she discreetly reached into the folds of her silver stola. When she drew out her hand again, the glint of something gold shone between us, and she pressed it into my palm. For more than a few seconds, she was holding my hand. That simple touch unwound the knot in my throat, making me lean in closer to her. But before I could say another word, her fingers slipped from mine, and then she was disappearing into the chamber, swallowed by the smoke.

I waited until I made it back across the room before I looked to see what it was. The Casperia crest was engraved into the metal, centered between the ridges of a wide, flat coin. I recognized it because Kastor had one just like it with our own family crest. It was the token used for entrance to her family's private chambers in the Citadel District's baths.

I turned the coin over, running a thumb along its edge before slipping it into my pocket. It was still warm from where it had been pressed against Maris' skin.

I took my place at the entrance to Kastor's chambers as another offering was set onto the coals. The smoke billowed into the atrium, the sound of mournful prayers rising with it. But I wasn't thinking about Kastor or his wasting body in the next room. I wasn't thinking about the fact that I was only hours away from being free of him. The only thought I had as I stood there, staring into the smoke, was that maybe Maris hadn't made up her mind after all.

CHAPTER 26

NOW: MARIS

The Citadel was cloaked in an eerie silence as I made my way up through the east corridor, headed for the Hall of Scribes. When I passed beneath the place where my mother's portrait had once hung, it was still empty.

The idea had come to me in the middle of the night as I sat in the window, watching the fires of the New Legion's camp on the other side of the Sophanes. I'd stared into the blinking lights, remembering Luca's eyes as they ran over my face. His hand as it reached through the air to find me. I'd been replaying that moment in my mind over and over, wishing that I had pressed my lips to the tears that striped his cheek. All I could think now was that I wasn't sure I'd ever get the chance again.

It was something Luca had said that sparked the idea. Whatever had been used as the key for the message wouldn't be easily accessed. I'd gone through every text in my mother's study, as well as her chambers in the Tribunal Hall. Scrolls were valuable and expensive, purchased as handwritten copies from the ones housed in the Citadel's Hall of Scribes. Even if I had the kind of access that would allow me to go through every single original that existed there, it would take years. But the scribes were diligent, dedicated to preserving each and every one. There was a record for everything.

The Consul was communicating with someone, but for what purpose? The only ones left outside the walls were the legionnaires who'd been lucky enough to be posted outside the gates when the fighting began. They hadn't been forced to pick a side, and there'd been no reports given about them in the Forum that were of any consequence. The highborn families who had left weren't soldiers, which meant there was little they could do for us now.

What twisted my mind was the question of *why* the Consul would keep what he was doing from the Magistrates. If there was one thing the Forum had been unified on, it was keeping the New Legion from advancing across from the Lower City. If the Consul had a plan to save Isara, what reason could he have to conceal it?

When I came through the open doors of the Hall of Scribes, I was relieved to see Drakon seated at the post. The young scribe who'd been only a novice to my uncle before the war began had been granted an expedited advancement with the dwindling number of officials who remained in the Citadel. Now he was overseeing the inventory of the entire library.

He sat with stylus in hand, not looking up as I entered. The afternoon light was filled with the mist of the sea, draping the grand room in a haze and making his fair hair glisten. He was hunched over the desk, concentrating on a line of writing he was copying from a faded scroll, and for a moment he looked untouched by all that had happened. But as the stylus made its last stroke, his gaze lifted to meet mine and I could see it—that gaping emptiness where hope had once been.

His eyes narrowed before moving past me to the hall. "Casperia." He looked surprised to see me.

"Drakon."

Carefully, he set the stylus down. The contents of the desk were organized, the entrance to the hall polished and gleaming. But it was empty and cold, making me wonder how often anyone walked through these doors anymore.

"I heard about your mother. Figured it might not be long before I saw you in here." He stood from his chair, smoothing his hands over his robes. "How can I help?"

The words flashed through my mind in a script I'd rehearsed that morning. "I'm looking for a scroll my mother was referencing in one of her chronicles. I'm afraid I don't know the name."

He frowned. "Do you know what class or theorem it might be under?"

"Agriculture, I believe."

A brief glimmer of some veiled reaction moved across his face, and I regretted my choice of theorem. Agriculture had been the only thing anyone had talked about for the last year, with a number of conspiracies festering about the fields, the Philosopher Vitrasian, and the Priestess Ophelius. It hadn't occurred to me until now that my request could be seen in connection with any number of them. Especially when I'd served as a novice in the temple.

"Well, that does narrow it down quite a bit," Drakon said.

He took a small slip of parchment from a stack on the desk and stood, going to the large open book on the stone pedestal behind him. I watched as he flipped back through the pages with careful hands, eyes scanning the names until he finally stopped.

"Here we are." He let the book fall open, the tip of the stylus scratching as he made a note. "Looks like there's only one that she requested in the last year."

When he turned back to me, his eyes dropped to the chain around my neck. "Just need to see your medallion."

"Of course." I pulled at the chain, letting the flat gold circle fall from the opening of my chiton.

Drakon took a thorough look at it before he wrote my name into the book and recorded the scroll.

"Just a moment."

He gave me a polite smile before he went through the archway, where I could see two other scribes working over their colored inkpots. They kept their attention on the careful movement of their styluses over the parchment, and I tried to make out what exactly they were doing. It all seemed so meaningless now, and maybe that was the point. Weren't we all just waiting for the end to come?

As soon as the curtain to the library fell closed, I listened for Drakon's footsteps to fade. The scrolls in the agriculture class were shelved at the farthest end of the hall, but it wouldn't take him long to find what he was looking for. I had to be quick.

I rounded the desk, stepping with light feet until I reached the pedestal and set my hand on the page Drakon had it turned to before flipping ahead. The latest entries weren't nearly as frequent as they'd been in the months before the war, but there were still officials requesting scrolls regularly.

I frantically searched for the Consul's name, but there was no Saturian listed. I couldn't find a single entry that belonged to him. Instead, I started looking for patterns. If the series of messages were all using the same key, the scroll would be requested multiple times. And I was right. There was one that repeated on every page for the last few weeks, at least.

Tale of Hermaus.

But the request was listed from a different person each time, and I didn't recognize any of the family names. I didn't know how that was possible. Drakon followed the rules to the letter. I couldn't imagine him falsifying the records. Not even for the Consul.

I let the pages fall to where Drakon had left them and returned to the other side of the desk. Only seconds later, Drakon came back through the curtain with the scroll protectively cradled in his arms.

"I'm so sorry, Drakon, I forgot I need one more. But this one, I do know the name of."

"Not a problem." He handed me the scroll. "Which is it?"

"*Tale of Hermaus,*" I said, sounding as if I were asking a question. "It should be in the—"

"Myths," he finished my sentence. "You can read the first language?"

"I'm learning," I lied.

He frowned. There was a moment when I was sure that he was going to press me. That his curiosity would make him think a little harder about what I was asking.

"Just one moment."

He pushed back through the curtain and I exhaled, hands slick on the carved ends of the scroll. The label identified it as a record of the grain harvest three years before, which meant my mother had been doing her own research.

I stared at the book on the pedestal as the seconds ticked by, my heart in my throat. I could feel the distance my loyalty was about to fall. I wasn't just a Magistrate's daughter anymore, and my mother was no longer here to protect me.

This was what I'd wanted—to wear the white robes and cast the judgment stone in defiance of the Forum. But here I was, playing the same twisted games they all were.

When Drakon returned, he held the scroll in his hands with the tips of his fingers. It was clearly very old, its handle carved of light ash wood and painted with fading colors. The tie that bound it closed was beaded at each end with spheres of blue glass.

"Here you are."

I took it, fingers tingling as if they could sense that the scroll held a secret. Drakon went back to the open book, noting the name of the scroll, and I swallowed hard. Whoever had been requesting it, they would likely come again. And when they did, they needed only look in that book to see my name beside it.

It was a clumsy move. A desperate one. But in two days' time, none of it would matter.

I walked slowly and calmly down the Tribunal Hall, and when I reached the door that said Casperia, I shut myself inside. The smell of paint was still thick in the air from the drying portrait that sat on the easel beside the window. My face stared back at me, the dark eyes focused, the set of my mouth defiant. Here I was in my mother's chambers, but I looked nothing like her in those robes.

That had been the plan, hadn't it? I would take my mother's seat, and Luca would take his uncle's. We'd devised a scheme to disrupt the fabric of the Magistrates' factions, and it would have worked. If that day in the Forum hadn't happened, if Vitrasian hadn't been executed, there would have been nothing to stop us.

I lit the lamp and closed the curtains to drape the room in

darkness. The sensation of eyes on me was like the feeling of insects crawling over my skin.

I sat down, drawing in a long breath before I untied the scroll and let it unroll across the desk. Firelight cast the parchment in a warm pink as my eyes flitted over the words. The shapes and patterns of the ink were like a long-forgotten memory.

The illustrations that filled the margins were the only translation I needed. I knew the story well after my years as a novice. It chronicled one of the first gifts ever bestowed upon mortals. Hermaus was a winged beast, with great white feathers tipped with gold, and there were many tales of his valiant courage and victories in battle. But one story—*this* story—was about one he lost. Hermaus was shot down from the sky and lay bleeding in a field when five traveling Valshadi women came upon him. They tended to his wounds and stayed with him, forsaking their journey until he was healed.

As repayment for their compassion and kindness, Hermaus plucked five feathers from his wings and gave them as gifts to each of the women. The illustration at the bottom of the scroll depicted that moment, as he held out a single feather to a woman with her hands lifted reverently, ready to take it. With that gift, he gave them their magic—and thus the favor of the gods, which would endure for their lifetimes and the lifetime of anyone they saw fit to pass it on to. The godsblood was a *gift*. One of the last ever given. Until Luca.

I jolted when the clang of bells echoed out in the Citadel, catching the end of the scroll before it could fall to the floor. They were the tribunal bells. The Consul was calling the Magistrates into the Forum.

I took out the message, finding the corresponding words on the scroll one by one and copying them down on a fresh piece of parchment. The bells chimed again as I stood and blew out the lamp, taking my Magistrate's robes from where they hung on the wall.

The message burned in my fingertips as I tucked it beneath the silk, against my heart. I couldn't read it, but I knew someone who could.

CHAPTER 27

NOW: MARIS

The Magistrates flooded into the Tribunal Hall, hands fluttering with half-tied robes as we all made our way to the Forum. I searched the faces around me for my uncle, but there was no sign of him.

There weren't many in Isara who spoke the first language, but Luca had been learning as a novice to Vitrasian.

Just the thought of it made me feel cold. Getting this message to him might do exactly what he'd said—it could be the only bargaining chip I had with the same people who wanted me dead. But if we were days away from watching the Citadel District fall, then what was the point? What had all this been for?

The Forum was buzzing when I made it to the entrance, the Magistrates streaming through the doors with an anxious air. A tribunal hadn't been expected today, and with the New Legion camped across the river, the nerves in the district were high.

I pulled the medallion from beneath my robes and held it up

to the man posted at the doors, swallowing hard as the tribunal scribe wrote it down.

"Casperia!"

My name echoed in the great, grand room and I shuffled past a string of white robes. This time there was no hush in the Forum, and only a few pairs of eyes followed me across the floor. I took my seat, my gaze immediately finding my uncle's place down on the marble floor. But the timber-framed chair he usually sat in was empty.

There hadn't been enough time for anyone to discover that I'd gone to the Hall of Scribes or that I'd taken the scroll from the library. So, why did I feel like I was seconds away from being found out? I scanned the rest of the room, looking for the source of whatever it was hanging in the air. Something just felt . . . wrong.

I searched the confines of my seat, but everything was just as I'd left it, with a neat stack of parchment, a stylus, and an inkpot. I straightened them along the edge of the small desk, eyes moving to the doors anxiously. And I wasn't the only one. The tension in the Forum was growing by the second. The bells could be heard throughout the Citadel District, so wherever Nej was, he'd be on his way, along with any late Magistrates. But with so many empty seats, I couldn't tell who else was actually missing.

My uncle finally appeared just as the doors were closing, and I let out the breath trapped in my chest. There were a few eerily quiet seconds before the doors at the back of the Forum opened, and Consul Saturian appeared on the other side. I rose to my feet with the other Magistrates. He didn't barrel in like he usually did. He took slow, patient steps to his chair, an appraising look falling on the tiered rows of seats in the room. His blue robes rippled like dark water around him, something that resembled a smile on his face.

"On this fourteenth day in the month of Eleni, I call this tribunal to order." The words were like flat, even beats. Behind him, Nej was already scribbling. "This morning I met with the warlord who calls himself the Commander of the New Legion."

There was another slight pause before a rumbling sound of disapproval swept through the room. I stilled. Meeting with the New Legion had been my suggestion. One the Consul had dismisssed. But more than that, he'd broken a significant protocol. The Consul, the head of government in Isara, held an unsanctioned meeting with the enemy without bringing it before the Forum for a vote. And not just any enemy—his *son*.

Beside me, two Magistrates were whispering, but I could pick out only pieces of the conversation. Going behind the Forum's back had created mutiny more than once. All it would take was a majority vote to expel and replace him. The Consul knew that, but he didn't look the slightest bit unnerved. If anything, he was enjoying this.

"In two days' time, the rebels will open the gates to the city." The words rang out. "And any resident of the Citadel District who wishes to will be permitted to leave unharmed."

There was a swallowed gasp somewhere behind me. This time, the murmuring quieted.

"The price?" he continued. "Those who choose to leave will surrender their medallion, their citizenship, and any rights they have to property or place within these walls."

The whispers resurfaced, and now they were growing.

"This, the traitors claim, is a show of mercy from the rebel legion, offered to all." He paused. "Except for the Magistrates."

The room erupted in shouts of outrage, several Magistrates

shooting to their feet. The clatter of items falling from desks punctuated the commotion. My fingers instinctively went to the medallion that hung around my neck. That was what Luca had been trying to tell me. If the New Legion was taking medallions at the gates, they would be checking names.

You can't be a Casperia anymore.

The Consul's hands lifted into the air patiently, waiting for silence. "This eliminates any sliver of doubt about the intentions of the rebels. They claim to want peace for Isara. But there is no denying that all they really want is to punish those who have dedicated their lives to this city."

The few who were standing slowly sank back into their seats. We were nothing more than a Forum full of rabbits now, running from a hunter with a bow. And by the look on the Magistrates' faces, they knew it.

"The rebels have done this distinguished body a service. When their legionnaires are put down, and the Citadel District is bled of its remaining traitors who would give up their sacred citizenship to save their own heads, Isara will be left to *you* and *me*." His voice rose, making me shiver. "You have yet to see what the strength of this city can do."

I flinched when a few cheers broke the silence, and the Consul sent a discreet glance in Nej's direction as his eyes swept over the room. There was a pause there. An exchange of some kind.

"We'll be holding the heads of the rebels in our hands, ready to begin this city anew."

More shouts sounded as my gaze trailed out the window to the Sophanes River, where the glint of sunlight on helmets glittered along the water's edge. Beyond them stretched a crumbling city. Even now, in the last throes of death, the Consul believed—truly believed—that the Citadel could win. But how?

I looked around me at the faces of the Forum. The expressions I found there almost looked like hope. Over the last few minutes, the Consul had managed to do the impossible. He'd betrayed the Magistrates by admitting to a meeting with the Commander of the New Legion. Then he'd promised victory to those who chose not to run. The whole act wasn't much different from the day I'd seen him turn the city against Vitrasian. But then why had he refused my request?

Below, Nej had now dropped his stylus and joined in on the clapping, and I wished I could see his face. I wished I could meet his eyes and try to interpret what lay there. Had he known, when I saw him last night, about the meeting with the Commander? Is that what he'd meant when he said that in the end, we needed to stand on the same side?

The Consul went on for another few minutes in an inspiring speech that had the Magistrates all but weeping, and when the gavel struck again, it was with the sound of thunder in my ears.

"Which is why I have called this tribunal." The Consul paused.

Below, Nej was writing, but he looked distracted, one hand clenched on the small desk before him.

The Consul sauntered along the platform, looking out over the Magistrates. "The matter involves the Priestess Ophelius." His smooth voice rippled through the room, the words devoid of any hint of emotion.

The murmurings began, and again, I looked to Nej, whose fist had tightened.

"I don't need to remind you all that we have gravely suffered at the whim of these Priestesses. With the dying magic has come our dying fields. The weaker it grows, the longer the fighting. Many of us have lost sons in this war. Homes. Our very bloodlines are at stake. It is the Priestesses who are responsible for the destruction of this city."

The Forum fell into a deeper silence.

"The will of the gods is clear—an abundant future for Isara. And the only thing standing in the way of that future is Ophelius. The Priestess tried and failed to end her own life, and now she refuses to gift her magic. With the approval of this tribunal, we will use any means necessary to convince the Priestess that we share the same goal—to protect the future of Isara."

I could see what he was doing. The Consul was framing his plan in a way that would get him what he wanted, and what he wanted was enough votes to act. The words were twisting and twirling into something entirely different from what they actually meant.

"As dictated by the gods, the only way to transfer the possession of this magic is to gift it to another. Ophelius has refused to do so, determined to die with it. But there *is* another way."

No.

"With your permission, I intend to enact the blood rites, as written in the sacred tomes. Ophelius will be bled, and the recipient of her magic will be chosen by this body."

A shaking breath escaped my lips and I blinked, unsure if I'd heard him correctly. The blood rites had never been performed within the walls of Isara. The act of bleeding and drinking every drop of godsblood was considered heresy.

"Who will perform these rites?" a voice called out from behind me.

The Consul's gray eyes landed on me. "Magistrate Casperia."

I stilled. The echo of my family name hovered in the air, followed by the faces turning toward me. My mouth opened, but no sound came.

The Consul's gaze burned everywhere it touched. Below, my uncle finally moved, his head swiveling from me to the podium. But he didn't look surprised.

To be addressed by the Consul directly in the Forum was a rare thing for any Magistrate. I'd attended many tribunals as a spectator, and I'd seldom seen it done. The Consul always kept his address to the body as a whole, but he'd met my eyes directly when he spoke my name, and the chill of it was still crawling across my skin.

"I'm sorry, I don't understand," I choked.

"You served as a novice to the Priestess for several years, did you not?"

My voice cracked.

"Casperia?"

"Yes. Yes, I did," I answered.

"And are you familiar with the ritual of the blood rites?"

I swallowed. "I am, but I've never performed them. I—"

"What better way to express your loyalty to this tribunal in your first days as Magistrate than to shoulder the burden of your city?"

I was breathing too loudly now, my mind racing for something to say. He wasn't asking. That was clear. And the buried threat in the words was there like the prick of a needle. Was I loyal, or wasn't I? This was why he'd been so curious about my ritual knowledge. Why he'd been so interested in my noviceship.

The decree he actually sought was folded beneath the words. Performing the blood rites was essentially an execution, and the laws were clear—a decree like that had to be approved by three-quarters of the Forum majority. If the Consul stepped outside those laws, he would be subject to the consequences and that wasn't something he would risk. Not now.

The Consul picked up his judgment stone, holding it in the air, and I watched as the Magistrates around the room reached for their own stones. It was customary to pick it up, even if you didn't plan to flip it. And one by one, they were placed down, white marble gleaming like little stars in the lamplight. There wasn't a single vote against.

Again, the Consul's attention drifted to Nej, and this time my uncle's eyes lifted from the parchment. Was I imagining it, or was there was an almost indiscernible dip of Nej's chin? As if he were confirming something. As if he were—my mind twisted with the thought—giving the Consul his approval.

It wasn't until I felt my uncle's eyes boring into me that I noticed that every face in the room had drifted in my direction. The Consul's included. I couldn't help wondering if they were thinking that I was about to seal my own fate. Or maybe they were just relieved to have not been given the task themselves. No one wanted the attention of the Consul. No one wanted to be relied on by him. We'd all seen with our own eyes what happened when you let him down.

I was the only one who hadn't picked up my stone, and they waited, silence roaring as my shaking hand reached for it. He had the majority, that was clear. But that wasn't why they waited for me to cast my vote.

I could see Nej's silent request in his tight expression, even if I couldn't hear it.

The gods have turned their faces upon us.

His words echoed. Whatever game he was playing, he wanted me to play it, too. But my mind was still struggling to keep up. I didn't know what was happening here.

In a matter of seconds, I was stringing together the pieces. The blank message that glowed with the sheen of godsblood. The same kind I'd seen in my own mother's study. I'd always known that Nej had the ear of the Consul, of everyone in the Citadel, but maybe I'd underestimated just how far his influence reached. Maybe the Consul wasn't the author of the messages. Maybe they were penned by my uncle.

The Consul waited, that question still hanging in the air. We both knew I didn't have a choice. But now I wondered who exactly I was giving an answer to. The Consul or his scribe?

The cold stone stung my hot, sweaty palm as I lifted it from the pedestal it sat on. I watched the golden light dance on the white surface, thinking of all the times I'd imagined casting my first judgment stone. All the ideals I'd had about conviction and integrity and changing the destiny of Isara. But as I stood there in the Forum, my own mother's shadow looming over me, it all shifted so sharply into focus. I set the stone down, white side up, a sickness brewing in my gut. The first time I cast my judgment stone in this tribunal, it was for death.

CHAPTER 28

BEFORE: LUCA

The baths of the Citadel District were nothing like the ones in the Lower City.

Smooth white limestone walls were erected in a maze, covered by climbing roses and vines that were spotted with the nests of swallows. Enormous mahogany doors served as the entrance, guarded by officials from the Citadel whose pale gray robes made them almost invisible against the fair stone.

I fidgeted with the Casperias' token in my pocket, turning it over in my fingers as I watched the doors open. Two men emerged from inside, their skin still dewy and flushed.

The baths in the Lower City were more practical than anything, used for communal washing. They were constructed of humble red clay bricks that were baked in the sun and adorned with simple frescoes of fig trees and serpents. But here, even the steam drifting on the wind from behind those walls smelled decadent. Like something that should be served in a silver cup.

Entrance to these baths was a sign of status, and those who held the highest wealth had their own chambers inside, the Casperias among them. I knew legionnaires who were granted regular entry, but it wasn't for the mineral pools or the rare wines poured for guests inside. There were deals to be struck behind those walls. Affairs and meetings that couldn't happen out in the light of day.

I pulled the token from my pocket and turned it toward the light, watching the gleam ripple over the name Casperia. Meeting like this was a risk neither of us should take. Both the Forum's factions were watching me, trying to predict what I might do when I took Kastor's seat. Maybe the worst possibility of all was me falling in love with Magistrate Casperia's daughter. I feared it was too late for that.

I crossed the street, steps steady, like I knew exactly what I was doing. I'd never been to the baths and could imagine that I didn't look like I belonged there. There were some things about the Lower City that just didn't wash away.

The men posted at the doors stopped their conversation as I drew closer, and one of them met my eyes in a way that made me think he recognized me. I no longer had the luxury of being an unknown face in the district, my obscurity fading by the minute. In a matter of months, I'd gone from being Kastor's sullied adopted son to a man who held the fate of a faction in his hands. I didn't like that kind of attention.

The man studied the coin pinched between my fingers, eyes flicking up to me again. It couldn't be the first time this family coin was used to invite a young man into the baths, but I could guess that it wasn't for Maris. And even these men knew better than to tempt the wrath of a Magistrate.

The doors opened and the humid, warm air wrapped around me as I stepped inside. Marble fountains lined the perimeter of the square entry, where perfumed water dripped and bubbled. The same lotus flower that was engraved on one side of the coin was pressed into the stone above one of the corridors, and I followed it, casting a glance around me.

The sky above disappeared as I wound deep into the honeycomb of the baths, looking for the symbol that marked the chamber belonging to the family Casperia. The sound of muffled voices and the hiss of water on coals grew louder the farther into the corridors I went. The hazy smudge of figures moved through the doorways, veiled in the steam pouring out of the doorways. When I found the one I was looking for, my hand hesitated, hovering over the door's latch. I wasn't sure where exactly the point of no return was, but I was beginning to think I'd already crossed it.

I pushed the door open and stepped through the stone archway, where beams of sunlight were cast across the room from the windows high up in the eaves. It smelled like jasmine and rosemary, the scent thick in my lungs as I drew it in.

It wasn't until the steam began to clear that I could see her. Maris, the Magistrate's daughter who'd somehow become the center of every one of my thoughts, stood on the other side of the basin in the middle of the room. She watched me, the thin fabric of her blue chiton clinging to her and the strands of hair that framed her face curling in the damp air.

"I didn't think you would come," she said.

I kept my feet planted where they were, slipping the coin back into my pocket. I wanted to argue with her—to say that she *had* known I would come. Just like I had. I hadn't even made the choice, as if my being here were something already decided. But that thinking was too close to admitting I was the victim of fate, and I had to remind myself that I didn't believe in the unavoidable, inescapable will of the gods. Not the way my mother did.

Maris came around the basin, and it wasn't until she stepped into one of those beams of light that I could see the small scroll in her hands. The wax seal of Ophelius was visible along the edge of the rolled parchment. It was another message.

She held it out to me. "For Vitrasian."

My jaw clenched. After everything that had happened over the last few weeks, I was more and more convinced that I had reason to be concerned about the correspondence inside. I'd suspected for months that something was going on with Rhea, and it had all started with a burning scroll that looked just like this one.

"The Citadel has forbidden Vitrasian to speak with Ophelius," I said, not moving to take it.

"I know."

I waited for some kind of explanation, but Maris didn't give one.

"What does it say?" I asked.

"I don't know."

When my eyes lifted to Maris' face, I realized that she was thinking the same thing I was. She wanted to open it. To know what Rhea and the Priestess were so intent on hiding. But I was also afraid of what I might find written there. The play Rhea had finished was set to be performed in just a few days, but I hadn't seen her since the tribunal, and I hadn't answered when she summoned me. I didn't want to face the fact that she'd known about the fields. That she'd lied. That she was, in fact, just like the rest of them.

I finally took the scroll, sliding it into my pocket. "Is that why you asked me to come here? A message?"

"No," she said.

"Then what is it? What do you want?" There was only one answer I wanted to that question.

"Your faction is turning against you, Luca. They plan to petition the Consul for a new leader's seat at the next tribunal."

I let out a half-hearted laugh, not believing that I'd let myself hope this meeting would be about anything other than the Forum. When it came down to it, Maris was one of them, too. The betrayal of the thought wound tight in my gut. "They're not my faction," I said.

"They *will* take it."

I shrugged. "And I'll let them."

Her brow furrowed. "What does that mean?"

"They can have it. All of it."

"You're not even going to fight to keep the faction's leadership?"

I studied Maris' face, trying to decide just how much I was willing to trust her with. "I'm not taking the seat, Maris." I said it out loud for the first time.

"*What?*" she whispered.

"When Kastor dies, I won't take his seat in the Forum."

"You can't be serious."

"I am. You were right. It's pointless—all of it."

A look of utter disappointment changed the shape of her mouth, her eyes. But there was also some sense of relief there. Like after everything, I'd finally proven her right about me. The feeling was mutual.

"My mother is planning to hang the harvests around the Consul's neck," she said. "There are at least six among your faction who are planning to join her."

I exhaled, impatient. "What is this?" What are you doing?

"Magistrates Gracilia and Aquintis are among them." She looked me dead in the eye. "The Consul's scribe is also involved in the plot."

A slow, creeping tension moved up my spine when I realized what was happening here. "Stop talking." My voice grated.

"As soon as you give up that seat, my mother will move to undercut your faction, and when she does, she will take the Consul down with them."

"Maris, *stop*."

"Who do you think will be Consul then?" The chamber was buzzing with the anguish in her voice.

What she was doing was more than reckless—betraying her mother and her faction.

"There isn't enough godsblood in the world to quench the thirst of this city," she rasped.

The picture she was painting was a grim one. Casperia had endeared herself to the entire Forum by falling on her sword and uniting the vote to amend the dole. Just in time for my uncle's seat to fall empty. Kastor's death would weaken his faction; if I didn't take his place and calm the fears of his supporters, I would be all but handing Casperia control. Alliances were kept with those who either gave or reinforced your own power. Casperia didn't have the votes with her faction to secure her as Consul, but she would if she united the Forum. And if she turned the Magistrates against the Consul and took the title for herself, the seat would never go to Vale. Not unless he was eventually able to oust her. Something that would be even harder to do if I had no vote.

"You risk too much," I said.

Her eyes grew even darker. "You're wrong. We haven't risked enough."

The tenor of her voice was uneasy, making me feel like there was still something else happening here that I hadn't quite riddled out. Like we were standing on an edge, about to fall.

"If what you say is true, then we've already lost."

"Not if we play the same game."

I closed the distance between us. "You think you can just summon me here like your mother does with her legionnaires and convince me to join up with some scheme to control the future of the Forum?"

Maris flinched.

"I know how this works. All of these games you Magistrates play, I don't want any part of it. I'm not a piece on the board. You can't just move me any which way you want."

"I'm not."

"You are! You know that my heart is already bound to you. And you're using it to put on some scheme you've orchestrated."

"That's not what I'm doing."

"Then what?" My voice rose. "Why did you ask me to come here?"

I looked down into Maris' face, following the sheen of moisture that covered her cheek. The light traveled down her neck, into the opening of her chiton, making me swallow hard. I wanted so badly to touch her. To go back to that moment in the Citadel when the world was coming apart around us and to just disappear.

"Luca," she breathed. "I came to ask if you would marry me."

All at once, the room went still around us. The steam, the voices, the light—it all froze in time.

"What?" The word was barely audible on my lips.

She looked a little afraid now, her skin flushed. "I want you to take vows with me."

I moved backward, suddenly eager to put her out of reach. But she followed, hands finding my tunic and holding me in place.

"Take Magistrate Matius' seat. Hold the faction together and when my mother is gone, I will control the other."

My eyes jumped back and forth on hers, trying to make sense of it. "And then what?"

"And then there are no more factions. We wait for the Consul's son to take his place and then we remake the Forum. Rebuild the Citadel."

I was catching on to what she was saying, but I almost couldn't comprehend it. If we took vows, one of us would lose our family name. Which meant that family name would lose a seat in the Forum. It would throw the entire body of Magistrates into chaos and shift the power balances that had reinforced each other for so long. We could even ensure that Vale became the next Consul. If that happened, if the three of us held the most powerful seats in the Citadel, there was little that could stand in the way of us changing everything.

"Will you do it?" she said.

I stared at her. The only thing standing between me and a future I'd thought impossible was the fact that I didn't want Maris as a political ally. I wanted *her*.

"I'll only take vows with you if they're true ones," I said, watching her carefully. I wanted to know that she understood me. That she knew what I was asking.

She took her time in answering, and with every second that passed, my pulse was steadily climbing. "You don't believe in the will of the gods, Luca, but I do. And I knew the moment I saw you in that garden that my life would be bound to yours. That our fates are entwined."

She waited for me to speak, but I couldn't. My mind was racing from one thought to the next, counting the rippling effects this would have. It was the kind of beginning that gave birth to an end.

"Let *me* be your family, and together, we can change everything," she whispered, hands still twisted in my tunic.

I didn't answer her because I didn't need to. It all felt like an inevitability, a point in time that had already been decided. Like one of Vitrasian's comets streaking across the sky.

I kissed her instead of speaking, my lips parting hers until the knot in my throat began to unwind. I didn't want to feel it, but I did—that sense of something bigger happening. The cosmic pull of fate that had twisted and reforged every moment since I met her.

I could feel the shape of her through the wet silk. Slowly, my hands traveled up the curve of her hip, over her ribs. I pushed the fabric down her shoulder so that I could press my mouth there. I was imagining it—this body belonging to me.

My fingers grazed the soft skin below her collarbone, hand sliding down her breast, and when I felt the race of her heart beneath my palm, I was close to believing what she'd said—that our fates were entwined.

Her hands unclenched from my tunic and then she was tugging it up and reaching for my belt. I walked her backward to the ledge cut into the stone, and I lifted her by the hips so her legs could come around me. I couldn't wait anymore. Seventeen days had felt like an eternity, and I didn't ever want to miss her again.

I reached between us, hands sliding over hot skin until I was touching her. Her mouth broke from mine, her head tipping back as she took me inside her. This wasn't like the lust I'd known. It never had been. She wasn't like the women I'd been with before. Maris was a bottomless, edgeless thing. As deep as the sky the Philosophers spent their lives studying. It was like there was no end to be found. And there wasn't. I didn't know yet that we were a story that had already begun. A tale the gods had written. And even if I'd been able to peer into the future and see how it would all end, I don't think I would have been able to stop it.

CHAPTER 29

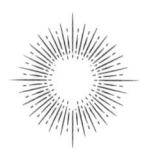

NOW: LUCA

I lay awake in the darkness of my tent, listening to the sound of the river. The black sky stretched like a veil across the city, and it was quieter than it had been in weeks. There was a hush that had fallen over the New Legion after Vale's declaration about taking the Citadel, and now there was a different feeling in the air.

After months of fighting through the tangled streets of the Lower City, after spilling the blood of countless legionnaires, it was all ending. Every fired ballista, soaring arrow, and knife drawn had been for *this*. A new beginning. But all I could feel as I lay awake in the dark was the sense that if Maris Casperia didn't make it out of Isara alive, then it had all been for nothing. What did that say about the man who'd started this war? What did it mean for the people who'd followed him?

I sat up, letting my feet hit the floor, and searched for my tunic in the dark. I hadn't even finished pulling it over my head before I'd made it outside, and the cool night breeze rushed around me, the smell of the river thick in the mist.

The idea had been turning in my mind since we'd left the bridge. There was only one way this ended for me and that was with Maris on the other side of the wall. If I wanted to make that happen, I had to cross a line Vale and I couldn't come back from if anyone found out. But what Vale didn't know, he couldn't be held accountable for. That was what I was counting on.

I followed the row of tents along the river until I found the one I was looking for. The tribune spent only a few hours in his own quarters, sleeping when I did. But what I needed from him wouldn't wait until morning. I glanced up the street, checking to be sure it was empty before I pulled the canvas opening back and ducked inside. The space was cold in a way that made it feel bare and empty, and when I reached the cot in the corner, I realized that it was.

The quilts were neatly folded, the bed not slept in. When I turned in a circle, eyeing the contents of the small table and the trunk beside the door, it didn't look like the place had been used in days. Weeks, maybe.

I stepped back outside, eyes scanning the peaks of the tents along the row until I spotted Asinia's. His quarters were next to Vale's.

The entrance to the Commander's tent was still, but I waited, watching to be sure he was asleep before I crossed the path. When I reached Asinia's tent and pulled back the canvas, the diffused glow of starlight fell on the cot inside. The quilts were only half draped over two entwined bodies, and the broad, bare expanse of the tribune's back was visible.

The sight made me swallow hard, a hundred memories of

lying like that with Maris flooding through my mind. The smell of her hair. Her warm weight in my arms.

As if the tribune could sense me there, he gently stirred, head turning and eyes squinting when he saw me. I met his eyes, tipping my head toward the street and, slowly, he sat up, untangling himself from Asinia's embrace.

I stepped outside, running one hand over my head and down the back of my neck, asking myself if I was really willing to do this. It wasn't just a betrayal to the New Legion. It was more than any Centurion should ever ask of a tribune. And somehow, I knew that mine wouldn't refuse me.

He came outside, still fastening the belt low on his hips, and the clouds broke just enough for the moonlight to touch him. I didn't know if it was the sight of him without his armor, or if it was seeing him sleeping in Asinia's arms, but he looked different to me then. More human than the quiet soldier who shadowed me day and night.

"What's wrong?" His voice was deeper with sleep, his face serious as he looked me over. As if searching for some evidence of what was going on.

"Can I trust you?" I said, looking him in the eye.

He visibly flinched at the question. For a moment, that empty look on his face made me unsure what his answer might be.

"Yes. You can," he said.

I exhaled and the tribune's eyes grew more focused. Concerned, even.

I instinctively glanced over his shoulder to Vale's tent. If he knew what I was about to do, he would be furious, and I had to ask myself again what I was willing to risk. If I put him between me and the whole of the New Legion, he would do the right thing. He would choose them.

The tribune followed my gaze to Vale's quarters. "My allegiance is to you, Centurion. Not the legion," he said.

I wasn't sure he understood the weight of what he was saying. What kind of danger those words held. They were the seeds of treason. The same ones we'd planted months, even years, before the war.

"What do you need?" he asked.

I took a step closer to him. "I need you to get a medallion."

His head tilted, like he wasn't sure he'd heard me. "A medallion," he repeated.

"One that bears a name of no significance. A name that won't draw any attention." I paused. "And then I need you to get it across the river."

Understanding slowly settled in his features, and he fell quiet. He looked at the ground between us, and I could see his mind turning with the implications of what I was saying. I was asking him to commit more than one serious crime, and not just against Isara. Stealing a medallion wasn't like stealing a possession. It was a sacred document. A holy thing. And crossing the river without the Commander's permission was an entirely different kind of offense. If he was caught, he wouldn't just be risking his own life. He could break the agreement we'd just made with the Consul.

"The woman." He watched my face for confirmation. When I said nothing, he sighed. "Are you asking me to help you protect a Magistrate?"

I stared at him, looking for any clue as to what he was thinking now. I'd suspected that he'd put together more about Maris than I wanted to believe, but he'd said nothing. Now I wanted to know why.

"You know who she is," I said as I realized it.

He didn't deny it. "I don't know who she is to *you*."

"It doesn't matter."

"It does," he argued. "My job is to protect you."

"This is how you do it." My voice was uneven now. I sounded desperate. And I was.

He stared at me, waiting.

"I end," I breathed, "with her."

The truth of it was laid bare in the words. There was no pretense in them. No posturing. That was the whole of it—of everything. The only reason I had to draw air into my lungs was across the Sophanes. And I couldn't think of anything I wouldn't do, anything I wouldn't ask for, to save her.

"How do you know you can trust her? She's one of them," he whispered.

"She's the only one I trust."

The tribune took two steps to the riverbank's edge, staring out at the water. He was silent for a long time. "You don't have to tell me everything, but if you want me to do this, then I need to know more than I do right now."

I would say the same in his position. He had everything he needed to report me as a traitor, and it was incriminating enough that not even Vale would be able to save me. The tribune held every advantage, every power in his hands. And I had no choice but to trust him with it.

"What is your name, tribune?" I said.

He turned around, facing me. It had been more than a month since he'd been assigned to me, and I'd never asked. I hadn't wanted to know.

"Théo," he answered.

The family name wasn't familiar to me, most likely a Lower

City bloodline like so many others that had never really mattered. Not in the eyes of Isara.

I cast my gaze across the river, to the faint outline of the Citadel's dome. "The only thing you need to know, Théo, is that there was a time when I had to choose between my duty and my heart."

"And what happened?" he asked.

"I chose wrong."

CHAPTER 30

NOW: MARIS

Sometimes you must burn a field to save it.

My robes fluttered over the marble floors as Ophelius' words echoed in my mind. They hadn't made sense to me the day she spoke them, but they did now.

When Luca crossed the river, I'd thought him selfish. But now I could see that he'd known something I hadn't—that there was no remedy for the kind of sickness that bled through Isara. The only way through was flame and smoke. Blood and dust.

I'd stood in the Tribunal Hall for years and watched as Nej smiled and shook hands. Clapped the Magistrates on the back. There'd been a moment a few days ago, as I sat for my portrait watching him pace the study, when I'd finally been sure I could trust him. I'd finally convinced myself that despite all his faults, we were on the same side. But all I could see now was a man who had his eye on the podium at the front of the Forum, where the gavel rested. And now I wondered if my mother, his own sister, had been sacrificed on the altar of that ambition.

The young legionnaire posted outside Nej's chambers straightened when he saw me, gaze dragging from my hair down to my feet. He looked too young to stand the post, but that was what the Loyal Legion was now—the sons of Citadel officials who'd been fit for armor they hadn't yet earned.

There was a strange look in the legionnaire's eyes, and I wondered if the dead feeling in my heart was visible on my face. When my steps didn't slow as I neared the doors, his javelin lowered in front of me.

"Stop." He shifted forward, putting himself between me and the open chamber behind him.

From a distance, I could see the shadow of someone moving. There was the faint sound of parchment. The tap of a stylus on an inkpot.

"What's your business?" the legionnaire said.

Now I looked at him, willing myself not to recoil when I saw the youth in his eyes. This boy would be dead in a matter of days. Maybe hours. We both would.

"Magistrate Casperia." I said only my name, the title bringing to mind the image of my mother. The white pallor of her bloodless skin. The empty blackness in her open, kohl-smudged eyes.

He looked me over again, as if trying to determine what was wrong with me. There was, indeed, something *wrong*. Even the tone of my voice sounded strange.

"Casperia."

I looked up when my family name filled the hall, and my uncle suddenly appeared, centered in the inner chamber's doorway. There was a proud, paternal smile on his face, but he looked different to me now. Like one of the trickster sprites in the old tales.

"Come," he said.

The legionnaire gave me a reluctant nod, moving aside so I could enter, and I stepped forward without another glance in his direction. Beyond the chamber doors, Nej stood behind his grand, gilded desk, a gold-rimmed chalice clutched in his hand. There was a glimmer of something in his eyes, a twist of the light that made them look more silver than blue.

Immediately, there was something warped and bent about the arrangement of the room. There he stood, in the light of the blazing lamps, with a jug full of wine and a tray of bread and fruit. It was as if everything was just slightly askew, like I was peering into a mirror world.

"I'm glad you've come." He came around the desk to face me. He had a placating expression, as if he was getting ready to handle me gently.

"What just happened in there?" I said, voice barely above a whisper.

"What just *happened*"—he crossed his arms over his chest—"is that you cast your first judgment stone."

My feet were so firmly planted on the ground that I couldn't move. The weight of all this—everything that had happened since the day Vitrasian died—was pressing down on top of me.

"It doesn't get any easier, Maris. The burden of the responsibility you now share in the Forum is a great one."

There was an unbridled compassion in his eyes that was more than convincing. It almost made me want to believe him.

"What did you do, Nej?" I said, my voice weak.

The softness in his face sharpened just a little, his gaze growing more focused. "I ensured that once all of this is over, you'll still have your name. Your family's reputation."

"You expect me to believe that it's *me* you're looking out for?" I scoffed.

"What benefits you benefits me, Maris. That's no secret." He let the mask drop just long enough for me to see what lay behind it. The Philosopher, Luca, my mother, me. He was writing the story himself.

"And what harms one of us harms the other?" I said.

"That's right." He nodded.

"Was that true for my mother?"

Nej's almost imperceptible reaction was like a turning flame on the wick of a lamp—there one moment and gone the next. That weight was settling within me. It was turning my heart to stone.

"Of course it was. She was my sister," he answered.

It all unspooled like a ribbon, uncurling back as far as the dying fields. The vote that changed the dole. The Philosopher's execution. What whispers had he spoken then? What wayward strategy had he fed the factions? That was what he did—he planned. Found a path where there wasn't one. It was the greatest lesson I'd learned from him.

Nej was maneuvering the Magistrates. Building a safety net. But how? The seat in the Forum engraved with my family name now belonged to me, and I was convinced that he was the one who'd put me there. What other plans did he have for me?

He stepped forward, taking my face in his hands. "You're a Casperia, Maris. You were made for this. Everything is about to change, and our family will be standing to inherit the will of the gods when it's over."

He looked so sure that it made me tremble. Now I *did* believe him. I'd underestimated my uncle. So had my mother. He wasn't just pulling strings. He was the one spinning them on the wheel. The vote. The Priestess. The blood rites were his idea. And I could guess who he had in mind to drink from that cup. He wanted the magic.

"I won't do it." I said, "I won't perform the blood rites."

The sound of boots echoed behind me and his gaze lifted to the doorway. When I turned, two legionnaires were waiting.

"The Consul is asking for you," one of the men said.

Nej smoothed my hair back affectionately, like he had when I was a girl. He gave me a soft, reassuring smile before he let me go. "You will do exactly what I tell you to, because I've worked very hard for this. For very long. And if you stand in my way, there is no god who will be able to help you. Do you understand?"

I was seeing my uncle clearly for maybe the very first time. He wasn't just blown by the winds of favor, like so many others in the Citadel. No, this man had the fate of this city clutched tightly in his fists.

He looked me in the eye for another moment before he followed the legionnaires out. I stood there, motionless, watching the shadow of fluttering wings on the eaves of the window.

I'd known for a long time that the Magistrates who worked behind these walls had their own interests at play. I'd overheard their talk over elegant dinners and beneath the beaded curtains at parties for as long as I could remember. And I wasn't foolish enough to believe that my mother or my uncle had ever been *good*. We were just a city of hungry beasts, waiting to devour one another. Nej, me, Luca. All of us. But this was a plot greater than I could have imagined, and I could feel all Nej's strings pulling tight. Something was coming. Everything *was* about to change.

I slowly glanced over my shoulder, checking the doorway before I moved toward Nej's desk. I quietly opened the drawers, moving the contents around carefully. I didn't know what I was looking for, but any chance I had to find it was quickly slipping away.

I rifled through the parchments on the desk, dumping out the alabaster bowl and opening the scrolls. When I found nothing, I went to the cabinets on the wall, pulling down texts and artifacts, relics from temples and other treasures Nej had collected.

My hands stilled on a half-opened scroll when I noticed a box carved from black obsidian by the window. The same one I'd seen in his study all those months ago.

The scroll slipped from my fingers, clattering on the ground as I moved toward the box, and when I took it in my hands, sliding it from the shelf, its weight seemed to pulse in the air around me.

I sank down, my white robes billowing onto the stone floor, and opened it. The gleam of golden light filled the air, and when my eyes landed on what was inside, I stopped breathing.

It was a stylus. Forged of shimmering light. It glowed before me, its tip as sharp as the point of a knife. I knew what this was. I recognized it from the frescoes and the tapestries that hung in the temple. The paintings on the domed ceiling in the Forum. It was a *gift*. From the gods.

Nej had been *gifted*.

I carefully lifted the stylus from the box, and the light seemed to almost melt into my skin. Every tale Ophelius had ever told me flitted through my mind, her voice like a low hum in my chest.

I swallowed as I touched the tip to the parchment, exhaling as its luminous golden ink marked the page. My hand moved in a memorized pattern as I wrote my own name.

Maris Casperia.

Slowly the light that formed the letters began to fade. It bled into the parchment until the letters were gone, leaving only the golden shimmer behind.

Breath by breath, the realization took shape in my mind. Mortals weren't the architects of this war. The gods were.

I swallowed down the rising urge to vomit. I thought I had hated. I thought that I knew what it was to hold malice in my heart. But this—this clawed thing inside me was darkness itself, unfurling like the leaves on the vines in the atrium. The cold, dead feeling bled through me again, that black pit expanding. I'd given up everything to wear these robes because I'd believed they were the answer. I'd dedicated my life to the gods. But now there was no more Forum or Illyrium or Citadel. There was no New Legion or Lower City. Now it was just me. Isara was an empty tomb and I just a corpse within it.

I let my eyes linger on the stylus for another moment before I placed it back in the obsidian box. Its light snuffed out as the lid closed, and I stood, a floating feeling coming over me.

My hands smoothed out the wrinkles of my robes, retying them the way my mother had taught me. The eyes of the Magistrate portraits followed me as I walked down the Tribunal Hall, sandals like a heartbeat on the stone. A deep calm settled in me as I took the narrow, winding staircases down into the catacombs. There was a bone-chilling silence that waited in the dark.

I kept my eyes ahead as I moved through the stone-walled passages, my steps steady when I saw the shine of armor at the entrance to the Priestess's chamber. The gazes of the legionnaires posted there were fixed on something invisible in the distance, reflecting that same empty look I knew was in my own eyes.

One of the legionnaires moved as I came closer, retrieving the alabaster box, and when I stopped before the door, I could see Ophelius in a haze of incense smoke.

I gave a nod to the legionnaires and they opened the door, letting it swing out into the corridor. I stepped inside the cell, going to the altar and setting the box down as the legionnaire unlocked the cell door. I took the whalebone knife from inside, and once the chamber was closed, I turned to face Ophelius.

The Priestess was crumpled on the cold floor, propped up by a single silk pillow, but when she saw me, her chapped lips moved just slightly.

"Casperia. I've been waiting for you."

Thinking of her as a *woman* didn't feel right anymore. This creature huddled in the corner barely looked human. The Ophelius I knew wasn't visible in the husk who sat before me. How this weak, deformed vessel could still have godsblood running in her veins, I didn't know. This was the creature Nej wanted me to bleed. Hers was the blood he wanted.

The ties of the robes suddenly felt like they were choking me, my lungs unable to draw in the air. There was too much death in the room. I came low, folding my legs beneath me as I pressed my forehead to the stone, and I could smell it—that tinge of rot in the air. But I could see by the look in Ophelius' eyes that she couldn't feel it anymore. She was suspended between this world and the next, her soul stretched thin.

Her bony hand slid across the floor toward me, but she didn't touch the fabric of my chiton. "Your path has changed since the last time I saw you."

"You've said that before," I said, heart sinking with the weight of it.

"Tell me." Her voice crackled, eyes slowly blinking. "Where is your husband?"

I pressed my lips together, a sharp pain igniting inside my chest the moment I heard her say the word. *Husband*.

"I don't know." The words broke.

A rattling woke in her chest and she coughed violently, curling into herself. I watched as she struggled to breathe. Her eyes seemed to focus and unfocus, as if she were watching something at play in the dark that I couldn't see. But there was a clarity in them that hadn't been there a moment ago.

"I told you," she said. "There are some bonds that cannot be broken."

"I know that now."

Ophelius' chest rose and fell raggedly. "You have a question for me," she whispered.

Even now, inches from death, she could see inside my mind.

"Why did he do it?" I asked. "Why did Hermaus give his blood to the mortals as a gift?"

She grinned. "You are thinking like a Priestess now."

The emotion buried deep in my belly woke, making my nose prickle with the sting of tears. And the way she looked at me said that she knew what question I was really asking. It began with a kindness. The love of a mortal. And when Hermaus gave the gift of magic, he gave us our doom.

"There are two versions of the story," she rasped. "The one we tell—the one painted in the temple—says that the mortals saved Hermaus' life that day."

"And the other?"

"The one told by my great-grandmother Ursu was different. It's the one painted on the temples in Valshad."

I waited, breath pinned in my chest.

"It tells the story of five women who happened upon the wounded god. And they did not help him. They did not tend to his wounds. They drew a blade against him in his helpless state. They drained his blood and drank it."

"They stole it." I stared into the torchlight behind her, lost in its glow as my mind pulled at the threads. If this version of the story was true, then Valshad had taken this magic with the blade of a knife. Then Isara had stolen it again, with the same violence.

She looked at me gravely, as if I'd spoken aloud some secret. "It is a terrible thing to touch the power of the gods."

She shifted suddenly, making me flinch, and her hands slid across the floor in jerking movements toward me. I watched in horror as she dragged her useless legs behind her, slithering like a snake on the stone. I was frozen as her skeletal fingers drifted through the air and found my face. I could hardly breathe as she pulled me toward her in an embrace.

To the legionnaire watching through the door's window, maybe it would appear as a dying Priestess saying goodbye to her novice. Or a desperate woman begging for her life. But there wasn't a tender or delicate bone in Ophelius' body.

Her grip on me tightened, pulling my hair as her bony, bloodless cheek pressed to mine. Her voice was so quiet that I could hardly hear it over the rush of the pulse pounding in my ears.

Her macabre grin widened. "There are some shadows you can see coming. Death is one of them. Remember that."

She let me go, hand falling to the floor, and her eyes rolled back before they found me again. "Are you going to tell me why you've really come, Maris?"

I leaned in closer, letting my voice fill the small space between us. "I need something from you. And in return, I'll give you what you want."

Another ragged breath filled her weak lungs before she nodded. Carefully, I pulled the transcribed message from inside my chiton, handing it to her. Her eyes brightened just a little as they moved over the words. And then a tear rolled from the corner of her eye.

"What does it say?" I whispered.

"They're coming, Maris." She drew out the *S* in my name like the hiss of a snake. "Valshad. They're coming."

She rocked onto her back, a smile breaking on her lips as she closed her eyes. The words fell heavy in the air, all of it suddenly making sense. The messages weren't to some lost contingent of the Loyal Legion or an unknown ally who was coming to save us. Nej had summoned the only people who wanted to see us burn more than the rebels. He was signaling Valshad.

"You see them for what they are now, don't you? The gods are not kind, child. They are not benevolent. They are mercilessly hungry beasts, just like us." A laugh cracked in her throat.

I leaned over her, hand stroking her thin hair with a prayer to the gods silent on my lips. I cursed them before I asked them to forgive me. And then I pressed the whalebone knife into her palm.

I was finally doing something that fulfilled the promise Luca and I made to each other. I'd considered it a betrayal when he'd crossed that river without me and turned against his own people. I hadn't understood him. But nothing *right* could fix what was wrong here. For the first time, I would have blood on my hands, making me finally understand what Luca had done.

He'd known what I hadn't. He'd seen long before me.

The tide was turning, and we were the wind.

CHAPTER 31

BEFORE: MARIS

The night of my wedding, there were crows circling in the sky.

I stood at the window, watching them turn in the air, black wings tipping on the gales pushing inland from the sea. There was a storm coming and its sweet, earthy scent bled through the breeze, catching the delicate edges of my chiton.

The courtyard of the Illyrium was filled with citizens from the Lower City, a steady, relentless current of panic brimming in the air. The first few days after the tribunal, the temple had been flooded. Every soul in Isara had come to make a sacrifice, begging the gods to have mercy on us all.

Behind me, the great bronze lamps that hung from the ceiling were lit with roaring flames, illuminating the painted ceiling overhead. Every inch was covered in individual panels that depicted scenes from the life of Toranus, the architect of lineages and creator of bloodlines. Beyond the glow of the lamps, the crucible sat in the corner, the temple smith waiting.

I'd chosen a stola of seashell iridescent silk, and it looked like melted pearl in the candlelight. Fine gold godsblood chains draped from the belt at my waist, falling in arcs over my hips, and the same strands were hung from my neck and my wrists. My fingertips fidgeted with them as I watched the dark street below.

"He will come." Ophelius' deep voice lifted over the crackle of the altar fire, where she stood with her hands clasped before her. "It is fated."

I turned to face her, the wind at my back. There was no warmth in her eyes. She'd said almost nothing since I asked her to perform the rites. In fact, she hadn't so much as asked a single question, and that made me nervous. It felt almost as if she'd been waiting for it. Like she'd known this would happen long before I did. The idea made a slow, cold shiver slide up my spine.

Her hand opened before me, beckoning me forward, and I obeyed. I crossed the stones with slow steps and her hand encircled my wrist, lifting it between us. She turned the heel of my palm toward her, eyeing the blue veins beneath my skin. Her lips just barely moved as her fingertips pressed to the vine-like pattern, and before I could even ask what she was doing, a hot jolt of pain shot through me. It ricocheted up my arm, through my chest, and down into my legs, burning. I pulled away from her, cradling my arm.

"What was that?" I hissed.

Ophelius' blank face looked back at me, her mouth flat. "I've closed your womb."

My eyes widened. "*What?*"

"You want me to perform the rites? Then I need to be sure."

"Sure of what?"

I looked down at my wrist, where the veins had darkened.

The skin was red and swollen, but the pain was slowly receding, turning to a dull warmth.

"It will be undone in time, but we haven't come all this way just so he could put a child in you," she scoffed. "There is too much work to do, Maris."

We. It was almost as if Ophelius believed she had orchestrated the whole thing. She looked into my face, surprising me when she placed a rough hand on my cheek. Her eyes searched mine like she wasn't quite sure what she saw there.

"Your path has changed, Casperia." Her hands tightened on me. "And he is a part of it. You can feel that, can't you?"

I stared into her eyes, feeling the prickle of tears in my own. The emotion brimming inside me was one I couldn't name, and I was grateful. I was afraid that if I did, it would come alive.

"Ophelius?" I whispered, the question spinning in my mind now poised on the tip of my tongue.

I was afraid to ask it because I was afraid of the answer. Defying the Forum was dangerous, and Ophelius had never been political. She was smart enough to stay out of the Magistrates' games. But I hadn't forgotten how all this started—on the morning of the First Feast, when she asked me about Luca Matius.

I glanced at the temple smith, keeping my voice low. "Did you have something to do with the leaflet?"

Ophelius' face turned just enough for me to see her profile. When she spoke, it was with the same resonance as a prayer. "Sometimes you must burn a field to save it, Maris."

The doors to the temple flew open and I turned, exhaling when I saw Luca. He was dressed in his ceremonial legionnaire uniform, the brilliant red cloak billowing out behind him as he made his way up the aisle. But when I saw who was with him, I stilled.

Magistrate Saturian's son followed on Luca's heels, his dark eyes flashing in the low light. The fear that had been thrumming in my gut all day swelled, making my palms slick.

Luca's steps slowed as he neared me, and his eyes dropped from my face, traveling down the length of me. His expression turned almost grave, his lips parting. I could feel it all over again—his hands sliding up my legs. His mouth on my skin. I was about to take vows with this man, but I'd already given all of myself to him. The part that couldn't be undone was already past us.

He stopped before me, his eyes running over me again. "I'm late. I'm sorry."

"I thought you changed your mind." I swallowed.

"Have you?" He met my eyes, waiting.

I shook my head in answer.

"You're . . ." he breathed. "You look beautiful."

A small smile broke on my lips, but it fell as my gaze went over Luca's shoulder, finding Saturian's son. He was watching us, an apprehensive look in his eyes.

"I wanted him here." Luca answered my unspoken question, and after a moment I nodded.

Luca's hand slipped into mine, and in an instant, I felt tethered to the earth. The coals on the altar hissed behind us and he pulled me toward the smoke, knotting our fingers together.

Ophelius took a bundle of cypress from the bowl beside the fire, twirling the stalks in the flames. In moments, a soft, rippling smoke was seeping into the air.

"Which name do you take?" Her voice echoed in the temple.

"Casperia," Luca answered, without even a moment's hesitation.

I looked up at him. We hadn't discussed which name we would take. We hadn't even gotten that far. "Wait," I said.

But Luca's eyes were on Ophelius. He was resolute. "We take the name Casperia."

The temple smith stepped forward and something in Ophelius' expression looked almost pleased. Like another one of her prophecies had come true. She held out a hand, waiting as Luca removed his medallion, and when he set it in her palm, she handed it to the smith.

She pulled the cypress from the fire, waiting for the flames to snuff out before she turned to us again. "I graft you, Luca Matius, into the family line of Casperia."

The deep vibration of her whispers hummed as she wafted the smoke over us, and Saturian watched in silence as the smith dropped Luca's medallion into the crucible. He looked almost afraid, his jaw tense and shoulders back.

I'd been in the temple smith's chamber only once in my life—the day the gods named me. Every child born Isarian was brought to the temple on the feast day that followed their birth so that their medallion could be forged. It was a sacred thing, the material representation of citizenship and family claim. It was also something that happened only once in your life unless you took vows and took the name of another. Upon death, your medallion went back to the crucible to be melted into an ingot that would be forged for another new soul.

Reforging Luca's medallion would cut him from his family line, and the vows were until death. The weight of that hung heavy in the temple. For the citizens of the Citadel District, giving up your family name was something people only did when they needed to advance their position, and something that was almost never done by someone who was the last of a line. But in only moments, the family Matius would be no more. And when Luca took his uncle's seat, the name engraved there would change to Casperia.

The body of the Forum would see it as a ploy by my mother—a swift, unexpected piece moving on the board. But not even Magistrate Casperia would see this coming. Nor would she benefit from it.

The smith pushed the rack into the forge and watched over it carefully as he cranked the bellows to keep the flames burning hot. When he poured the melted gold into the mold, the metal reflected the light like a mirror. It cooled slowly, the hiss of steam erupting into the air as the blacksmith submerged it in water, and when he pried it free, my family name stretched across the medallion's face.

Gone was the line of Matius. Now Luca was a Casperia.

Ophelius clasped the medallion around his neck, the word flashing on its surface, and a feeling like fire began to burn over my skin. She wasn't speaking to us anymore. Now she was conversing with the gods.

When I looked up at him, Luca was steady. Unshaken. His eyes didn't leave mine as she spoke the sacred words and they wrapped around us, making me tremble. When he felt my hands shaking in his, Luca closed his fingers around mine tightly, as if trying to anchor me there.

"Flesh to flesh, bone to bone, blood to blood," Ophelius whispered.

She chanted the words over and over, sealing the ceremony in a ritual that couldn't be undone. The sound made my head swim in the thick smoke from the herbs on the coals.

I'd imagined it—taking my vows. But it had never looked like this. Magistrates' daughters didn't get married in the temple in the middle of the night, hidden in shadow and secrets as an act of radical rebellion. But that was exactly what this was, and there was some part of me that felt like it was only the first wind in a much greater storm. Like we were weaving threads we couldn't see the pattern of.

Ophelius opened the leather-bound tome on the altar, dipping the stylus into ink that shimmered with godsblood. I watched with my heart in my throat as she recorded the names there.

MARIS AND LUCA CASPERIA
SIXTH DAY IN THE MONTH OF CALISTO
END OF THE LINE MATIUS

CHAPTER 32

NOW: LUCA

Asinia straightened as I neared the library of the Illyrium, where Vale had been shut up for most of the day. The tribune's jaw clenched before he stepped in my path, blocking my entry.

I stopped short, gaze moving past him to where Vale was bent over a long table with a stylus in hand.

"Where is he?" Asinia's voice was a crackle in his chest.

It took a few seconds for my mind to catch up to the question. He was asking about Théo. My tribune.

He hadn't returned to camp since I'd sent him for the medallion, and the fact that Asinia didn't know where he was only made me more inclined to believe that Théo was telling the truth when he said that I could trust him.

Asinia took a step toward me, his face only inches from mine. "Where is he, Luca?"

"He's following orders," I said.

"They'd better not be ones that get him killed."

I met his eyes. "Every order we have given or followed since this started has killed someone. I hope Théo isn't next, but maybe he is. Maybe I am. Maybe you."

"He didn't enlist, didn't take the place as your tribune, to give his life for *her*." Anger twisted Asinia's words. He was worried about the man he loved, and I understood that kind of rage.

"Luca." My name echoed behind him.

Vale was watching us from where he stood inside the temple's library.

Asinia finally stepped aside, letting me pass, and I strode across the marble floors toward the Commander. Vale was missing the cloak he usually wore, clad only in his tunic. For the first time in a long time, he looked his age. He was a month away from twenty-eight years old, but he had the face of a man who'd seen a hundred lifetimes.

"What was that?" he asked, dropping the stylus on the table.

"It was nothing."

My eyes ran over the parchments between us. He'd been poring over the inventory of the armory, taking stock of what we had left for the push into the Citadel District. From what I'd seen of the Loyal Legion over the last few weeks, it was more than enough. I could only hope that we didn't have to use it.

"Are they ready?" Vale looked up at me, distracted.

I nodded. "Every cohort has their orders. They're ready."

Vale gave a slight shake of his head. "I don't know," he said, almost to himself. He scratched at the scruff covering his jaw. "Something still doesn't feel right."

I tried not to show how nervous that made me. Vale was more than intelligent. He was intuitive, sensing things in a way that I never did. He was also a patient man, another thing we didn't have in common.

He finished the line of script he was writing, and once the ink was dry, he picked up the parchment and rolled it tightly, taking up the stick of red wax beside it. I watched as he held it over the flame of the oil lamp. It bubbled and he let it drip over the parchment's seam, then he curled his fingers into a fist so that he could press his signet ring into the circle of wax. The seal of Isara.

He ran a hand through his hair and faintly winced, as if the movement woke a twinge in his ribs. "Every falcon that leaves that tower will come down until we cross that river."

"Agreed," I said, looking at Asinia. "Post more archers."

Asinia obeyed, turning on his heel and ducking out. But not before he threw another tight glance at me over his shoulder.

Vale motioned for me to follow, and we took the long hallway that ran down the south side of the Illyrium to the temple's entrance. The camp was busy, the fragrant smell of venison stew in the air. Vale had made sure the legionnaires could fill their bellies with food and wine, an indulgence meant to bolster them for the fight ahead. I hoped it would also smooth over the news of the meeting with the Consul.

Striking the agreement to allow the citizens of the Citadel District to leave before we crossed the Sophanes had garnered mixed reactions in the New Legion, and it only confirmed that Roskia had been right. If we hadn't refused that courtesy to the Magistrates, I wasn't sure the legionnaires would have supported the plan. But that didn't solve my own problem in the district.

Tomorrow, the legionnaires would stand on the riverbank to watch the steady stream of people crossing the bridge. Wealthy Isarians draped in decadent chitons and shining gold jewelry would walk in a somber parade through the Lower City, and we'd be lucky if we could get them through the gates without someone drawing a sword.

Vale led us to his tent, weaving through the congested camp and touching the shoulder of a legionnaire or two on his way. He was moving better, not as rigid as he'd been in the days before, either. That was good.

As soon as we were inside, he tugged the tunic over his head, dropping it on the cot. For once, the bandage on his ribs wasn't showing any evidence of bleeding.

"What are we going to do about Roskia once this is done?" I asked.

"That's tomorrow's problem. Not today's."

"I'm not so sure."

He pulled a clean tunic on. "The only legionnaires left in this city have lost enough to know where their allegiances lie. Roskia will prove useful if we handle him right."

I still wasn't convinced. The fabric of the New Legion felt like it was on the verge of fraying. The soldiers were loyal, but as we'd fought our way through the Lower City, their passion had transfigured into what felt more like zeal. That worried me.

"The gates open at dawn. When the sun sets, we take the Citadel," Vale said. "We just need to stay alive one more day. Can you do that?"

"I can do that." I swallowed.

"Good. Because I need you, Luca." He paused. "For what comes next, most of all."

A sinking feeling woke at the center of my gut, as if the earth were pulling me into it. The truth was, I'd lied to him when I told him we could wage this war against the Consul and come out the other side a better people. I'd betrayed him when I refused the post of Commander and left it to him. Because Vale had always been a better man than I was. We both knew that. But it was a responsibility that had come at a cost, and he'd paid it tenfold.

"Where else would I be?" I said, voice low.

Vale looked at me with something like sympathy before he shouldered into his scale armor, turning his back to me. "Why didn't you tell me she was here?"

I went still, understanding slowly settling between us. That was what this was about.

"That was reckless, Luca. Even for you."

"She was picked up in the Lower City," I said, handing Vale his cloak.

"That doesn't explain why you didn't tell me."

"She took a seat in the Forum, Vale. I'll be in enough trouble if it comes out that I've taken vows with a Magistrate. There's no reason to take you down with me."

"I was *there,* Luca. I watched you take the vows."

I glanced over my shoulder, checking the opening of the tent for anyone who could be listening. This was too dangerous a conversation to have in the camp. "I remember."

"Which is why I'll say it again." He finished with the buckles. "I need you. *Here.*"

"I *am* here."

"And what are you going to do about Maris?"

"I'm taking care of it."

He studied my face, as if trying to determine how concerned he should be. I wasn't going to tell him that I was more worried than he was. It didn't matter what had come before or what would come after. If it came down to a choice between Maris and the New Legion, or even Maris and taking the Citadel, I knew what I would do. So did Vale. I just needed her outside the city gates so that I never had to make the choice.

"I'm with you," I said.

He nodded.

For years, we'd served as legionnaires to the Citadel, even when officials cared more about statues than they did grain to feed their citizens. And when I drew my blade in the Forum the day Vitrasian died, I'd set off a chain of events I couldn't see coming. But neither of us knew that word about what happened had spread through the legion. The morning of my own tribunal, where I was sure to be executed myself, they came for me. *Vale* came for me. We left six dead bodies in the catacombs that day, and then we'd crossed the Sophanes.

The Consul called those dead men the first casualties of this war, but he was wrong. Rhea was the first.

A deep, bellowing sound rang out in the distance, softened by a gale of wind, and Vale's brow pinched.

"Is that . . ." He didn't finish.

We both fell quiet, listening, my pulse kicking up in the passing seconds of silence. When it rang out again, my eyes snapped to Vale's.

I knew the sound. It was the call of a horn. The kind that was used for only one thing—war.

Vale pushed out of the tent and I followed. Across the camp, the legionnaires were frozen, waiting. A whistle cut through the next stretch of silence and I looked up to see Asinia at the end of camp, jogging in our direction. Vale strode toward him, his scale armor jingling.

The closer he came, the clearer that grave look on Asinia's face was. "Commander! The gates!"

He cut toward the Illyrium and we followed, climbing the exterior stairs as soon as we reached the courtyard. He took us up the east side of the temple, where the withered rooftop garden was nothing more than dust in sculpted planters. Asinia zigzagged between them with us on his heels until we reached the ledge on the other side of the building.

In the distance, I could see the western wall, where the city gates were shut up and barred. The legionnaires standing watch along the plank walkways that overlooked the hills were moving. The sunlight flashed on their armor as they scrambled past one another and more figures scaled the ladders below.

Asinia set his hands on the railing of the ledge beside us, eyes wide as a faint *ping* echoed out. I exhaled, knowing exactly what I would see in the next breath. It was the unmistakable sound of a ballista.

As soon as I thought it, a string of enormous stones appeared in the sky, hurling over the wall in an arc. We watched in horrified silence as they dropped, second by second, smashing into the buildings below.

We were under attack. But not by the Loyal Legion. This was coming from *outside* the walls.

"The gates!"

Vale's voice tore through the air and the legionnaires below scrambled away from the river as we ran back down the steps. Smoke from the fires was already trailing up to the sky as we darted through the tents, following the sound of shouting. Ahead, the people of the Lower City were streaming out of their houses, filling the streets. Running in the opposite direction.

Asinia shoved through the crowd, making way for us to cross the main artery of the city, and when I spotted the red tunics ahead, I shoved him in their direction.

"There!"

He pivoted, cutting up the next street. The stones were still flying, accompanied by bolts that whistled through the air over us, crushing rooftops in their wake.

The growing swarm of legionnaires pooled, surrounding the gate, the archers climbing the ladders to take their places on the wall. When I heard the roar of Vale's voice calling orders, it wasn't close now. Somewhere in the last few seconds, I'd lost him. I climbed the nearest toppled cart, searching the smoke, and I let out the breath I was holding when I spotted him standing before the gates. Beside him, a crew of legionnaires lowered another bolt into place.

I jumped down, shoving through the bodies between us. "I'm going!" I reached for the nearest ladder and climbed, hand over slick hand until I was launching myself up onto the walkway at the top of the wall. I shoved the legionnaires aside so I could see, and a choked sound cracked in my throat when my eyes landed on the hills.

A haze of smoke moved against the bright sky, clearing just long enough for me to see them. Hundreds of soldiers clad in green were taking formation below. They were coming over the hills like a cloud of locusts.

"It can't be," a hoarse voice spoke behind me.

The same words were flitting through my own mind. I recognized the scene from countless stories of the Old War and the military scrolls that illustrated the battles. Those green tunics and gold-tipped flags rippling in the wind were like ghosts come back from the dead.

It was Valshad.

CHAPTER 33

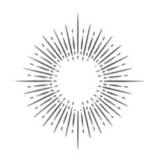

NOW: MARIS

Back at the Citadel, Ophelius was already bleeding. I'd kissed her hair as I pressed the whalebone knife into her hand, not uttering a goodbye as the door to the cell closed behind me. In only seconds she would have pressed the blade to her wrists. Freed the godsblood from where it was imprisoned, just like her. Ophelius had finally gotten her wish. And now I could see that death was a mercy I should have granted her long ago.

I threw open the doors to the villa, hinges rattling as I untied the Magistrate's robes. The silk fluttered to the ground, a trail of white that followed me through the atrium to the hall. I had minutes before Nej and the Consul knew what I'd done, only minutes to get myself across the bridge into the Lower City.

It all made sense now. The last thing anyone would expect was for the Consul to signal Isara's oldest enemy. An invitation to come and take what was left—a last, gasping breath of a dying city before it succumbed to the flames. And the New Legion had no idea what was coming for them.

I opened the birdcages suspended in the atrium, unlatching the little gold clasps of their doors. The finches chirped and sang, fluttering on their perches with wings beating against the wires until, eventually, they darted up and out. I watched with cold, numb tears striping my cheeks as they followed the bright light of the atrium's alcove.

Wind poured through the open windows of my mother's room, tugging at my pale blue stola as I tore open the drawers of the chest, grabbing fistfuls of her jewelry. I stuffed it into a bag, searching for anything of value I could find. There was no question about the fate that awaited me here in the district or across the river, but I'd have to take my chances on the bridge with a bribe if I was going to get to Luca in time.

Sweat beaded along my brow as I cinched the bag closed, but my hands froze on the strings when the wind shifted, making the room fall quiet around me. Slowly, my eyes lifted to the mirror. There was a sudden oppressive feeling, like the walls were creeping toward me. Like I was sharing the space with someone else.

I jolted when I saw him, jostling the chest before I caught myself on it. A young man stood in the doorway of the room, hair blowing across his face as he watched me. It took several seconds for me to recall where I'd seen him. It had been in the lamplight of Luca's tent. This was his tribune, Théo.

His armor was missing, and, without the helmet, I could see just how young he was. He'd snuck into the district, that much was clear, but how long had he been here? Since I walked through the door? Had he been waiting for me?

"What are you doing here?" I said, confused. But that confusion almost immediately turned to dread. "Where is Luca?"

Théo took something from his pocket, holding it out to me. The glint of godsblood-infused gold flashed on a linked chain.

"What is that?"

He took a step toward me, making me inch closer to the window, but he lifted a hand in a gesture that was meant to calm me. "He asked me to give you this. That's all. That's the only reason I'm here."

When I didn't protest, he set it on the chest and slowly backed away.

It was a medallion. I stared at it before I picked it up, the cold metal heavy in my hand. The family name read *Esdran,* one I'd never heard of before. I supposed that was the point.

You can't be a Casperia anymore.

I rubbed my thumb across the engraved letters, the sharp prickle of tears igniting behind my eyes again. Luca was still looking for a way to get me out of this mess. After everything. But there would be no opening of the gates. No exodus to freedom. He just didn't know it yet.

A jingling sounded down on the street, perforated by the pound of boots, and I went still as the last few hours came rushing back. The tribunal. Nej. The Priestess. My time was up.

Before me, Théo went still. "What? What is it?" He was already pulling the knife from his belt.

"They're coming." I swallowed. "For me."

Three heavy knocks resounded through the empty villa, but I could hardly hear them. I wasn't even sure I was breathing.

Théo went to the window, moving me from view as he peered down to the street. "Get over there. In the corner."

I slipped the medallion into my pocket and did as he said,

pressing myself against the wall as the footsteps grew closer. Théo looked around the room, eyes jumping from one thing to the next before he took a long, carved wooden hairpin from the chest and a white ribbon from the mirror.

The pounding of a fist echoed again, making the door shake on its hinges, and I flinched.

"Don't move. Don't make a sound," Théo said, positioning himself on the other side of the doorway. His eyes were on the small circle of light on the floor between us. "Understand?"

A broken exhale escaped my throat.

"I won't let anything happen to you. Do you believe me?" he said lowly.

I looked him in the eye and nodded, forcing my breath to slow. My back pressed against the wall, the fabric of my chiton clutched in my trembling arms. Théo set a shoulder on the doorframe, a look of utter calm coming over him.

The doors to the street flew open down the hall, and the sound of metal clanged against the floor as bodies tore through the atrium. I didn't breathe, following Théo's gaze to that small circle of light on the tile floor. His eyes were intently focused on it.

Through the sliver I could see of the atrium, figures moved, and with each one that came through the door, the light streaming in from outside flickered. The circle on the floor flashed, and each time Théo's mouth moved. He was counting them, I realized. Tallying how many he was up against.

The men spread out, two heading in what sounded like the direction of my mother's study, and three more funneling in. I watched Théo exhale as the first of the legionnaires came through the door. His eyes swept the room as the other two continued down the hall, and Théo was so still that, for a moment, I wondered if he would move at all.

He shifted out and away from the wall with silent steps just as the legionnaire turned, and Théo wrapped his arms around him, one hand clasped over his mouth as he dragged his knife across the legionnaire's throat. He held him up until the man's legs gave out, and he slowly lowered him to the floor, waiting for the next to enter. When he did, shouting erupted in the villa, but the sound was cut short when Théo's blade hit its mark, running him through the gut. He fell to his knees, toppling forward on the white stone.

I closed my eyes, hands pressed to my face, as I breathed through a muffled cry, trying not to make a sound. By the time I opened them again, Théo had another man lying at his feet.

When the fourth man's eyes found me across the room, Théo barreled toward him and the hairpin spun in his fingers before he plunged it down into the crease between the man's armor and his collarbone. The legionnaire screamed, sinking to his knees, and Théo pressed the hairpin in with the heel of his hand.

Eyes wide, the last legionnaire backed out of the room clumsily. Théo got back to his feet, body heavier now, and slipped the white ribbon from his tunic. I set my forehead on my knees as I listened to the sound of the body hitting the floor. The crash of something off the wall. The sick, wet choking sound as Théo wrapped the ribbon around the man's neck and pulled. So tight.

I sat, frozen, as the spreading pool of red on the floor crept closer, touching the hem of my chiton. The smell of blood was thick in the air now, making me swallow against the taste of bile on my tongue.

Théo returned as soon as the choking stopped, a legionnaire's arrows clutched in his bloody hands. "Let's go."

He dropped the bow over his shoulder and went to the window, watching the street below. But the only thing I could hear was the sound of my heart pounding in my chest.

"*Now,*" he said louder when I didn't move.

I got back to my feet as another wave of nausea hit me and I leaned into the wall, letting it hold me up. He waited for me to pass through the doorway before he followed. I could feel him close behind me, one hand hovering at my side as if he were afraid I might tip over. The bodies in the atrium were surrounded by pools of blood.

He stood at the door, one hand on the bolt. "Ready?"

A gust of wind rushed in through the open windows, whipping around me and pulling the loose strands from my unraveling braid. It carried the distant howl of a sound that made me stop short, my eyes moving back to the view of the city below.

The sound resurfaced, louder, as another shifting breeze poured into the villa. Beside me, Théo was frozen.

The swift, biting realization of what it was made a pit bloom in my stomach. It was a horn. The distant call of voices came next, followed by the clang of metal.

An unsettling silence crept through the villa and I blinked, looking up at the window. There was a stillness outside. A quiet resonance that sent a chill running over my skin and emptied the room of all its air. I stood, taking a tentative step toward the doorway, listening. Across the district, the bridges were no longer empty and a swarm of red tunics was spilling from the Ilyrium.

The sound was coming from outside the walls.

"No." The word was a whisper.

Théo paled, watching as artillery hit the buildings in the distance, and all I could think was that this was a dream. That it couldn't be right.

My eyes jumped from the gates to the New Legion's camp across the river, fear coursing through my veins so fast that my head was light with it. There was only one thing, one single thought, snaking through my mind. One source of the panic that swelled like a storm within me.

Luca.

More boots sounded below and I leaned out the window, heart sinking when I saw more legionnaires. They were headed for the stairs.

There was nowhere to hide. Nowhere to run. I had no more allies or strings to pull. I'd made my choices, and now the cost had come for me.

"You have to leave. Now." I took hold of Théo's tunic, pushing him back toward my chamber.

He caught my wrists with his hands, holding me in place. His eyes searched mine, and I could see the scenarios playing out behind them. There was no way out of this. A handful of legionnaires was one thing. But there were more than a dozen coming up the steps.

"They won't kill me. Not yet. But they *will* kill you."

Théo's chest rose and fell, his grip on me tightening.

"Your vow is to him, not me," I said, swallowing hard. "*Go!*"

I shoved him backward, and he finally released me, hesitating before he disappeared into the chamber. A second later, his shadow was flitting across the sunlit floor. Then he was gone.

I drew in a long, steadying breath as I turned to face the atrium, waiting for the door to open. There was no written history of this in the Citadel. No scrolls or paintings to archive a tale of darkness like this one. We had stolen the blessing of the gods. Pretended we deserved their favor. But before my very eyes, the great walled city of Isara, the jewel of the sea, was breaking into pieces all around me.

Below, the district wasn't silent anymore. Magistrates and their families streamed into the streets alongside legionnaires from the

Loyal Legion. Their eyes were wide with terror as they watched the smoke rise in the distance. The punctuated, metallic sound of artillery dragged on, firing at a speed I hadn't heard in weeks. Whatever the New Legion was shooting at, it wasn't something that could be taken down with return fire. And I knew what I would find if I could see over those walls. The banners of Valshad.

CHAPTER 34

BEFORE: LUCA

I fastened the bronze chain across my chest, situating the cloak in place. The leather breastplate was freshly oiled, the ceremonial version of the legionnaire's uniform missing the scale armor and helmet used for battle. Only last night, I was wearing it to take vows with Maris Casperia.

I'd woken in her arms, her skin softer than the delicate silks I had unwrapped her from the night before. The hours had been spent memorizing every curve and freckle, each shade of color in her hair that changed as the morning light lifted through the windows. I hadn't realized it then, but every time I'd kissed her, I was tightening that knot between us. Now I was fairly certain there was no way to get it undone.

The spell was broken by the collective anticipation flooding the Citadel District. There was always a buzz in the air that preceded the first performance of one of Vitrasian's new plays. For the first time in weeks, the district felt familiar. The aftermath of the tribunal and the truth about the harvests had tainted the

Magistrates in the eyes of the Lower City. There was a glaring crack in the perfect, gleaming surface of the Citadel. A play on the night of a feast was something that felt normal, and I suspected that was exactly what the Consul and the Magistrates wanted. But no one knew yet that everything had changed.

I pulled the medallion from my pocket, glancing down at it one more time. The name Casperia was now mine. Forfeiting the name Matius was the first move of many that would one day unravel the Forum. Maybe even this whole city. There was no more family Matius, and the yoke it had put around my neck was suddenly gone. Somehow, by the grace of some god that hadn't yet turned their back on me, I'd bound myself to a woman I loved. I wasn't sure how it was possible.

"Sir?"

A soft voice outside my chamber made me turn, and I slipped the medallion back into my pocket. Kastor's personal servant, a man named Yuretes, was standing in the doorway with a grave expression.

"It's your uncle. I'm afraid it's time."

I followed him through the corridor to the closed wooden doors at its end. The smell of death was thick in the outer chamber, but for the first time in days, it was quiet. The coughing and wheezing that had echoed through the villa was gone. Now there was only silence.

Yuretes opened the door and the stale, still air grew heavier. The lamps burning at the corners of the room made it too warm, their glow making it hard to see the lump of a man on the bed. One pale hand had slipped from the quilts and I stared at it, revolted.

"I'll leave you," Yuretes said quietly, slipping away.

It took a few seconds for me to cross the floor to my uncle's bedside. He was so still that, for a moment, I thought he was already gone. But his almost empty eyes moved as I drew closer, rolling in his head to follow me.

I stopped beside the bed, looking down at him. The man who'd lorded over me with cruelty and disdain, who'd shunned my mother and damned her, was now just a shriveled thing. A weak, pathetic creature clinging to the last threads of life that held him to this world.

His head tipped to one side, his eyes focusing on me. But his mouth didn't move, his jaw slack.

"I've come to say goodbye, Uncle," I said.

His chest rose and fell slowly.

"And to tell you"—I leaned closer—"that I plan to honor you by repaying every kindness, every opportunity, every bit of generosity you've given me, by letting you part this world knowing one thing."

Kastor's eyes seemed to focus a little more clearly, his breaths a little less shallow. Slowly, I reached up and unclasped the medallion from around my neck, holding it between us. The gold disc spun in the air, and I waited until it stopped, watching his face. I could see the exact moment he realized what I'd done. The moment he read the name *Casperia*. I could see the white-hot current of horror brimming, trapped beneath the surface of his dying body. A choking sound gurgled in his throat, the fingers of his open hand twitching.

"The moment you die, your bloodline will die with you. I'm not a Matius anymore." I closed my fist around the medallion and came low, letting my hands rest on either side of him so that I could look into his face. "I'm a Casperia now."

Kastor's eyes widened with horror. He was struggling for even a sip of breath now, blood spattering the corners of his mouth. He couldn't fight me as I took the Matius medallion from around his neck. He couldn't even move.

I fixed it around my own throat, tucking the Casperia medallion into my pocket, a secret that wouldn't be told until I'd taken Kastor's seat. There was a deep sense of justice in it. A balancing of scales that made the world seem just a little more fair.

The choking sound returned to his throat, his eyes bulging with the torture of knowing. And then I turned and walked away.

The entrance to the theater was full, with Magistrate families and Citadel officials dressed in their finest togas and stolae. Gems and precious metals glittered with godsblood in the torchlight, the sound of voices and music alive in the night. It was as if nothing had happened. No lies, no amendment to the dole, no faction leader left dying in his bed. The sight only made me more certain that what we'd done—Maris and I—had been right.

My uncle's medallion was heavy around my throat as the man at the entrance checked it. Kastor's seat in the theater was a prominent one with a good view of the stage, and I was surprised to see who was waiting there when I made it up the steps.

Rhea Vitrasian was dressed in a deep violet stola, her fair, curling hair tied up on top of her head. Ornate gold earrings dangled above her bare shoulders, and a parchment was clutched between her hands. There was a shadow of concern in her eyes that vanished when she saw me.

I pressed through the bodies that filled the aisles of the amphitheater. "Do you need me?" I asked, still searching her face for the source of that worry I'd seen a moment ago.

She shook her head. "No. Just wanted to be sure you were here."

But I wasn't convinced. Rhea was the most self-possessed

woman I'd ever met, as steady as stone. There was something wrong, but I couldn't tell what.

"You've been avoiding me," she said, not meaning it as a question.

I didn't deny it. There were questions I needed ask her that I didn't want to. Things she needed to tell me that I wouldn't want to hear.

"We're about to start." She took hold of my arm, squeezing, before she handed me the pamphlet for the play.

I watched her descend the steps toward the stage, and the view opened up as people took their seats. I looked down at the pamphlet, eyes running over the words slowly as I read the title along the top.

THE FIFTH FEAST
FIELDS OF FAVOR

I hadn't seen the play she was working on, but Vitrasian had been instructed to present something that would bolster the hope of Isara. She'd probably been commissioned to write it before the empty carts from the fields were even paraded through the city. It wasn't like Rhea to play along with the Citadel's schemes, but maybe even she could see what was at stake here. Isara was a caged animal inches away from turning on its master.

My gaze moved over the audience, searching for Maris, and when I found her, her eyes were already on me. My pulse slowed. She sat several rows below, half turned in her seat.

I reached into my pocket, taking the medallion into my hand, and letting my thumb move over the name there. If my uncle wasn't dead already, he would be in a matter of minutes. In a few days, I would take his seat in the Forum, and as soon as I did, everyone would learn what we'd done. There would be nothing they could do to stop it.

The fires in the lamps were put out, draping the theater in darkness. Maris disappeared from view and I took my seat just before the first actor clambered onto the stage. His white robes identified him as a Magistrate, and the mask he wore was painted in a distressed expression, the wide mouth turned down at the corners. His arms were full of scrolls that spilled out onto the ground, trailing behind him, and when the curtains pulled back and the lights came up on the enormous backdrop, I stiffened.

It was a rotting field. Hills of withering grain were painted to look like they went on for miles, the scene dotted with hundreds of circling black crows. It covered the entirety of the theater's width, making the man look small. His mask looked even more ridiculous now as he stumbled around the stage, picking up the scrolls and dropping them as he laughed maniacally.

A creeping sense of dread pooled in my chest, an eerie silence filling the theater. The distinct feeling that something wasn't right here was like a stench creeping over the crowd. What happened next, no one could have guessed. The tale that followed wasn't a tactic to bolster the hope of a city. It was a brazen critique of the Citadel and, specifically, the Forum.

A score of actors trailed out onto a scaffold erected over the stage, suspended high above the Magistrate. Their blue robes and golden halos signified that these were the gods, their masks painted in smiles so wide they were disturbing to look at.

More Magistrates filled the stage below, all dumbly weaving in circles that went nowhere. When one appeared in a sapphire-blue robe, the discomfort in the room fell heavier. It was meant to be the Consul.

Light glinted on something up on the scaffolding, and every

face lifted to watch as one of the gods drew a javelin from his robe. The others followed as the music swelled, and as the drums pounded, reverberating in my bones, each of the javelins was thrown. They soared down to the stage, the Magistrates falling one by one, toppling into a pile as red stained their white robes.

Rhea was drawing from the myths of the gods to illustrate that their favor was reflected in the harvests, and it wasn't a far leap to decipher the meaning. There was a clear line that could be drawn from one point to another—that the problem with the fields lay in the favor of the gods. That their retribution was coming for Isara.

A chilling silence descended in the theater as, slowly, the audience began to understand. Faces turned to look at each other, bodies awkwardly shifting. I looked down at the door that led to the side of the stage, where Rhea usually watched the performance. But I couldn't see her shadow there.

I rose from my seat quietly, following the steps down until I was pushing through the curtain. The small viewing chamber was empty.

The passage into Vitrasian's study from the theater couldn't be accessed without crossing the stage, so I slipped out of the theater, taking the dark arched corridors to the entrance from the Citadel's gardens. When I reached the courtyard, a single light shone from a window across the pond. Rhea's study.

When I came through the doors, she was sitting at her desk, her earrings glittering as she worked her stylus over a parchment. She didn't look up when I entered, as if she'd merely been waiting for me. As if this were any other day, her working over her studies, me serving as her novice.

"What have you done?" I said gravely.

She stopped writing, taking her time to lift her gaze. "They asked for a play, and I've given them one."

I stared at her, heart sinking. The role of the Philosopher in Isara was to be a thinker, and every generation of Philosophers was different. Vitrasian's tenure had been marked by wide-ranging accomplishments. While most Philosophers focused on one area of thought, Vitrasian's mind was spread across many disciplines. And she excelled at them all.

In my years with her, we'd spent significant time on the school of intellectual thought about the gods, religion, and their roles in society. She'd been enlisted by the Consul and the Magistrates to help shape the public's opinion. But this wasn't what the Citadel had in mind.

"What were you thinking?" I rasped.

She arched an eyebrow at me. "Do I have to explain myself to a novice now?"

"Rhea." I used her given name, something I rarely did. But I hoped it would help bring the seriousness of the situation into focus. "You need to find a way to explain this. To make it look like you didn't intend for—"

"For what?" Her chin lifted in defiance. She'd always liked an argument. But there was something different about this. She looked almost . . . scared.

"Why are the fields dying, Luca?" she asked, impatient.

I crossed my arms, ready for the string of questions I could feel coming. "There are countless variables that impact the harvests. No two seasons are the same. You taught me that."

"Alright." She nodded. "Why has *this* harvest failed? And the one before that? And the one two years ago?"

I looked around the study, thinking. "Rain? Changes in the soil?"

"But our measurements are consistent, are they not?"

"They are. But like I said, there are many variables that—"

She interrupted me. "Variables aren't the only thing that can be measured. We must also measure the outcomes. The harvests have been waning for the last seven years. Most likely before that, too. The Citadel's granary has run out of reserves, and this will be the first year we do not have enough grain to feed our people."

My hands tightened into fists.

"Next year, there will be less. And the year after that, there will be none. What comes after failed harvests? What happens after drought or infestation or overly wet seasons?" she pressed.

"Famine," I answered, more to myself than her.

But she didn't look pleased. "The grain will stay on this side of the river. It will feed the Citadel District. The Lower City will starve, and the Forum will have their justifications. They will say that it was the will of the gods. That the city has been culled in some divine way that is acceptable. And people will accept it because they don't want to believe the truth. Then the Consul will take our legion to war. We will tear apart a people, like we did to Valshad, and the collective identity of Isara will be renewed. This is a cycle. A pattern as reliable as the seasons and the path of the moon."

There was no hint of emotion in her voice. No echo of it visible in her eyes, either. She was thinking like the Philosopher she was. She was looking at the problem from the perspective of its inevitable consequences.

"And the play? What is the point of that?"

Vitrasian exhaled. "It's time the Forum considered less scientific solutions to the problem."

I waited.

"Harötha," she said, testing me with the Valshadi word.

I had to think about it before the translation came to me. "Atonement," I said. "You think the gods are angry."

"The gods are always angry," she scoffed. "But now they are hungry for blood."

"Then how do we appease them?"

I went rigid when I heard the sound of boots in the corridor. The unmistakable sound of a cohort of legionnaires. They were coming. For Vitrasian.

Finally, she stood, fingertips grazing the top of her desk before finding a strip of parchment. She held it over the lamp, watching it catch flame.

Her eyes met mine with a tender look. "I'm afraid it's too late for that, my love."

The burning parchment fell from her fingers, and the fire caught quickly, racing to the floor in a river that rushed to the shelves. She'd doused the room in oil.

She watched, blank-faced, as a tangle of angry orange light engulfed the study—every scroll, every specimen, every record—in flames.

CHAPTER 35

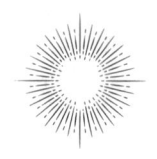

NOW: LUCA

"The messages."

The words left my mouth, inaudible over the roar of ballistae. The Citadel was sending messages to Valshad. It was so simple. So easy. And we had never seen it coming.

I'd been wrong about the Consul. We all had been. He wasn't delusional, refusing to believe that he'd been beaten. No, he *knew* that he'd lost. And now he was going to take us down with him.

I turned as another line of bolts soared overhead, punching holes into the Lower City below. Down the wall, Roskia was staring at the hills, his eyes wide and full of shock.

"Archers!" Vale shouted, raising a hand over his head as every bow on the wall lifted in unison, strings creaking as the archers nocked their arrows.

His hand dropped heavily and a sea of arrows shot into the air, spinning in the wind until they rained down onto the hills. Bodies dropped by the dozens and Vale's hand rose again.

"Take down those ballistae! *Now*," he roared.

I moved around him, running up the top of the wall to the nearest watchtower. "Scorpios!" I called out, climbing the steps. The order was echoed down the wall and every watchtower called it back.

When I dropped onto the landing, two legionnaires were already arming the scorpio, winding the ropes with a steady click as the shutters flew open. Light filled the watchtower's defense quarters and I took position behind the wheel, lifting the arms from the ground. The bronze circle before the frame looked out at the expanse and I swiveled the scorpio until I could see one of the ballistae on the hillside. I pulled in a breath, centering the weapon in the sights and waiting for the legionnaire beside me to make the call.

"Ready!"

I pulled the lever and the stays snapped loose, shooting the heavy bolt into the air. I held my breath as it arced and hit the ground, splintering into pieces. I'd missed.

"Load!" I dropped the arms of the scorpio, tearing at the buckles of my breastplate until it was sliding over my head. Then I took up the arms again, getting closer to the sights.

"Come on," I murmured, blinking against the sting of smoke in my eyes.

The wind was rolling over the hills, steering the bolts awry. I watched the pull of the army's tunics and shifted my aim to the left. Too far for an accurate shot, but with the wind, I hoped it was enough.

"Ready!"

The lever released and the scorpio loosed the bolt, the recoil striking me in the chest as it rolled back. I hit the stone wall behind me, catching myself as the bolt glided through the air. Its path bent and swayed as it flew, and I bit down so hard as it neared the ballista that I thought my teeth would crack.

It hit its mark with a boom, sending a cloud of earth and splintered wood into the air. But behind us, Isara was already burning.

"Pull!"

Vale shouted to the legionnaires at the bottom of the wall and they heaved against the ropes, lifting a crate of more iron-tipped bolts into the air.

Across the hills, cohorts of green-clad soldiers dotted the landscape, orchestrating a synchronized attack targeting the base of the city walls. Below, I couldn't see any sign of a breach, but it was only a matter of time before Valshad hauled a battering ram from behind the hills.

The crate swung clumsily as it reached the watchtower and I grabbed hold of the lines, guiding it to us just as an arrow slammed into the ramparts and splintered into pieces. As soon as it hit the planks, I started passing the bolts to the legionnaire beside me, who stacked them at the foot of the scorpio for reloading. Far down the wall, Roskia and his men were doing the same thing in the east tower.

The stays of the scorpios creaked as they were cocked, and over and over, the bolts were hurled into the air, aiming for the most crowded sections of the army in the distance. This wasn't a spontaneous attack. It was an onslaught. A well-prepared and efficiently organized battle strategy that was working.

A shriek of wind shot over us and I ducked when another storm of arrows pierced through the clouds. Beside me, a legionnaire launched forward, snatching up the lid of the crate and tossing it to me. I caught it and swung it up over my head before

I crouched low, and the pop of iron piercing through the wood pounded in my ears as they came down on top of us. When the last of them had fallen, I tossed the makeshift shield to the planks.

I instinctively glanced behind me to what was visible of the Citadel District, looking for any sign of smoke. The shots coming from the other side of the wall hadn't made it that far yet, but as the army came closer, they would.

The thought made my gut twist. At least Maris was as far from the wall as she could get, but everything beyond the Sophanes was unprotected.

Vale called out another order down the wall and the clang of the ballista rang out again, making every legionnaire stop. Our eyes jumped from one Valshadi cohort to the next until we saw the bolts soaring through the air. They hit the wall only feet away, and the ropes of the pulley swung again. We lurched back into the scaffolding before the suspended crate slammed into the stone and I tipped sideways on the edge, my balance tilting away from the wall. I could feel the fall in my stomach first, that sensation of dropping through the air, but a pair of hands caught hold of me.

I turned to see Théo, his fists twisted in my tunic as he wrenched me back from the edge. He was out of breath, his face red and shining.

"Where is she?" I rasped.

"She's in the district."

I stared at him, the panic I'd been keeping at bay since I first saw Valshad in the hills finally beginning to spill over.

A quick, hot jolt pierced my arm, knocking me backward. Théo's eyes went wide and then he was on top of me, lifting his shield overhead to cover us. It wasn't until I looked down that I saw what he did. A long, feathered arrow was sticking out of my upper arm, torn through a line of shredded flesh and buried deep in the muscle.

Théo pressed down hard around the wound, where pressure was building by the second, and blood gushed through his fingertips.

"Breathe," he said, and I obeyed, drawing in an inhale, and then pushing it out in one long, steady stream. He didn't wait before taking hold of the shaft, supporting the base, and then snapping it in two.

"Get him off the wall!" he shouted down the scaffold, but I took hold of his armor, shoving him back.

I got to my feet and didn't so much as blink as I ripped the broken piece from my arm and tossed it over the wall. I couldn't even feel it.

The legionnaires in the watchtower were calculating how to work with the wind, but the army in the hills had figured it out, too. With every ballista fired overhead, their aim was truer. Farther.

Again, I looked to the Citadel District. An explosion erupted down the wall, and I turned as the stones of the east watchtower cracked, buckling in on themselves. The wood-planked roof was next, snapping and collapsing before another growl of stone rang out and it crumbled.

Screams filled the wind and bodies ran down both sides of the wall, trying to escape the tumbling stones. But it was too late for the legionnaires inside.

Immediately, I searched the chaos around me for any sign of Vale. He was missing from where he'd stood only minutes ago. I moved past the stream of legionnaires running along the scaffold, pulling myself along the railing until I spotted him at the bottom of the pulleys. He was already reloading the crates.

"What is that? What are they doing?"

A voice shouted over the sound of the scorpio, and the legionnaire stopped firing. I stepped forward as Vale climbed the ladder, eyes trained on the shape of the brigades. Slowly, the wind cleared the smoke and the view opened up. The legion was shifting now in a movement that was mirrored across every cohort.

Beside me, Vale watched with darkening eyes. Every legionnaire on the wall waited for an order that wouldn't come. Continuing the fight would bleed us dry of what little we had left. Now we could only sit and watch as they constructed a camp, built towers, replenished their weapons, and prepared to scale our walls. After months of fighting and days away from its end, the Lower City would become a battlefield. Again.

"Centurion?" Théo was staring at me now.

I followed his gaze down to my arm. It was covered in a slick, shining red that dripped from my limp hand, leaving a trail on the dusty planks beneath my feet. But my eyes moved back to the hills.

The ballistae didn't reload. The archers didn't fire. Steadily, the soldiers drew down the slopes toward the road. They lined either side in three rows as something appeared in the distance. A series of dark blots moved toward the city.

A caravan. An ever-multiplying line of carts with covered loads came into view, protected on each side of the road. The truth about what this was slowly began to sink in, making my heartbeat stutter. Valshad wasn't just here to attack us. They weren't puncturing the walls to weaken the New Legion and give the Consul a fighting chance. Of course they weren't.

Wood, iron, chains, forges. Tents, tools, pitch, crucibles. They were the tools of conquerors. Of laying siege to a city. They didn't want to destroy Isara.

They wanted to take it.

CHAPTER 36

BEFORE: MARIS

The tribunal bells rang just after dawn, calling the Magistrates to the Forum. My mother hadn't even returned from the theater, spending the hours of the night shut away in her chambers at the Citadel with her closest allies.

There was no coming back from a public rebuke for what the Magistrates had done, which made Vitrasian's actions unforgivable. The Philosopher was known for being opinionated and outspoken, not afraid to contradict the Consul or the Forum, but she'd gone far beyond that last night. She'd publicly rebuked and humiliated the Citadel, holding everyone inside to account. And she'd done it at a time when peace in Isara was on the verge of breaking in two.

What most people in the district didn't yet know was that she had set fire to her own study, destroying countless texts and records. This was its own kind of betrayal.

If the citizens of the Lower City weren't already turning against the Citadel District, they would be now. Word of the play, penned by one of Isara's most influential leaders, would embolden the masses. The question was whether the Magistrates would be able to head off what was coming.

I'd waited for Luca at the mouth of the theater as the horde of furious spectators flooded out, but his seat was empty. When I'd taken the risk of going to his villa, there was no answer. Now I waited at the entrance to the Forum's gallery, searching for him in the agitated crowd.

Luca had been Vitrasian's novice for nearly three years, and there would be plenty of people in the Citadel who would question whether he was involved in the Philosopher's plans. Especially when he was known to be critical of those in the district. What had once made me admire him now struck a cold fear in my bones.

The names of the Magistrates had just begun to ring out when I finally saw him climbing the steps to the gallery. A long, shaking breath escaped my lips. As soon as he made it to the landing, I caught him in my arms, holding on to him tightly. I couldn't find it in me to care who might be watching.

Luca's tall frame enveloped me, his mouth pressing to my hair. "They took her."

I pulled back from him, brushing a hand over his flushed face. The dark circles beneath his blue eyes made them look like storm clouds. There were people glancing at us now through the door to the gallery.

"They're saying they think she was behind the leaflet, too," I said softly. "Please tell me you didn't know about this."

"I didn't know. I've been with my uncle's faction all night, trying to come up with some way this could work out to their advantage. But they weren't convinced."

"And your uncle?"

"Gone. The physicians marked his death last night."

"That means . . ."

Luca met my eyes. "The seat is mine. At least, it will be."

But our plans weren't as seamless as they'd once been. Now the Forum was thrown into chaos. It wouldn't be as simple as Luca taking his vows and casting the judgment stone from what was once his uncle's seat. It would be days before he could take his oath, and in that time, Kastor's faction would be missing its leader.

The names of the Magistrates being called out in the Forum finally stopped and I took Luca's hand, turning toward the gallery doors before they closed. I pulled him into the crowd, knotting my fingers tightly with his. We had to push through the spectators to make it to the balcony.

Below, the Magistrates were dressed in their robes, many of them still wearing the jewels and braided hair from the night before. No one in the Citadel District, it seemed, had slept.

The Consul called the tribunal to order and the gallery fell silent.

"I have called this tribunal to address the actions of the Philosopher Vitrasian, who last night betrayed the trust of this body and the city of Isara by making false and dangerous claims that put our people at risk."

The doors behind him opened and two legionnaires escorted Vitrasian in, placing her at the center of the twelve-pointed star inlaid on the marble floor. Her hands were bound before her, the sight almost too degrading to look at. She was one of the most revered women in the city, reduced to the mortification of being a prisoner. She looked calm as she peered out over the Magistrates.

The purple stola she'd been wearing last night was mussed, her hair beginning to unravel around her face, but her stark beauty was still arresting.

"The consequence of these actions has been the sowing of discord and terror among the most vulnerable of our citizens, and this is an offense that cannot be overlooked. Especially in the aftermath of this Forum's decision to withhold the state of our grain fields from the public."

My stomach turned. By humbling themselves before the city, the Magistrates had taken the role of apologetic mothers and fathers who'd done their best for their children. By painting the Philosopher as a liar, they then took the role of victims, placing themselves alongside the people. The ire wouldn't be difficult to stoke because the only thing more terrifying than the possibility of the city starving was the idea that it was an act of the gods. From that, there was no rescue.

"The nature of this crime"—the Consul's voice echoed—"is treason."

The throng of onlookers erupted into discord and Luca's hand slipped from mine, finding the railing before us. He leaned forward, as if steadying himself; his knuckles were white and the muscles in his arms flexed beneath his skin.

"The punishment for which is death."

The voices in the Forum exploded, making the air stifling hot. I struggled to draw in a breath.

"No." Luca's voice was so low that I barely heard the word.

Treason was a charge only rarely brought by the Consul, mostly used to make an example of those who defied him. There was a message to be communicated here—that anyone who disturbed the facade, anyone who attempted to challenge the Forum, would face the same vote as Vitrasian. But down on the floor, the Philosopher's expression was unchanged. She looked out into the middle distance, her eyes unfocused.

"It is our duty today to hold Vitrasian to account."

When the Consul spoke again, it was with the fervor of a soldier. This was where it would begin. They would hold the vote, narrowly sparing Vitrasian from punishment, then they would discredit her and her findings with a swift hand. The work of convincing the city that suffering through famine was a collective effort, a banding together for future generations, was something I'd already heard the Magistrates discussing. They were nothing if not inventive. Somehow, they would manage to take Vitrasian's act of rebellion and turn it into a unified battle cry. It was, in a word, brilliant.

The tribunal continued with a barrage of accusations against the Philosopher as the crowd watched in a kind of horrified awe.

Beside me, Luca looked like he was coming out of his skin. The veins in his neck were visible, a sheen of sweat cast across his brow.

"All in favor . . ." The Consul's monotone voice distorted in my head.

My own mother was the first of the Magistrates to turn her judgment stone, and the moment the white face was visible, Luca was pulling free of me.

"*No,*" he cried out, making the people around us turn to look.

"Luca," I whispered, grabbing hold of his tunic and trying to pull him back to me. But he was already disappearing in the mass of people.

He slipped through my fingers and I chased after him. By the time I made it to the stairs that led down from the gallery, he was already at the bottom.

"Luca!"

I clambered down the steps, hands sliding on the railing, and when I rounded the banister, Luca was pushing into the Forum. Vitrasian's gaze fixed on him as he burst through the doors, the glint of tears in her eyes. But in the next breath, sunlight gleamed on a blade as the legionnaire lifted it in the air, and I watched with a cry trapped in my chest as it came down across her throat.

The sound of Luca screaming filled the Forum as he raced down the aisle. Every head turned to watch him as he caught Vitrasian's body in his arms, her blood spilling down her chiton and soaking into his tunic. He was racked with sobs as he fell to the floor, pressing uselessly to the gushing wound.

It wasn't until her hands fell limply to the ground that I saw the look in his eyes change. Before anyone could so much as breathe, he was lunging forward, taking the short sword from the second legionnaire's belt. He drove it into the gut of the man, dropping him to the ground before he turned on the other. I screamed Luca's name as he plunged the blade into the legionnaire's heart.

That was when I saw it—the shimmer of gold. The flash of a gleaming circle taking shape over his head. A sharp gasp shot through the Forum and I stopped short, eyes going wide. The sword slipped from Luca's hand, his chest rising and falling erratically, and his face paled and he dropped to his knees.

Every eye in the Forum was fixed on that gilded circlet, an air of utter disbelief thick in the room. It appeared like a specter, painting Luca as if he were a character in the oldest myths that covered the walls of the temple. It was a halo, an omen of providence.

It was a mark of fate from the gods.

CHAPTER 37

NOW: LUCA

Vale stared stoically at the fissured wall as each of the Centurions took turns reporting on the losses of their legionnaires.

"And the other watchtowers?" Vale asked, arms crossed over his chest.

Roskia stepped forward. "From what we can tell, the three left standing didn't sustain much damage. They're sound."

That was at least one bit of good news. The towers were the only places that were feasible to operate the larger artillery. Without them, we'd be stuck fighting hand to hand with soldiers coming over the walls.

"What about the Lower City?" Vale continued.

"Many structures sustained damage. Only six structures fell."

"Only?" Vale's tone took on an edge. "And the citizens?"

Another Centurion's eyes cut to me, hesitant. "There's no way to know just yet. It will take days to search the debris."

Vale didn't like that answer. "Then we get every set of hands available to do the job. The bodies will be wrapped and burned. No exceptions."

The Centurions responded with a collective grunt. With the legionnaires defending the walls, there were those who wouldn't likely know the fate of their own families for days. Maybe that was best.

In the distance, a line of men, women, and children stretched from the bank of the river, hauling buckets of water toward the remaining flames in the Lower City. The blackened rooftops looked like a barrel fire of smoking coals, and I tried not to think about who may have been inside the homes when the flaming stones and bolts landed.

Valshad's fire hadn't reached the river and I now suspected that wasn't luck. The towers of the Illyrium still stood, only one pillar of smoke rising from its roof in the distance. The attack had missed the temple, and the buildings that surrounded it were also untouched, which meant Valshad had taken care with their aim. I didn't like what that might mean.

The Citadel was being protected. So was the district. We'd thought the Consul and the Magistrates were mad, but this wasn't madness. It was desperation. For weeks, months maybe, the Consul had been orchestrating the one strategy no one could ever predict. The city had fallen, the Loyal Legion all but gone, and even the Forum was half emptied of its Magistrates. We'd been hours from crossing the Sophanes to take the Citadel, and the only things he had now were the Priestess Ophelius and the grain. Both of which could be used in a bargain with Valshad.

"Matius." Vale's voice broke through the storm of thoughts

in my head and I looked up to see him staring at me. "Do you agree?"

I nodded, unsure what he'd even said.

"As soon as you have numbers, I want to hear them." Vale was talking to the Centurions again.

He dismissed them with a nod and they dispersed, headed to gather their own cohorts. All except Roskia. He waited for the others to get out of earshot before he spoke.

"You know what must be done, Saturian," he said, his voice level and calm.

Vale waited. I watched his face, trying to read where this conversation was going. But he looked unsure.

"This could have been avoided if you had allowed yourself to part from your own sentimentality. It's past time to act," Roskia said.

"Are you saying this is our doing?" I snapped.

Roskia shook his head. "If we'd stormed the Citadel weeks ago like we should have, Valshad wouldn't be at the gates."

"You don't know that," I said.

"I think I do." He kept his tone respectful, but I could see in Roskia's eyes that he was resolved. That coldness within him was crackling just below the surface.

I was losing my patience now. "Murdering the Consul and his Magistrates isn't a solution, Roskia."

"Murder and justice are not the same thing. There are plenty of legionnaires behind me who would agree," he replied.

That single statement was enough to put Vale on guard. With Roskia, we were always dancing on the edge of a threat. He knew that with the right words, the right angle, he could turn this legion into a bloodthirsty mob. He was just waiting for the right moment to do it.

Roskia kept his voice even. "We need to get across the river and deal with the Consul. Now. We never should have waited this long."

"I agree," Vale said.

My eyes snapped up.

Roskia's brows lifted. "What are you saying?"

"We should have pushed into the district weeks ago. We shouldn't have stopped the line at the river," Vale continued.

My jaw clenched and I bit back the words I wanted to say. We were close, much too close, to our own desperate measures.

"But right now, we have to secure the gates," Vale continued.

The three of us fell silent, the false hope in the words making me tense. There wasn't one among us who couldn't see how this ended. We didn't have the men or the weapons to hold off an attack by Valshad.

"And then we decide how to handle the district." Vale exhaled.

Roskia nodded, a sense of arrogance in the way his chin lifted. I waited for him to look at me with a measure of satisfaction, but he didn't. He didn't have to. In this war we'd been waging between us for months, he had finally gained some ground.

Roskia turned to leave us and Vale started toward the gates. I followed him into the smoke as the winding, empty streets took us into the heart of the Lower City.

"You can't be serious, Vale," I finally said.

Instantly, he stopped walking, turning to face me. He was only inches away, his dark eyes blackening. "What exactly would you like me to do, Luca?"

"It sounded like you were close to sanctioning the execution of everyone in the district. You know that's what Roskia wants."

"Maybe he's right to want it." Vale's voice rose. "Maybe we should have cut their throats a year ago."

I squared my shoulders to him. "We agreed from the beginning that we wouldn't be who they are."

"There is no *we*, Luca."

I flinched.

"You tell yourself there is, but it isn't true. You had your chance to lead, and you didn't want it. So, now I have to take what's left and do what I have to. There aren't any options here. We were fooling ourselves to think there was a clean way to do any of this."

"Nothing about this has been clean. People have died. The city is in ruin."

"What did you think was going to happen?" He was shouting now. "You want revolution, but you don't want to pay the cost. You don't want to sacrifice."

"I have sacrificed *everything*."

"Is that true?" His voice lowered.

"What?"

"You watched the Consul and the Magistrates murder Vitrasian right in front of you, but you won't walk across the bridge and give them your vengeance. But if it were *her* . . . if it were her, you'd bathe yourself in the blood of your own brother. If I had my knife to her throat, you'd draw your own blade against *me*."

I could feel the rising tide of rage consuming me inch by inch. What he was saying was the closest he'd ever been to turning against me. I hadn't thought that was possible.

"Deny it," he dared me.

When I said nothing, he laughed bitterly.

I leveled my gaze at him, letting the truth of the words bleed into my voice. "Don't put me in that position, Vale."

There was nothing lost in my meaning. I'd started a war with him, fought beside him, but none of that would stand against the lengths I would go to in order to be sure that I never saw Maris hanging from the bridge.

"All of this"—he lifted his arms around him, his face falling—"I've done for you. For all of us. But everything you do is for Casperia."

I swallowed down the words I was thinking, as if that would make them untrue. But Vale wasn't wrong. About any of it.

"Centurion." Théo's low voice was suddenly at my back, making both Vale and me look up. Asinia stood behind him.

Théo's face was still streaked with ash, and when Vale saw him, his expression darkened.

"Where the hell were you?" he growled.

I went to step between them, but I wasn't fast enough. Vale shoved Théo in the chest with both hands, and Théo took the brunt of its force, feet planted on the ground. But he didn't say a word.

Behind him, Asinia was visibly restraining himself, grip tight on his javelin.

"You're a tribune! Your Centurion nearly died today!" Vale roared, shoving him again.

Théo's gaze met mine for a split second, his jaw tight. "I'm sorry, Commander."

If he was ever going to betray me, now would be the time. But Théo was unwavering in the set of his mouth, the line of his shoulders. Not for the first time, I had to ask myself *why*.

Théo lifted a small scroll in Vale's direction. "A falcon just arrived with this."

Vale snatched it from him, turning the scroll over in his hands until I could see the seal that was pressed into the wax. It was the seal of Valshad.

He hesitated before he broke the seal with the blade of his knife and unrolled it.

"They want to meet," Vale said heavily.

The irony of it was palpable in the air between us. Only days ago, we'd sent the same request to the Consul. We'd had the upper hand, in a position to make our own demands. Now we were on the other end of that message.

"What will you do?" I asked.

"I'll accept." He folded the message, eyes moving over the city in the distance. "It's not as if we have much choice."

I was surprised to hear him use the word *we,* though whether he'd said it out of intention or habit, I didn't know. The divide that had opened between us only moments ago was something I didn't know how to cross with him.

"Send the falcon back and tell them that we accept." His gaze dropped to my arm. It was still bleeding. "And then get his arm taken care of."

Théo looked to me, waiting for permission, and I nodded.

Asinia followed him out, and we stood in a knife-edge silence before I finally spoke. "What you said . . ."

Vale lifted a hand, stopping me. "I'm sorry. It's not fair to use her against you."

"But you weren't wrong."

The look he gave me told me that he knew it was true. "I know."

"It's the reason you're wearing the mantle of the Commander. Not me."

For the first time in maybe months, Vale let his gaze lift to the ring of gold that arced in the air over the crown of my head.

"You'll come with me?" he asked.

"Of course." My eyes landed on the scroll. "What do you think they want?"

"I think they want what they've never been able to get—vengeance. And I think they will have it."

CHAPTER 38

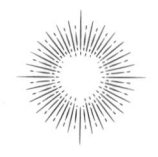

NOW: MARIS

I stood at the window of my chambers in the Tribunal Hall, watching the lights of the New Legion's camp across the river. Not one round of artillery had crossed the Sophanes, leaving the district untouched, and by now I imagined that word about what the Consul had done was beginning to spread.

The fighting at the gates had finally stopped, the city quiet as the sun fell. The light from the lamps in the Illyrium came to life and I could only pray to the gods that it meant there was a chance Luca was there.

The Citadel had been humming for hours, more alive than I'd seen it in months. Sandals brushed up and down the halls, the creak of doors opening and closing. I'd seen more than one falcon leave the aviary, with no attempts by the New Legion to shoot it down. This was what the Consul—what Nej—had promised, wasn't it? A return to *before*. But I wondered if anyone in the Forum was thinking the same thing that was spinning in my mind.

Now that Valshad was here, *before* didn't exist anymore. Now there would only be an after.

This time, it wouldn't be the Philosopher standing at the center of that twelve-pointed star in the Forum. It would be me. It would be my blood painting the marble. I was only glad that Luca wouldn't be there to see it.

I went to the cabinet against the wall and opened it. The fine white silk glowed inside and I reached up, slipping the Magistrate robe from its hanger. I pulled it on, tying it closed methodically, and then I smoothed my hands over the soft fabric. If they were going to kill me, they would look in the mirror while they did it.

The iron bar bolted to the door of the chamber lifted with a screech, and slowly I turned to face it. The door swung open over the polished floor, the shadows of the legionnaires painted on the gleaming white marble. Nej was with them.

He stood centered across the threshold, his pale blue tunic stained with large splotches of dark blood. I didn't have to hear him say it to know who it belonged to—the Priestess Ophelius. And that thought sent a wave of relief through me. She, at least, was finally free.

He entered without an invitation, striding across the floor with his gaze cast out the window, where the Lower City lay dark, save for its smoldering fires.

"We are but mortals." He spoke the words softly and they caught in the wind, stretching and pulling in the silence.

The saying was one that was etched across the breast of one of the statues in the Forum. A woman holding a single coin in one hand and a fish in the other.

"It's Valshad, isn't it?" I asked, following his gaze to the city walls in the distance.

"Even one's enemy can be useful at the right moment. That's something your mother should have taught you." He walked to the tray along the wall, picking up a jug of wine and unstopping it. He filled one of the agate cups, swirling the liquid. "I do admit that I bear some responsibility for your lack of perspective. Where my sister failed, I should have succeeded. I thought I had."

He took a long sip. "I think the biggest surprise here is your lack of reverence. Murdering the Priestess is not just an act against your own people and a betrayal to your seat as a Magistrate. What you've done, Casperia, is a sin against the gods."

My throat tightened. "I didn't kill her."

"That's exactly what you did." He swallowed the rest of the wine in a single gulp. "You had a place of power. A seat in the Forum that would have given you a future in the new Isara. And you gave it up. For what?" His head was tilted to one side as he examined me, as if he could somehow unearth the answer if he looked closely enough. "What in the name of the gods were you thinking?"

"I was playing the game you taught me to play. That's what you want me to do, isn't it?"

"Don't be stupid. If you had any idea what I've done to—"

I cut him off. "My mother didn't kill herself, did she?"

Nej moved toward me with slow steps, the cup dangling from his fingertips. "She sealed her own fate. That's essentially the same thing."

I could imagine how it had all played out. My mother was no hero, but there was no world in which she would have agreed to a plan that involved offering the city up to Valshad. I didn't doubt that she'd made her sentiments known or that she'd made a plan to move against my uncle. But she'd underestimated Nej. We all had.

"The gods are watching, Maris. You had your chance to stand alongside me and rise with this city when they redeem us."

"You're wrong," I breathed. "The gods aren't impressed, Nej. They're laughing at you."

Before I even saw him move, the cup clattered to the ground and a flash of metal shone at his fingertips. He took a handful of my hair into his fist, and I gasped, heart beating wildly inside my chest as the room spun around me. When I tried to pull away from him, he tightened his grip and held me in place, bringing my face close to his. The cold, sharp edge of a knife blade pressed to the soft skin at my throat.

"I am *gifted*. Chosen." he hissed. "Neither blood or family name will stand between me and that fate."

He let me go, shoving me away from him. "I suppose there's a symmetry to it. This war began with the execution of a woman. It can end with one, too."

He shot a glance at the legionnaire behind him. "Call the magistrates to the Forum."

The doors slammed shut and I reached up, finding the blood dripping down my throat. I stared at the crimson stain that spread across my fingers. My hands were still scraped from the night the legionnaire Neatus had dragged me through the Lower City. Crescent moons of soot were gathered beneath my fingernails. The gold rings I usually wore were gone.

I wiped the blood across the folds of my robe, the deep red blooming on the white silk. These hands, I thought, could tell the entire story. Of the night I met Luca Matius. Of the first time I touched him. The night I gave him my name, my body, my soul. That had been only the beginning. Did that mean we were now at the end? Of everything?

Slowly, my eyes lifted to the unfinished portrait across the room. That version of me looked resolute. Determined.

I took slow steps toward the painting. There was a lie in those eyes. I'd been pretending, when I put on those robes that any of this mattered. I picked up the stylus from the desk, fist clenched around it before I lifted it over my head and stabbed it into the canvas. Then I dragged it down, tearing the painting through the middle until my face was broken.

The tribunal bells began to ring, and only seconds later quick footsteps echoed in the hall. They were followed by the sound of a voice, and the stylus slipped from my fingers. There was no going back now. No way to undo what had been done. The Magistrates were gathering, donning their robes, and adorning themselves with jewels to meet with the Consul in the Forum.

The sound of footsteps and voices grew louder, but when a scream sliced through the night, I turned to the window.

Below, a few figures moved in the darkness and I scanned the villas, watching as doors and windows were shut. A chill ran over my skin. The street fell into an eerie silence, and the voices in the hall lifted again—this time, more panicked. Shadows swarmed in the street, and I spotted the red tunics as a cloud moved from the face of the moon. I pressed myself to the wall as they crossed the bridge. Footsteps echoed between the stone walls of the villas and another cry rang out. It was followed by the sound of a door being kicked in.

The New Legion. They'd come.

I pushed back from the window, pulse racing as the commotion in the Tribunal Hall swelled. I blew out the oil lamps before I went back to the door, pressing my ear to the wood and trying to listen. I could hear shouting now. Running. Doors slamming.

I got down on my knees and pressed my face to the floor, trying to see beneath the door. The boots of the guards were gone.

A bloodcurdling scream tore up the corridor and I frantically slid back, palms slick on the marble as I watched that slice of light beneath the door. It bent and swayed as one long exhale hissed through my lips. The sounds of death crept into the chamber, my chest rising and falling in a frantic rhythm.

They were hunting Magistrates.

Shadows moved over the floor as doors slammed on their hinges, the sound of a crash ricocheting in the hall. The legionnaires were going room to room. I could hear them dragging people across the floor, their screams abruptly cut short by the sick, wet sound of blades piercing flesh.

I got to my feet on shaking legs, moving backward until I reached the window ledge. I had seconds before they opened that door.

I tore off the Magistrate robe and tossed it out the window, the white silk fluttering in the wind as it fell. Then I unclasped my medallion, looking at it one last time. *Casperia*. My breath hitched as my hand reared back over my head and I threw it out into the dark. The glint of it flickered through the air before it disappeared in the river below.

The wind pouring in through the window whipped around me as I stared at the black water, and the sound of boots grew louder in the hall. I imagined the light flooding the room. The shadows coming toward me, hands dragging me across that floor. This was the moment the New Legion had been waiting for. This was when the Citadel would finally be purged.

A deep, cold calm seeped into the corners of my mind as the moonlight sparkled on the water below. The fall seemed a mercy compared to what waited on the other side of the door. The crush of bone hitting the river's surface was nothing to the terror of being strung up on a rope. Dangling and rotting in the sun.

I stepped up onto the ledge, breaths slowing as I realized what I was about to do. The fear bled out of me, drip by drip, the night melting into a liquid silence. Starlight touched my face as I drifted toward the drop and exhaled softly before I let myself tip forward.

My feet slipped from the ledge as I fell through the air, my chiton rippling like birds' wings around me. My mouth opened, but no scream came, the stars blurring in the dark sky as I plunged through the night. Their silver color warmed as I fell, blinking gold as the light gathered and swelled. It was suddenly all around me, so bright that I had to close my eyes, and the heat of it sent a rush of goose bumps over my skin.

The roar of the wind howled in my ears as the dark river came closer, and I twisted in the air as the gold glittered and sparked, wrapping itself around me. When I hit the water, it was with a sound like thunder, and suddenly I was beneath it. The current pulled the gold threads of light into ribbons as they faded, and the sudden cold made a stream of air escape my lips.

I broke the surface with a ragged gasp as the river carried me away from the Citadel, its light growing dim in the distance. The south bridge raced over me, and I raked my hands through the water until I caught hold of one of the iron grates that lined the canal. My body shook as I pulled myself toward it, my chiton twisting around me. It wasn't until that moment that I realized the golden light that had enveloped me as I fell wasn't completely gone. It still glowed just beneath the surface of the water.

The air was cold on my skin, but a deep-rooted burn seared

across my upper arm, making me groan. I lifted myself up, and when I looked down, I felt the blood drain from my face.

A pair of gilded unfurled wings encircled my arm just above the elbow, like a golden cuff. But when I tried to slide it free, it wouldn't budge. I recognized the light—the almost viscous metallic dust in the air.

My eyes lifted to the sky, the realization of what had just happened slowly taking shape in my mind.

The gods had *saved* me.

CHAPTER 39

BEFORE: LUCA

Three seconds. That was how long it had taken to lose everything.

I could still feel the pounding of my heart. See the blur of the light. Hear Maris screaming my name in the Forum. But it was all nothing to the memory of Rhea Vitrasian dying in my arms.

I don't remember lifting my gaze or taking the sword from the legionnaire's belt. I don't remember getting to my feet or driving the blade into his chest. The first memory I had after looking down into Rhea's face was standing over those young soldiers' bodies as blood dripped from my fingertips. Then I was hitting the floor as two more took me to the ground.

Now there was only quiet.

The soft drip of water somewhere deep in the dark catacombs fell in a steady rhythm that mimicked the beat of my heart. It was cold and damp, but I couldn't feel it. The air didn't stir as the torchlight flickered. There were no voices, no footsteps. The legionnaires outside my cell were silent and I didn't have to see their faces to know that they pitied me.

At first light, the tribunal bells would ring. And the Magistrates would end my life to pay for the two I'd taken. They'd be wiped clean of it then—what they did to Rhea. And after everything, she'd be remembered as a traitor.

The loud groan of a door echoed through the catacombs and I let my eyes drift to the glow of light in the distance. There were shadows moving, the sound of boots hitting the stone, and as soon as the figure came around the corner, my hands found the slick iron bars.

Vale.

He walked straight toward the cell as I got to my feet, the amber light finding his face in flashes. He was wearing his legionnaire's armor, his helmet tucked under one arm, and the two soldiers standing guard outside straightened when they saw him.

"Leave us." Vale stopped in front of the cell, eyes locked on mine.

The legionnaires didn't question the order from the Consul's son, and the silence fell heavy once they were gone. Vale stared at me, the tension in his face visible even in the dark.

"What the hell were you thinking?" he said lowly.

I set my forehead against the bars, swallowing. "I wasn't."

"This is bad, Luca. There isn't a single one among the Magistrates who won't take the opportunity to cast you as an accomplice to Vitrasian."

"I know."

I'd known it the moment I felt the heat of the legionnaires' blood on my hands.

Vale pinched the bridge of his nose before running one hand

over his head. He was looking at me again, as if trying to decide something.

"What is it?"

"You've done more than offend my father, Luca."

"What? What's wrong?"

Vale glanced over his shoulder, lowering his voice. "Word about what happened at the tribunal has made it to the Lower City. They're calling you a savior. Saying that what you did was an act of the gods."

Slowly, the words sank in, making me feel colder.

His eyes lifted above my head, and for a fraction of a second, I saw the glow of the mark light his face. I had only ever heard of the gifts that the gods gave mortals. I'd never believed in them. I'd certainly never seen them for myself. They were the kind of sacred acts that happened in the time of the Old War.

"There's talk of rebellion," he whispered. "And not just across the river. In the legion, too."

My hands slipped from the bars and I stepped backward into the dark.

"Someone's painted your likeness across the river. An image of you kneeling with blood on your blade."

Pain woke in my jaw as I clenched my teeth. "What are you saying?"

He reached into his tunic, handing something through the bars. I took it, tilting it toward the light until I saw the reflection. It was a knife.

"The Priestesses in the Illyrium opened their own veins, Luca. Two of them died. Something bigger is happening here than you and Casperia's daughter, or even what they did to Vitrasian. And I'm not sure you're ready to understand your part in it."

I stared at the blade, my blood running cold.

"You have until nightfall to come to terms with it," he said.

I didn't have to know the details of what he was saying to comprehend it. There was a storm coming. One I'd woken.

Vale reached through the bars and I took his arm, tightening my grip as I met his eyes.

"Don't do anything for me that can't be undone, Vale," I said.

He let me go. "You're my brother, Luca. I already have."

Movement behind him drew my eye and the soft sound of footsteps surfaced from the resonant hum of the catacombs. I saw the red of her stola first, like a twisting flame in the shadows.

Maris stepped into the light, the image of her like a ghost. The thin silk rippled around her in the cold breeze that blew through the tunnels, and it picked up her hair, pulling it beneath her chin, across her face.

Vale moved past her, giving me one last look before he disappeared. This was his doing. A chance to say goodbye.

Emotion curled tightly in my throat as she moved toward me, and when her hands came through the bars, I reached for her. Her arms wrapped around me, making me feel so heavy that I could hardly stand. I pressed her palm to my face, desperate to feel her touch, and she kissed my temple through the bars.

The smell of jasmine filled my lungs, washing away the stench of blood, and I wept as her fingers moved up my back, holding me to her. Only days ago I'd kissed her, telling her that I would marry her. The next time the sun fell, I was taking her name in the temple. But it all felt so meaningless now, the idea that anything could change.

"I'm going to fix this," she whispered. "My mother can fix this."

But the words were hollow and empty. She couldn't believe that. She couldn't possibly think that there was any way out of this that didn't involve a lot more blood.

"When they burn my body," I said, hand running over her hair, "don't let them do it in the temple."

She stilled under my touch. "Luca . . ."

"Promise me." I pulled back to look at her. "Don't let them do it in the temple. And don't tell them you married me." Now she was trying to pull free from my hold on her, but I only tightened my grip. "I'm serious, Maris. No one can know."

She was crying now, and I pulled her back into me. She knew it like I did. Deep down, she knew this was the last time she would see me. Touch me. Hold me.

"Don't come to the tribunal," I said. "I don't want you there."

She clung to me as I drew the knife from my belt. I took one of the long thin braids behind her ear and I pressed the edge of the blade against it until it was free.

Maris watched as I tied it off, winding it around my wrist, and when she looked at me again, her swollen eyes shone with tears.

"It's time to go." Vale's voice surfaced in the dark behind her as he stepped back into the light.

Maris' hold on me tightened and I kissed her, letting my hands run through her hair, down her back. My fingers followed up her arms until I could take hold of her wrists and I pushed her from me as she cried. When she wouldn't let go, I met Vale's eyes over her shoulder. He stepped forward, pulling her away. And the last time I saw my wife, she was being swallowed by the dark, the sound of her cries trapped like a storm inside me.

CHAPTER 40

NOW: LUCA

My hands shook as I lit the incense.

I spoke the words with my eyes closed, my voice echoing in the Illyrium's temple. The fragrant smoke filled my lungs, washing out the taste of the acrid fire still burning in the Lower City. But there was no forgetting what Vale had said. There was no denying it, either.

If Valshad had come for blood, we had little hope of maintaining what control we'd gained over Isara. Vale and I had been at it all night, constructing scenarios that might give us a chance at keeping the city walls intact. We had not one front now but two—the Sophanes and the gates. But we had nowhere near enough men to hold them both, which meant we were working at a puzzle that was impossible to solve.

Valshad's army had done what they came to do—weaken our defenses. And I wasn't the only one thinking it. The same thought was on the face of every legionnaire who had stood at the foot of the wall with soot smeared over his skin and blood streaking his tunic. Valshad had started a war before we'd even finished fighting the one with the Citadel, and I could feel the quiet trepidation of the soldiers from the Lower City who'd taken up arms with us.

We'd been low on supplies and resources weeks before Valshad appeared. We also had the looming threat of the entire Lower City at our backs. They were still waiting for what we'd promised them: grain and peace.

From what I'd seen of Valshad's legion, we were outnumbered in a way that didn't offer much hope, and many of the legionnaires most experienced in strategy and large-scale battle were across the Sophanes or gone. We had only a day before we needed to open the gates to Valshad's Commander, so by the time the sun was setting again, we needed to have a plan. Walking away from that meeting with any kind of solution would come down entirely to what exactly they wanted, and I had a feeling that would depend on what the Consul had promised.

I prayed, Maris' name burning on my lips as I cupped my hands, washing the smoke over my head. What Vale had said still haunted me. I had loved Maris Casperia since the first moment I saw her, and I hated the gods enough to reject the idea that it was the result of their fortune or favor. Sometimes I felt like she was a curse they had cast upon me. The ideas that Vitrasian had planted in my mind hadn't found fertile ground until Maris. I hadn't seen a way past my uncle, the Magistrates, the role I was destined to play in Isara. It was the night I stood with her in the gardens that I first found that sight.

"Matius."

Théo said my name in a way that made my prayer stop short. I turned back to see him at the entrance to the temple. He'd refused to sleep, he and Asinia standing guard throughout the night as Vale and I worked.

"What is it?"

"There's something you should see." The tone of his voice was somewhere between confusion and concern.

I left the incense burning and got to my feet, striding toward the temple's entrance. My body was so heavy with the need to sleep that I hardly felt my own feet beneath me. We took the long, statue-lined corridor of the Illyrium to the doors that opened on the silent courtyard.

Théo stopped at the top of the steps. "There."

He pointed at the river, where the north bridge was visible in the distance. But there was something strange about the view that made a painful pricking feeling race across my skin. I couldn't place what it was until Théo spoke again.

"The legionnaires. They're gone."

I took the steps down to the courtyard, eyeing the empty archway. Where soldiers were always posted, there were none. I couldn't see any at the entrance to the south bridge, either. The hair stood up on the back of my neck as I looked around us, suddenly aware that things weren't just quiet. They were *too* quiet. I squinted, studying the dark, and my eyes narrowed when I saw the flash of light flickering against the sky.

I took a step forward as it drifted toward us, turning and twisting in an erratic pattern. A few seconds later, I realized it was fire. The object fell from the sky, landing on the stones before us, and a sick feeling turned inside me.

It was a falcon. Engulfed in flames.

My eyes lifted back to the sky, where more were tipping and swaying on burning wings. They were coming from the Citadel. And that wasn't all. A warping shadow of black moved against the night sky, the smell of it thickening.

Smoke.

My feet started moving, taking me across the plaza as my mind tried to make sense of what I was seeing. Ahead, the bridge was empty. Deserted. The barricades were still standing, but not a single one was manned. Théo watched the buildings around us, both of us thinking the same thing.

"Where is Roskia?" he murmured.

I walked wordlessly toward the end of camp where his cohort had been gathered, and Théo disappeared into one of the tents as I turned in a circle, eyes scanning the scene around me. Tables set with pots of stew and unleavened bread were left abandoned, the fires gone out. Stools were toppled, the rooftop missing its sentries.

Théo reemerged from the tent in the midst of strapping on his armor, the sword swinging at his side. But he stopped short, turning toward the river when we heard the sound of shouting. We stood there, eyes trained on the mouth of the haze-draped bridge ahead. There were no legionnaires posted on the other side, either.

Théo took a careful step forward, watching the rooftops as if he were waiting for the sound of an arrow. But there were no archers on the Citadel. I drew the knife at my belt with the sound of Théo's footsteps at my back, holding my wounded arm to my chest. We were running now, and my heart was sprinting ahead of me as the bell of the camp rang behind us. Someone else had noticed that something was wrong. That, or they were calling in reinforcements. To a battle we hadn't sanctioned.

I ran toward the empty bridge, driving my legs faster as we crossed the water. The barrier that separated the market from the north end of the district was already a pile of bricks, toppled by the ammunition of the ballistae in the New Legion's attack on the Illyrium. Théo climbed the heap, reaching behind him to pull me up. I dropped on the other side and he came down beside me.

I didn't wait for him before I walked into the wall of smoke, swallowed up by the sounds of voices and orders being called out in the buildings ahead. The air burned in my eyes and throat, and when I saw what lay on the other side, panic flooded my veins.

Dozens of legionnaires in red tunics and scale armor were barely visible through the thick smoke, covering the steps of the Citadel. Each of them wore a blue sash on their arm. They weren't the Loyal Legion. These soldiers belonged to us.

"There!" Théo watched the entrance, where Demás stood at the top of the steps. And wherever Demás was, Roskia couldn't be far behind.

A heavy breath escaped me as I realized what this was. Roskia's cohort had crossed into the Citadel District. The men at the river's edge straightened when they saw me, their voices echoing in a salute as I searched their faces for Roskia. We took the steps two at a time and I resisted the urge to draw my sword. There was something wrong about the way the legionnaires stood in the entrance to the portico. Their weapons were sheathed, their postures relaxed. It wasn't the manner of soldiers holding a defense. This was the way legionnaires looked when a battle was won.

Smoke rose from the roof, spiraling into the black sky over us, the Citadel lit with the glow of firelight.

"Sir."

The legionnaires recognized me with a string of acknowledgments, but I halted as my eyes tried to understand what I was seeing. Beams of early sunlight slanted through the hazy, warm air, and every inch of me registered the disturbing silence that filled the domed room.

That sick, gnawing feeling crawled up my throat as I stared at them—the bodies. Hung from the balcony along each side of the wall. Below each one, a Magistrate's portrait taken from the Tribunal Hall was propped on display. Like a trophy for each of the slain.

This wasn't happening. This *couldn't* be happening.

The room spun around me and I pinned my eyes to a pair of dangling, sandaled feet ahead. The portrait beneath it was slashed, the canvas ripped in two.

I moved forward, not breathing as I peered up into the blank face of a dark-haired woman. My heart threatened to explode in my chest before I realized it wasn't Maris.

I went to the next, and the next, hands skimming the bloodstained chitons and stolae.

"She's not here." Théo's voice was suddenly close to me again, and his hand came out, taking hold of my arm to steady me. It wasn't until then that I realized I was trembling. So violently that I could hardly stand.

"She's not here, Matius," he said again, his grip tightening.

I turned in a circle, my gaze still searching for any sign of her. There were at least fifty, maybe sixty bodies hanging from the banisters. Magistrates and their families. More than one had a face I recognized.

My vision tunneled as I found the knife at the back of my belt, and Théo's voice flickered out, replaced by the pounding in my ears. I walked straight toward the other side of the portico, where the archway opened to the Tribunal Hall.

I didn't see the faces of the soldiers who passed me or the dead ones from the Loyal Legion who lay scattered across the floor.

The door to the Magistrate chambers marked with the name Casperia was ajar, the iron bar busted at the joint as if it had been forced open.

I couldn't breathe, imagining it. Maris' body on the floor. The cold touch of her skin, the color drained from her face. I stepped over the pool of expanding blood creeping across the marble and pushed inside, a sound breaking in my chest. The chamber was dark, except for the faintest light of dawn. I stepped inside, the underwater feeling creating pressure in my head as my eyes swept the room. It was empty.

My gaze landed on a dark streak that marred the white stone below the window. I moved toward the ledge, teeth clenching. It was blood. Pressed to the ledge in the shape of a small, slender hand.

I peered down to the river below, the water writhing like a snake as the New Legion's camp came to life. Any moment, they would wake to what had happened. But it was far too late to stop it.

CHAPTER 41

NOW: MARIS

River water dripped on the polished floor of Villa Matius as I stared into the mirror in the atrium. I was trying to force myself to believe it was really there. The unfolded wings curled around my upper arm, the tips of the feathers fanning out until they touched and overlapped. The cuff looked like gold melted in the forge of the temple, glowing with a telltale light that made the air sparkle.

I tried to wedge my finger beneath it, attempting to slide it over my skin, but it wouldn't budge. It was fused to my body, with no clear place where the cuff ended and I began.

It was a *gift*. It had to be. Like the stylus in the obsidian box in Nej's chambers and the ringlet of gold that marked Luca as chosen. I'd been recounting the tales in my mind since I pulled myself from the river. The gods were not kind, like Ophelius said. But there was a time when they used mortals to do their bidding, intervening in our world to enact their own wills. So, what did they want from me?

The heavy iron doors to the street on the other side of the villa groaned open. I pushed the sleeve of the chiton down, covering the cuff, and sank to the floor, pressing myself against the stone wall. I was hidden by the chest in the servants' quarters, but I watched that square of light on the floor cast through the doorway, like Théo had done.

Outside, the sound of doors being kicked in and glass shattering echoed in the street. They were searching for us. Driving us out like rats until every seat in the Forum was empty. If I was lucky, Villa Matius would be spared the search. The New Legion would expect it to be empty.

That square of light flickered, blinking out as the door hit the wall, the shadow of a legionnaire slipping through the darkness. I pulled my knees up to my chest, trying to become smaller. I could see him as he flitted in and out of the beams of moonlight. The reflection of scale armor and the blue sash tied around his arm. This wasn't a soldier of the Loyal Legion. The district had finally fallen.

His knuckles were white around the hilt of the short sword he had drawn at his side. The muscles that corded his arm flexed as he moved with silent feet through the atrium. The chamber across the hall creaked open and then he went to the next, searching the villa one room at a time.

My shaking hands came up over my head when he reached the servants' quarters, and I tried to swallow down the cry erupting in my throat. But it was too late. Footsteps came barreling toward me just before hands took hold of my chiton, and then I was screaming. The man dragged me across the floor as more boots sounded down the corridor, followed by more shadows on the wall. When the face came into view this time, I froze.

Luca.

He stopped midstep when he saw me, the faint sound of an

inhale in his chest. A second later, his tribune appeared in the doorway behind him.

"Centurion."

The man standing over me gave Luca a respectful nod, but Luca was still staring at me. Like he couldn't believe I was really there.

In the next breath, he pulled the short sword from his hip and stalked toward the man, his arm arcing backward before he reached out and grabbed his armor. With his next step he drove the sword up into the man's ribs. A crackling, gasping sound broke in the legionnaire's throat as Luca twisted the blade, and then he shoved him backward, where he lost his footing on the steps.

My hands fell limply into my lap as I stared at him. A sob loosed in my chest as Luca closed the distance between us, sinking down to his knees and wrapping himself tightly around me. His arms encircled the whole of my frame, draping me in darkness, and I ran toward it. I desperately wanted to disappear into him. To hide where no one could find me.

Théo checked the street before he quietly closed the door, and my hands climbed up the sleeves of Luca's tunic until my fingers hooked around his neck. I pulled him closer to me and his face pressed into my hair. He was speaking. Saying something in a voice too broken to understand.

"I've got you." His mouth came low to my ear, his grip tightening around me. "I've got you." He sounded like he was reassuring himself.

I let myself get heavier in his arms, my breaths slowing. "What happened to them?" I whispered, my face still buried in his shoulder. "What happened to those people?"

"They're dead," he said.

"Why? How could you just—"

Luca pulled back from me, hands finding my face, and I could finally see his eyes. They were bloodshot. Red and swollen. "I didn't." He wiped the tears from my cheeks with his thumbs and I leaned into the feeling.

I searched his face, desperately wanting to believe him. "I told you this would happen. I *begged* you," I said.

There was a moment of cold silence before my hands twisted tighter in his tunic, and then I pushed away from him. He watched me get to my feet, still kneeling before me.

"I thought they were going to kill me," I rasped, trying to catch my breath. "I thought . . ."

He stood, coming toward me, but I moved out of reach.

"You did this." I sounded as if I was still trying to wrap my mind around it. To follow every decision that had led us here, to this place.

Tears burned in his eyes, and the sight of them made it painful to breathe.

"I know." He swallowed.

"You may not have put your blade to their throats, but you did this, Luca."

"I know!" he shouted, making me flinch. The words were delicate. Fragile and afraid. "You think I don't know that? I know what I am."

A tear slid down the arc of his cheek, finding the edge of his jaw. An anger burned in his expression that I could hardly bear to look at. It was hatred. Pure, undefiled hatred. For himself.

He wasn't the only one who felt that way. The two of us had been broken too deep to be stitched back together. So, why couldn't I leave him? Why couldn't I walk out of this city unless he was with me?

The door to the street opened again and I peered over Luca's shoulder to see Théo, his face unreadable as he looked between us.

"The Commander has crossed into the district," he said quietly.

Luca ran a hand over his face, the mask he wore returning. Gone was the man who'd given himself to me. The one I still thought I could save. Now the Centurion stood before me, with armor that sank deep beneath his skin.

"Don't let her out of your sight," he said, his eyes not leaving mine.

From the corner of my eye, I could see Théo nod sharply before he positioned himself by the door.

Luca didn't look at me again before he turned and left, but the cut of the words he'd spoken felt like it was drawing blood.

I know what I am.

CHAPTER 42

BEFORE: LUCA

The first to die for the Citadel was an old man, a highborn legionnaire who'd chosen the wrong side.

I stood over his body in the catacombs as the cell door slammed shut behind me, the shadows of my liberators like ghosts in the dark. Vale had come for me, like he said he would. And there was no going back now.

"Come on." His voice echoed in the stone corridor ahead.

Behind him, another legionnaire was on his knees. Asinia had his blade to the man's throat, the blank expression on his face enough of a threat. He didn't need to use words when the old man was lying dead beside them.

My heart was beating hard in my chest, my stomach turning with the gravity of what was happening. This wasn't an act of protest, like what Rhea had done. We were defecting. Turning on our own brothers and fathers. And soon, all of Isara would know.

Vale took me by the arm, pushing me ahead of him, and I led us up the spiraling steps. The legionnaires who'd pledged their loyalty were silent behind us save for the sound of a few prayers on their lips.

The most devout of the soldiers had joined up with Vale, the sight of that halo over my head enough to convince them it was worth it. But the gods wouldn't repay their fealty. I'd seen that with my own mother.

The air warmed as we rose up out of the catacombs, and Vale pressed a hand to my chest to stop me when we reached the top of the stairs. There wasn't a single official in the Citadel who didn't know who he was. No one in the entire district who wasn't compelled to obey him. He was the son of the Consul. A shining example of what it meant to be Isarian. And now he was a traitor of the worst kind.

He checked the hall, a knife discreetly poised at his back, before he motioned us forward. The legionnaires flanked me on either side and we moved as one entity as the light of the oil lamps fell upon us.

"Saturian?" a Magistrate named Ovidia called from the doorway of his chambers.

His eyes moved over us, from face to face, and when they landed on me, he stumbled backward. As soon as his mouth began to open, I shoved past the legionnaires, the knife steady in my hand as I brought it through the air. I closed the distance between us quickly and he teetered backward, catching the door with his hand. But my knife was already buried in his gut.

I clamped a hand over his mouth, pressing him into the door, and his legs gave out beneath him. It wasn't until his jaw was slack that I let him drop, and his head hit the floor with a crack.

The legionnaires dragged his body inside and shut the door as

I wiped the blade on my tunic. I had no pity for anyone who'd turned their judgment stone against Rhea or the Lower City. If I could cut them down one by one, I would.

Three more men would die before we made it out of the Citadel, and we moved through the district in silence, listening for the moment they realized what we'd done. We didn't have much time.

The lights of Villa Casperia were like a beacon in the dark, and I walked toward them with my heart in my throat, following the river. No one stirred as I climbed the balcony of the gardens and slipped through Maris' window. And as I stood there, watching her sleep, I almost didn't wake her. I almost kissed her with a silent goodbye and slipped back into the dark.

Later, I would wish I had.

I lowered myself beside the bed, letting my hands slide under the quilts. Her skin was hot beneath my cold fingers. Her eyes fluttered open, squinting as her vision adjusted, and when she sucked in a breath, I pressed a finger to my mouth.

Slowly, she wound herself into my arms, pressing her cheek to mine. "What's happening?" she whispered.

I let my hands move down the curve of her, the line of her body fusing to mine. Like there were places we'd been made to fit together. I didn't want to forget that feeling.

"You need to leave the city, Maris."

"What?" She was unraveling herself from me now, leaning back to look into my eyes. Whatever she saw there made her afraid. "What are you talking about?"

"The legionnaires are coming with me. We're crossing the Sophanes and we're not coming back." She struggled against my grip and I tightened my hold on her. "You can't be here when we take it from them."

She went still. "Take what?"

"The Citadel."

The fear in her eyes was a wild thing now, snaking into her body and turning it to stone. "What did you do?"

The cold, numb feeling I'd had as I stood over the dead Magistrate was far away now. Maris was a fire that made it impossible to reach.

"Whatever you did, we can find a way to—" She pulled at my tunic, desperate.

"It's done. It was already done when Vitrasian died."

Maris' eyes jumped back and forth on mine as she let out a shaking breath. "This isn't your fate, Luca. You have to see that."

"I have no fate."

She shook her head, weary. "You do. With *me*."

I put my arms around her when she began to cry and her forehead came to rest on my chest as I held her. "Promise me you will leave the city."

"I'm not leaving." She wept. "I swear by the names of the gods that I'm not leaving unless you're with me."

A low whistle sounded outside the window, and I pulled myself from her arms, peering out to see Vale. He stood on the path that edged the river, looking up at me before his gaze drifted east. Toward the Citadel.

I could hear the distant, low hum of chaos. A rupture in the stillness of the night. They were coming for us.

"Don't do this," Maris said, hands clutching me. "*Please* don't do this."

I drew in a deep breath, trying to take the scent of her into me. Trying to bind her soul to mine. She held on to me so tightly that her fingernails dragged painfully against my skin, and when I tried to let her go, she wouldn't let me.

"*Please,*" she whispered through broken breaths. "Luca . . ."

I kissed her softly before I touched my forehead to hers, and I didn't meet her eyes again. I broke her hold on me and I didn't look back as I went to the window, a bloody, gaping hole tearing open where my heart had once been. That was the last time I felt it beating inside me.

CHAPTER 43

NOW: LUCA

I knew where I'd find him.

My boots hit the marble in a steady, heavy rhythm that pulled my vision back into focus as I made my way up the Tribunal Hall. There wasn't a single Magistrate portrait hanging now, the walls bare for the first time in a hundred years. The stillness that had come over me when I saw Maris was already fading, the feeling returning to my fingertips, the heat setting fire to my blood as the entrance to the Forum appeared.

Two of Roskia's legionnaires were posted outside the open doors, and they nodded as I passed the threshold, only briefly eyeing the blade in my hand. I didn't stop when I saw Roskia sitting before the window in the Consul's chair. A soft smile lifted his lips at the sight of me, and when he spoke, I couldn't hear him. The only thing resounding in the room as I stalked toward him was my own breath. My own heartbeat.

Alarm lit on his face when I was only steps away, and he shot up from the chair, his hands going to his belt. But I already had my blade at his throat, one hand clutched to the collar of his breastplate as I walked him backward toward the window.

His feet dragged clumsily and he caught himself on the shutter as I pinned Roskia to the ledge. I looked down into his shocked face with an emptiness inside me that I'd never felt before. The pit in my soul was like the drop down to the river behind him, over a hundred feet below.

"What did you do?" I growled.

Roskia met my eyes, his hand closing over my wrist to keep himself from falling. "I did what you didn't have the guts to do," he said through clenched teeth.

Behind me, the sound of more footsteps filled the chamber and the air grew warmer. From the corner of my eye I could see Roskia's legionnaires filing in to see what the commotion was. None of them had drawn a weapon but I didn't doubt there were some who would if I let Roskia fall to his death. There had to be at least one or two who would kill a Centurion. For a moment, it was a welcome thought.

Roskia smiled, as if he could hear the words flitting across my mind. "We were headed to this moment the day you turned against the Citadel and took half the legion with you. *I* knew it." His eyes cut to the legionnaires behind me. "*They* knew it. The only one who didn't," he breathed, "was you."

I let him go, nausea rolling in my gut.

What Roskia hadn't realized was that I *had* known. I had seen it that night at the front when two of our cohorts were ambushed by the Loyal Legion and scores of our soldiers were slaughtered. After the first few battles for the Lower City, there hadn't been a legionnaire among us who didn't want every head left in the Forum to roll. And Roskia had been willing to lead them.

The next day, he'd orchestrated one of the bloodiest battles of the rebellion. Not long after that, Magistrates who'd been caught trying to flee the city slowly started appearing on the bridge, their bodies drained of color.

"I did you a favor, Matius," Roskia chided. "You should be grateful."

Demás lowered his sword as Roskia righted his balance, and I stepped backward. "You will not take another life on this side of the river without an order," I said hollowly.

Roskia straightened his armor, brushing the shoulders of his cloak. "Understood, Centurion."

The smug look on his face only confirmed that he wasn't worried about being held accountable for what he'd done. He knew as well as I did that Vale would have to save face if he was going to keep the confidence of the New Legion. The truth was, they would be happy to believe that Vale ordered the executions himself. Proud, even. Roskia's twisted words were a heavy, undeniable truth.

I did this.

"Commander! Commander!"

The faint shouts echoed down the hall, signaling that Vale had arrived, and Roskia's smile widened. We looked at each other, and I imagined that we were both playing out exactly how this next part would go.

"Commander Saturian." Roskia feigned a respectful tone as Vale entered.

Outside the Forum, the entire Citadel was coming alive with the sound of voices and victorious shouting.

"Welcome to your Citadel, Commander Saturian." Roskia's hands lifted out into the air.

"Leave us," Vale ordered, not blinking.

Demás and Asinia instantly stepped forward, obeying without

hesitation. The legionnaires in the Tribunal Hall disappeared from view as the doors closed, and suddenly we were alone.

I studied Vale's face, trying to read him. After walking through the Citadel, where the bodies of the Magistrates were hung like festival garlands, Vale looked—maybe for the first time since this all began—truly scared.

"How could you possibly think we would let this stand?" My voice deepened.

"This victory belongs to the New Legion. To the Lower City," Roskia said.

"All you've done is re-create us in the Magistrates' image."

"I don't think they see it that way," Roskia said, letting the silence draw out by way of explanation. We could still hear the echo of celebration. "There wasn't a single man out there who hesitated to strike the names of the Magistrate families from the canon of this city's history."

Beside me, Vale said nothing. His patience had always worked in his favor, but I could see him struggling to weigh his options. He had very few.

"No sign of Casperia, though," Roskia said calmly. He didn't look at me, but a grin lifted on his lips. "That is her name, isn't it? Casperia?"

My hands curled into fists at my sides, the black hole within me expanding.

"What I haven't told the men out there"—he paused, eyes sliding to meet mine—"is that *you* should be hanging up there, too."

"Roskia." Vale's tone was a warning.

"You thought because I was lowborn I wouldn't recognize her, right? You think my life has been so insignificant that I wouldn't know the daughter of one of the vilest Magistrates ever to taint this Forum?" He took a step toward me, his smooth orator's tongue inhabiting the words. "I knew exactly who she was the moment she walked out of your tent."

I was seething now, summoning every ounce of will I had not to put my hands around his throat.

"I assume you have her. Otherwise you'd have driven that sword into my chest the moment you walked in here. I have to say, Matius, I've always wondered what Magistrate tastes like."

The thread holding me together snapped and I moved toward him, arm heavy at my side and ready to swing.

"Matius." Vale's voice was missing its fervor, as if he were trying to decide whether to stop me. But I ignored him, bringing my fist down hard across Roskia's face.

Blood spattered the white marble as his head whipped to the side. He was smiling again, this time with blood smeared on his teeth.

He spat at my feet, taking his time to wipe it from his chin. "Do you have any idea what those legionnaires would do if I told them that you're her *husband*? That you lied to protect her? That all this time, you've been shielding the Citadel District because your own loyalties are divided?" Roskia's eyes searched mine. "What's worse is that our own Commander condoned it. He even allowed you to poison his ear with compassion for the very people we waged this war against. The only reason there's an enemy outside our gates is because *you* allowed the Consul the time to enact this strategy. He should have been dead months ago. We have fought tooth and nail through the bowels of this city only to find an enemy outside our door." He pointed to the window, where the gates of the city lay in the distance. "I did you a favor. You would have lost these men by morning if you hadn't given them some justice."

What was so sickening about it was that I knew, deep down, that he was right.

"The moment we find the Consul and string him up with the others, that will be all the fire the New Legion needs to defend this city from Valshad. It will douse this fire in oil." Roskia was so proud of himself that he looked like he might cry.

"He's in the catacombs," Vale said, voice deadened.

Roskia's expression faltered. "What?"

"The Consul. If you want him, you can go down there and scrape up his blackened bones from the smoking granary. He's dead. The Priestess Ophelius, too."

My lips parted, his meaning sinking in.

"The moment you crossed that bridge, the Consul locked himself in the granary and set fire to it."

Vale came to stand in front of Roskia, leaving only inches between the toes of their boots. "You didn't save this city, Roskia," he said lowly. "You just starved it to death."

CHAPTER 44

NOW: LUCA

I stood with both feet planted on the bloodstained stone as the gates of Isara opened for the first time in almost six months. But in my mind, I was only thinking of Maris.

I traced each memory, following them back to the moment I first saw her. The way her dark eyes had been so open in the garden that night. The way she'd looked me in the eye. I didn't like to think about what she might see there now. I wasn't the man she'd given herself to. The one she'd taken vows with. And that had never been clearer than now.

The pulleys clicked and groaned as the great iron gates slid open. In the distance, the golden grass that covered the hills folded beneath the wind, and the setting sun cast everything in a violet haze.

The boots of patrols echoed up on the walls as I scanned the hills in the distance. From so low a vantage point, the army of Valshad was nowhere to be seen. But they were there, like a sleeping dragon. I could feel the rumble of its breath beneath my feet, making the ground unsteady.

The breeze caught my cloak as I walked out from beneath the archway and the sun hit my face. My boots sank into the soft earth and Vale's footsteps landed in tandem with mine as the land widened around us.

Vale lifted a hand, motioning for the line of legionnaires marching behind us to halt. Their steps ceased in unison and Vale and I continued on, our two shadows stretching across the ground as we walked. The air grew cold and thin without the sound of them at our backs, and the disorienting expanse seemed to suddenly go on forever. After so long within the city walls, where our world had been divided by a single river, we were standing in the middle of nothing. Nowhere.

When a figure appeared on the crest of the hill ahead, we stopped, and my fingers wrapped around the hilt of my sword. It was useless in the face of what was actually waiting for us, but I couldn't help it. I was a man who spoke only the language of death now.

The gleaming gold helmet of Valshad's Commander glinted in the sunlight as the morning crept across the land. He was a tall, broad man, adorned with ornate ceremonial armor and a silver-studded bow strung across his chest. The young woman at his side had the same weapon, but it was clutched in her hand, as if she were hoping she'd get to use it. Long blond hair was pulled back from her face, spilling over her shoulder like the tail of a horse, but she wasn't dressed for ceremony. She wore an ash-stained tunic and muddy boots that were likely the ones she'd fought in the day before. She was a legionnaire.

When they made it to us, the General reached up with both hands, carefully pulling the helmet from his head. His angled face was set with dark eyes, and the fair hair that was cropped short on his head was as pale as that of the woman beside him.

"Viria," his deep voice grated, bellowing out in the space between us. "General of the Valshad legion." He tucked his helmet beneath his arm.

"Saturian, Commander of the New Legion of Isara. This is Centurion Matius." He gestured to me.

The General's eyes ran over us, and I could almost hear the conclusions he was drawing. That Vale was too young to be a Commander. That we had no idea what we were doing and that this was going to be the quickest battle he'd ever won. The Magistrates had thought the same things, but they'd been wrong.

"So, it's true." The woman beside him had her eyes fixed on me. Her gaze flicked up to the arc of gold over my head. "You have been gifted."

I said nothing, not breaking her gaze.

Viria took a step toward us. "I'd like to speak to the Consul."

"The Consul is dead." Vale's voice didn't waver.

That seemed to catch the General off guard. He frowned, glancing up at the city gates in the distance. "Then I'd like to speak to the highest-ranking Magistrate."

"He's dead, too, I'm afraid." Vale's words were flat and lifeless. "We took the Citadel last night."

Viria looked to the woman beside him, who was staring me in the eye. Her gaze sharpened as she studied me, but she said nothing.

"Then who has taken control of the city's leadership?"

"I have," Vale answered.

An unmistakable look of dissatisfaction crossed the General's face.

"I made a deal with the Consul." Viria's tone turned impatient. "If you've accepted his responsibilities, then I expect you to honor it."

"I have no intention of honoring the promises a traitor made to the man who's put our city under siege."

The glint in Viria's eyes grew brighter.

"If you've come to slaughter the city for its grandfather's sins, these hills will be painted with your army's blood," Vale continued.

"We're not *beasts*." The woman finally spoke again, her voice venomous, each word sharpened to a point. The implication was clear. She was talking about Isara. The legion had decimated Valshad in the Old War and left its bones to be picked clean by scavengers.

"Then what is it you want?" I replied.

Her head turned, looking to the city that lay behind us. "The Priestess. The one who has godsblood in her veins."

So, that was what the Consul had promised them. He'd raised a flag of surrender, inviting Valshad to come and take advantage of our broken city. And in exchange, he was going to give them back the one priceless gift no one else could. But I'd seen the Priestess's body myself. The only godsblood left was smeared across the stone floor.

"And what will you give us in return?" Vale said.

The woman beside Viria stepped forward, eyes moving between us before dropping down to my chest. "Nothing. We grew the wool that made that tunic. Grew the grapes that made your wine. We even mined the ore you use to build and wage war. And do you know what we did with all your coin? We made arrows to pierce your legionnaires' armor. Swords to strike down your Centurions. Boots to march on this forsaken city. The wealth of Isara was built on the spoils of war. Our gold, our jewels, our magic. And now the gods have punished you for it."

The truth was a painful one. That look in the woman's eyes

had been forged in the ashes of that war. Valshad had waited a hundred years to find its revenge, and now it was within their grasp.

"Tomorrow, we're opening the gates for anyone who wants to leave the city. You will allow safe passage to the Isarian people, or we will kill your Priestess," Vale said.

I blinked, trying not to show a visible reaction. There was no Priestess to give them, but that knowledge was the only scrap of leverage we had to wield. It was our only chance at sparing Isara more bloodshed.

"You wouldn't risk the gods' wrath," Viria sneered, disgusted.

"Look behind me," Vale said hollowly. "The gods aren't here."

Vale and the woman looked at each other for a long moment, the tension growing taut. It wasn't until the General turned in her direction and something unspoken passed between them that I realized she wasn't a tribune or something else like it. She was missing the decoration of a high-ranking soldier, but she was important somehow. I could feel it.

The wind picked up, catching her long flaxen hair, and she gritted her teeth as if biting her tongue.

Viria turned toward us again, his tone formal. "We will allow the safe passage of your citizens through the gates." His voice deepened. "And when they open again, it will be the day we take this city."

CHAPTER 45

NOW: MARIS

Villa Matius was the home of the family line we'd erased. I stood at the window, watching the thin clouds twist across the expanse of sky. In the distance, the birds flitted through the last bit of sunlight. For a moment, I could almost pretend that it was the Isara I remembered—dusk rippling over the rooftops, the dome of the Citadel gleaming, and the smell of the sea on the wind. But that world was gone.

Valshad had the city under siege, and every time I looked out to the walls, where their encampment dotted the hillside, I couldn't help thinking that this was finally the end of our story. There was no Consul. No Forum. No seat of power. Isara was gone.

Ophelius' words snaked through the streets below and drifted on the smoke in the air. *Sometimes you must burn a field to save it.*

But there was nothing left to burn.

Beams of fading light spotted the floor beside my feet and my eyes lifted across the hall to a small open room. Théo was still posted there, standing erect beside the threshold. He hadn't left my side since Luca departed.

I took a step toward the doorway of Luca's chamber, eyeing the strange shadow that danced on the opposite wall. Like a spinning star. I walked toward it, and as soon as I reached the doorway, a gust of cool wind poured into the room. The shadow swayed on the wall, rocking back and forth, and I reached up to touch the plaster before I turned to the window to see what it was. A small star folded from dried palm hung from a string, twirling in the breeze.

The chamber was simple and bare, missing the warm touches of having been lived in, but that single star was like a story in and of itself. I reached up, taking it down from where it hung, and I let my fingertips touch the points one by one as I sat on the ledge.

"It's a tradition in the Lower City."

A voice I knew as well as my own sounded behind me. Luca. He had one shoulder leaned into the doorframe, arms crossed over his chest. I didn't know how long he'd been standing there, watching me.

"Children make them for the Tenth Feast."

His sharp features looked almost sinister in the low light, his eyes empty of any emotion. His cloak, breastplate, and scale armor had been removed and his dirt- and blood-smeared tunic had been replaced with a new one. The gold circle that hovered over his head was just barely visible, and I bit down on my bottom lip. He looked so much older. Like years had passed since we'd said our vows. It felt like that, too.

He waited a moment before he began to cross the room, eyes studying me as if he were unsure whether I would let him get close to me. But I didn't move. I was hardly even breathing. As he stepped into the light, my gaze ran over him, catching all the things I hadn't seen in the dark. All the ways he'd changed. All the wounds, physical and otherwise, that were visible on his body, in his face. My eyes dropped to the sword at his hip, wondering how many lives it had taken.

Behind him, Théo disappeared from view, his footsteps trailing up the hall. When Luca reached me, he stared down at the braided palm in my hand, his eyes tracing the bruises that covered my arm. Every inch of him seemed to turn to stone, his jaw clenching before he took the star between his fingertips.

"What happened?" I asked.

He exhaled. "The gates will open tomorrow at sunrise. Valshad is giving safe passage to anyone who leaves the city."

Sunrise. That was just hours from now.

"Once they close the gates . . ." He didn't finish.

"And my uncle?" I said, voice small.

Luca shook his head. "I checked the corpses in the Citadel. He wasn't there."

I didn't know what feeling that knowledge woke in me. Had I hoped that he would be strung up with the others? Burned to ash in the catacombs like the Consul? Some part of me had known that he wouldn't be. Nej had been chosen—gifted. There was no way to know if the gods were through with him yet.

Luca seemed to be asking himself the same question. I let myself take a careful look at him, gaze running from his head down his face and throat to the opening of his tunic. But my eyes stopped on the dark red staining a tied strip of cloth below his shoulder. I followed it down to the end of his sleeve, where fresh blood coated his skin, striping his hand.

"I'm okay," he said, answering the question he could read on my face.

He didn't look fine. He was pale, his voice rough and tired.

"Let me see," I said, lifting the sleeve of his shirt, but Luca moved from my reach, taking a step backward. He was as afraid of me touching him as I was.

"I'm sorry for what I said before," I whispered.

"Why? It was the truth."

I didn't like the way he was avoiding looking at me. The way he was keeping a stretch of distance between us. He didn't look up as I took a step toward him, but his face turned back toward the shadows of the room, leaving only half of him in the light.

"No, it wasn't," I breathed.

He sat down on the edge of the bed, turning the star in his hands. "Why did you stay? Why didn't you leave when I told you to?" There was a deep sadness in his voice. A brokenness that filled the room with a suffocating feeling.

"You told me you would only take vows with me if they were real ones. Remember?"

If I closed my eyes, I would still be able to see it. The glow of the fires in the temple. The glint of liquid gold and the press of Luca's mouth on mine.

Flesh to flesh, bone to bone, blood to blood.

My gaze followed the line of red streaking down his arm to the end of his sleeve again. When I saw what encircled his wrist, my eyes narrowed. I reached for his hand, ignoring the way he tried to pull away from me, and my fingers touched the bracelet. It was a braid of dark hair. The one he'd taken from me that night in the catacombs.

It wouldn't be a strange sight on anyone else. Most people in Isara had objects of superstition. But Luca didn't put his faith in such things.

"What is this?" I asked. "A talisman?"

The way he looked at me then was like he was looking into the past. "You're the only god I believe in."

I swallowed hard before I silently took the star from his hand and set it down on the table. When I turned back to him, he was watching me with a wary expression. The muscle in his jaw twitched again when the skirt of my chiton brushed his knuckles.

Nerves danced beneath my skin as I reached out and took his hand, guiding it to my face. I pressed his palm against my throat where my pulse was racing and turned my cheek into it, breathing him in.

He went still as I lifted the length of my chiton and climbed onto his lap. I tucked my legs on either side of his hips so that I could look down into his face. His eyes changed, searching mine, and I could see that he was looking for something to hold on to. Something to keep him from disappearing. So, I folded his arms around my waist and drew him into me until our bodies were sewn together.

He pulled in deep, steady breaths against my throat, and the more the corners of him melted into the shape of me, the tighter I held him.

He pressed his face against my skin. "I love you."

"I know," I said.

"I'm sorry." His voice splintered. "I'm so sorry."

"I should have come with you."

It was true. I could see now that he'd needed me. That when I'd let him cross the river, I'd left him alone.

He let me go, looking up, and his eyes bored into mine, as if he were trying to pry each of my thoughts from one another. Like he was waiting.

"If you're going to ask me to go, Luca—"

"I am." He cut me off.

"I told you I'm not leaving without you," I said.

"I know. So we'll go together."

My lips parted, my mind turning the words over to be sure I'd understood them. "What?"

"We'll go together," he said again.

My hands were shaking now, my heart racing. "What about Isara? What about Vale?"

"He'll understand. It's what we should have done a long time ago. I think we're the only thing left to save, Maris. You and me."

He looked at me a long time, and when a hot tear slid from the corner of my eye, I took his face in my hands so I could find his lips with mine. When they parted, the warmth of his mouth spilled inside me until my chest felt like it was caving in. I kissed him deeply, the way I'd dreamed of doing a hundred times since the night he left me.

Luca's arms unwound from me and his touch found my legs, sliding beneath my chiton so his fingers could travel up my thighs. There, his grip tightened almost painfully, making my stomach clench so that I couldn't breathe.

I gave in to the rush of it, breaking the kiss long enough to unwind the cords of my chiton. It fell over my shoulders, puddling at my waist. He stilled when he saw the cuff that circled my arm, drawing in a breath. Before he could speak, I pulled at his tunic, tugging it over his head.

His chest rose and fell as my hands traced over rivers of scars I didn't recognize. Beneath my palm, I could feel his heartbeat, steady and strong.

He was staring at the shimmering gold, and I could see that he wanted to ask. But I could also tell that he was afraid to. He pressed a kiss below my ear before his lips moved down my throat, and when his mouth opened against my breast, I groaned at the feeling it sent through me. Every place that his skin touched mine was a resurrection. We were the dead summoned back to life.

His fingers brushed over my stomach, trailing down until they were between my legs, and I let him touch me, pressing myself against the hardness of him.

His mouth found mine again. "I need you." The words were lost in an anguished breath. "Can I have you? *Please.*"

I answered him with a slower kiss, and he pulled my leg up and over his hip, groaning when he pushed the length of himself inside me. A long, uneven breath escaped his lips, and with it, a stillness fell over the world. He thrust into me slow and deep until a sharp-edged, painful pleasure moved through me. It was just me and Luca. Not the young fools who'd thought they could change their world. Now we were wounded and ruined. Healing all wrong.

He made love to me slowly, like he wanted to make time stop. And I did, too. I wanted the gods to keep the planets from spinning, the sun from setting. I wanted to stop my heart from beating. Despite what he thought, the soul of Luca Casperia wasn't dead. And as long as that was true, then mine wasn't dead, either.

I moved with him, every inch of my skin singing until we were knit back together, into one—flesh to flesh, bone to bone, blood to blood.

I'd bound my heart to this man. Then I'd bound my name. What I hadn't really believed, not until now, was that I'd bound my fate, too.

CHAPTER 46

NOW: LUCA

Once, the theater had overlooked the sea.

I stood at the top of the seats, where sunlight bathed the white stone, and stared into the haze. Now the view was hidden behind a sky filled with smoke.

Only a year ago, I'd watched Vitrasian stand on the stage and speak to dozens of highborn Isarians about the revolution of the planets. It was one of the last lectures she gave before she penned the play that would change the fate of our city.

She had been a lover of tragedies and I'd seen all the ones she'd written, no idea yet what that word even meant. I remembered watching as the players killed each other with wooden swords below. Now I wondered if that was where it had been born—the thing in me that had filled the sky with the smoke that hid the sea.

I'd realized something the day Vitrasian was executed. For the first time in my life, I had a reason to die. But if I was going to finish what I started, I had to untie myself from my only reason to live.

By the time I reached the Citadel, the Forum was flooded with the legionnaires transferring the legion's camp across the river. We'd waited for this day for so long, and now that it was here, none of it mattered. On the other side of the wall, an army waited to devour us. Every risk, every sacrifice, every death. It was all so close to meaning nothing.

I was numb as I climbed the steps and passed back through the corridors. Inside, soldiers were taking down the stiff hanging corpses and hauling them out. An order from Vale, I guessed.

The Consul's inner and outer chambers had been mostly cleared of soldiers, and the legionnaires in the corridor didn't even look at me twice, giving small gestures of acknowledgment as I passed.

Asinia stood at the door and I breathed through the tightness in my chest when I saw Vale's shadow stretched across the marble. He stood before the altar, burning a plate of incense.

"Close the door, Matius." The words were heavy as he said my family name, missing the familiarity that they usually held.

I clenched my teeth, obeying. Asinia glanced at me from the corner of his eye before the door slid shut and I stepped inside, lifting my chin. Vale's silence roared in the room, a quiet rage rippling off him in waves. I could almost always read him, but I didn't know what this was. This was something different.

I waited in silence as he washed the smoke over his body with cupped hands, eyes closed. He was stripped down to his tunic, the blood from battle still crusted on his skin. But his hands and face had been scrubbed clean.

"What are you asking the gods for?" I said, voice low.

He blew on the smoldering incense, sending another waft of pungent smoke into the air. "The offering isn't for them."

He didn't elaborate, and I didn't press, trying to read the

feeling that seeped through the air. The look on his face was strange. Distant.

"How many times have we talked about the day we would stand in this room together?" he said, keeping his back to me.

I didn't answer. The truth was too hard to think about. Those dreams were born long before this war, and we'd had no real idea of what the cost would be. We didn't know what it would take. And now here we were, with everything we'd wanted, and it only felt like we'd lost.

"Did you really believe we could win?" he asked.

"I did."

"Do you think that's what we did?"

"We knew there would be a price, Vale. If you're asking whether the price was worth it, then my answer is I don't know yet," I said hoarsely.

He looked at me with a deep sympathy, his face softening.

From the beginning, it had been Vale and me. From our first day as legionnaires to the day we walked across that bridge. Even now, as the bodies were being dragged out of the Citadel, our fates were intertwined.

"You and I lost control of this thing a long time ago. We promised them a swift victory and the reward of power. Grain for their families. Peace. Now we don't have any of those things."

"You think we were fools," I murmured.

He nodded. "Yes, we were. But that doesn't change what happened here. If we'd never gone to war with the Magistrates, the streets would still be filled with the dead. *Our* dead."

He was talking about the citizens of the Lower City now. The ones who'd taken up arms with us. But we weren't the same as them. Not really. I was a grafted vine of both noble and common blood. I'd been born in the Lower City, but I'd become a man in the Citadel District. I'd fallen in love and taken vows with the daughter of a Magistrate, and though I'd dreamed of revolution, I'd never cut the ties that bound me to the Citadel.

"You and I might see this for what it is, but this isn't about you and me," Vale said. "It's about Isara. Right now, Valshad is waiting outside the walls. And we've promised them a Priestess that we don't have."

"So, what do we do?"

"We open the gates. Then we see if the gods have any mercy left for us. If you plan to stay, that is."

I waited. I could see he had a question. Whether he would ask it was another matter.

After a long moment, Vale leveled his gaze at me. "You have every reason to go, Luca. And if you stay, you will always be a breath away from them finding out what Roskia knows. He's wrong about a lot of things, but he's also right. Eventually, justice will find us both."

"Are you asking me if I plan to leave?" I said.

"You're not Commander. You made sure of that."

"We decided together that you would lead," I said, defensive.

"We did. But for different reasons. I think we've come far enough together to say the truth out loud, don't you?"

"What truth?"

"That I became Commander because you were afraid to. I did this *for* you."

The words carved deep inside me, splitting me in two. To the legionnaires, I was the stoic, ruthless rebel who'd avenged the Philosopher and started the rebellion. But to Vale, I was just the only thing he had that resembled family. And he was protecting me in more ways than one.

I turned to the window, where I'd held Roskia over the drop only hours before, looking out over the Forum to the sea. Almost immediately, I could see Maris. Feel her touch beneath the water.

"When we started this," Vale said, "we gave our lives to Isara. We let go of what we wanted. Do you remember that?"

I swallowed. "I remember."

He took hold of my shoulder and clenched it tight, his eyes meeting mine with a deep sadness. "But you're my brother, Luca. And if you want to go, I'm not going to stop you."

I'd never heard his voice sound like that. The pain on his face was so vulnerable that it filled my insides with dread. What had it taken for him to muster the courage to say it? That if I wanted to go, he would let me.

My eyes drifted back to the altar, where the incense still burned. Maybe that was what he'd meant when he said it wasn't an offering for the gods. Maybe it was an offering for me.

"We started this together, Vale. That's how we'll finish it, too," I said.

"And Maris?"

The name resounded inside me as soon as it was spoken, but Vale didn't so much as blink. I'd already decided before I'd seen the cuff on her arm. I'd known the words I'd spoken were a lie. But now, with the knowledge that Maris had been gifted, I was even more certain about what I had to do. I didn't trust the gods. I especially didn't trust them with Maris.

"I'm not leaving." A strangled feeling curled in my throat as I said it. Even thinking it made my heart feel like it was tearing open with each beat.

Vale exhaled. He rubbed his hands over his face, breathing into them.

"But if I don't get her out of the city, I can't do what I need to do. I can't make the decisions I need to make or keep the promises I made to you."

We'd come far, he and I. Once, we'd been boys holding wooden swords on the training grounds for the legion's recruits. But that was before we'd seen what we'd seen. Before we'd done what we'd done.

He looked up at me, the old Vale I knew flashing in his eyes. "Then why are you here, Luca?"

"Because I need your help," I said.

CHAPTER 47

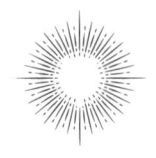

NOW: MARIS

Théo watched the street as the sun climbed the sky inch by agonizing inch. He was dressed in a plain tunic, his knife tucked into his belt. He'd been there since dawn, both of us silent in the hours that passed until the gates would open.

He looked back at me and I pulled the palla up over my head, tucking it around my hair. All we had to do was make it to the gates, where Luca would be waiting.

"Ready?" he said.

"Ready."

He opened the door and I followed him outside, down the steps to the streets of the Citadel District. I tried to swallow down the nauseous feeling when I realized they were empty. If they'd had the chance just days before, there would have been families from every corner of the district streaming toward the gates. It was a moment many of them had been waiting for, but it hadn't come. Not before the New Legion crossed the river.

Smoke from the Lower City drifted in a cloud overhead, blanketing the city in a stunned silence as the last few fires finished burning below. The sundial in the courtyard of the Citadel cast a moving shadow over the ground as we passed, the night gently giving way to morning. I tugged up the palla again, keeping my face cast down.

Anyone who stopped to look would see the name Esdran on my medallion, but it would take only one pair of eyes recognizing me to keep us from walking through the gates.

Théo's shoulder brushed mine as we crossed the bridge, passing legionnaires and those from the Lower City who'd resolved to wait out the fight. He hadn't left my side once since they found me in Villa Matius, never more than a room away, and now I found myself wondering what would become of him once we were gone. When Valshad made it over those walls and took the city, I didn't have to wonder what they would do with the Isarian legionnaires.

Théo stuck close to me as we made our way through the streets, and with every step that took us closer to the gates, I felt the weight lifting off me. We were so close to being free, Luca and me. So close to being out from behind these walls, where there was no family Casperia or Matius. No Magistrates and heirs and seats of power.

We disappeared into the crowd headed in the same direction, and when the gates finally came into view, my heart was in my throat. Scores of legionnaires were posted along the street. Beyond the horde of people, I could see blue sky.

"Where is he?" I said, searching the faces of the legionnaires ahead.

Théo was looking, too. He took hold of my arm, pulling me from the crowd, and we slipped into an alley that had been cleared. I let out a knotted breath, smiling, when I saw the dark-haired figure walking toward us. He was hidden in the shadow of the buildings, but his armor was gone, and he was dressed in a simple gray tunic, his boots laced up. It was the image of the Luca I'd once known. The one who'd been a novice in the Philosopher's theater. Once we crossed through the gates, he wouldn't be a Centurion anymore and I wouldn't be a Magistrate. Whatever we were now, we were together.

But a chill crept over my skin as he drew closer, and slowly my eyes adjusted against the bright early sunlight. The hands were the first thing I noticed. Those weren't Luca's hands.

When he finally crossed to the center of the alley and dropped the hood of his cloak, it was Vale Saturian's face I saw. His tribune was at his side.

"Casperia." His voice lifted just loud enough for me to hear it.

He stopped walking, and I searched the street behind him, looking for Luca.

"What are you doing here?" I swallowed.

His eyes watched the empty rooftops around us, as if he were worried about being seen. Beside me, Théo's eyes were locked on Vale's tribune. Something unspoken passed between them.

"Luca sent me," Vale said.

"Sent you? Why?" My cheeks flushed hot. "Where is he?"

The icy feeling on my skin was like fire now, burning over the whole of me in a rapid scorch of flame. Something was very wrong.

"He's not coming," Vale said.

My heart beat so hard in my chest that I could hardly feel its rhythm anymore. It was just one deep ache behind my ribs.

"What?" I breathed.

"I'm here to be sure you've left the city."

Beside me, Théo was blank-faced and silent.

"But . . ." I spoke slowly, my breath coming faster. "I don't understand."

Vale looked at me with sympathy before he reached into his tunic. He pulled a message free, handing it to me. My hand shook as I took it from him and opened it. The sick, twisting truth soured in my gut all at once, tears stinging behind my eyes as I read the words.

Every part of me that matters, every part that's real, you're taking with you.

The sea wind stopped, the sound of the city extinguishing with it. All around us, the world was going still, like it had last night. But this time, I could see what a fool I'd been. Luca was never going to leave. Never going to desert the legion. Of course he wasn't. It had been buried beneath every word he'd said.

I looked back at the gates. The next time they opened would be with a battering ram. I reached out, pressing a hand to the rough wall of the building, and my fingernails scraped against the stucco. Every bit of air that surrounded me was in my lungs, threatening to tear them open.

"I'm not leaving without him," I rasped.

Vale's gaze leveled on me. "You don't have a choice. As acting Consul in the Citadel of Isara—"

"Don't." My voice strained as I realized what he was about to do. "Saturian, *don't*."

His eyes fixed over my head. "I hereby strip you, Maris Casperia, of your Isarian citizenship and expel you from the city."

His open hand lifted before me, waiting for my medallion. But I didn't move. My eyes searched the windows and rooftops that surrounded us, looking for the face I knew was hiding there. I could feel Luca like I could feel the heat of the sun. I could sense the pierce of his gaze on me.

I swallowed down the cry threatening to break loose in my throat, reaching up to unclasp the medallion around my neck. I dropped it into Vale's hand. Without a medallion, there was no returning to this city. That was exactly what Luca wanted.

Beside me, Théo stepped forward, pressing his medallion into the hand of Vale's tribune. He watched Théo, stunned, his eyes wide.

But Théo didn't look up, his gaze fixed to the dust-covered stones at our feet.

"What are you doing?" I stared at him.

His jaw clenched before he finally looked up at me. "I'm coming with you."

Vale's tribune stepped forward, but Vale caught him in the chest with one hand, stopping him. Behind us, more than one person in the crowd had now turned to watch us.

"We have to go," Théo said lowly. "We don't have much time."

The pain in my chest was now in my throat, the reality of what was happening suddenly becoming real. Luca had left me. Again.

Théo took my arm, walking me back to the street. But I was still watching the dark windows overhead, trying to find the source of that burn on my skin. He was there. I could feel him.

Wrapping one arm around me, Théo didn't stop walking until we'd been swallowed by the crowd. We joined the line of people at the gates, keeping our eyes down as we passed the legionnaires. It wasn't until I stepped foot onto the dirt outside the gates that a deep, guttural cry began to simmer inside me. But I wouldn't let it escape. I wouldn't let it devour me until it had eaten me from the inside.

Silent tears coated my cheeks, rolling down my throat and soaking the fabric of the palla as we made our way to the nearest cart ahead. I fumbled through my satchel until I found a pair of pearl earrings and handed them over without a word. Payment for passage to whatever lay beyond this.

I climbed up, finding a seat, and Théo sat beside me. But I could still feel Luca when the reins snapped in the air and the cart jolted forward. I could sense him like the warmth of a candle's flame.

I kept my eyes on the horizon, letting the pain bleed out, one breath at a time. The gates of Isara pulled away as the horses trotted up the path. I wanted to hate him. To scream his name into the wind until it disappeared. But when I turned back to see the city growing small in the distance, my heart was still locked behind those walls.

CHAPTER 48

EPILOGUE: MARIS

Green flags moved over the hills, snapping in the wind like birds taking flight. The banners of Valshad were coming.

I watched the legion descend the slope, squinting through the burn of smoke in the air. Every few days they came to the camp, delivering grain and water, but this time they'd made the journey with their General.

Beyond the hills, too far from the sea to smell the salt in the air, lay the new Isara. A place for the broken pieces of our people that had been blown to the wind. Tents dotted the rolling land, where rings of dwellings curled around fires that washed the blue sky in a smoky haze. In the twenty-six days that had passed since we'd walked through the gates, the hundreds of Isarians who had traded their medallions for safety outside the walls had ended up here—a two days' journey from the place we'd once called home.

Théo crouched over the fire, the corner of his cloak pulled

up to cover his mouth and nose as he turned the turnips over on the coals. He was watching the commotion at the front of the camp, a subtle tension seeping into him.

I'd been with him long enough now to see it—that reflexive instinct buried deep under his quiet exterior. He was like a bird of prey, watching patiently before he took the effort to unfold his wings.

Théo had barely spoken since we'd walked through the gates, and I was glad for it. I had nothing to say that wouldn't bring a curse upon me, and it was better for us both if I kept us away from the attention of the gods. Especially when I woke each morning to find their gift still fastened to my arm.

My fingers found the cuff beneath the sleeve of my chiton as I watched the crowd gathering ahead. Valshad's insignia was driven into the ground where voices lifted in what sounded like a chant.

The only time Théo left me was to give me the courtesy of washing and dressing alone. He'd taken a particular interest in making sure I was fed, even when there was nothing to eat. Everything in the camp tasted like dust. Not the kind that stirred up along the banks of the Sophanes River. This was the kind of dust you found beneath a funeral pyre. All that was left of something once living.

He pulled the turnips from the coals, that uneasiness more visible now. Whatever was happening, he didn't like it.

I got to my feet, shielding my eyes from the sun so that I could see what they were gathered around. It was the woman. The Valshadi woman who was a legionnaire.

I took an involuntary step in the direction of the crowd as her voice lifted over the others.

". . . to take back your city!"

The throng of people gave a collective sound of approval.

Behind me, Théo abandoned the fire, taking me by the arm. "We should stay out of sight."

But I pulled from his grasp, moving closer. There was something about the woman that I couldn't tear my gaze from. The sound of her voice was like the fire in the temple, her pale blue eyes glinting in the sun. Her long blond hair caught the wind, making her look like a goddess.

"Any man or woman who joins us will be treated as our own. Rations, training, armor, weapons," she shouted.

I looked to the faces that surrounded me. There was a kind of awe hanging in the silence. A tenuous quiet that made me stop walking.

"The siege has begun, and with the help of the gods, we will breach the gates. Isara is your birthright! Your home! And when the city is freed of the sickness that has devoured it, you will inherit it all!"

Cheers erupted around me, and my head swam with the words. Valshad wasn't just cultivating the goodwill of those who'd been cast out. They were recruiting them.

The cuff at my arm burned like fire, the haze that cloaked the blue sky suddenly seeming to clear. This was my way—the *only* way—to get back into the city. To get back to Luca.

"Who will answer the call of the gods?" she shouted.

My hand lifted in the air before I'd even decided. Before she'd even finished speaking. But it wasn't the favor of the gods I was after. Not anymore.

"Stop." Théo pulled it down, trying to lead me away.

But the woman was already looking at me, those blue eyes like crystal. Again, I lifted my hand, and a wry smile played on her lips.

"What are you doing?" Théo hissed

I pushed into the crowd, slipping from his grasp, and when I finally looked back, he was already too far to reach me.

"He made his choice." My voice lifted over the crowd. "Now I'm making mine."

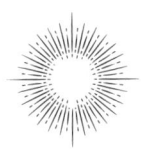

ACKNOWLEDGMENTS

Fallen City is dedicated to my son, Ethan, a philosopher of his own kind. I was only twenty-one years old when he was born, and very much still a child myself. It has been an incredible gift to be able to grow into who I am today alongside him. The greatest lessons in my life have come from motherhood, and in that way, all my children have been teachers. None more than Ethan.

This book would not have come to pass if not for the dedication of my friends. I sold this book at the very beginning of the pandemic, and in the years that followed, it was put on the back burner as I worked on other projects. I now understand that this story needed that time to develop into what it is today, and I'm really grateful for the path it took. All along that road, my writer friends made sure I didn't forget about *Fallen City*, championing it to the finish line. For that, almost all my thanks go to them.

Thank you also to my wonderful editor Eileen Rothschild and the whole team at Saturday Books, whose enthusiasm carried me through the process of finishing the book. And to my agent Barbara Poelle, who is always there, rain or shine, with a joke and a pep talk.

All my love and gratitude to my family, inside and outside my house, for your love and belief in me. I would be lost without you.

ABOUT THE AUTHOR

ADRIENNE YOUNG is a foodie with a deep love of history and travel and a shameless addiction to coffee. When she's not writing, you can find her on her yoga mat, sipping wine over long dinners, or disappearing into her favorite art museums. She lives with her documentary filmmaker husband and their four little wildlings in the Blue Ridge Mountains of North Carolina. She is the author of the *New York Times* bestselling Sky and Sea duology and the World of the Narrows series.